John Herbert Slater

Early Editions

A Bibliographical Survey of the Works of Some Popular Modern Authors

John Herbert Slater

Early Editions
A Bibliographical Survey of the Works of Some Popular Modern Authors

ISBN/EAN: 9783337280987

Printed in Europe, USA, Canada, Australia, Japan

Cover: Foto ©Andreas Hilbeck / pixelio.de

More available books at **www.hansebooks.com**

EARLY EDITIONS

A BIBLIOGRAPHICAL SURVEY OF THE WORKS OF SOME POPULAR MODERN AUTHORS

BY

J. H. SLATER

LONDON
KEGAN PAUL, TRENCH, TRÜBNER, & CO. L^TD
PATERNOSTER HOUSE, CHARING CROSS ROAD
1894

INTRODUCTION

If there be a fashion in acquisitiveness, there is little doubt that books of the kind mentioned in the following pages are collected mainly in accordance with its dictates. Early in the century it was the classics—Latin or Greek —and other scholarly volumes that chiefly attracted the book-man, just as in remoter times the ponderous commentaries of the Fathers held almost undisputed sway over his fancy.

To say why a man should delight in accumulating books, would be no more difficult than to assign a reason for any other preference, foolish or the reverse, that he might have ; but why first or early editions should be accounted more desirable than later ones, is not always so easy to explain. A late edition may, and in some cases should, be more complete than an earlier one; the errors in the first may be corrected in the second; additions, in the form of notes or otherwise, may have been made ; yet notwithstanding these advantages it not unfrequently happens that the comparatively imperfect edition is the more sought after of the two. Legitimately speaking, its value should be confined to the opportunity of comparison afforded to the student, enabling him to note textual differences, and thus, as it were, to follow the author through the maze of his thoughts and the development of his genius. Perhaps this was really the consideration that originally suggested the accumulation of different editions of the same book; but if so, though the practice yet remains, the reason has clearly become amplified. Scarcity and pecuniary value are the primary qualifications that every book must now possess, before it can rank as an object worthy the attention of the typical collector.

The search for early editions of popular modern authors seems to have been carried on, in this country at any rate, for at least a quarter of a century, during which period the price of books answering that description has continued to increase. So great is now the desire to obtain them, that a distinct trade has sprung up, not only for the purpose of ministering to the exigencies of the demand, but also to extend its scope.

It might be possible to trace the vagaries of fashion in the past, and perhaps to explain some of the rules that seem to shape the ends of the book-man now, though many of his predilections are doubtless in favour of slight variations and distinctions, which, though sufficient to create a technical difference, are perhaps not in themselves of any consequence, and would, moreover, be exceedingly difficult to classify. It might be urged that slight distinctions are never recognised until the weighty ones are exhausted, and that the collector of anything, no matter what, is invariably forced at last to shelter himself behind technicalities, owing to competition, the expansion of his desires, his approach as he thinks towards finality, and a number of other circumstances which will occur to the onlooker, who, while committing himself in no way, is sufficiently interested to advance reasons for the attitude of others. Though at first sight few will be able to appreciate the desirability of a volume that is perhaps a trifle worse, though earlier in date, than some other almost identical so far as the text is concerned, still there may after all be good and sufficient reasons to account for the choice.

In the first place, few, if any, authors spring suddenly into fame, and their earlier works are consequently peculiarly liable to have been overlooked, and in many cases destroyed. To be ignored is to be lost for the time being, and these first-fruits, crude though they generally are, come only into prominence with their author. There is a demand for them then, and the fact that many people want the few copies that have escaped the wrack of neglect, makes them objects of unusual interest. The inevitable reprint comes at last, but it is not the same; sentiment still hangs around the shabby volume of years ago, with all its errors, and the glass case or the iron-bound door shuts it out from busy fingers that would speedily send it else, after those other copies that have gone before. This is one reason of the book-man's fancy.

Another reason has more of an artistic basis. How the book-men, by whom is meant at the moment those who accumulate books from a mere love of possession, came to fix their attention on early editions at all is a matter for speculation. If a guess might be hazarded, it would be that they were first attracted by those containing plates by such well-known and popular artists as Rowlandson, Theodore Lane, H. K. Browne, Alken, and many more, and that subsequently, when the fashion was firmly set, they extended their desires to other books not so illustrated, and that the same rules of procedure then began to operate with respect to them also. If so, this will be another reason why a first edition is usually accounted of more importance than a second. The illustrations are necessarily superior, the plates having passed under the artist's hands, and not yet worn; but even if there are no illustrations, the transition is natural, and the development quite in harmony with what might have been expected.

The reason, whatever it is, once recognised, it follows that it would sooner or later be stretched to meet a variety of exceptional instances never thought of originally, and that a mass of subsidiary rules would speedily be promulgated. This has been the case, and these rules, for the most part purely technical, cause much comment on the part of those who abhor collectors of any thing or any school, and deplore the large sums of money lightly spent, as they assert, upon trifles.

The book-men may, however, be safely trusted to look after their own interests. In the aggregate they rule supreme, and can do as they please; and though they perhaps cannot explain why a set of original parts should lose most of their importance when bound up in more convenient volume form, or give the reason—other than an arbitrary one—of their preference for some particularly unreliable and inferior edition, the fact remains that their word is law, and that no power on earth, short of their own will, can detract from its authority.

Personally, I do not collect books, or, indeed, anything else; but if I did, it is almost certain that after some years of success I should, like others, be led from the track, trod smooth by the feet of thousands, to stray in less familiar places, and to derive some little satisfaction in pleasanter, because more expectant paths.

It is, however, quite possible for the sole owner of nothing but what is useful for every-day consultation to be a collector of much in theory. In this case his choicer possessions are held in common; they are more numerous than any accumulation that has ever been made, even by some ancestral house or any public institution, and they are being added to continually. A very few of a certain kind are described hereafter, but many more are within the reach of all who choose to search for them. This is the communism of books, and should any one claim to possess the monopoly, then he must be deaf to the sound of the auctioneer's hammer and the lesson it conveys.

In this compilation books published in extremely limited quantities, for the obvious purpose of inducing speculation, have no place. The importance of many of these books is fictitious, and their quoted value illusive, and under all the circumstances it appears advisable to ignore them. The work merely contains a selection of books of a particular class, and the principles upon which that selection has been made depend upon the extent of the legitimate demand for volumes of the kind, as I conceive it to be, in addition to their importance from the limited standpoint of their price in the market.

That there are other modern or contemporary authors who might, on their own merits, be fairly represented, is unquestionable. Many authors of the first rank, such, for example, as Sir Walter Scott, though favourites in the broadest sense, were never sufficiently exclusive to excite the competition of accumulators of rare editions. They had a large audience almost from the first, and their books are to be met with every day. Their very popularity is their bane in the estimation of those who love most when there is least left to love.

J. H. S.

TEMPLE, E.C.

CONTENTS

NOTES

The quoted values are estimated with reference to good and perfect copies of the books to which they are appended, bound as described. Where auction values are given, they are based on a close average, and do not necessarily represent any sum actually realised on any particular occasion.

The editor cannot hold himself responsible for the technical accuracy of the stated sizes of books in small 8vo *et infra*. The confusion exists principally in the case of books in 12mo, a size not now used except on very rare occasions; and foolscap 8vo, crown 8vo, and post 8vo respectively.

At page 102 it is stated that Dickens had hardly anything to do with the pamphlet, "A Curious Dance round a Curious Tree." The original MS., kindly produced by Mr. Wise, is, however, entirely in the handwriting of Dickens.

At page 125 the opinion is expressed that the sonnets, "Brother and Sister," were probably reprinted from the "Legend of Jubal and other Poems," 1874, and that the pamphlet of 1869 would, in this case, be a fictitious and ante-dated edition. The British Museum Catalogue contains an entry to the same effect. I am assured, however, on the highest authority, that there is no foundation for the assertion, actual proofs of the writing and printing of the sonnets in 1869 being available.

EARLY EDITIONS.

WILLIAM HARRISON AINSWORTH.

THE interest manifested in the works of this prolific author seems to be confined chiefly, if not entirely, to those which are embellished with illustrations by Cruikshank, Hablot K. Browne, Franklin, J. H. Rimbault, or Sir John Gilbert. In this case it is the artist and not the author who is the real object of interest to the collector, for such of Ainsworth's works as were published without plates bring comparatively small prices.

William Harrison Ainsworth was born in King Street, Manchester, in February 1805. He seems to have developed an early talent for letters, for he could not have been much more than fifteen when he wrote a privately acted drama, afterwards published in *Arliss's Magazine*, and contributed regularly to the *Edinburgh Magazine*, the *European Magazine*, the *London Magazine*, the *Manchester Iris*, now a very scarce little periodical, and many other journals, including *Fraser's*. He even started a magazine of his own, called *The Bœotian*, which reached its sixth number, and published a collective volume of poems (the "Works of Cheviot Tichburn," 1822) before he was seventeen. By the age of twenty, he had written and published a short story (" A Summer Evening Tale," 1825), and a year later a volume of scattered essays (" Letters from Cockney Land," 1826), his views on the best means of affording immediate relief to the operative classes in the manufacturing districts, and a romance entitled " Sir

A

John Chiverton," noted as having earned the eulogy of Sir Walter Scott. In fact, Ainsworth was a well-known writer at twenty-one, which, if not an unique experience, is at any rate a highly exceptional instance of literary enterprise at such an early age.

No bibliography or satisfactory memoir of Ainsworth has yet been published, and as many years have elapsed since his death in 1882, it is improbable that the omission will now be supplied. A short memoir by Laman Blanchard is prefixed to the 1857 edition of "Rookwood," and various notices, more or less reliable, are to be found in the Cyclopædias. These apart, Ainsworth is without a biographer.

The final page of a Brochure, printed for the guests at a complimentary dinner given by the Mayor of Manchester to Ainsworth in 1881, contains a list of his works in chronological order; but even this attenuated though official bibliography is incorrect in many particulars. It has, moreover, been copied, apparently without enquiry, by nearly every writer who has paused for a moment to notice Ainsworth and his works.

It was this Brochure which started the theory that the number of the author's published novels amount to thirty-nine. That the list given in the following pages contains notices of considerably more will not be surprising when it is stated that the Brochure omits all mention of "Sir John Chiverton," "James the Second," and "Preston Fight," and describes "The Good Old Times" by its second title of "The Story of the Manchester Rebels of '45."

Collectors of Ainsworth will, I think, find a descriptive account of most of his works in the ensuing list, except the following:—

(a.) *The Bœotian*, a magazine, complete in six numbers, published in or about the year 1822.

(β.) The "Works of Cheviot Tichburn." London, 1822. Reprinted at Manchester three years later. .

(γ.) "A Summer Evening's Tale." London, 1825.

All these works are scarce, though one would think that copies must be met with occasionally. Probably they would not be recognised by most people even when seen, and so may escape repeatedly, hidden among the refuse that litters the street stalls. Personally, I have never come across any one of the three, and am consequently unable to describe them. I am at present in the same position with regard to "Tower Hill," 1870, "The South Sea Bubble," 1868, and "Talbot Harland," 1870.

It must be remembered that Ainsworth edited various periodicals at different periods of his career, *e.g.*, *Bentley's Miscellany* from March 1840, *Ainsworth's Magazine* from 1842 to 1853, and the *New Monthly* from 1853 onward (vol. lxxiii. to vol. cxlvii. inclusive). *Ainsworth's Magazine* is referred to hereafter, as it is peculiarly identified with its proprietor and founder.

1. December Tales. . . . London. Printed for G. and W. B. Whittaker, Ave Maria Lane. 1823.

These tales, scattered over the pages of several magazines, were now issued in a collective form.

The book, which is a small one (fcap. 8vo), was published at 5s. 6d., and should contain half-title, title as above, dedication to the Rev. Geo. Croly, preface, contents, and eleven different tales on pp. 1–198. It must be carefully observed that each of the tales should have a half-title prefixed, or the work will be incomplete.

Value about 10s. (boards).

2. Considerations on the Best Means of Affording
   Immediate Relief to the Operative Classes in
   the Manufacturing Districts. By William H.
   Ainsworth. London. John Ebers, Old Bond
   Street. MDCCCXXVI.

An 8vo tract of 24 pp. Following title as above there is an
unpaged dedication to "The Right Hon. Robert Peel." The
"Considerations" commence on p. 5.

3. Letters from Cockney Land. By William H.
   Ainsworth. . . . London. John Ebers, Old
   Bond Street. MDCCCXXVI.

This was published in boards, 12mo. Copies are occasionally
met with for very little, but the bookseller's average price seems
to be about 10s. (boards, as issued).

4. Sir John Chiverton : a Romance. . . . London.
   John Ebers, Old Bond Street. MDCCCXXVI.

Small demy 8vo, no illustrations, half-title, title as above,
dedicatory stanzas pp. v–vii, another half-title to the same effect
as the first, and text of novel pp. 3–317. It is questionable what
part of this romance can be attributed to Ainsworth. The authorship has been claimed by him, and also by J. P. Aston, until
recently a Solicitor in Manchester. The probability is that both
had a hand in it.
Value about 15s. (boards, as issued).

5. Rookwood : a Romance. London. Richard
   Bentley, New Burlington Street (successor to
   Henry Colburn). 1834.

The original edition is in 3 vols. post 8vo, and does not contain
any illustrations.

Value about £1 10s. (original cloth, auction). Other and later editions are of greater importance than the first, e.g. :—

First Illustrated Edition, 1836, published by Macrone in cloth with a gilt back. There is a portrait of Ainsworth after Maclise, and 12 full-page etchings (including title) by George Cruikshank.

Value about £5 15s. (original cloth, auction) ; £2 10s. (rebound in calf extra, auction).

Edition of 1851, post 8vo, published in cloth, with portrait and Cruikshank's etchings as before.

Value about £3 10s. (original cloth, auction).

Edition of 1857, demy 8vo, published in bright blue pictorial cloth, 8 full-page plates by Gilbert, and a memoir of the author by Laman Blanchard. This is the first edition illustrated by Gilbert.

Value about £1 15s. (original cloth, auction).

Edition of 1862, post 8vo, contains the same plates by Gilbert.

Value about 15s. (original cloth, auction).

6. Nick of the Woods : a Story of Kentucky. By the Author of " Spartacus," &c. Edited by W. Harrison Ainsworth, Esq., Author of " Rookwood." . . . London. Richard Bentley, New Burlington Street. 1837.

This work was written by Dr. Bird. It is a post 8vo book, in 3 vols. No copy is complete which does not contain a half-title before the title-page of each volume.

Value about 17s. 6d. (original boards).

7. Crichton. By W. Harrison Ainsworth, Esq., Author of " Rookwood." . . . London. Richard Bentley, New Burlington Street. MDCCCXXXVII.

In 3 vols. post 8vo, boards, no illustrations.

Value about £1 5s. (original boards). Copies of this edition rarely bring as much as £1 by auction.

Another Edition, 1849, Chapman & Hall, known as the " First Octavo Edition." It was published in pictorial cloth, and contains 18 etchings by " Phiz."

Value from 20s. to 30s. (cloth, auction).

Another Edition, 1853. Many copies are found in yellow boards, but some are in pictorial cloth. This edition contains the same etchings by " Phiz " as the last named.

Value about 15s. (pictorial cloth, auction).

" Crichton " was first published as a serial in *Ainsworth's Magazine*.

8. Jack Sheppard : a Romance.　By W. Harrison Ainsworth, Author of " Rookwood." . . . With Illustrations by George Cruikshank. London.　Richard Bentley, New Burlington Street.　1839.

This is one of the most important of Ainsworth's publications, and also one of the most expensive. The original edition of 1839 consists of 3 vols. post 8vo, with 27 full-page etchings by George Cruikshank, and a portrait. The volumes are made up as under :—

Vol. I. Portrait to face title, dedication, contents, list of illustrations, half-title, and text of novel pp. 1–352.

Vol. II. Half-title, frontispiece, title, contents, half-title, and text pp. 3–292.

Vol. III. Half-title, frontispiece, title, contents, half-title, and text pp. 1–312.

As usual, copies in the original green cloth are worth much more than those which have been rebound. The following auction prices will make this clear :—£12 15s. (original cloth); £7 (*ibid.*); £3 3s. (morocco extra, by Zaehnsdorf) ; £5 10s. (original cloth) ; £3 10s. (half morocco) ; £3 (half calf).

Another Edition, 1840, called the " First Octavo Edition." It contains the same etchings and portrait as the last edition, and is nearly as scarce when in good condition. It was issued originally in monthly parts, with pictorial covers specially designed by Cruikshank.

The following are auction values :—£5 10s. (original cloth) ;
£2 (half calf).

Another Edition, 1854, contains the 27 etchings by Cruikshank,
and was issued in cloth covers specially designed for it by the
same artist.

Value about £1 (original cloth).

Another Edition, 1862, published in yellow boards, with the
same illustrations.

Value about 16s. (boards, as issued).

" Jack Sheppard " was published originally as a serial in *Bentley's
Miscellany*, 1839–40.

9. The Tower of London : a Historical Romance.
By William Harrison Ainsworth. Illustrated
by George Cruikshank. London. Richard
Bentley, New Burlington Street. . . . 1840.

Issued in 13 monthly parts, the covers of which were designed by George Cruikshank. These parts together contain 40 full-page etchings and 58 woodcuts by the same
artist.

Value from £6 to £7 (auction).

First Royal 8vo Edition, 1840. The peculiarity of this book
is that copies sometimes contain 40 etchings by Cruikshank, and
sometimes 41. In either case the number of woodcuts is the
same, viz., 58. Copies of the book bound up from the parts only
contain 40 etchings ; in any other event, one extra plate ("The
Escape of Courtenay ").

The published price of this edition was 15s. Present value
about £3 10s. (pictorial cloth, auction) ; £1 10s. (half-calf,
ibid.).

Another Edition, 1845, 8vo. Pictorial cloth, plates and woodcuts as in the last-mentioned edition.

Value about £1 (cloth, as issued).

Another Edition, 1853, 8vo. Pictorial cloth, plates and woodcuts as before.

Value about 18s. (cloth, as issued).

10. Guy Fawkes ; or the Gunpowder Treason : an Historical Romance. By William Harrison Ainsworth. . . . With Illustrations by George Cruikshank. London. Richard Bentley, New Burlington Street. 1841.

Another important book, issued in 3 vols. 8vo, with 22 full-page etchings (including front) by George Cruikshank.

Vol. i. contains half-title, frontispiece, title, dedication to Mrs. Hughes, preface, contents, list of illustrations, the plot (on one unpaged leaf), text of the novel pp. 1–303. There should be seven plates in this volume.

Vol. ii. contains frontispiece, title, contents, half title, and pp. 3–307. Seven plates.

Vol. iii. is made up as vol. ii., with pp. 3–358, and eight plates. Value about £10 10s. (original cloth, auction).

First Royal 8vo Edition, 1857, with the same illustrations by Cruikshank. George Routledge & Co., cloth. This edition contains frontispiece opposite title, dedication, preface v–vi, contents vii–viii, and text pp. 1–359.

Value about £2 2s. (original cloth, auction).

11. Old Saint Paul's : a Tale of the Plague and the Fire. By William Harrison Ainsworth. . . . With Illustrations by John Franklin. London. Hugh Cunningham, Saint Martin's Place, Trafalgar Square. 1841.

Published in 12 monthly parts, in pictorial wrappers designed by George Cruikshank. The wrappers, which have the title in type under a Gothic arch, with a Crusader at each side, were originally intended for "The Tower of London," but used instead for "Old St. Paul's." The illustrations number 20, inclusive of front.

Value about £6 6s. (auction).

First Royal 8vo Edition, 1847, was issued in pictorial cloth, designed by " Phiz," but with 22 full-page etchings, 20 by Franklin as before, and two extra ones by "Phiz." This latter artist etched "The Song of the Plague." which forms the front, and the "Piper on the Dead Cart" on title to face. It will be noticed that the list of illustrations only gives 21 plates, omitting the plate to face p. 28.

Value about £2 10s. (original cloth, auction) ; £3 10s. (*ibid.*).

Another Edition, 1855, 8vo, George Routledge & Co., has the full set of plates by Franklin and "Phiz," and was issued in pictorial red cloth, representing Solomon Eagle at the summit of St. Paul's Cross. There should be half-title, front, pictorial title, plain title, advertisement, contents, list of plates (22, including front and vignette on first title), and text pp. 1–426.

Value about 15s. (original cloth, auction).

12. Ainsworth's Magazine : a Miscellany of Romance, General Literature, and Art. Edited by William Harrison Ainsworth. Illustrated by George Cruikshank. London. Hugh Cunningham, Saint Martin's Place, Trafalgar Square.

This periodical commenced in February 1842, and was discontinued in 1853, when Ainsworth is said by some to have acquired the *New Monthly Magazine*. It had many contributors who were either then or afterwards became eminent in the world of letters, among them C. J. Apperley ("Surtees"), Thackeray, and G. P. R. James. The first volume, to be complete, should contain (after title and contents, with list of illustrations at the foot), title-page of the first number for February, with Cruikshank's complaint against Bentley on the reverse, "To the Subscribers," and a "Preliminary Address."

A complete set of *Ainsworth's Magazine* is rarely met with, but odd volumes are comparatively common, selling for about 5s. each in half calf, or 15s. in original cloth, if clean and perfect. Original numbers with the covers are worth from 1s. 6d. to 2s. each.

13. The Miser's Daughter: a Tale. By William Harrison Ainsworth. . . . With Illustrations by George Cruikshank. London. Cunningham & Mortimer. . . . 1842.

Published in 3 vols. post 8vo, with 20 full-page etchings by George Cruikshank. The first volume contains front to face title as above, dedication, contents, half-title, and text; vols. ii. and iii. are made up in precisely the same way, except that the dedication is omitted. The frontispieces are included in the list of 20 full-page etchings.

Value about £3 10s. (original cloth, auction).

Another Edition, 1843, 3 vols. 8vo, with the 20 etchings as before.

Value £1 10s. (cloth, auction).

First Demy 8vo Edition, 1848, with the 20 etchings by Cruikshank, and a portrait of Ainsworth by Finden. Published in pictorial cloth, and made up as follows :—Portrait, title, dedication, contents, list of illustrations, frontispiece, half-title, and text pp. 1–396.

Value about £2 10s. (original cloth, auction); £1 7s. (calf extra, *ibid.*).

Another Edition, 1855, demy 8vo, published in pictorial blue cloth, with the 20 etchings as before. Contains half-title, front, title, dedication, contents, and text pp. 1–302.

Value 12s. to 15s. (original cloth, auction).

14. Windsor Castle : an Historical Romance. By W. Harrison Ainsworth, Esq., Author of "The Tower of London." . . . London. Henry Colburn, Publisher, Great Marlborough Street. 1843.

Published in 3 vols. 8vo, each containing half-title, front, title, contents, another half-title, and text of novel. The frontispiece to each volume is by George Cruikshank, but there are no other illustrations.

Value about £2 5s. (half morocco, uncut, auction).

First Demy 8vo Edition, 1843, containing 18 full-page etchings and 87 woodcuts by George Cruikshank, Tony Johannot, and Delamotte; also a portrait of Ainsworth after Maclise. Originally issued in monthly parts. The pictorial cloth covers of the bound book were designed by Cruikshank.

Value about £2 2s. (original cloth, auction); £4 4s. (original parts, *ibid.*).

Another Edition, 1844, royal 8vo, with the portrait, plates, and woodcuts as before. This edition was originally issued in 11 monthly parts with pictorial wrappers.

Value about £1 5s. (original cloth, auction); £1 (*ibid.*); £1 10s. (*ibid.*); £3 10s. (original parts, auction).

Another Edition, 1847, royal 8vo, with portrait and woodcuts as before, but 19 etchings by Cruikshank instead of 18.

Value about £1 (original cloth, auction).

Another Edition, 1853, royal 8vo, with portrait, 18 etchings, and 87 woodcuts as in the first demy 8vo edition.

Value about 15s. (original cloth, auction).

15. Saint James's; or the Court of Queen Anne: an Historical Romance. By William Harrison Ainsworth, Author of " The Tower of London." . . . With Illustrations by George Cruikshank. London. John Mortimer. . . . 1844.

Published in 3 vols. post 8vo, with 9 plates (inclusive of front to vol. i.) by George Cruikshank. Vol. i. should contain front, title, dedication to G. P. R. James, contents, half-title, and text. Vols. ii. and iii. are made up in the same way, but with the omission of the frontispiece and dedication.

Value about £2 10s. (half morocco, uncut, auction); £7 10s. (original cloth, *ibid.*).

Another Edition, 3 vols. post 8vo, 1846, with the 9 full-page etchings as before. This edition was published in pictorial cloth cover designed by George Cruikshank.

Value about £3 5s. (original cloth, auction).

16. Auriol; or The Elixir of Life. By William Harrison Ainsworth. . . . London. Henry Colburn. . . . 1845.

This novel was written for the *New Monthly Magazine*, and appeared in two parts during July and August 1845, with 15 full-page etchings by "Phiz." These two parts are scarce, selling for 30s. or 35s. by auction if in the original wrappers and clean.

There is no good edition of "Auriol." That of 1865, published at 1s. by Routledge, is unimportant, and another copy published by the same firm without date (but 1875), is merely one volume of a series which made its appearance in green cloth, gilt, demy 8vo. Though it contains the 15 etchings by "Phiz," the value is trifling.

17. James the Second; or the Revolution of 1688 : an Historical Romance. Edited by W. Harrison Ainsworth. London. Henry Colburn, Publisher, Great Marlborough Street. 1848.

In 3 vols. post 8vo, made up as follows :—
Vol. I. Half-title, front by Buss, title, introduction, list of illustrations, and text.
Vols. II. and III. The same, except that there is no introduction or list of illustrations. The illustrations comprise simply the three frontispieces ; there are none other.
Value £1 7s. (original cloth, auction) ; £2 (*ibid.*).

18. The Lancashire Witches : a Novel. By William Harrison Ainsworth, Esq. London. Printed for Private Circulation only. 1849.

This novel appeared in the *Sunday Times* during 1848, and when completed Ainsworth had a few copies printed from the

same type for presentation to friends. This privately printed
edition is in double columns, folio, and was issued in purple
cloth, lettered on the back, pp. 1–185. It is scarce, and copies
are worth some £4 or £5 each.

First Published Edition, 3 vols. post 8vo, 1849, Henry Colburn.
The title reads, "The Lancashire Witches : a Romance of Pendle
Forest." There are no illustrations.

Value about £1 (original cloth).

First Illustrated Edition, 1854, 8vo, published in pictorial cloth,
with 12 full-page plates (including front) by Gilbert.

Value about £1 (as issued).

19. The Star Chamber : an Historical Romance.
By William Harrison Ainsworth, Author of
"The Tower of London." . . . London. G.
Routledge & Co., Farringdon Street. 1854.

Published in 2 vols. 8vo, without illustrations. Each volume
should have half-title, title, and table of contents, and vol. i. an
inscription to Mrs. Mostyn.

Value 10s. to 12s. (cloth).

First Illustrated Edition, 1857, 8vo, cloth, with 8 full-page plates
by "Phiz."

Value about £1 5s. (original cloth, auction).

20. The Flitch of Bacon ; or the Custom of
Dunmow : a Tale of English Home. By
William Harrison Ainsworth. . . . With
Illustrations by John Gilbert. London.
George Routledge & Co., Farringdon Street.
. . . 1854.

This work was published in red cloth, crown 8vo, and contains
front, title as above, dedication, preface, contents ix–xii, half-
title, and text pp. 3–376. It is divided into five parts, each of

which should have its half-title. There are 8 plates including front.

Value about £1 (cloth, as issued).

See *post*, No. 43.

21. Ballads, Romantic, Fantastical, and Humourous. By William Harrison Ainsworth. Illustrated by John Gilbert. London. G. Routledge & Co. . . ˙. 1855.

Published in green cloth, gilt, post 8vo, with 8 plates (inclusive of front) by Gilbert. This is the first collective edition of Ainsworth's poems. A complete copy should contain half-title, front, title, contents v–ix, list of illustrations (unpaged), another half-title, and text pp. 3–274.

Value about 5s. (original cloth).

22. The Spendthrift : a Tale. By William Harrison Ainsworth. . . . With Illustrations by Hablot K. Browne. London. George Routledge & Co., Farringdon Street. . . . 1857.

Published in pictorial cloth, 8vo, with 8 full-page illustrations (including front) by "Phiz." There should be a half-title before front.

Copies even in the original cloth very rarely bring as much as £1 by auction, and frequently sell for much less.

23. Mervyn Clitheroe. By William Harrison Ainsworth. Illustrated by Hablot K. Browne. London. George Routledge & Co., Farringdon Street. . . . 1858.

This novel was published in monthly parts in yellow wrappers. The first part appeared in December 1851, but the publication stopped with the March number, and the fifth part did not appear until December 1857, nor the last until June 1858. Each part contains 32 pp. and 2 etchings.

The story was first published in volume form in 1858 as above, and this work contains 24 full-page etchings, inclusive of front and illustrated title. There are thus two title-pages, one with a vignette and the other plain; a half-title precedes the list of plates.

Value about £1 5s. (original cloth). A set of the parts would be worth considerably more, as owing to the temporary stoppage of the publication, the earlier numbers are exceedingly difficult to meet with.

24. The Combat of the Thirty : from a Breton Lay of the Fourteenth Century. With an Introduction comprising a New Chapter of Froissart. By William Harrison Ainsworth. London. Chapman & Hall, 193 Piccadilly. MDCCCLIX.

Issued in stiff wrappers, square post 8vo, at 1s., and contains title, contents, introduction 1–12, "The Combat" pp. 13–32.

This little publication is scarce, and a clean copy could not be procured for much less than £1.

25. Ovingdean Grange : a Tale of the South Downs. By William Harrison Ainsworth. Illustrated by Hablot K. Browne. London. Routledge, Warne & Routledge. . . . 1860.

This work was published in blue cloth designed by "Phiz," and contains 8 plates by "Phiz" (inclusive of front). A half-title should follow the list of illustrations.

Value about 25s. (pictorial cloth, as issued).

In connection with this work may be mentioned an oblong 8vo pamphlet entitled "Views of the Devil's Dyke, the Legend of which is derived by permission from Ovingdean Grange." This pamphlet is in a yellow cover, lettered in green and gold, and contains four views of the "Devil's Dyke" and "The Legend of the Devil's Dyke," pp. 1–8. Two blank leaves should follow the text. The pamphlet is not dated, but it was published in 1860.

Value, a few shillings.

26. The Constable of the Tower : an Historical Romance. By William Harrison Ainsworth. Illustrated by John Gilbert. London. Chapman & Hall, 193 Piccadilly. MDCCCLXI.

Published in 3 vols. post 8vo, red cloth, with six illustrations, three of which are in vol. i. and two in vol. ii. In each vol. a frontispiece faces title, and a half-title follows the list of illustrations in each case.

Copies in the original cloth rarely sell for as much as £1 by auction.

27. The Lord Mayor of London ; or City Life in the Last Century. By William Harrison Ainsworth. London. Chapman & Hall. 1862.

This work was published in 3 vols. post 8vo, magenta cloth, with the City of London arms on the side. There are no illustrations. Each volume has a half-title, which follows the table of contents.

Value about 15s. (original cloth).

28. Cardinal Pole ; or the Days of Philip and Mary : an Historical Romance. By William Harrison Ainsworth. London. Chapman & Hall, 193 Piccadilly. 1863.

Published in 3 vols. post 8vo, brick-red cloth. There are no illustrations. Each of the eight books into which the novel is divided is preceded by a half-title.

This is one of the least valuable of all Ainsworth's publications, the three volumes being worth no more than about 10s. (cloth, as issued).

29. John Law, the Projector. By William Harrison Ainsworth. London. Chapman & Hall, 193 Piccadilly. 1864.

Issued in 3 vols. post 8vo, brown cloth. There are no illustrations.
Value about 15s. (cloth, as issued).

30. The Spanish Match; or Charles Stuart at Madrid. By William Harrison Ainsworth. . . . London. Chapman & Hall, 193 Piccadilly. 1865.

Issued in 3 vols. post 8vo, purple cloth. No illustrations. Each volume has, or should have, a half-title after the table of contents.
Value about 15s. (cloth, as issued).

31. The Constable de Bourbon. By William Harrison Ainsworth. . . . London. Chapman & Hall, 193 Piccadilly. 1866.

Issued in 3 vols. post 8vo, magenta cloth. No illustrations. Each volume has half-title after the table of contents.
Value about 10s. (cloth, as issued).

32. Old Court: a Novel. By William Harrison Ainsworth. London. Chapman & Hall, 193 Piccadilly. 1867.

Published in 3 vols. post 8vo, terra-cotta cloth. No illustrations In each volume a half-title precedes the title, and another follows

the table of contents. There are consequently two half-titles to
each volume.
  Value from 15s. to £1 (original cloth, as issued).

33. Myddleton Pomfret: a Novel. By William
     Harrison Ainsworth. London. Chapman &
     Hall, 193 Piccadilly. 1868.

In 3 vols. post 8vo, dark red cloth. No illustrations. The
first volume has a half-title preceding the title, but vols. ii. and iii.
have not.
  Value 10s. or 12s. (cloth, as issued).

34. Hilary St. Ives: a Novel. By William Har-
     rison Ainsworth. London. Chapman & Hall.
     . . . 1870.

In 3 vols. post 8vo, red cloth. There are no illustrations. Each
volume contains title, contents, and half-title preceding the text.
  Value 10s. or 12s. (cloth, as issued).

35. Boscobel; or the Royal Oak: a Tale of the
     Year 1651. By William Harrison Ainsworth.
     Illustrated by J. H. Rimbault. . . . London.
     Tinsley Brothers, 18 Catherine Street, Strand.
     1872.

Published in 3 vols. post 8vo, green cloth, each of which contains four illustrations (including front) by Rimbault.
  Value from 20s. to 25s. (original cloth).
  Routledge's illustrated edition of this work was published in
1874. It is, however, one of the series in green cloth, not usually
bought by collectors.

36. The Good Old Times : the Story of the Manchester Rebels of '45. By William Harrison Ainsworth, Author of "Boscobel." . . . London. Tinsley Brothers. . . . 1873.

In 3 vols. post 8vo, bright blue cloth. No illustrations.
Value 10s. or 12s. (cloth, as issued).

37. Merry England; or Nobles and Serfs. By William Harrison Ainsworth, Author of " The Tower of London." . . . London. Tinsley Brothers. . . . 1874.

In 3 vols. post 8vo, light green cloth. There are no illustrations. Each volume contains two half-titles, one before the title and the other after the table of contents.
Value 10s. or 12s. (cloth, as issued).

38. Preston Fight; or the Insurrection of 1715 : a Tale. By William Harrison Ainsworth, Author of " Boscobel." . . . London. Tinsley Brothers. . . . 1875.

In 3 vols., green cloth. No illustrations. Each volume contains title, contents, and half-title.
Value 10s. or 12s. (original cloth).

39. The Goldsmith's Wife : a Tale. By William Harrison Ainsworth, Author of " Preston Fight." . . . London. Tinsley Brothers. . . . 1875.

In 3 vols., bright blue cloth. No illustrations. Each volume contains title, contents, and half-title.
Value 10s. to 12s. (original cloth).

40. The Leaguer of Lathom : a Tale of the Civil
War in Lancashire. By William Harrison
Ainsworth, Author of " Preston Fight." . . .
London. Tinsley Brothers. . . . 1876.

In 3 vols. post 8vo, in bright blue cloth. There are no illustrations. Vol. i. contains a dedication, and all three vols. have a half-
title after the table of contents.
Value 10s. or 12s. (original cloth).

41. Chetwynd Calverley : a Tale. By William
Harrison Ainsworth, Author of " Preston
Fight." . . . London. Tinsley Brothers. . . .
1876.

In 3 vols. post 8vo, slate-coloured cloth. There are no illustrations. The story is divided into six books, each of which should
be preceded by a half-title.
Value from 10s. to 12s. (original cloth).

42. The Fall of Somerset. By William Harrison
Ainsworth, Author of " Preston Fight." . . .
London. Tinsley Brothers. . . . 1877.

In 3 vols. post 8vo, reddish-brown cloth. In vol. i., after title
as above, comes dedication (unpaged), contents, half-title, and text
pp. 3–290. The other volumes have title, contents, and half-title.
Value from 8s. to 10s. (original cloth).

43. History of the Dunmow Flitch of Bacon
Custom. By William Andrews. . . . Poems
by William Harrison Ainsworth and others.
London. William Tegg & Co., Pancras Lane,
Cheapside. MDCCCLXXVII.

This is a small fcap. 8vo, of 64 pages, in blue pictorial boards.

It should contain a portrait of Ainsworth, whose contribution to
the work is a poem entitled "The Custom of Dunmow, showing
how it arose." Some 6s. or 8s. would probably have to be paid
for a clean copy, as issued.

44. Beatrice Tyldesley. By William Harrison
    Ainsworth, Author of "The Tower of London."
    London. Tinsley Brothers. . . . 1878.

Issued in 3 vols. post 8vo, red cloth. There are no illustrations.
Value about 10s. (original cloth).

45. Beau Nash; or Bath in the Eighteenth
    Century. By William Harrison Ainsworth,
    Author of "The Tower of London." . . .
    London. George Routledge & Sons. . . .
    N.D. (but 1879).

Issued in 3 vols. post 8vo, dark brown cloth. No illustrations.
Value from 10s. to 12s. (original cloth).

46. Brochure presented to each Guest, and Report
    of the Proceedings at a Complimentary Dinner
    given by Thomas Baker, Esq., Mayor of
    Manchester, to William Harrison Ainsworth,
    Esq., at the Town Hall, Manchester, Sep-
    tember 15, 1881.

The Brochure is an 8vo pamphlet of eight pages, containing a
photograph of Ainsworth, surrounded by descriptive scroll work,
scenes from some of his chief novels, and a chronological list of
his works. The Report gives an account of the proceedings at
the dinner, and occupies pp. 3–24. Subsequently both Brochure
and Report were bound up together in stiff green covers, bearing
the above title.

It is difficult to assess the value of this production, which was not of course published, but a collector of Ainsworth's works would probably be asked 15s. or 20s. for a copy.

47. Stanley Brereton. By William Harrison Ainsworth, Author of "The Tower of London." London. George Routledge & Sons. N.D. (but 1881).

This, the last of Ainsworth's novels, was published in 3 vols. crown 8vo. Vol. i. is dedicated to Thomas Baker, and contains a Revised Report of the Manchester Banquet. Each volume contains half-title after the table of contents. There are no illustrations.

Value about 10s. (cloth, as issued).

Many of Ainsworth's novels which appeared originally without illustrations were afterwards published in a series by Routledge with plates. There is the green cloth series in demy 8vo, about 1874, and the red cloth series, with a facsimile of the author's signature on the cover of each volume, which was published some five years later. Single volumes from these sets are occasionally used to supplement plain original editions. The value in every case is the same, viz., about 2s. 6d. per volume.

MATTHEW ARNOLD.

ALTHOUGH the works of Matthew Arnold are numerous, only a few need be mentioned here. The remainder are educational works or essays in prose of great importance from a scholastic and literary point of view, but of little account from that of the collector of early editions. Some few of these minor works may, however, be referred to.

"Popular Education in France," 1861, is a desirable book which sometimes sells for 10s. or 15s. by auction, in the original cloth, and "Culture and Anarchy," 1869, "Mixed Essays," 1879, and "God and the Bible," 1875, will sometimes bring a few shillings each. "Poetry of Byron," 1881, was issued on large paper, with the portrait on India paper. The booksellers charge from 17s. 6d. to £1 for a good copy of this, and for "Friendship's Garland," 1871, 8vo, they will frequently ask more. There was a difference between the boards of original issue and the remainder copies of "Friendship's Garland." All the other books credited to this author, except the seven mentioned below, are, however, easily met with, and for that reason do not excite much interest.

Matthew Arnold was the eldest son of the celebrated schoolmaster, Dr. Arnold. When eighteen years of age he secured honourable distinction at Rugby for his prize poem, " Alaric at Rome," and three years later obtained the New-digate prize for a poem entitled "Cromwell." Later on he published "The Strayed Reveller" and "Empedocles on Etna," two exceedingly scarce volumes of verse, which were apparently withdrawn from circulation to make way for the first and second series of poems, published in 1854 and 1855 respectively, these being almost exclusively composed of selections from the earlier works mentioned. "Merope, a Tragedy," appeared in 1858, and with that the author's poetic activity practically ceased, though in 1867 he issued a series of "New Poems" all of which were then published for the first time, with the exception of seven from " Empedocles on Etna."

Matthew Arnold was born at Laleham near Windsor in 1822, and died on April 15, 1888.

A capital Bibliography of Arnold, by Mr. Thomas Burnett Smart, was published by Davy & Sons, of the Dryden Press, Long Acre, in 1892.

1. Alaric at Rome : a Prize Poem, Recited in Rugby School June xii. MDCCCXL. . . . Rugby. Combe and Crossley.   MDCCCXL.

This is a post 8vo pamphlet of eleven pages, without cover, and until recently the only copy known was in the library of Mr. Edmund Gosse. A second copy has, however, since been reported.

It is impossible to estimate the value of an almost unique book. Some little time ago a copy of " Alaric at Rome " is said to have been sold by a dealer " for its weight in gold," which, however, would not be a particularly large amount.

2. Cromwell : a Prize Poem, Recited in the Theatre, Oxford, June 28, 1843. By Matthew Arnold, Balliol College. . . . Oxford. Printed and Published by J. Vincent.   MDCCCXLIII.

A pamphlet in 12mo, published at 1s. 6d. in brown-paper covers, lettered as above. It contains title as above, synopsis (unpaged), and text, pp. 5-15. A second edition appeared the same year. Reprints are in green covers.

Seven hundred and fifty copies are said to have been printed of this work, which, though scarce, is not unprocurable. The bookseller's price is about £4 4s.

3. The Strayed Reveller, and other Poems.   By A. London.   B. Fellowes, Ludgate Street.   1849.

Foolscap 8vo, dark-green cloth, published at 4s. 6d.   There are eight pages of preliminary matter, and pp. 128 of text.

Although 500 copies of this book were printed, only about 100 were sold, the remainder being withdrawn from circulation.   The value of any stray copy depends almost entirely on the freshness of the original cloth cover.   The book has realised as much as £7 by auction, but a far more usual price is from £3 15s. to £4.

4. Empedocles on Etna, and other Poems.   By A. London.   B. Fellowes, Ludgate Street.   1852.

Foolscap 8vo, dark-green cloth, published at 6s.

This book, like the last, was withdrawn from circulation after a small number of copies had been sold, some say 50, while others estimate the sale at over 100.   However this may be, the value is about the same as "The Strayed Reveller."   From £3 10s. to about £6 are the usual limits, the actual value depending in this instance also upon the condition of the cloth covers.

5. Poems.   By Matthew Arnold.   A new edition. London.   Longman, Brown, Green & Longmans.   MDCCCLIII.

Published at 5s. 6d. in dark-green cloth, 12mo.   The book contains half-title, title, preface (v–xxi), contents (xxxiii–xxxv), second half-title ("Poems"), third half-title ("Sohrab and Rustum"), and text (pp. 5–248).

Though the title describes the work as a "new edition," it is in fact the first edition of Arnold's collective poems.   The edition was new in the sense that the poems had mostly appeared before, either in "The Strayed Reveller" or "Empedocles on Etna."

For value see next entry.

6. Poems.   By Matthew Arnold.   Second Series. London.   Longman, Brown, Green & Longmans.   MDCCCLV.

Published at 5s. 6d. in dark-green cloth, 12mo.   The book contains title, but no half-title, contents (iii–v), Greek inscription (unpaged), half-title ("Poems"), and text, pp. 3–210.

Clean and sound copies of the two volumes, comprising the first and second series of the "Poems," 1853 and 1855 respectively, sell by auction for about £1 1s. (original cloth), or, if very clean, for more.

These "Poems" passed through many editions, all of less value than the originals.

7. Merope: a Tragedy.   By Matthew Arnold. London.   Longman, Brown, Green, Longmans & Roberts.   MDCCCLVIII.

Published in dark-green cloth, 12mo, lettered in gilt on face. The work contains half-title, title, preface (vii–xlviii), historical introduction (xlix–lii), a second half-title, and text, pp. 3–138.

This is not a very scarce book, copies being frequently met with at auction for 5s. or 6s. (original cloth).

––––––––

Matthew Arnold's concluding volume of verse, which he published in 1867, post 8vo, under the title of "New Poems," contains several pieces reprinted from "Empedocles on Etna," together with a number of fresh poems never before printed.   This book is of about the same bibliographical importance as "Merope," above mentioned.

R. H. BARHAM.

THE Rev. Richard Harris Barham, at one time a minor Canon of St. Paul's, and afterwards Rector of St. Mary Magdalene and St. Gregory, was a man of one book, but that one of such merit that he acquired an undying reputation on the strength of it.

The "Ingoldsby Legends" has passed through numerous editions, and is probably destined to pass through many more. This series of stories in verse and prose commenced in *Bentley's Miscellany* with "The Spectre of Tappington," and was continued from time to time in that journal and in the *New Monthly Magazine*, and when published collectively in one volume, 1840, firmly established the author's reputation as a humorist of the highest rank. A second series of "Legends" appeared in 1842, and a third in 1847.

From the book-man's point of view, original editions of these three series are of the greatest importance, their scarcity being notorious, and the talent displayed in text and illustration undeniable.

The author's "My Cousin Nicholas," which appeared originally in *Blackwood* in 1834, but was not published in volume form until 1841, has little to recommend it. It is mentioned here, however, for it is occasionally asked for, though from a pecuniary aspect the value is not great.

The Rev. R. H. Barham was born at Canterbury in 1788, and died in June 1845.

1. The Ingoldsby Legends; or, Mirth and Marvels. By Thomas Ingoldsby, Esquire. London. Richard Bentley. MDCCCXL.

This well-known work was originally published in 3 vols. post 8vo, 1840-42-47, blue cloth, containing the first, second, and third series respectively. There are two issues of the original edition of the first series, the earlier and better of which may be known by a misprint which occurs on page 81, and was subsequently altered.

The collation of these three scarce volumes is as follows:—

Vol. I. Half-title, engraved title, dedication to Richard Bentley (iii–v), contents, and on the reverse list of illustrations, front, and text, pp. 1–338. An appendix in verse follows page 338, and this is very often wanting. There are six plates by Buss, Leech, George Cruikshank, and others.

Vol. II. Half-title, title as before but dated MDCCCXLII, dedication to Richard Bentley (v–vii), contents (unpaged), and text, pp. 1–288. Seven full-page plates.

Vol. III. Half-title, title as before but dated MDCCCXLVII, preface, (iii–vi), contents, with list of illustrations on reverse (unpaged), portrait of R. H. Barham, and text, pp. 1–364. Six plates by Leech and others, including two portraits.

A second edition of the first series was published in 1843, and this is noticeable as containing a preface which did not appear in the prior edition of 1840. A second edition of the second series was published in 1842, and a second edition of the third series in 1848.

A third edition of the first series appeared in 1846, of the second series in 1846, and of the third series in 1848.

Clean and sound copies of the three original series are very seldom seen, and invariably command high prices whenever they make their appearance in the auction room. As much as £31 10s. was paid at a sale held by Messrs. Christie, Manson & Woods on January 29, 1891, for the three volumes, in the original cloth as issued; but in this case the covers were quite fresh, and the impressions of the plates unusually clear. A very ordinary auction price under less favourable, but far more usual, circumstances is some £15 or £16, from which it is evident that, in assessing the value of these books, special attention must be paid to the quality and impressions of the plates in the first instance, and secondly to the appearance of the binding. As these points are in favour of or against the work, so will its value rise or fall between the limits of about £30 and £10, for a copy which will not produce the latter sum must be a very indifferent one indeed.

In most cases the three volumes will be found to belong to different editions. Thus, the first may belong to the second, and the second and third to the first; nor may they all be bound the same way, for one volume may be in the original cloth, and the other two in a calf or russia binding. Variations such as these must, of course, be taken into account on every purchase, and the price calculated according to the special circumstances of the case, a difficult process, and one requiring a great deal of experience to work out satisfactorily.

Thus copies of the 1st series, 3rd edition, 1846; 2nd series, 2nd edition, 1842; and 3rd series, 1st edition, 1847, in half-russia, but uncut, would sell for about £9 by auction. The single volume of the 2nd series, 1st edition, 1842, half-russia, uncut, would bring about £2 10s., and the three volumes, 1st series, 2nd edition, 1843, and 2nd series, vols. ii. and iii., 1st editions, 1842 and 1847, respectively about £10 10s. (original cloth).

Every copy must therefore be dealt with on its merits, always remembering that rebound and cut-down specimens, as well as those which are imperfect in some particular, or much worn by constant handling, must be granted a liberal reduction. Attention should also be directed to the quality of the plates, for some impressions are much better than others. The general rule that it is better to have a copy of a dirty uncut book, than a copy which is quite clean but has been cropped by the binder, applies in its full force here, and must not be overlooked.

Another Edition, the three series, in 3 vols. 8vo, 1852, blue cloth, with all the plates by George Cruikshank, Leech, &c., and portrait by Lane.

Value about £4 (morocco extra, uncut, auction), £2 5s. (half-morocco, uncut).

Another Edition, the three series, in 3 vols., 1855, blue pictorial cloth, with all the p'ates by G. Cruikshank, Leech, &c., and portrait by Lane.

Value about £2 10s. (original cloth, auction), £1 (half-calf,
ibid.).

Another Edition, the three series, in 1 vol., 1866, 4to, with 72
illustrations by G. Cruikshank, Leech, Tenniel, Doyle, and Du
Maurier.

Value about £1 15s. (half-calf, gilt edges, auction).

Another Edition, with notes by R. H. Barham, 2 vols., 1870,
8vo, and 25 plates by Cruikshank, Leech, Gilks, and Buss.

Value about 15s. (original cloth, auction).

2. Some Account of My Cousin Nicholas. By
    Thomas Ingoldsby, Esquire. . . . To which is
    added the Rubber of Life. London. Richard
    Bentley, New Burlington Street. 1841.

This novel, which was now published in 3 vols. post 8vo, cloth,
1841, had previously appeared in *Blackwood's Magazine* in the
form of a serial.

The present value of a clean copy, as issued, averages about
17s. 6d. by auction.

GILBERT À BECKETT.

GILBERT ABBOTT À BECKETT (born 1811, died 1856) is better known as a successful burlesque writer than in any other capacity, though two of his works, "The Comic History of England" and "The Comic History of Rome," have always commanded a large share of attention, probably by reason of their intrinsic merit, but chiefly no doubt from the fact of their having been profusely illustrated by Leech.

Gilbert à Beckett was on the original staff of *Punch*, and it is probable that he had at any rate something to do with its establishment, for his journal, *Figaro in London*, was discontinued to make way for what has since proved to be one of the most successful literary ventures of modern times.

As an all-round journalist, à Beckett had few rivals. For many years he was on the staff of the *Times*, the *Morning Post*, and the *Illustrated London News*, and it is recorded that on one occasion he wrote the whole of the leading articles that appeared in one of the numbers of the first-named journal. If this be true, no further proof is needed of his great expedition and singular versatility, which indeed displayed itself continuously throughout his comparatively short career.

The dramatic productions of Gilbert à Beckett will be found scattered through the pages of several collections of acting plays, notably Duncombe's "British Theatre," Webster's "Acting National Drama," Cumberland's "British Theatre," Hilsenberg's "Modern English Comic Theatre," and Cumberland's "Minor Theatre." He did not publish many works in volume form, and only half a dozen are sought after by collectors. These are given below in their proper order, and in the meantime reference must be made to that well-known publication, "The Comic Almanack: an Ephemeris in Jest and Earnest," which contains many contributions from his pen, and was illustrated throughout by George Cruikshank.

"The Comic Almanack" was published annually, from 1835 to 1853 inclusive, by Tilt of Fleet Street, at a charge of 2s. 6d., except in 1848 and 1849, when its size was reduced, and the price altered to 1s. This change did not produce the desired result, so that in 1850 the periodical was restored to its normal dimensions, and published at 2s. 6d. as before. The 19 numbers or parts are not often found complete and perfect, that is to say, the first 15 parts in the original wrappers, and the remaining four in the original cloth, as issued. Such a set, with original impressions of the cuts, sells readily enough by auction at from 12 to 17 guineas, according to condition, though bound and cut copies are of nothing like the same value, and are, comparatively speaking, of small importance. In March 1891, a set sold by auction for £40, but the etchings in twelve of the parts were brilliant proof impressions on India paper, and all the original covers and advertisements were beautifully bound up by Rivière. In all cases, it is a question of the character and quality of the plates, and the earlier these are, and the more brilliant, the better.

In or about the year 1870, Hotten issued a reprint of the "Comic Almanack" in two series, and the same number of volumes, the first from 1835 to 1843, and the second from 1844 to 1853. They were published in green cloth covers, with designs by George Cruikshank, and a facsimile of his signature, both in gilt on the sides. The two volumes of this reprint sell on the average for about 18s. by auction, though some copies, if very clean, occasionally produce a little more.

The following six works are attributed to Gilbert à Beckett, and will be readily remembered.

1. The Comic Blackstone. By Gilbert Abbott à Beckett. London. Published at the Punch Office, 194 Strand. MDCCCXLIV.

Published in four parts, fcap. 8vo, in yellow boards, lettered in black and red with the comic cut of a "Bill of Costs" on the side. The first part made its appearance in 1844, the last in 1846, and each was published at half-a-crown. The earliest issue of Part I. has an engraved title-page, representing two Counsel playing at battledore and shuttlecock.

Value about £1 (as issued).

Another Edition, 1886, &c., 8vo, revised by A. W. à Beckett, and published in parts by Bradbury, Agnew & Co., who afterwards issued the whole work in one volume at 12s. Some of the illustrations are coloured.

The value of this publication is, usually speaking, less than the published price.

2. George Cruikshank's Table Book. Edited by Gilbert Abbott à Beckett. . . . London. Published at the Punch Office, 92 Fleet Street. MDCCCXLV.

This work, which contains 12 full-page illustrations and numerous woodcuts by George Cruikshank, was published originally in 12 monthly parts in wrappers designed by Cruikshank, and afterwards in volume form, royal 8vo, cloth, with gilt edges.

It contains illustrated title-page, title as above, list of illustrations (v–vi), contents (vii–viii), frontispiece (entitled "A Reverie"), and text pp. 1–284.

It was to this periodical that Thackeray contributed (under his pseudonym of Michael Angelo Titmarsh) the "Legend of the Rhine." Many of the articles are by à Beckett, who, as the title announces, was the editor.

Value about £3 10s. (original cloth, auction). Copies which

have been rebound are of comparatively little value, unless the edges are left quite uncut. Copies of the original 12 parts are very scarce, and worth some £8 or £10 by auction.

> 3. The Quizziology of the British Drama. . . . By Gilbert Abbott à Beckett. London. Published at the Punch Office, 85 Fleet Street. MDCCCXLVI.

This little book, in 12mo, was published in reddish brown cloth, lettered in gilt on side and face. It contains frontispiece ("Stage Passions"), title as above, introduction (iii–iv), and text pp. 1–87. In addition to the frontispiece, there is a cut on the title and seven woodcuts in the text by Leech.

A clean copy in the original cloth is worth some 10s. or 12s.

> 4. The Almanack of the Month: a Review of Everything and Everybody. Edited by Gilbert Abbott à Beckett. London. Punch Office . . . MDCCCXLVI.

This Ephemeris was issued in 12 monthly parts, in pictorial wrappers, which, when bound up, are generally in two volumes, the first embracing January to June, and the second July to December.

Vol. i. contains half-title ("The Almanack of the Month"), title, and text pp. 1–380, inclusive of index.

Vol. ii. contains half-title (as before), title, preface (v–vii), and text pp. 1–376, inclusive of index.

The preface in vol. ii. was issued with the last number for December, though its position is altered in the bound volume.

The value of the 12 parts as issued is somewhere about £2 when bound, but if cut by the binder, much less.

5. The Comic History of England. By Gilbert
   Abbott à Beckett. . . . Published at the
   Punch Office, 85 Fleet Street. MDCCCXLVII.

In 2 vols. demy 8vo, 1847–1853, brown cloth, with gilt design
on sides and face by Leech. Published originally in 20 parts.

Vol. i. contains half-title in red, title in red and black, with
vignette, preface (v–vi), contents (vii–viii), list of illustrations
(ix–xii), and text pp. 1–320. There are 10 full-page coloured
plates and numerous woodcuts in the text by Leech.

Vol. ii. contains half-title in red, title, advertisement (v–vi),
contents (vii–viii), list of illustrations (ix–xii), and text pp. 1–304.
In this volume also there are 10 full-page coloured plates and
numerous woodcuts in the text by Leech.

Value about £2 10s. (original cloth, auction); £5 (original
parts, *ibid.*).

Another Edition, 1863, in 1 vol. 8vo, Bradbury, Agnew & Co.,
published at 12s., and now worth a little less.

Another Edition, 1881, 2 vols. imperial 8vo, published at Edinburgh. Value about £1 (in cloth, as issued).

Another Edition, called the "Edition de Luxe," 2 vols. 4to,
N.D., Bradbury, Agnew & Co. The coloured (20) and other
illustrations are on China paper. Value about £1 5s. (as issued,
auction).

6. The Comic History of Rome. By Gilbert
   Abbott à Beckett. . . . Published by Bradbury & Evans, 11 Bouverie Street, Whitefriars. N.D.

This work was, like the author's "Comic History of England,"
originally published in parts, and afterwards in volume form, demy
8vo. It contains half-title in black, pictorial title in red and black,
preface (v–vi), contents (vii–viii), list of illustrations (ix–xii), and
text pp. 1–308. There are 10 coloured plates and numerous woodcuts by Leech.

The original 10 parts are not often met with, and when clean and perfect sell for as much as £3 10s. or £4.   When in volume form the work sells for about £2 10s. by auction (original cloth). Early editions of this work are much scarcer in any form than the "Comic History of England."

Another Edition, 1863, 8vo, Bradbury, Agnew & Co., published at 7s. 6d., and now worth about the same amount.

Another Edition, 1881, imperial 8vo, published at Edinburgh. Value about 10s. (in cloth, as issued).

Another Edition, called the "Edition de Luxe," N.D., 4to, Bradbury, Agnew & Co.   The coloured and other illustrations are on China paper.

Value about 15s. (as issued, auction).

ROBERT BRIDGES.

SOME of the works of Mr. Robert Bridges have now become exceedingly scarce, and, being affected by an increasing number of collectors, are becoming more difficult to meet with every day. Others seem to have been issued in much larger quantities, and can be got without any great amount of trouble, though they also show a distinct tendency to rise in value.

Mr. Bridges' books are of three kinds. Firstly, those published in the ordinary way, which did not sell much when they first came out. Some of these "remainders" were destroyed. Secondly, those printed (not published) by Mr. Daniel at his private press; and thirdly, those published in the ordinary way, which sold well, and are still for sale. Judging from the booksellers' catalogues, there appears to be an impression abroad that all Mr. Bridges' works are out of print, but this is erroneous.

Among what may be called the less important publications are "Prometheus the Firegiver," 1884; "Eros and Psyche," from the Latin of Apuleius, 1885; "Eden, an Oratorio," 1891; "On the Prosody of Paradise Regained, and Samson Agonistes," 1889; a series of "Plays" published by Edward Bumpus, in 4to, 1890, &c.; "Nero" [1885]; "Achilles in Scyros," 1892 (a small book of 68 pp.); and in a minor degree "Poems," 1886, and "Shorter Poems," 1890. Only 110 large-paper copies of this last-named book were published, but for some reason or other, which it is impossible at present to explain, except it be that the work is not complete, the value is small. Most of the books above mentioned are yet in print, and can consequently be obtained at the published price. The others (with the exception of "Nero") sell by auction at present for about 5s. each, in the original cloth or wrappers.

The following works are, however, in quite a different position, and it is worthy of note that the value of each, to-day, is at least 25 per cent. higher than it was a couple of years ago. The market values given are the latest procurable :—

1. Poems. . . . Pickering. . . . 1873.

This is a small 8vo book, which I have not been able to meet with.

It is scarce, selling by auction for about £2 10s. (original cloth).

2. Poems. By Robert Bridges. Printed at the Private Press of H. Daniel, Fellow of Worcester College. Oxford. 1884.

In crown 4to, half-vellum, blue boards, lettered on face in gilt.

A blank leaf precedes title as above, then follows a "Note" on an unpaged leaf, contents (not paged), another blank leaf, and text, pp. 1–52. A rough woodcut on a leaf follows, and two blank leaves conclude. Toned paper, with rough edges.

Only 150 copies were printed. The present auction value averages £1 10s. (as issued).

3. The Feast of Bacchus. By Robert Bridges. Privately Printed by H. Daniel. Oxford. 1889.

In crown 4to, half-vellum, green boards, lettered on face in gilt.

A blank leaf precedes title, and there is a woodcut on the leaf
that follows, then comes half-title, "Dramatis Personæ" on the
reverse of next leaf, and text, pp. 1–94. A "Note" on an unpaged leaf follows p. 94, and a blank leaf concludes. Toned paper,
with rough edges.

Only 105 copies printed. Present value about £2 5s. (as issued,
auction).

4. The Growth of Love. (1890.)

The collation of this book is very irregular. After a preliminary
blank leaf, follows what may perhaps be called the title, consisting
of the words, "The Growth of Love," without author's name,
date, or any other particulars. A second blank leaf follows, and
then comes text, pp. i–lxxix. At the end of the book there is a
"Note" on an unpaged leaf, then the imprint ("Printed by II.
Daniel, Oxford"), on a second leaf, and a final blank leaf. The
work appeared in half-vellum, green boards, lettered along the face
in gilt. Thick toned paper, rough edges, crown 4to. Black
Letter. 100 copies privately printed.

Value about £2 10s. (as issued, auction).

This is in reality the third edition of the "Growth of Love,"
the first having been published by Edward Bumpus in 1876, in
pamphlet form, at 1s. This prior issue is not of much importance,
though copies are not often met with.

A second edition, consisting of 22 copies only, was privately
printed at Mr. Daniel's press.

ELIZABETH BARRETT BROWNING.

Original copies of Mrs. Browning's poems are not of the same importance as those of her husband, though there are one or two exceptions to this rule. Elizabeth Barrett Barrett married Robert Browning in the autumn of 1846, and her more important works to collectors were published before that date. "The Runaway Slave" is the only one of Mrs. Browning's poems dated after 1846 which can be regarded as difficult to obtain or particularly valuable. In the case of Mr. Browning also the rule is the same, all, or nearly all, his expensive originals being published before his marriage. Of course, the reason of this is obvious. A poet's early efforts are apt to be overlooked; the demand for copies of the works of any unknown author is seldom large, and what few copies do get on the market are treated none too kindly, and are apt to be destroyed. Hence one of the scarcest *brochures* in the whole range of English bibliography is Mrs. Browning's "Battle of Marathon," which her father published for her in 1820, when she was a school-girl of twelve. This little book was privately printed by W. Lindsell of 87 Wimpole Street, and consists of 72 pages 8vo. The authoress dedicated the poem (from Hope End, 1819) to her father, and in the preface which follows she remarks that "a female may drive her Pegasus through the realms of Parnassus without being abused in the Review or criticised in society: how justly, then, may a child hope to pass unheeded." She was ten years old when she wrote this poem, which, like most other early productions of authors who subsequently become famous, is valued not so much on account of its intrinsic merit as for the circumstances attending its production, the personality of the writer, and its excessive rarity.

"The Battle of Marathon" apart, Elizabeth Barrett Barrett's first work is entitled as follows :—

1. An Essay on Mind ; with other Poems. "Brama assai, poco spera, e nulla chiede."—*Tasso.* London. James Duncan, Paternoster Row. MDCCCXXVI.

This is a small book (12mo) containing 152 pages. Besides preface (iii–xiii), and contents (1 p.), it has a half-title and "Analysis of the First Book" (pp. 3, 4). The second part of the work is devoted to the "Miscellaneous Poems" (pp. 109–152), and has also a half-title.

This work, which was issued in boards, is scarce, good copies in the original covers selling by auction for about £3 10s. It has been reprinted by Mr. R. H. Shepherd in his "Earlier Poems of E. B. Browning," 12mo, 1878.

2. Prometheus Bound, translated from the Greek of Æschylus : and Miscellaneous Poems. By the Translator, author of "An Essay on Mind;" with other Poems. (Then follow two quotations from the Greek.) London. Printed and published by A. J. Valpy, M.A., Red Lion Court, Fleet Street. 1833.

The collation of this book is important. Prior to the title, as above, there should be a half-title. The preface occupies v–xxi, and contents xxiii and xxiv. Then follows another half-title

("Prometheus Bound"), and the poem itself is found on pages 1–68. The "Notes" are on pages 69–78, after which follows another half-title ("Miscellaneous Poems"), and then pp. 81–163. As the loss of even a half-title would materially affect the value of the book, purchasers should be careful to see that the three are there.

In June 1889 a copy in the original binding (blue watered cloth with label on the edge), sold at Sotheby's for £16, an enormous increase on the published price of 5s. On another occasion a copy, bound in calf extra by Bedford, brought £2 16s. The book is rare in any condition, but especially so in the original binding, though the larger amount quoted above appears to be unusually large.

3. The Seraphim and other Poems. By Elizabeth B. Barrett, author of a translation of the "Prometheus Bound," &c. (Quotation.) London. Saunders & Otley, Conduit Street. 1838.

Great care has to be taken with this book on account of the half-titles. There is one prior to the title as above, then follows preface (v–xviii), contents (xix–xxi), another half-title ("The Seraphim, Part the First"), text (pp. 3–25), a third half-title ("Part the Second"), text (pp. 29–78). The "Other Poems" occupy pp. 81–360, and there are half-titles to four of them and no more, viz., "The Poet's Vow," "The Romaunt of Margret," "Isobel's Child," and "A Romance of the Ganges." At first sight it looks as though there should be a half-title to each of the four parts of "The Poet's Vow," but only the first part is so distinguished.

A copy of "The Seraphim" in the original cloth might be expected to sell by auction for about £1 10s., more or less.

4. The Runaway Slave at Pilgrim's Point. By Elizabeth Barrett Browning. London. Edward Moxon, Dover Street. 1849.

This is an 8vo pamphlet printed on thick paper, containing

half-title ("The Runaway Slave"), title as above, advertisement
dated from Florence 1849, and text, pp. 9–26. The wrapper is
yellow, with the title within double lines.

The pamphlet is very rare, being absent from nearly all collections, but it is not as valuable as might be supposed, £3 or
£3 10s. being the limit by auction (as issued).

5. Casa Guidi Windows.   A Poem.   By Elizabeth
  Barrett Browning.   London.   Chapman &
  Hall, 193 Piccadilly.   1851.

Preceded by half-title, advertisement (v–vii), text (pp. 1–137),
notes (pp. 138–140).   Issued in dark blue cloth, 12mo.
Value about 12s. 6d. (original cloth).

6. Two Poems.   See under ROBERT BROWNING,
  No. 7.

7. Aurora Leigh.   By Elizabeth Barrett Browning.
  London.   Chapman & Hall, 193 Piccadilly.
  1857.

A half-title precedes the title, and there is a dedication to John
Kenyon, from Devonshire Place.   Text, pp. 1–403.
Value about 15s. (original cloth).
There are several later editions of little value.   A fifth edition
appeared in 1860, and a sixth in 1864.

8. Poems before Congress.   By Elizabeth Barrett
  Browning.   London.   Chapman & Hall, 193
  Piccadilly.   1860.

This work, which was issued in red cloth, gold-lettered on the side, has a half-title, title as above, preface (v–viii), contents, and text (pp. 1–65).

Value from 15s. to 18s. (cloth, as issued).

This was the last work written and published by Mrs. Browning.

9. Last Poems.   By Elizabeth Barrett Browning.
   London.   Chapman & Hall, 193 Piccadilly.
   1862.

A posthumous work, edited by Robert Browning. It commences with half-title, title as above, undated dedication to "Grateful Florence," advertisement, contents (ix–xi), text, pp. 1–142. Published in violet cloth, post 8vo.

Value about 15s. (original cloth).

A second edition, published by Chapman & Hall in 1862, crown 8vo, sells for about 3s. (cloth, uncut).

10. The Greek Christian Poets and the English
    Poets.   By Elizabeth Barrett Browning.   London.   Chapman & Hall, 193 Piccadilly.   1863.

A work posthumously published (by Robert Browning) consisting of a number of articles which appeared in the *Athenæum* for 1842. No half-title, title as above, advertisement (iii–iv), text, 1–211.

Value about 15s. (green cloth, as issued).

11. Kind Words from a Sick-Room.   Greenock.
    1891.

A series of four letters from Elizabeth Barrett Barrett, dated from Wimpole Street in 1845 and the following year, and one letter from Robert Browning, dated from 19 Warwick Crescent, W., December 24, 1883. This pamphlet, which is in a greenish paper cover, demy 8vo, was privately printed by Mr. William Hutchison of Greenock.

In addition to the above separate publications, comprising all that are credited to the authoress, Elizabeth B. Barrett modernised Chaucer's Tale of "Queen Annelida and False Arcite" for R. H. Horne's "Poems of Geoffrey Chaucer Modernised," 8vo, London, 1841.

The first edition of her collected poems appeared in 2 vols, 1844, fcap. 8vo, E. Moxon, scarce, £2 (cloth, as issued); second edition, 1850, 2 vols. fcap. 8vo, 8s. (cloth, as issued); third edition, 1853, post 8vo, 5s. (*ibid.*); fourth edition, 1860, 3 vols. post 8vo, 16s. (*ibid.*); fifth edition, 1862, post 8vo, 10s. (*ibid.*); sixth edition, 4 vols. post 8vo, 15s. (*ibid.*); also 1877, 8vo, 5 vols. 15s. (*ibid.*).

The poem entitled "Lady Geraldine's Courtship" was reprinted 1876, with illustrations by Barton, and the "Rhyme of the Duchess May" in 1873, with illustrations by Morrell.

The rarest of all Mrs. Browning's pieces, "The Battle of Marathon" excepted, is a privately printed post 8vo pamphlet of pp. 47 entitled "Sonnets, By E. B. B.," 1847, the probable value of which is some £15 or £20.

ROBERT BROWNING.

MANY persons have attempted to form a complete collection
of original copies of the works of Robert Browning, but
almost all have failed, owing to the excessive rarity of the
first of the series, "Pauline," written by the poet when in
his twenty-first year. So far as is known, the number of
copies of this poem hitherto discovered is well under a
dozen; eight I believe is the exact total, of which one,
though badly shorn of most of its glories, reposes in a
"Select Case" in the British Museum Library, and is thus
intituled :—

> 1. Pauline; a Fragment of a Confession. Plus
> ne suis ce que j'ai été, Et ne le sçaurois
> jamais être.—*Marot*. London. Saunders &
> Otley, Conduit Street. 1833.

Mr. Thomas J. Wise, who in 1886 edited a very close reprint
of this scarce book, says that an uncut copy of the original
measures $7\frac{3}{4} \times 4\frac{7}{8}$ inches, and his reprint (small paper) accurately
retains these dimensions; in fact, but for the paper, which it was
found absolutely impossible to match, there is very little difference
between the original and its copy. I once saw one of Mr. Wise's
reprints which had been "doctored" in a masterly manner. His
title and prefatory note had been removed, and "Pauline" rebound in a very expensive cover. The difficulty with regard to
the paper had to a large extent been got over by the simple
device of rotting it to make it porous, and afterwards slightly
smoking the leaves to give them that mellow appearance which

is naturally produced by age. The effect was good, and as a comparison with an original copy would in many cases be entirely out of the question, I have no doubt that this artistically treated reprint has by this time taken up comfortable quarters.

This is a fair example of the way reprints are sometimes fraudulently passed off as originals. The price asked is usually low, and the would-be purchaser must make up his mind without delay or lose what he has perhaps been searching for all his life, and so the bait is taken on a venture.

The paper of Mr. Wise's reprint is much thicker than that of the original, but this is no assistance to any one who has not the opportunity of comparing the two. One test is however conclusive, and it is this. On the final page (71) appear the words "Richmond, October 22, 1832." If the word "October" is printed in *thin* italics, the book is without doubt a reprint. So far as I am aware, there is no other difference between Mr. Wise's excellent reprint and the original (the paper excepted).

No genuine copy of "Pauline" has been sold by auction within recent years. If one does come on the market I should think it may be expected to bring £40 or £50. The reprint is worth about 10s. or 12s. (boards, as issued) or £1 (large-paper). Of the large-paper copies, only 25 copies were issued.

2. Paracelsus. By Robert Browning. London. Published by Effingham Wilson, Royal Exchange. MDCCCXXXV.

This is a fcap. 8vo book, published at 6s. There are several editions, of which only the first is much sought after. A perfect copy of this should contain the inscription to the Comte A De Ripert-Monclar, an "address to the reader," dated 15th March 1835 (vii–ix), table of "Persons," Paracelsus, pp. 1–200, and a note containing a short biography of Paracelsus, pp. 201–16.

A good uncut copy sells by auction for about £4 4s. (boards), though inferior ones may sometimes be bought for less. The work, however, very seldom appears in the market in any condition.

3. Strafford : an Historical Tragedy. By Robert Browning, author of Paracelsus. London. Printed for Longman, Rees, Orme, Brown, Green & Longman, Paternoster Row. 1837.

Issued in wrappers, with a label. There is more than one edition, notably that by Emily H. Hickey, published by George Bell & Sons in 1884. There is, however, no mistaking the original, which contains dedication to "William C. Macready, Esq.," dated April 23, 1837, preface (iii–iv), "Dramatis Personæ," and text, pp. 1–131.

Value of a copy of the original edition of Strafford, about £2 (as issued, auction).

4. Sordello. By Robert Browning. London. Edward Moxon, Dover Street. MDCCCXL.

This little book was published at 6s. 6d. in brown boards, and contains on half-title "Sordello," title as above, and text, pp. 1–253. Sordello is written in six books, and in size is technically described by some as 12mo, by others post 8vo, and by others again as fcap. 8vo. A clean copy in the original boards sells for about £2 10s. by auction.

5. Bells and Pomegranates.

Eight distinct and separate poems go to make up a full set of "Bells and Pomegranates." These are as under :—

No. 1. "Pippa Passes," 1841 (pp. 3–16). Published 1s.
  „ 2. "King Victor and King Charles," 1842 (pp. 5–20). Published 1s.
  „ 3. "Dramatic Lyrics," 1842 (pp. 3–16). Published 1s.
  „ 4. "The Return of the Druses," 1843 (pp. 3–19). Published 1s.
  „ 5. "A Blot in the 'Scutcheon," 1843 (3–16). Published 1s.
  „ 6. "Colombe's Birthday," 1844 (pp. 3–20). Published 1s.

No. 7. "Dramatic Romances and Lyrics," 1845 (pp. 3–24).
 Published 2s.
 „ 8. "Luria; and a Soul's Tragedy," 1846 (pp. 5–32). Published 2s. 6d.

Each of these numbers was issued at the date mentioned, by
Edward Moxon, in large 8vo (royal), in yellowish greenish covers.
When the series was complete, the publisher bound the remainder
up in cloth and sold them as one book.

As usual in all such cases, the parts with their wrappers are
regarded most favourably, a clean set bringing as much as £10.
A complete series, bound in cloth (as issued), brought ten guineas
by auction not long ago, but this price is unusual; about £7 or
£8 would appear to be an average price.

Note.—This is the last of Browning's works in order of date
that is exceptionally difficult to procure. All works issued subsequent to 1846 are much less valuable, because Browning's fame
by that time being well assured, larger numbers of each work were
published.

6. Christmas Eve and Easter Day. A Poem. By Robert Browning. Chapman & Hall. 1850.

The poems are distinct. "Christmas Eve" begins on p. 1 and
"Easter Day" on p. 80. The pagination is, however, continuous.
This work was issued in dark-coloured greenish cloth at 6s.
(fcap. 8vo).

Value about £1 (auction, as issued).

An edition was published by Lothrop & Co. at Boston (Mass.)
without date (but 1886). There is, however, no mistaking the
two. Subsequent English editions are also unmistakable.

7. Two Poems. By Elizabeth Barrett and Robert Browning. London. Chapman & Hall. 1854. Price Six-pence.

This is a tract of 15 pp. in a yellowish cover (crown 8vo). The title is repeated on the fly-leaf. The first poem, by Elizabeth Barrett Browning, is entitled "A Plea for the Ragged Schools of London, written in Rome;" the second, by Robert Browning, is entitled "The Twins."

Value about £1 5s. (auction, as issued).

8. Men and Women. By Robert Browning. London. Chapman & Hall. 1855.

The work is complete in 2 vols., fcap. 8vo (both dated 1855), published at 6s. each. There are fifty separate poems and "one word more," making altogether fifty-one. Vol. i. includes contents, text, pp. 1–260; vol. ii. contents, text, pp. 1–241.

Value £1 15s. (original cloth, auction).

9. Dramatis Personæ. By Robert Browning. Chapman & Hall. 1864.

Issued in red cloth, fcap. 8vo. It contains Table of Contents, "James Lee" on half-title, and text, pp. 3–250. Each poem (18 in number) is prefixed by a separate title, but the pagination is continuous.

Published at 8s. 6d.; present value about £1 (cloth, as issued).

The second edition, also dated 1864, is much inferior from the collector's point of view. Copies of that sell for about 2s. 6d. each.

10. The Ring and the Book. By Robert Browning, M.A., Honorary Fellow of Balliol College, Oxford. 1868.

The four volumes which make up this work were all published by Smith, Elder & Co.; the two first in 1868, and the two last in 1869. Each volume contains three distinct poems, and was issued at 7s. 6d.

Present value of the 4 vols. about £1 10s. (brown cloth, as issued).

The second edition of "The Ring and the Book" appeared in 4 vols., 1872, and is worth now about 17s. 6d. (cloth, as issued).

11. Balaustion's Adventure, including a Transcript from Euripides. By Robert Browning. London. Smith, Elder & Co. 1871.

Published at 5s. in fcap. 8vo. Contains title, dedication "To the Countess Cowper," and text, pp. 1–170. A clean copy can often be bought for about 10s., sometimes for less. There are several later editions of this poem (three appeared in 1883 alone), but the value of these is trifling, nor can any of them be mistaken for the original.

12. Prince Hohenstiel - Schwangau, Saviour of Society. By Robert Browning. London. Smith, Elder & Co. 1871.

This little book (fcap. 8vo) was issued in blue cloth at 5s. It contains title, on the reverse a Greek and English inscription, and text, pp. 1–148.

A clean copy in the publishers' cloth can be got for 10s., and often for less.

13. Fifine at the Fair. By Robert Browning. London. Smith, Elder & Co. 1872.

Published in fcap. 8vo at 5s. Purchasers must be careful to see that any copy offered for sale is made up as follows :—Half-title, title, quotations from Molière's "Don Juan" and English translation, prologue (vii–xii), text, pp. 1–168, and epilogue.

A clean copy of this book is worth little more than the published price.

14. Red Cotton Nightcap Country, or Turf and Towers. By Robert Browning. London. Smith, Elder & Co. 1873.

Contains dedication to Miss Thackeray, and text, pp. 1–282.
This poem was issued in green cloth (post 8vo) at 9s., and the value of an average copy is under £1. A very clean one, however, might be expected to sell by auction for about that amount.

15. The Inn Album. By Robert Browning. London. Smith, Elder & Co. 1875.

This book contains a half-title as well as the title, and 211 pages of text. It was issued in green cloth, fcap. 8vo, at 7s., and sells by auction for about 16s. (as issued).

16. Aristophanes' Apology, including a Transcript from Euripides, being the Last Adventure of Balaustion. By Robert Browning. London. Smith, Elder & Co. 1875.

Published at 10s. 6d. in fcap. 8vo. There should be pp. i–viii of introductory matter, then follows the apology, pp. 1–208, the transcript ("Herakles"), pp. 209–327, and finally the continuation of the apology, pp. 327–366.
A clean copy is worth about the published price.

17. Pacchiarotto, and how he worked in Distemper; with other Poems. By Robert Browning. London. Smith, Elder & Co. 1876.

There are 15 poems, a prologue, and an epilogue, in addition

to " Pacchiarotto." There should also be a half-title, as well as
the title itself.

This work was published at 7s. 6d., but has hardly maintained
its value.   Good copies are frequently offered for 5s.

18. The Agamemnon of Æschylus.   Transcribed by
     Robert Browning.   London.   Smith, Elder
     & Co.   1877.

Contains i–xi introductory matter, and pp. 1–148 of text.   Fcap.
8vo.
Published at 5s., and now worth about the same amount.

19. La Saisiaz: The Two Poets of Croisic.   By
     Robert Browning.   London.   Smith, Elder
     & Co.   1878.

Issued in blue cloth, fcap. 8vo, at 7s.   The title is, or should
be, preceded by a half-title and a table of contents.   " La Saisiaz "
occupies pages 3–82, and " The Two Poets of Croisic " pages 85–201.
Value about 5s. (cloth, as issued).

20. Dramatic Idyls.   By Robert Browning.   Lon-
     don.   Smith, Elder & Co.   1879.

It should be noted that these Idyls appeared in two distinct
series, each of which was published by Smith, Elder & Co. in
brown cloth at 5s.   Vol. i. is dated 1879, and vol. ii. the year
following.   They contain respectively 143 and 147 pages.   The
second series should contain a final poem (on an unpaged leaf
following p. 147) commencing "Touch him ne'er so lightly."
Clean uncut copies of this work are worth rather more than
the majority of Browning's later poems, about £1 for the two
volumes being a very usual auction price, though sometimes more
is obtained.

21. Jocoseria.   By Robert Browning.   London.
Smith, Elder & Co.   1883.

This book consists of ten distinct poems, and commences with
a half-title, followed by title, contents, half-title containing some
verses, commencing "Wanting is—what?" half-title "Donald"
(the title of the first poem), and pp. 7-143 of text.   A second
edition of this work appeared the same year.

An uncut copy of the first edition of "Jocoseria" is worth about
7s. (auction).

22. Ferishtah's Fancies.   By Robert Browning.
London.   Smith, Elder & Co.   1884.

Published in olive cloth, fcap. 8vo.   The work should contain
half-title (on the reverse two quotations), title, contents, prologue
(pp. 1-4), and text (pp. 5-143).
Value of an original copy about 5s. (cloth as issued, auction).
A new and unimportant edition appeared in 1885.

23. Parleyings with Certain People of Importance
in their Day, &c.   London.   Smith, Elder
& Co.   1887.

This work was published in brick-red cloth, fcap. 8vo, at 9s.
It contains half-title, title, "In Memoriam," contents, prologue
(pp. 3-28), and text (pp. 31-268).
The average value of a copy in the original cloth is about 7s. 6d.

24. Asolando: Fancies   and   Facts.   London.
Smith, Elder & Co.   1890.

Although "Asolando" is dated 1890, it was in reality published
in 1889.   It is memorable as being Browning's last work.   The

published price. was 5s., cloth, and copies of the original edition are now worth some 12s. or 15s. Several later editions appeared before the end of 1890, but only the first, above mentioned, is of importance.

The preceding twenty-four items comprise the whole of the separate works of Robert Browning, but there are others which it may be advisable to mention. One of these is Shelley's "Letters," published by Moxon in 1852, which contains a preliminary essay by Browning. As all the world now knows, these "letters" were forged, and the remainder of the edition had to be suppressed. Copies are scarce, selling for as much as £4 4s. by auction (original cloth). The "Essay" has since been separately published for the Shelley Society (London. Reeves & Turner. 1888. 8vo. Price 6s.).

The first collective edition of Browning's "Poems" was published by Chapman & Hall, in 2 vols. 8vo, 1849. It is not particularly scarce, however, for the two volumes may sometimes be met with in the auction room for about £1 5s. (original cloth, as issued). Other collective editions include those of 1849 (second edition of this date), 2 vols. 8vo, about £1 (cloth); 1865, 3 vols. 8vo, £1 5s. (morocco); 1868, 6 vols. 8vo, about £1 5s. (cloth); 1872, 4 vols. 8vo (published at Leipzig), £1 5s. (mor. ex.); 1878, 6 vols. 8vo, £1 5s. (hf. mor.); and 1888–89, 16 vols. 8vo, £2 5s. (cloth). Large-paper copies of this last-named edition are scarce, realising as much as £8 or £9 by auction (original cloth).

Reference may be made here to three very scarce pamphlets by Browning, entitled "Cleon," "The Statue and the Bust" (said to be worth £10 or £12 each), and "Gold Hair" (selling for about £5).

ROBERT BURNS.

THE collective poems of Robert Burns have been reprinted
on a great number of occasions, and in every variety of form.
It is calculated that by the end of 1816 no less than 22
editions had appeared in London, 19 in Edinburgh, 16 in
the United States, 4 in Dublin, 4 in Belfast, 3 in Glasgow,
2 in Berwick-upon-Tweed, 1 at Kilmarnock, 1 at Paisley,
and 9 in other towns scattered about England or Scotland.

The original edition appeared at Kilmarnock in 1786, and
for eighty-four years from that date, say up to 1870, only
two years are recorded (1791 and 1795), in which at least
one edition of Burns' works was not published. This record
of continuous publication is only surpassed in the case of
three other books, viz., the Bible, the works of Shakespeare,
and the " De Imitatione Christi."

It is evident, therefore, that collectors of Burnsiana may
count themselves lucky if, during the course of a lifetime,
they can manage to accumulate one-half of the volumes that
are associated even directly with Scotland's national poet ;
for not only are there considerably more than 100 editions
of his collective works, but a large number of editions of
poems, separately reprinted and illustrated by well-known
artists, among whom the names of R. C. Lucas, Thomas
Bewick, D. O. Hill, George Harvey, Sir Noel Paton, Sir
John Gilbert, Landseer, and John Faed are prominent.

Some of these are most difficult to meet with, as, for
example, the " Letters to Clarinda," published in Glasgow in
1802, and almost immediately suppressed, the " Cantata," a

twopenny tract published by Stewart and Meikle in 1799, an oblong folio volume of 15 etchings on copper by Lucas, illustrating *Tam o' Shanter*, of which perhaps not a dozen copies were circulated, and many others which, for one reason or another, are objects of great interest to the collector.

The most extensive collection of Burnsiana in existence is probably that in the museum at the Kay Park, Kilmarnock. It consists of nearly 1000 volumes, a large proportion of which comprise various editions of the poet's works published in the United Kingdom, and the remainder of books touching on his life or writings, or the scenes with which he was associated.

Among all this mass of literature, it would be extraordinary indeed if the collector should not find himself lost occasionally. It must be remembered that there are, in Scotland especially, many collectors who devote much of their spare time, and a considerable proportion of their money, to accumulating copies of as many of these numerous editions as possible, and in their eyes every edition, no matter whether it be generally regarded as "scarce" or otherwise, becomes an object of absorbing interest. Sometimes a book which is not of itself particularly scarce, becomes so under special circumstances. When a tolerably extensive collection of anything has been formed, it is frequently a matter of great difficulty to add appreciably to it, partly no doubt because the commoner examples will naturally have been already appropriated, but partly also because common examples have a remarkable tendency to recur to the exclusion of others, perhaps neither better nor worse than themselves. This accounts for the well-known rule, that the importance and consequent value of a collection, whether it consists of books, coins, or in fact anything else, increases out of all proportion to the importance and value of the individual objects that constitute it. A book which, by itself, is hardly worth the

paper on which it is printed, becomes of great consequence
when it is required for the purpose of completing the series
to which it belongs, and it is precisely books of this class
that are apt to evade pursuit, and give the greatest trouble
to the collector.

The coveted first edition of Burns was printed at Kilmarnock by John Wilson, under the title of "Poems, chiefly in
the Scottish Dialect." Rather more than 600 copies are
said to have been published, and of these 350 were previously subscribed for. No doubt the majority of these books
were thumbed till they became mere things of shreds and
patches, and were then thrown lightly away by their owners
as of no account. Some again may have been wilfully
destroyed, or perhaps stored in the attic with a heap of
rubbish, to be carted away when quite forgotten, and so
brought to an untimely end. Whatever their fate, certain
it is that copies are now hardly to be met with in any condition, and are at all times, and under any circumstances,
extraordinarily expensive.

In March 1888, at the sale of the second portion of the
extensive library of the late Mr. Gibson-Craig, a good copy
of the Kilmarnock edition of "Poems, chiefly in the Scottish
Dialect," sold for £111, and on another occasion a rebound
copy brought £86. Nor are mutilated or imperfect examples
much more easily procurable; £27 seems a large, but is by
no means an unusual amount to pay for a copy "with the
title and first leaf of preface defective, wanting dedication
and last leaf of table, with all faults." For its size—it is only
a small book in 12mo—this work is one of the most costly
in the world, being only exceeded in this respect by the early
Shakespearian quartos, the first edition of Walton's Angler,
and one or two others which we read of occasionally, but
rarely see outside the walls of some great public library.

In 1867, James M'Kie of Kilmarnock published a reprint

of this first edition, in facsimile, taking extraordinary pains with each detail, however minute, of type, paper, and binding. The type was cast from the identical matrices which had been used for the true edition, and which he was fortunate enough to discover in the lumber-room of the Edinburgh type-founders. Three other volumes were also printed by Mr. M'Kie from the same types, viz., "Poems and Songs," 1869, reprinted from the early Edinburgh editions, and "Posthumous Poems," 1869. These four volumes together constitute a complete collection of all Burns' poems and songs, and must be of the greatest interest to collectors who despair of meeting with the originals. Some 30 copies of each were printed on large paper.

In 1787 there appeared at Edinburgh a second edition of the "Poems," with a portrait of Burns by Beugo, after Nasmyth. This was published in calf gilt, with yellow edges, and though nothing like so important as the Kilmarnock edition, is still highly prized. Copies in the original binding sell readily enough by auction for two or three guineas, and sometimes for even more.

The third edition of Burns' poems appeared at London, also in 1787. It has the portrait by Nasmyth, a glossary, and a long list of subscribers' names. This is not of the same importance as the Edinburgh edition, being a reprint of it. A copy once sold by auction for £8 15s. It was a very fine one, quite uncut, and had been handsomely bound by Rivière. As a rule, the value does not exceed a fourth or fifth of that amount.

In 1787 a pirated edition appeared at Belfast, and another at New York the year following. Both these editions are scarce, selling for 30s. or 35s. by auction. Perfect copies of each should contain the portrait after Nasmyth.

In 1787, an edition in two small volumes, with engravings by Bewick from Thurston's designs, was published at Alnwick. An ordinary copy of this edition, in half-calf, sells by auction for about £1. Another edition, with Bewick's cuts, was also published at Alnwick in 1808, 2 vols. fcap. 8vo.

In 1789 the first Dublin edition appeared. This is a reprint of the Belfast edition, with a fresh title-page.

The Glasgow edition of 1801 is important, as it contains a number of poems ascribed to Burns "not contained in any edition of his works hitherto published." Copies in the original boards can sometimes be met with for £1 or less. The second Glasgow edition of 1802 is worth considerably less than the first, but some copies have bound up with them the "Letters to Clarinda," and these are proportionately more valuable.

The "Letters to Clarinda" were, as previously stated, published at Glasgow in 1802, but almost immediately suppressed, with the result that stray copies sell by auction for about three guineas. This, however, is a good price, that is rarely ever exceeded.

Burns wrote comparatively little, and his bibliography consists not so much in the multitude of his books as in the extraordinary number of editions through which they passed. Really and truly he may be said to be an author whose fame rests substantially upon a single volume, the little book of "Poems" published at Kilmarnock in 1786, though other poems not to be found there, notably those in later collections, must in no wise be forgotten.

Another book with which the name of Burns is inseparably linked, and with this I must conclude the article, is the "Address to the People of Scotland" respecting Grose, the antiquary. This little volume was published in 1791, though it is not dated, and in addition to the "Address" contains some verses on "Ruins," other verses to the memory of J. Thomson, on Alloway Kirk, "The Whistle," and other poems. The book is not so valuable as might be supposed, though it is scarce enough. The average auction value of a fairly good copy is about £2.

Little, if any, advantage would be gained, at least by us, from a catalogue of editions of the works of Robert Burns, which are, indeed, only collected by the very few who have the necessary time and money at their disposal to enable them to achieve a reasonable amount of success. The ordinary collector is content with a few of the best editions among them, most of which I have enumerated and shortly described.

LORD BYRON.

ALTHOUGH a few of Byron's works are so rare as to be practically unprocurable, and others very difficult to meet with in good condition, by far the greater number are of little moment to the collector. This arises from the fact that his popularity, like that of Scott, demanded the publication of large editions at a time when little or no attempt appears to have been made to cater for the select few. Like Scott, Byron was a man of the people, whose works were scattered broadcast, and such of them as happen to have now become scarce, have attained to that distinction, if it be one, by accident rather than design. One or two pieces, privately printed, may perhaps be excepted from this general statement.

I give below a description of eleven of Byron's more inaccessible books, and in the meantime proceed to detail, in order of date, twenty-four others which are met with almost every day, and are therefore of minor importance from the peculiar standpoint upon which this work is based. I would not, by this, have it believed that none of these two dozen volumes are worthy the bookman's attention. On the contrary, no collection of Byron's works could of course approach completeness without them, and they are therefore just as important in one sense as any other books would be, which were urgently required to make up a set. All I wish to imply is, that they are, generally speaking, easy to meet with, and need not cost much to acquire. They are in fact what the collector calls "common" books, to be picked up as a rule for a few shillings each, in the intervals of leisure snatched from the graver work of tracking down rarities in which he especially delights. Occasionally, he will have to pay somewhat higher than the usual market price, but whenever he is called upon to do this, he will find that the particular book is an unusually clean and perfect specimen, perhaps in the original wrappers, as fresh as when it left the publisher's hands. An exceptional book demands an exceptional degree of attention, but it cannot for that reason be produced to disprove the rule.

The following is a list of some of these minor productions, with the date of the first publication of each :—

    I. The Bride of Abydos. 1813.
   II. The Corsair. 1814.
  III. Lara (and Jacqueline). 1814.
  IV. Hebrew Melodies. 1815.
   V. Farewell to England, and other Poems. 1815.
  VI. A Monody on Sheridan. 1816.
 VII. The Prisoner of Chillon, and other Poems. 1816.
VIII. Poems. 1816.
  IX. The Siege of Corinth and Parisina. 1816. Published separately in the first edition, afterwards together.
   X. Fare Thee Well, Sketch, Napoleon's Farewell, &c. 1816.
  XI. Manfred. 1817.
 XII. The Lament of Tasso. 1817.
XIII. Poems. 1818. (Second edition of the Poems of 1816.)
XIV. Beppo. 1818.
 XV. Mazeppa. 1819.
XVI. Sardanapalus, The Two Foscari, Cain. 1821.
XVII. Marino Faliero and the Prophecy of Dante. 1821.
XVIII. Letter on Bowles' Strictures on the Life and Writings of Pope. 1821.
XIX. Werner. 1822.
 XX. The Age of Bronze. 1823.
XXI. The Island; or Christian and his Comrades. 1823.
XXII. Ireland. 1823.
XXIII. Parliamentary Speeches. 1824.
XXIV. The Deformed Transformed. 1824.

Second or subsequent editions of all the above are seldom sought for, though it must be remembered that there are illustrated reprints of some of them. Books of this class stand upon an entirely different footing. They are not collectors' books in the full acceptation of the term.

1. Fugitive Pieces. . . . Newark. Printed by S. & J. Ridge. 1806.

This book was privately printed by Lord Byron, in thin 4to. The story goes that after 100 copies, of which the edition consisted, had left the printers' hands, he showed one of them to a friend— Mr. Beecher—who advised the total suppression of the book as containing matter of an objectionable character. Lord Byron followed this advice, and burned the entire issue, with the exception of three copies. This work is consequently extraordinarily rare, and cannot be valued.

In 1886 a facsimile reprint was privately printed in 4to, and, like the original edition, strictly limited to 100 copies. This reprint in its parchment binding sells for about £2 by auction.

In 1807 Lord Byron produced the work in an altered form and with some additions, under the title of "Poems on Various Occasions" (see *post*, No. 3), and subsequently under yet a fresh title, "Hours of Idleness" (see *post*, No. 4). The scarce "Fugitive Pieces" appears therefore in three separate and distinct forms, under three different titles, and with many omissions, additions, and alterations.

2. Verses to a Beautiful Quaker. . . . 1806.

These verses were written at the Brown Hotel, Harrowgate, and privately printed on 2 pp. 4to.

Copies of this pamphlet are occasionally met with. When seen in the auction room they sell for about £3 3s.

3. Poems on Various Occasions. Virginibus Puerisque Canto. *Hor.* Lib. 3, Ode 1. Newark.
Printed by S. & J. Ridge. 1807.

An 8vo book in boards, with label on the side, containing pp.
xi and 144. It was privately printed.

This work, as explained above (*ante*, No. 1), is in effect a reprint
of the suppressed "Fugitive Pieces," with certain alterations and
additions.

The rarity of this small volume is proverbial. A hundred
copies are said to have been printed, but very few can now be
accounted for. Some time ago a clean copy in the original boards
sold for £68, and rebound copies have several times been disposed
of at sums ranging from £20 to £40.

4. Hours of Idleness : a Series of Poems, Original
and Translated. By George Gordon, Lord
Byron, a Minor. . . . Newark. Printed by
S. &. J. Ridge. 1807.

It is frequently stated that a prior edition of this work appeared
in 4to, 1806, but this is only partially correct. The book referred
to is the "Fugitive Pieces" which, as already explained (*ante*,
No. 1), was suppressed, and afterwards privately reprinted, with
alterations and additions, under the title of "Poems on Various
Occasions" (*ante*, No. 3), and again under the title "Hours of
Idleness," as above.

"Hours of Idleness," a book of 200 pages in small 8vo, was
savagely criticised in the *Edinburgh Review* for January 1808,
which criticism, by the way, was the direct cause of the publication of the satire "English Bards and Scotch Reviewers," referred
to in the next entry.

An uncut copy of "Hours of Idleness" would sell by auction
for quite £4 10s. or £5, and large-paper copies, of which a few
were issued, readily bring £15 under similar circumstances. A
large deduction must be made in the case of cropped examples.

Another Edition, 12mo, Newark, 1808, worth some 10s. or 12s. (boards, auction).

5. English Bards and Scotch Reviewers : a Satire. . . . Cawthorne. N.D. (but 1809).

A small book in 12mo, published in boards, and containing title, preface, and pp. 54 of text.

Value about £1 12s. (original boards, auction).

This masterly satire, though excusable enough as a reply to the unfair and violent criticism of "Hours of Idleness" contained in the *Edinburgh Review*, was nevertheless itself unfair, in that Lord Byron went out of his way to attack many contemporary poets who had in no way offended him. This he himself subsequently deplored, going so far as to suppress an entire edition (the fifth, of 1812) as a sacrifice to his changed feelings. It is said that one copy of this edition escaped destruction, though the probability is that more are extant. I have never seen one.

The fourth edition, of 1811, is also worthy of special attention, as a few large-paper copies were issued. These are scarce, and sell by auction for some 25s. or 30s., or more if in the original binding.

6. The Curse of Minerva. . . . T. Davison. 1812.

This is one of the scarcest and most valuable pamphlets in the English language. I have not seen a copy, but, from a short description of it in a recent catalogue, it is a thin 4to in boards.

Value £100 (as issued, auction) ; £68 (*ibid.*).

7. Childe Harold's Pilgrimage : a Romaunt. . . . London. J. Murray . . . 1812, &c.

This is the work that firmly established Lord Byron's reputation as a poet. It was published in three instalments, viz., Cantos i. and ii., in one vol. 4to, 1812 ; Canto iii., 8vo, 1816 ; and Canto iv., 8vo, 1818. The four Cantos, complete, are sometimes met with in a single volume, but it is better, where possible, to have them in the three parts as published.

The first and second Cantos, 1812, are scarce when in the original boards, bringing as much as £2 and sometimes more by auction. Copies of all three parts (as published) have, however, sold for less than £1 5s. on several recent occasions, and much depends on condition.

Another Edition, 1814, 8vo, complete in a single volume, and scarce. A good copy of this, in the original boards, as issued, has sold by auction for as much as £3 15s., but this price is an unusually high one.

Another Edition, 1841, imperial 8vo. An edition with numerous vignettes by Finden, on vellum paper. Some copies have the illustrations on India paper.

Value about £2 (original cloth, auction), or £4 (large-paper, India proofs, *ibid.*).

8. The Waltz : an Apostrophic Hymn. By Horace
     Hornem, Esq. London. Sherwood, Neely,
     & Jones. . . 1813.

This extraordinarily scarce pamphlet was published in 4to with a wrapper. So far as I remember, it contains title and about 8 pp. of text in large type.

I have never seen a copy in the wrapper, but one sold by auction a little while ago for £86. An example without the wrapper would bring about £50, a large advance on the published price of 3s.

Another Edition, 8vo, 1821. This reprint is comparatively common, being worth no more than about 12s. or 15s.

9. The Giaour : a Fragment of a Turkish Tale. . . .
     1813.

Published in 8vo, in a wrapper.

This is not a scarce work, unless quite clean in the original

wrapper.   Under these circumstances it is worth from 20s. to 25s.
by auction.   If rebound and cut down the value is trifling.

10. Poems on Domestic Circumstances.   i. Fare Thee Well.   ii. A Sketch from Private Life. . . . Hone.   1816.

Murray's authorised edition of 1816, 8vo, was suppressed, but not before a considerable number of copies had got on the market. Hone then issued a surreptitious edition as above, also in 8vo, the work creating such a sensation that no less than 23 editions of one kind or another had appeared by the end of 1817.

The two volumes, uncut as issued, seldom sell by auction for more than about £1 15s.

11. Don Juan. . . . Davison. . . . 1819, &c.

Cantos i. and ii. of this poem were published by Davison. in quarto, 1819; Cantos iii., iv. and v., also by Davison, in 8vo, 1821; Cantos vi., vii. and viii., by Hunt, in 8vo, 1823; Cantos ix., x. and xi., by Hunt, in 8vo, 1823; Cantos xii., xiii. and xiv., by Hunt, in 8vo, 1823; and Cantos xv., xvi., by the same publisher, in 8vo, 1824.   There are therefore six volumes, the first in 4to, and the remaining five in 8vo.

Value of the set about £1 5s. (original boards, auction).

Another Edition, N.D., 8vo, with coloured plates by J. R. Cruikshank.   The value of this edition amounts to about £1 (original boards, auction).

There are several completions of Don Juan, all unauthorised, and none by Lord Byron.   Among these may be noted :—

A Sequel to Don Juan (a poem in five cantos), illustrated with fancy portraits, Paget & Co., N.D., 8vo, about £2 2s. (uncut, auction).

Some Rejected Stanzas of Don Juan, 1845. 4to, with Byron's (?) notes.   Value about £3 (wrappers).

The best complete edition of the works of Lord Byron is that with Life, by Moore, 17 vols. 8vo, 1832–33, and later.   Another good edition is in 10 vols. 8vo, 1851, with 20 plates by Finden, and a third in 6 vols. 8vo, 1855–56. As might be expected, Byron's complete works have been published in numerous forms, and at all sorts of prices.

It may be mentioned with advantage that none of the early collective editions published during Byron's lifetime, or shortly after his death, are of much importance. Thus the first collective edition of 1819, in 3 vols. 8vo, only sells for a few shillings, and the editions of 1827 in six small volumes, and of 1820 in four small volumes, are in a similar position. The reason of their disparagement is that they are not complete, and were subsequently superseded by Moore's edition above mentioned.

WILLIAM COMBE.

William Combe or Coombe, satirical poet, political pamphleteer, and journalist, was born at Bristol in 1741, and commenced his literary career in 1772 with an "Heroic Epistle to Sir William Chambers." Having wasted his substance, he found himself under the necessity of subsisting practically from hand to mouth within the "rules" of the King's Bench and Fleet Prisons, and the works that issued from his pen were *ex necessitate rei* very numerous. Very few are, however, of much interest to collectors, who for the most part confine their attention to those illustrated by Rowlandson and other contemporary artists of repute.

Combe cannot be classed among authors who have maintained their position by sheer force of genius, though some of his work was much above the average; but should rather be regarded as exceptionally fortunate in having been employed to write up to the illustrations of one of the first caricaturists of his own or any other day. Combe's chief creation, "Dr. Syntax"—the travelling schoolmaster—was suggested to him by Rowlandson, who had already supplied the drawings, and there is no doubt that the connection thus established between artist and author, has more than anything else contributed to preserve the name of the latter from decay.

It appears from Combe's preface to the second and later editions of the "Tour of Dr. Syntax in Search of the Picturesque," that a drawing was supplied to him every month, and that he composed a certain proportion of pages in verse in which, of course, the subject of the design was introduced, the rest depended upon what would be the subject of the second, and in this manner Rowlandson continued designing and Combe writing, till a work containing nearly 10,000 lines was produced.

At this time and long afterwards the author was a prisoner of the King's Bench for debt, and this fact may possibly be the reason why none of his works were avowed during his lifetime. He preferred anonymity, and from 1772, when poverty and the consequent loss of friends compelled him to look to literature as a means of subsistence, till his death in 1823, not one of his works, numbering nearly a hundred, appeared under the sanction of his name.

1. An History of the River Thames. . . . London. Printed by W. Bulmer & Co., for John and Josiah Boydell. 1794.

This is a folio book in two volumes, the second being dated 1796.

Vol i. contains a preliminary title ("An History of the Principal Rivers of Great Britain"), dedication to George the Third, front, title as above, dedication to Horace Walpole, preface (ix–xiv), table (unpaged), list of plates (unpaged), two folding maps of the Thames, and text pp. 1–312.

Vol. ii. contains preliminary title as before, title, table (unpaged), list of plates (unpaged), and text pp. 1–294.

The numerous full-page coloured illustrations in these volumes are by J. C. Stadler, after J. Farington, and the text was written by Combe.

Value about £5 (morocco, auction). In this case, however, chiefly on account of the size of the work, the value varies very much according to binding. An average copy may often be met with in the auction room for about £2 10s. or £3. The large coloured prints are most interesting to the antiquarian and topographer.

2. The Tour of Dr. Syntax in Search of the Picturesque : a Poem. . . . Published . . at R. Ackermann's Repository of Arts, 101 Strand, London.   1812.

This poem was first published in the *Poetical Magazine* under the title of "The Schoolmaster's Tour." being afterwards separately published as above at 21s., impl. 8vo.   The book contains front consisting of portrait of "The Revd. Doctor Syntax," engraved title, advertisement (i–iii), and text pp. 1–276.   A leaf of "Directions to the Binder for Placing the Plates" follows title.   These plates, which are all by Rowlandson and coloured by hand, number thirty-one inclusive of frontispiece and engraved title.

There are many later editions of this book, a fourth and fifth appearing in 1813, and a ninth in 1819 ; they contain the same plates, though the later impressions look much inferior, notwithstanding the fact that they were re-etched on several occasions. In 1838 a new edition, with illustrations by "Crowquill," was published by Ackermann.   A new edition also appeared in 1844.

In 1820, the "Second Tour of Doctor Syntax in Search of Consolation" appeared in the *Poetical Magazine*, and the same year a "Third Tour in Search of a Wife."   As in the case of the first "Tour," these were afterwards published in volume form, and passed through many editions, though they never attained the same popularity.   Each of these books contains 24 coloured plates by Rowlandson.

In 1823, Ackermann published what is known as the "Miniature Edition" of the three tours, in 3 small vols. (16mo), at a guinea.   This is a very important edition, for the whole of Rowlandson's coloured plates are reproduced, though of course on a smaller scale.   Later, a reprint was issued by Nattali & Bond in 3 vols., N.D., 8vo, with all the coloured plates.

The rough value of the editions of the "Tours of Doctor Syntax" will best be judged from a comparison of the following auction prices, collected to meet various combinations and the variety of circumstances mentioned.

1812–20. The Three Tours, 3 vols. 8vo, £5 15s. (calf gilt, first edition of each volume).

1815–20. The Three Tours, 3 vols. 8vo, later editions, £5 10s. (calf extra), £4 10s. (morocco extra).

1819–21. The Three Tours, 3 vols. 8vo, £6 (half calf, the third edition of the first tour, and first edition of the second and third).

1813. 8vo. "Tour in Search of the Picturesque" only, fourth edition, £1 7s. (uncut).

1814–22. Sixth edition of the "Picturesque," third edition of the "Consolation," and third edition of the "Wife," £4 4s. (clean copies, boards).

1820–21. The Three Tours, later editions, £4 (half calf), £7 (morocco extra).

1823. The Miniature Edition, Ackermann, 3 vols. 16mo, £1 14s. (calf), or about £2 10s. (uncut).

1838. "Crowquill's" Edition, in 1 vol. post 8vo, illustrations after the manner of Rowlandson, but very inferior, 10s. (cloth, as issued). Copies of the later editions of 1844 are only worth a shilling or two each.

N.D. Nattali & Bond, 3 vols. 8vo, £1 15s. (cloth, as issued).

3. Poetical Sketches of Scarborough. . . . London. Printed for R. Ackermann, 101 Strand. . . . 1813.

It is doubtful whether Combe had much, if anything, to do with this work, though, being often attributed to him, it is included here for that reason. The book is a royal 8vo, in verse, containing twenty-one coloured plates by Rowlandson, after drawings by J. Green.

The work contains front, title, advertisement (unpaged), "Some Account of Scarborough" (i–xv), and text pp. 1–215.

Value about £1 15s. (half calf, auction). Prices however vary greatly, and are, as in the case of all the works by William Combe, more than usually dependent upon condition, binding, and the quality of the plates in each instance.

4. The Life of Napoleon : a Hudibrastic Poem in Fifteen Cantos. By Doctor Syntax. . . . London. Printed for T. Tegg, 111 Cheapside. . . . 1815.

This work is nearly always ascribed to Combe, though it is doubtful whether he had any share in its composition. The work, which is in royal 8vo, contains 30 coloured engravings by George Cruikshank, inclusive of title, and text pp. 1–260.

This book is scarce, particularly when in fine condition. Prices vary from about £2 to £5, according to circumstances, the average lying between those amounts.

5. The English Dance of Death. . . . London. . . . Published at R. Ackermann's Repository of Arts, 101 Strand. . . . 1815.

Published in 2 vols. royal 8vo, 1815–16, with 72 coloured plates after Rowlandson's designs.

Vol. i. contains front representing a figure of Death crowned and sitting on a globe, illustrated title, plain title, advertisement (iii–vii), index (4 unnumbered pages), and text pp. 1–295.

Vol. ii. contains plain title, index (4 unnumbered pages), and text pp. 1–299.

This is a very scarce book when in anything like condition. A very ordinary auction price for the two volumes, bound say in half calf, is from £6 to £7, though copies frequently sell for more.

6. The Dance of Life : a Poem. . . . London. Published by R. Ackermann, Repository of Arts, 101 Strand. 1817.

Royal 8vo, published in boards, with 26 coloured plates (inclusive of front and title) by Rowlandson. The work is collated thus :—Coloured front, illustrated title, plain title, advertisement (unpaged leaf), advertisement (i–ii), index to the plates (i–ii), and text pp. 1–285.

A clean copy of this scarce book, in the original binding, would sell readily by auction for £5.

7. The History of Johnny Quæ Genus, the Little Foundling of the Late Doctor Syntax : a Poem. London.   Published by R. Ackermann. . . . 1822.

Royal 8vo, published in boards, with 24 coloured plates (inclusive of front) by Rowlandson.   The work contains coloured front ("Quæ Genus on his Journey to London"), plain title, preface (2 pp. unpaged), and text pp. 1–267.

Value about £3 3s. (calf extra, auction).

———

The success of "Dr. Syntax in Search of the Picturesque" (*supra*, No. 2), was productive not only of the two other Tours by William Combe, but of a number of imitations, which, despite their character, are of great importance, and all more or less difficult to procure.   One of these, entitled "The Tour of Dr. Prosody in Search of the Antique and Picturesque," first appeared in 1821.

It contains 20 humorous coloured plates drawn and enlarged by W. Read, and sells readily enough for £2 10s. or £3 by auction (calf extra).

Another work of the same kind, entitled "Tour of Dr. Syntax through London," 1820, 8vo, sells for about £1 10s. (half calf), or more, if in good condition, and the "Tour of Dr. Syntax through Paris, " 1820, is equally noteworthy.   The "Adventures of Dr. Comicus," published without date, but about the same time, is a fourth book of which we are irresistibly reminded when glancing at Combe's once popular and ever interesting creation.   It contains 15 coloured plates.

CHARLES DICKENS.

Collectors of the works of Charles Dickens seldom confine their attention to the novels and stories with which he is primarily credited, but they seek, in yearly increasing numbers, for any book, pamphlet, or print that can in any way be considered as supplementary to or even connected with his acknowledged productions. As might be supposed, this comprehensive view of an already intricate subject has made the bibliographer's task an exceedingly difficult one. It is also responsible to some extent for the mass of subsidiary rules and arbitrary distinctions that have grown up to complicate the subject still farther, and to make a complete or even an almost complete collection of *Dickensiana* a practical impossibility.

Notwithstanding the researches of Mr. C. P. Johnson, Mr. James Cook, and Mr. F. G. Kitton, a very great deal yet remains to be said about the works of Dickens and those parodies on or imitations of them which appeared some forty or fifty years ago in such large numbers. No popular author has been so closely observed, and certainly no author has been so much written about and imitated as he who commenced his literary career with the inimitable "Sketches by Boz," and closed it with the half-finished "Mystery of Edwin Drood."

In December 1892, Messrs. Sotheby sold a copy of a book sometimes attributed to Dickens. It is entitled "More Hints on Etiquette for the use of Society at Large, and Young Gentlemen in Particular." The illustrations are by

George Cruikshank, and on the occasion in question, the copy, in the original cloth gilt, 12mo, 1838, sold for £7 5s. It contains pp. vi, 78.

The whole of this work might easily have been occupied with a description of the minute distinctions which collectors have thought fit to create between one copy and another of almost all Dickens's novels, the extra plates or the varieties of title-page or binding which add to or detract from the importance and consequent value of any particular copy, and the historical circumstances accountable for innumerable variations which it is absolutely necessary to be aware of and to some extent to remember at will. Even then the task would have been far from complete, for some of the imitations and parodies are of the greatest importance, and many of the extra plates far more rare and expensive than the originals.

In this article I have noticed all the works attributed to Dickens, and in one or two instances others with which his name is sometimes associated, but there are many which, though objects of interest to the universal collector, hardly come within the four corners of our scheme. These I divide into two classes, as they are either obvious imitations or distinct genuine pieces appearing in the pages of some foreign book or publication.

First, as to the imitations, among the most important of which are the following :—

I. Post-humorous Notes of the Pickwickian Club, by "Bos" (G. W. M. Reynolds). 2 vols. E. Lloyd. N.D. 120 engravings. £1 5s. (original cloth).

II. Pickwick in America, edited by "Bos" (G. W. M. Reynolds). 8vo. E. Lloyd. N.D. 46 engravings. £1 10s. (original cloth).

III. Pickwick Abroad, or the Tour in France, by G. W. M. Reynolds. 8vo. T. Tegg (1839). 41 steel plates by "Crowquill," and 33 woodcuts by Bonner. About 21s. (original cloth).

IV. The Pickwick Gazette. 1837. 8vo. Published in numbers, worth some 3s. or 4s. each.

V. Posthumous Papers of the Wonderful Discovery Club, formerly of Camden Town, established by Sir Peter Patron, edited by "Boz." 8vo. 1838. Issued in numbers, worth probably some 8s. or 10s. each if clean and perfect.

VI. Sam Weller's Pickwick Jest-Book. Hodgson. 12mo. N.D. (1837). With 24 portraits. About 17s. 6d. (cloth).

VII. Life and Adventures of Oliver Twiss, the Workhouse Boy. E. Lloyd. N.D. (1838). 8vo. Illustrations. £1 5s. (original cloth).

VIII. Scenes from the Life of Nickleby Married. 8vo. 1840. 22 illustrations by "Quiz" (Rev. Edward Caswall). £2 10s. (original cloth).

IX. Nickelas Nickelbery, by "Bos" (G. W. M. Reynolds). 42 woodcuts. 8vo. E. Lloyd. N.D. About 17s. 6d. (original cloth).

X. Dombey and Daughter, a Moral Fiction, by R. Nicholson. Woodcuts. 8vo. N.D. (1848). 12s. (original cloth).

XI. Characteristic Sketches of Young Gentlemen, by "Quiz" Junior. Front. 8vo. N.D. 5s. (original cloth).

XII. The Battle of London Life; or Boz and his Secretary, by Morna (Mrs. Catherine Ladd). 8vo. 1849. £1 15s. (half-calf), or £2 2s. (as issued).

XIII. The Cricket on the Hearth, a New Christmas Quadrille, respectfully inscribed to Charles Dickens, Esquire. 1846. 8vo. About 2s.

Secondly, genuine pieces by Dickens appearing in foreign publications; amongst them the following :—

XIV. The Library of Fiction, or Familiar Story-Teller, consisting of original Tales, Essays, and Sketches of Character. 28 illustrations. 2 vols. 1836–37. Chapman & Hall. 8vo. £3 3s. (original cloth). Dickens contributed "The Tuggs at Ramsgate."

XV. The Atlantic Monthly. The numbers containing "George Silverman's Explanation," by Charles Dickens. 1868. 8vo. £1 (with covers, uncut).

XVI. Our Young Folks. The numbers containing " A Holiday

Romance," by Charles Dickens. Illustrations. 8vo. 1868. £1 5s. (bound in 1 vol. morocco extra, uncut).

XVII. Mr. Thackeray, Mr. Yates, and the Garrick Club. : The Correspondence and Facts stated by E. Yates (contained in a long letter from Dickens to Thackeray). 1859. 8vo. *See* under W. M. Thackeray, No. 31.

XVIII. An Account of the Origin of the Pickwick Papers, by Mrs. Seymour, widow of the artist who originated the work, with Mr. Dickens's version, and her reply thereto, &c. Printed for the author. N.D. A very rare pamphlet, worth some £50 or £60 in the original state, as issued.

XIX. Rymer's Christmas Portfolio of Wit and Humour. 1867. 8vo. Containing, *inter alia*, an original contribution entitled "Broadstairs," by Dickens (*vide* Index). £2 (original cloth).

XX. Bentley's Miscellany (No. 1, for January 1, 1837, and later numbers), to which Dickens contributed, as well as "Household Words," "All the Year Round," &c. &c.

Dickens's first printed work issued in separate form consists of the two series of "Sketches by Boz," of which the first appeared in the February and the second in the December of the year 1836, though the latter is invariably dated 1837. All the works in the following list are arranged in order of date, according to the usual practice of the cataloguers.

1. Sketches by "Boz"; Illustrative of Every-day Life and Every-day People. . . . London. John Macrone, St. James's Square. MDCCCXXXVI.

The two volumes post 8vo which make up the first series of this work were published at a guinea, in green cloth, and are now scarce. To identify the genuine first edition, it is necessary to consult the preface, which is dated "Furnival's Inn, February

1836;" the second edition (also published in 1836) being dated
August 1836. Vol. i. should contain pp. viii–348, and vol. ii. a
"Table of Contents" (unnumbered) and pp. 342, and there are in
each volume eight illustrations by George Cruikshank. There are
35 distinct articles in this series.

The second series of sketches is dated "Furnival's Inn, December 17, 1836," and is complete in one vol. post 8vo, 1836, same
publisher, pp. viii–375, with twelve illustrations by George Cruikshank. This series consists of 20 articles, and was published at
15s., in pink cloth with black labels. From what has been said,
it is evident that the earliest and most valuable copies of the two
series are complete in 3 vols. post 8vo, dated as described, with 26
illustrations by Cruikshank, the first series (vols. i. and ii.) being
in green, and the second series in pink or brown cloth.

In November 1837, Messrs. Chapman & Hall commenced to
publish the three series in monthly parts, at 1s. each, and in June
1839 the twentieth and final part was issued. Each of these is in
pink wrappers, and contains two etchings by Cruikshank (making
40 in all). The earlier plates contain no publisher's name, but this
remark does not apply to the plate "Greenwich Fair" (at p. 120),
and all that follow, which should have Chapman & Hall's imprint
at the foot. If this does not appear, it may be assumed that the
particular plate is only a reprint, or at any rate not of the first
issue. Of the illustrations, 25 appeared originally, though they
were now re-engraved in larger size (the etching entitled "The
Free and Easy" was altogether omitted), thirteen were added for
the first time, and two ("The Last Cabdriver" and "The First of
May") were taken from a later edition of the second series published in 1837. The earliest edition of the second series does
not legitimately contain these two plates, and, whenever they are
found, they must have been added from the later edition. Some
collectors, however, procure them to make the book quite complete.

In 1839 the publishers, having issued the last part, proceeded
to publish the whole work in volume form at 21s. This issue is
complete in one vol. green cloth, demy 8vo, pp. viii–526, with the
series of 40 etchings by Cruikshank (inclusive of the etching on
title) that appeared with the monthly parts. Some copies offered
for sale were bound direct from the parts, and these are or may be
much better in quality than those which were bound up from the

sheets, for it is very often found that the latter are "made up" in all sorts of ways, but more particularly by the addition of inferior plates, not bearing the imprint of Chapman & Hall as above mentioned. Sometimes copies bound from the sheets are themselves made up from later editions. and the greatest care has to be exercised in collating them. It may be mentioned that the "advertisement" to genuine copies of the first demy 8vo edition is dated "May 15, 1839," though this is not conclusive, for the volume may have been "perfected" in other respects.

No copy of "Sketches by Boz" could even be approximately valued without the minutest details of edition, binding, and the number, quality, and description of the plates. As might be supposed, the value varies immensely, and each book has therefore to be dealt with on its merits. Speaking generally, it may be said that the following prices are about what would be realised at auction for average copies of the kind described :—£15 15s. (complete set of 20 parts); £9 (the three volumes, first and second series, 1836–7, original cloth, as issued); £1 5s. (the second edition of 1836, in 2 vols. 8vo, original cloth); £1 (the third edition of 1837, in 2 vols. 8vo, original cloth); £5 (first demy 8vo edition of 1839, original cloth); £2 10s. (*ibid.*, in half-calf, half-morocco, or even full binding, unless from the hands of a first rate binder, in which case a little more); £5 (*ibid.*, where the series of 26 smaller sized etchings from the first edition of 1836–7 are inserted and placed opposite the corresponding plates, half-calf or half-morocco, uncut). In May 1892 the three series of "Sketches by Boz" sold for the large sum of £28 10s., a quite unusual amount. The three volumes were beautifully bound, were quite uncut, and had the original cloth covers inserted.

> 2. Sunday Under Three Heads : As it is ; as Sabbath Bills (*sic*) would make it ; as it might be made. By Timothy Sparks. London. Chapman & Hall, 186 Strand. 1836.

This is a pamphlet of pp. v. 49, with three illustrations (in addition to the illustrated yellow paper cover) by H. K. Browne.

Owing to its scarcity it has been twice reprinted, first by Jarvis &
Son, and secondly by Edwin Pearson of Manchester. The booksellers generally detect a reprint by reference to the plates, which,
in the case of Jarvis's reproduction, are so very badly executed
that nobody could be deceived by them for a moment. Pearson's
reprint, on the contrary, is extremely like the original, and has
doubtless done duty for it in numerous instances. It is easily told,
however, by turning to page 7, line 15, where the word "Hair,"
as it should be, is spelled "Air." Jarvis's reprint has the correct
rendering in this respect, but an important omission occurs on page
35, the words "Sunday under Three Heads" being wanting as
heading to Chapter III.

The value of a genuine copy of "Sunday Under Three Heads"
is about £8 8s. by auction (in the original wrappers), but if the
pamphlet has been bound up, and the edges in any way cropped,
it falls to £5 or £6, or even less, according to the extent of the
injury. The facsimile reprints are frequently kept with the
original, and though of themselves of no value, they might be
worth a few shillings for purposes of comparison.

3. The Village Coquettes : a Comic Opera, in Two
    Acts. By Charles Dickens. The Music by
    John Hullah. London. Richard Bentley.
    . . . 1836.

A demy 8vo pamphlet of 71 pp., with dedication, dated
December 15, 1836. A reprint which was issued in 1878 cannot
be mistaken for the original, for it has a notification on the back
of the title to the effect that it is a reprint. In point of execution the work of imitation has been very well performed. In
1837 the songs, choruses, and concerted pieces in the "Village
Coquettes," as produced at the St. James's Theatre, were printed
separately by Bradbury & Evans, and published at 10d. This
pamphlet is much scarcer than original copies of the opera itself.
A specimen in the original wrapper once sold for £25 by auction.

Value about £9 9s. (original pamphlet of the "Village
Coquettes" as published, auction) 15s. (reprint, as issued).

4. The Strange Gentleman : a Comic Burletta, in Two Acts. By "Boz." First Performed at the St. James's Theatre, Thursday, September 29, 1836. Chapman & Hall, 186 Strand. MDCCCXXXVII.

A pamphlet of 46 pp. in a pink wrapper, with frontispiece by "Phiz." It is scarce when in perfect condition, the frontispiece being nearly always wanting, and the preliminary unpaged leaf ("Costume") very frequently. In 1878 a reprint was issued, but without the frontispiece, though one was afterwards etched for it by Pailthorpe.

Value about £10 (in cloth, with the original wrappers bound in, auction) £20 to £30 (original wrappers, *ibid.*). The farce of "The Strange Gentleman" was founded on "The Great Winglebury Duel" in the "Sketches by Boz."

5. Is she his Wife? or, Something Singular : a Comic Burletta, in One Act. By Charles Dickens. . . . 1837.

This is the title of a comic burletta which was brought out at the St. James's Theatre in March 1837. Play-bills which were distributed on the occasion in question are extant, but there is no trace of any book of the words. This play is mentioned here because it is said to have been privately printed in 1837. In 1877 James R. Osgood & Co. of New York published the Opera in 32mo, brown cloth, pp. 80, and copies of this are worth on the average about £2 10s. (as issued, auction).

6. The Posthumous Papers of the Pickwick Club. . . . London. Chapman & Hall, 186 Strand. MDCCCXXXVII.

The well-known "Pickwick Papers" was issued originally in twenty 1s. monthly parts in green wrappers, commencing in April 1836 and ending in November of the following year. After Seymour had etched seven plates for this work he committed suicide, and the task was entrusted to Buss, whose two plates ("The Cricket Match," p. 69, and "Arbour Scene," p. 74), were not, however, considered satisfactory. Hablot K. Browne then took the place of Buss and etched 36 plates, so that the total number of illustrations amounts to 43, to which are frequently added the "Buss plates" above mentioned, though they only appear in the earlier copies of the third number. While the parts were in course of publication, the author addressed several communications to his readers, and these are found in Nos. 2, 3, 10, and 15, a point worth remembering, for these "addresses," as they are called, should always be preserved.

In 1837 Messrs. Chapman & Hall issued the first edition of "Pickwick," in green (or purple) cloth, pp. i–xiv; 1–609; price 21s. The dedication to Sergeant Talfourd, author of the play of "Ion," and other works, is dated from 48 Doughty Street, September 27th, 1837.

Good copies of "Pickwick" in the original being scarce, care must be taken to see that the contents are in every way perfect, special attention being directed to the plates. The first seven of these are, as I have said, by Seymour, the two following (in a few numbers of part iii.), by Buss, and the remaining 36 by "Phiz." Now, it must be observed that not one of these plates as originally issued bore any title, and further, that the 8th to the 11th plates inclusive, which appeared in Nos. 3 and 4, are said to bear Browne's sobriquet "Nemo," which he then used for the last time. The two "Buss plates" are, like the rest, destitute of any lettering. If they are printed off on buff-coloured paper, they are probably spurious, though there are facsimile reprints on white paper as well, and great care must necessarily be taken with regard to these.

It is said that when "Pickwick" commenced its career in 1836, the publishers, not over sanguine of its success, limited the issue to 400 (some say 1500) copies of the early numbers, so that accidental loss, wear and tear being taken into account, very few people can lay claim to possess the absolute first issue of the first four numbers. One peculiarity about this first limited issue is that the name "Weller" on the signboard of "The Marquis Granby," which appears as a vignette on the title, is spelled "Veller," the W being substituted for the V in all subsequent issues.

Such are the chief points to be observed on the purchase of any copy of the "Pickwick Papers," though it must by no means be supposed that, if it should happen to vary from the above details, it is necessarily and on that account a bad one. It is a very difficult thing to get an ideal copy of the "Pickwick Papers," for the plates vary immensely. For instance, in some copies of the original edition, each plate *has* its appropriate inscription at the foot, and Browne's sobriquet "Phiz" takes the place of that of "Nemo," and the plates in one copy may vary from the corresponding plates in another, though all are genuine. These distinctions arise by reason of alterations purposely made in the plates themselves by the artist as the publication proceeded; and as issue followed issue in rapid succession, each was marked by some characteristic of its own. All may be genuine, but it is only the earlier issues that excite great competition, and only the very earliest that sell for the large sums of money to which we are now becoming accustomed.

In 1837 E. Grattan, of Paternoster Row, issued a series of 32 plates by Onwhyn under the pseudonym of "Samuel Weller." These plates are found in two states, *i.e.*, either in 8 parts, each containing 4 illustrations, published at 1s. each in green wrappers, or in a bound volume (boards), at 9s. Some copies were issued in 4to, India proofs, at 2s. each.

The same year "Alfred Crowquill" (A. H. Forrester), lithographed and published, through Ackermann, a series of 40 plates which he entitled "Pictures Picked from the Pickwick Papers." They were issued in ten parts, with buff wrappers, at 1s. each part (plain), or 2s. (coloured).

The same year W. Heath etched a series of 20 plates entitled "Pickwickian Illustrations," demy 8vo, in a wrapper.

The same year Thomas Sibson etched a series of 10 plates, demy 8vo, which were published in a green wrapper at 2s. 6d., labelled "Sibson's Racy Sketches of Expeditions from the Pickwick Club."

A set of 24 etchings by Pailthorpe, in 4to, realises about
£1 10s. (India proofs, wrappers).

The extra plates by Onwhyn and "Crowquill," if in the original
wrappers, and early impressions, are very scarce indeed, bringing
perhaps twenty times as much as the published price.

As in the case of "Sketches by Boz," it is impossible to value
the "Pickwick Papers" without reference not necessarily to special,
but to particular copies.

The questions to be asked in each case are, in addition to the
usual ones relating to binding and general condition—(a) Does
the particular copy contain genuine impressions of the Buss plates?
(b) Is it bound from the numbers? (7) Does it contain the four
author's addresses? (8) Does it contain any extra illustrations by
Onwhyn, "Crowquill," Heath, or Sibson?

A set of the 20 numbers, with all the wrappers and advertisements, the two Buss plates in No. 3, and the four addresses
in parts ii., iii., x., and xv. respectively, would sell by auction
for about £30, possibly for more, but copies like this are of
course highly exceptional. A set of the numbers as usually
seen, with the Buss plates, but without the addresses, brings as
a rule no more than about £6, or occasionally £7. If part x.
contains the address dated Dec. 1836, it is by itself worth 25s.
or 30s., and if part xv. contains the two-leaved address, that
alone is worth from 10s. to 15s.

Copies in the original cloth, if bound from the numbers, are
worth more or less according to what those numbers contain. The
numbers are not improved by being bound, and may be greatly
injured. An average auction price for a copy of the "Pickwick
Papers," as issued in cloth and not bound from the numbers, is
about £3 10s. (with the Buss plates), but inferior copies, rebound
in half-calf and more or less cut down in the process, bring
no more than £1. That indeed is a good price for some of
them.

7. Oliver Twist; or the Parish Boy's Progress.
    By "Boz." . . . London. Richard Bentley,
    New Burlington Street. 1838.

This novel originally appeared in *Bentley's Miscellany* (vols. i.–v., 1837, &c.), and was first published in a separate form in 3 vols. post 8vo, brown cloth, as above, with 24 illustrations by George Cruikshank, nine of which appear in the first volume, seven in the second, and eight in the third. A second edition made its appearance in 1839, and a third in 1841. The distinction between the first and second editions or issues of 1838, is that the title of the latter reads, "Oliver Twist, by Charles Dickens," and if this is borne in mind it cannot be mistaken for the first. What is known as "The Fireside Plate," depicturing Rose Maylie, Oliver Twist, and others sitting in front of a fire, is seldom found. It only appeared in a few copies of the earliest issues of vol. iii., and is consequently very scarce.

Value about £5 (with the cancelled plate, original cloth, auction); £2 5s. (second issue, no cancelled plate, *ibid.*).

Another Edition, 3 vols. 8vo, 1839, with the 24 etchings by Cruikshank; £1 5s. (original cloth, auction).

Third Edition, 3 vols. 8vo, 1841, with the etchings and an introduction by the author, now appearing for the first time; £2 10s. (original cloth, auction).

1st Demy 8vo Edition, 1846, Bradbury & Evans. Originally published in ten monthly numbers (with the 24 illustrations). in green pictorial wrappers designed by George Cruikshank. The first number is dated January 1846, and the entire work was afterwards published in one volume, slate-coloured cloth, pp. xii–311, at 11s.

Value about £2 10s. (original cloth as issued, auction); £1 (half-calf, *ibid.*). The monthly parts are rare, selling for £8 or £10 by auction.

A skit on this work appeared without date (but 1838), entitled "Life and Adventures of Oliver Twiss, the Workhouse Boy." It is an 8vo book published by E. Lloyd, and is now scarce, selling by auction for about £1 5s. (uncut).

The set of 21 coloured plates etched by Pailthorpe in 1866 as extra illustrations to "Oliver Twist," sell by auction for about £3 3s., or for about £2 if printed in black or bistre.

8. Sketches of Young Gentlemen. . . . London. Chapman & Hall, 186 Strand. MDCCCXXXVIII.

This is a companion volume to "Sketches of Young Couples" (see *post*, No. 12), and both works were written by Dickens. Another book of the same kind, entitled "Sketches of Young Ladies," though it is frequently sold with the other two, was from the pen of Edward Caswall, and therefore not within the scope of the present article. The "Sketches of Young Gentlemen" is a fcap. 8vo book, published at 3s., containing six illustrations and a pictorial cover all by "Phiz;" also pp. viii–76.

A clean copy in the original boards brings on the average about £2 10s. by auction.

In 1843 "Young Gentlemen," "Young Ladies," and "Young Couples" were issued in a single volume, 12mo, with one title to the three. Value of this collective edition about 15s. (as issued). The second edition of "Young Gentlemen," 1838, is not worth more than about 10s. (pictorial boards).

9. Memoirs of Joseph Grimaldi. Edited by " Boz." . . . London. Richard Bentley. 1838.

Dickens contributed to this work in addition to writing an "introductory chapter," dated from Doughty Street, February 1838. The book is in two vols. post 8vo, pink or brown pictorial cloth, containing a portrait of Grimaldi by Raven, forming the frontispiece to vol. i., and twelve illustrations by George Cruikshank, six in each volume. There are two issues of the first edition, the earliest in pink cloth, and the later one in dark-brown cloth, with design in gilt by Cruikshank. The peculiarity of the later issue is that the final plate, entitled "The Last Song," has round it a pictorial or pantomimic border by "Crowquill," never found in the plate appearing in the first issue. In auctioneers' and booksellers' catalogues, the words "with the pantomimic border" are invariably made use of to intimate that the particular copy described belongs to the second issue.

Though the second issue is undoubtedly somewhat more difficult to meet with than the first, the value of each is about the same, viz., £5 (original cloth, auction). Rebound copies sell for considerably less as a rule.

Another Edition, 1846, 2 vols. post 8vo, white cloth, about £2 2s. (as issued, auction). This edition has a coloured portrait of Grimaldi as clown in the pantomime of "Mother Goose," which appears in no other edition. There are later and less valuable editions of 1853, 1866, &c.

10. The Life and Adventures of Nicholas Nickleby. By Charles Dickens. . . . London. Chapman & Hall, 186 Strand. MDCCCXXXIX.

This work was originally published in 20 monthly parts, in the usual green covers, at 1s. each. Part i. is dated April 1838, and the last part (containing Nos. 19 and 20) October in the following year. There is a portrait after Maclise, and 39 illustrations by "Phiz." The first complete bound edition is in one volume as above. It contains all the illustrations, and pp. i–xiv, 624.

Forty extra illustrations to "Nicholas Nickleby" were published by E. Grattan of Paternoster Row in 1839, in eight parts, with green and buff wrappers, at 1s. each. They are all after Onwhyn's designs, who on this occasion adopted the pseudonym of "Peter Palette." In the same year Robert Tyas of Cheapside issued a series of 24 portraits of the chief characters, by "Miss La Creevy" (Kenny Meadows). They were published in six parts at 6d. each, containing four portraits in an illustrated wrapper. The original parts of both these publications are very scarce (if with the wrappers and advertisements, &c.), but bound volumes of both are comparatively common.

Value about £3 3s. (original parts, auction), £2 10s. (first complete edition in one vol. as above, original cloth, auction).

11. The Loving Ballad of Lord Bateman. . . . London. Charles Tilt. . . . MDCCCXXXIX.

The original edition of this book in 32mo was published in pictorial green cloth, designed by George Cruikshank. There are 11 illustrations, and a sheet of music (often missing) by the same artist. The first issue of the original edition is scarce, and can easily be recognised from the fact of the pages being numbered, not in the right hand top corner, but in the middle. The authorship of this version of the ballad has been variously attributed to Dickens, Thackeray, and Cruikshank, though the probability is in favour of Dickens, more especially as regards the notes and preface.

The *Athenæum* of the 10th December 1892 gives the text of a letter from Mr. Henry Burnett, which throws considerable light on the question. Mr. Burnett married Charles Dickens's sister Fanny, and, in reply to a question respecting the authorship of the ballad, observes :—

"On one occasion, at Dickens's request, Cruikshank sang, as often before, 'The Loving Ballad of Lord Bateman.' It was a favourite with him, from the unique manner of Cruikshank's rendering. When it was ended Dickens said, ' Cruikshank, why don't you publish that song with the tune as you sing it, and with illustrations after your own manner?' The answer was, ' If Burnett will take down the music as I sing it, I will set about preparing it at once.' An appointment was made for the next evening at my house, and punctually the artist appeared. I rapidly jotted down the notes as he sang them, intending to make a fair copy, but he took hold of the manuscript and put it in his pocket, saying, ' It will do quite well.' The clef was one-sided, the notes leaning this way and that—and just so it appeared from Cruikshank's hand. It would have been no pleasure to the man to have engraved what was neatly written. Who is responsible for the preface and notes to Cruikshank's version of ' Lord Bateman '? I would rather not give an opinion at this date, though I may say I have a feeling there was something proposed to Dickens during the first conversation."

Value about £8 (original cloth, first issue, auction). The second issue is worth about a third less.

Second edition, 1851, Bogue, 12mo ; about £1 5s. (cloth, as issued).

Another edition, no date, Tilt & Bogue, 12mo ; £1 (cloth, as issued).

According to *Notes and Queries* for May 8, 1875, and Walford's
Antiquarian for July 1887, Dickens about this time wrote a
portion of a work entitled "Serjeant Bell and his Raree Show,"
which was illustrated by George Cruikshank, London, Tegg, 1839,
pp. viii–447, square 16mo. This book is very scarce, a clean copy
in the original gilt cloth selling by auction for about £9.

12. Sketches of Young Couples; with an Urgent
Remonstrance to the Gentlemen of England.
. . . By the Author of "Sketches of Young
Gentlemen." . . . London. Chapman & Hall.
. . . MDCCCXL.

This work was published at 3s. in boards, and is now scarce.
There are or should be six illustrations by "Phiz," who also
designed the cover. Pp. 92, fcap. 8vo.

Value about £2 10s. (original pictorial boards, auction). The
value of rebound copies is usually very much less.

The second edition, which is also dated 1840, is not worth more
than 8s. or 10s. (as issued, auction). Copies of any edition with
uncut edges are, however, very uncommon.

13. Master Humphrey's Clock. By Charles Dickens.
. . . London. Chapman & Hall, 186 Strand.
MDCCCXL.

This is one of the least expensive of Dickens's originals, as a
large number of bound copies were issued. However, exceptional
examples are occasionally met with, and these are scarce. In the
first instance the work was published in 88 weekly numbers (containing six addresses) at 3d. each, demy 8vo, but later on in 20
monthly parts at 1s. (or in a few cases 1s. 3d.) each, in the familiar
green covers. "Master Humphrey's Clock" contains "The Old

Curiosity Shop," "Barnaby Rudge," and preliminary and final addresses from "Master Humphrey."

The whole work was finally published in cloth, with the representation of a clock in gilt on the sides. Vol. i. is dated, in Roman letters, 1840, and vols. ii. and iii., 1841.

Notwithstanding the reputation of the author, "Master Humphrey's Clock" did not sell as well as was expected, and the two novels "Barnaby Rudge" and "The Old Curiosity Shop" were issued separately at 13s. each, from the unsold sheets, the preliminary matter being cut out. Both parts and bound volumes contain Browne's and Cattermole's illustrations on wood, one plate by George Cruikshank and one by Maclise, but several sets of extra plates were almost immediately published, e.g. :—

(α.) Seventy-two plates by T. Sibson, in 18 parts, each containing 4 plates, imperial 8vo, green paper wrappers, published by R. Tyas at 1s. each.

(β.) What were known as the "Hands to Humphrey's Clock" were published in November 1841 by G. Berger of Holywell Street. They consist of six etchings by "Jacob Parallel," intended to illustrate vol. i. An advertisement states that a similar series would appear simultaneously with the completion of vols. ii. and iii., and six etchings actually did appear to illustrate vol. ii., though the publication then appears to have dropped. At any rate the series is now usually regarded as being complete in 12 plates, instead of 18.

(γ.) Eight plates by "Phiz," issued in sets of four, in a green wrapper, by Chapman & Hall, 186 Strand, at 1s. each. Four of the plates illustrate "The Old Curiosity Shop," and a similar number "Barnaby Rudge." These plates are scarce, especially when on large paper (4to), India proofs.

The three bound volumes of "Master Humphrey's Clock" are common, even although in the original cloth binding, with a representation of a clock in gilt on the sides. Copies are frequently to be met with for about £1 5s. the three volumes, while the separate editions of "The Old Curiosity Shop" and "Barnaby Rudge," as made up from the same sheets, are worth no more than 6s. or 8s. each. Exceptional copies of "Master Humphrey's Clock" may, however, sell for much more than the sum quoted. These are generally extra illustrated with Sibson's plates (the title-page and "List of Illustrations" bound in), or some of the other etchings that have from time to time been specially designed and published. Again, some copies are bound from the parts and have all the wrappers and advertisements preserved. These are also in an exceptional position. A set of the 88 weekly parts sells by auction for about £3 3s.; the 20 monthly parts for about the same.

A number of portfolios were sold simultaneously with the weekly numbers, for their better preservation. They have a gilt design of the "Clock" on the sides, and may yet occasionally be met with for 4s. or 5s. each.

14. The Pic-Nic Papers. By Various Hands. Edited by Charles Dickens, Esq. . . . London. Henry Colburn. . . . MDCCCXLI.

In 3 vols. post 8vo, in green cloth, with 14 illustrations by George Cruikshank, "Phiz," and others, four of which are in each of the first two volumes, and six in the third. Dickens wrote the preface, and the first story entitled "The Lamplighter."

Value about £3 3s. (original cloth, auction).

15. American Notes for General Circulation. By Charles Dickens. London. Chapman & Hall, 186 Strand. MDCCCXLII.

This work, which was published in 2 vols. crown 8vo, in purple cloth, passed through no less than three editions before the close of the year.

The original edition was issued in two forms, owing to the elimination at the last moment of an introductory chapter which would have occupied pp. viii of preliminary matter. When this chapter was suppressed, the publishers forgot to alter the pagination, and consequently vol. i. of the earliest issue is paged up to xvi, although there are only viii pages of text. Later copies of the same edition have the necessary alteration, and thus there are what may be described as two separate issues, the first an accidental one. The suppressed chapter will be found in the opening pages of vol. ii.

Value about £2 (1st issue, original cloth, auction); £1 1s. (2nd issue, *ibid.*).

16. A Christmas Carol in Prose; being a Ghost Story of Christmas. By Charles Dickens. . . . London. Chapman & Hall, 186 Strand. MDCCCXLIII.

Fcap. 8vo, containing half-title, title, preface, contents, and pp. 166, together with four coloured illustrations and four woodcuts by Leech. It must be specially noticed that the earliest issue of this story was published not in red, but in brown cloth, with gilt edges, gilt design, and green end papers. On page 1 the head words read, "Stave 1." The words "Stave One" indicate a later issue, no matter how the book may be bound. The title is printed in red and blue, though some copies appear to have been printed in red and green. It may be said that if the words "Stave 1" appear as the heading to the first chapter, the book belongs to the earliest issue, even though the title be printed in red and green, but that if, under these circumstances, the title-page is dated 1844 instead of 1843, though the book belongs to the first edition, it belongs to a later issue of that edition. Some authorities are of opinion, however, that both equally belong to the earliest issue, and the point is therefore exceedingly speculative. If "Stave One" appear, there is no doubt that the copy is a late issue, though it may be of the original edition.

Value £3 10s. (title in red and green, dated 1844, original brown cloth, auction); £3 10s. (title in red and blue, dated 1843, original brown cloth, auction); 10s. to 15s. (red cloth, late issue of 1st ed., *ibid.*); 5s. or 6s. (third edition of 1843, original cloth, auction).

17. The Evenings of a Working Man; being the Occupation of his Scanty Leisure. . . . By John Overs. . . . London. T. C. Newby. . . . 1844.

Dickens wrote only the preface and dedication to Elliotson, the rest of the book being by Overs. It is in 16mo, and was published at 5s. in brown cloth, with the title in blue and red.

Value about £1 15s. (original cloth, auction). A very good and bright copy would sell for rather more.

18. The Life and Adventures of Martin Chuzzlewit. By Charles Dickens. . . . London. Chapman & Hall, 186 Strand. MDCCCXLIV.

This work was published originally in 20 monthly parts, demy 8vo, stitched in the usual green wrappers, the titles of which vary considerably from that which appears to the first complete edition of 1844 (*supra*). The bound volume contains pp. xiv, 624, green cloth, and is dedicated to "Miss Burdett Coutts." The illustrations, forty in number (inclusive of front and engraved title), are by "Phiz," and some copies have the "£" on the sign-post (illustrated title) transposed; thus "100 £." These are scarcer than the ordinary copies of the first edition, where the mistake has been corrected ("£ 100").

Value in the 20 monthly parts about £3 10s. (auction); in volume form, with the "£" transposed, £2 5s. (original cloth, *ibid.*).

19. The Chimes: a Goblin Story of some Bells that Rang an Old Year Out and a New Year In. By Charles Dickens. London. Chapman & Hall, 186 Strand. MDCCCXLV.

As in the case of the "Christmas Carol," there are at least two separate issues of the first edition of this work. The first may be known from the fact of Chapman & Hall's name forming part of the plate used for the illustrated title. It was in fact etched on the plate itself. In the later issue or issues it is printed below and outside the plate mark. This work was published in pictorial red cloth, fcap. 8vo, pp. 175. The list of illustrations comprise engraved front and title, and 11 woodcuts.

Value about 16s. (cloth, first issue); 10s. (*ibid.*, second issue). These are average auction prices in both cases.

20. The Cricket on the Hearth : a Fairy Tale of Home. By Charles Dickens. . . . Bradbury & Evans, 90 Fleet Street; and Whitefriars. MDCCCXLVI.

Fcap. 8vo, in red cloth, containing pp. 174, with front and illustrated title, and 12 woodcuts.

Value about 10s. (original cloth, auction). Many editions were issued before the close of the year 1845.

21. Pictures from Italy. By Charles Dickens. . . . London. Published for the Author, by Bradbury & Evans, Whitefriars. MDCCCXLVI.

Fcap. 8vo, pp. 270, with vignette illustrations on wood by Samuel Palmer. "Pictures from Italy" originally appeared in the form of a series of letters in the *Daily News*.

Value about 12s. (original cloth, auction).

22. The Battle of Life : a Love Story. By Charles Dickens. London. Bradbury & Evans, Whitefriars. MDCCCXLVI.

Fcap. 8vo, in red cloth, containing pp. 175, half-title, front, engraved title, plain title, inscription, list of illustrations, and 11 woodcuts. There are three separate and distinct issues of this edition, which can only be distinguished by reference to the engraved title. The first issue has merely the words "A Love Story." In the second issue the same words are supported by a Cupid, and the third issue omits the publisher's name at the foot, which the other two do not. The third issue is often met with, the other two are more uncommon, especially the second. So far as I am aware, no other edition of this work appeared during the author's lifetime, though several, which are of no importance, have been published since.

Copies of the third issue sell by auction for about 10s., those of the first and second issues at about a guinea.

23. Dombey and Son. By Charles Dickens. . . . London. Bradbury & Evans, 11 Bouverie Street. 1848.

Published originally in 20 parts at 1s. each, in the usual green covers, commencing January 1846. The illustrations, 40 in number, are by "Phiz." The bound volume, which was published in green cloth at a guinea, contains pp. xvi, 624, and the 40 illustrations as before (inclusive of title).

Value £3 3s. (original 20 parts, with the 12 extra plates by "Phiz"); £1 10s. (original 20 numbers); £1 (original cloth, auction).

See "The Story of Little Dombey," *post*, No. 33.

Twelve extra plates by "Phiz" were published separately by Chapman & Hall in 1848. These are in two numbers, stitched in a wrapper, the first containing 8 plates, published at 2s., and the second containing 4 plates, published at 1s. Both are now scarce, especially when on large paper (4to), with India proof plates.

24. The Haunted Man and the Ghost's Bargain :
a Fancy for Christmas Time.   By Charles
Dickens.   London.   Bradbury & Evans, 11
Bouverie Street.   MDCCCXLVIII.

Published in red cloth, fcap. 8vo, pp. 188, with front, engraved
title, and 14 woodcuts as per list.   There are two issues of
this edition, the first being dated "MDCCCXLVIII." as above, and
the second, "1848."   The first is rarely met with, the probability
being that only a very few copies were issued with the date in
Roman letters.

Value about 10s. ("1848," original cloth, auction).   Copies of
the "MDCCCXLVIII." edition are worth about two guineas.

25. The Personal History of David Copperfield.
By Charles Dickens. . . . . London.   Bradbury
& Evans, 11 Bouverie Street.   1850.

This work appeared originally in 20 monthly parts, published
at 1s. each, in green wrappers.   The bound volume entitled as
above was issued at 21s.. in green cloth, and contains pp. xiv, 624.
Genuine copies of the first edition *always* bear the date "1850"
at the foot of the title; if this date is absent, then the particular
book belongs to a second or some later edition.   Both parts and
bound volume contain 40 illustrations by "Phiz."

Value about £1 10s. (original cloth, auction); £2 10s. (in
the 20 parts, auction).

Dickens prepared a version of "David Copperfield" for his
public readings.   It is in four chapters, in wrappers, 8vo, privately
printed, without date (but 1851).   This revised and curtailed
version is much rarer than the original edition of the work itself,
as only a very few copies were printed for private distribution.

Value from £3 to £4 (as issued).

26. The Christmas Numbers of " Household Words " and " All the Year Round."   1850, &c.

The Christmas numbers of *Household Words* were published from 1850 to 1858 inclusive, and of *All the Year Round* from 1859 to 1867 inclusive, making in all 18 parts.   The question is often asked, How many of these numbers were enclosed in wrappers, and how many were published without?   The answer is that wrappers were not used at all until 1863, when " Mrs. Lirriper's Lodgings " appeared in a dark blue cover.   The last five Christmas numbers of *All the Year Round* were thus published, but all the other parts were issued without any wrappers at all.

Value about £2 (the nine numbers of *Household Words*, auction); £1 5s. (the nine numbers of *All the Year Round*, *ibid.*).

27. Mr. Nightingale's Diary : a Farce in One Act. . . . London.   1851.

This is a pamphlet of 26 pp., which was printed privately by the author.   There is a copy in the South Kensington Museum, but the *brochure* must be exceedingly scarce.   In 1877 a reprint was published at Boston (Mass.) in 16mo which is difficult to meet with, and invariably brings a high price in the salerooms, viz., about £2 5s. (as issued).

So far as I am aware, no copy of the first or privately printed issue has ever been sold, at any rate publicly.   If one should come to the hammer, it may be expected to bring about £25.

28. A Child's History of England.   By Charles Dickens. . . .   London.   Bradbury & Evans. . . . 1852–54.

This work originally appeared in serial form in *Household Words* during almost the whole of 1851-2-3. Before completion, the articles that had hitherto appeared were collected and published in volume form, and are complete in 3 vols. crown 8vo, vol. i. being dated 1852, vol. ii. 1853, and vol. iii. 1854, red pictorial cloth. Each volume contains a front designed by Topham. Later editions cannot be mistaken for the first, if care be taken to observe the date of the respective volumes.

Value about £3 (original cloth, auction).

29. Bleak House. By Charles Dickens. . . . London. Bradbury & Evans. . . . 1853.

Published in 20 monthly parts at 1s. each, in green covers, commencing in March 1852. The work was first published in volume form (in green cloth), as above, at 21s., and contains pp. xvi, 624, with 40 illustrations by "Phiz."

Value about £1 (cloth, uncut, auction); £1 10s. (in the original numbers, auction).

30. Hard Times, for These Times. By Charles Dickens. London. Bradbury & Evans. . . . 1854.

This story first appeared in *Household Words*, and was afterwards published in volume form as above (green cloth), at 5s. It contains pp. viii, 352, and an inscription to Thomas Carlyle, but no illustrations.

Value about £1 1s. (original cloth, auction). Very clean and bright copies often sell for considerably more.

31. Speech of C. Dickens, Esq. : Delivered at the Meeting of the Administrative Reform Association, at the Theatre Royal, Drury Lane. . . . London. Effingham Wilson. 1855.

This is an 8vo pamphlet, in wrappers, giving an account of the speech delivered by Dickens on Wednesday, June 27, 1855. It contains title, and text pp. 3–11.

A clean copy of the 1st edition (there are at least two issues), sells by auction for about £2 (as issued). The first issue has M. S. Rickerby's imprint, and is worth considerably more than £2.

32. Little Dorrit. By Charles Dickens. . . . London. Bradbury & Evans. . . . 1857.

Originally issued in 20 monthly parts, commencing in December 1855, in the usual green wrappers, at 1s. each. The work was afterwards published in volume form at 21s., green cloth, pp. xiv, 625, with the same 40 illustrations by "Phiz" that appeared with the parts.

A good set of the monthly parts will sometimes bring £1 10s. at auction, but the majority of specimens sell for less. Bound copies more frequently sell for less than £1 than above that amount.

33. The Story of Little Dombey. By Charles Dickens. London. Bradbury & Evans. . . . 1858.

This is a short and revised version of portions of "Dombey & Son," which Dickens was accustomed to deliver in the form of public readings. It contains pp. 121, and was issued in a green wrapper with woodcut on side.

Value about 17s. (original wrappers, auction).

Another Edition seems to have been published in pictorial wrappers by Chapman & Hall in 1862, 8vo. The value of this is about the same.

34. The Poor Traveller : Boots at the Holly-Tree Inn : and Mrs. Gamp. By Charles Dickens. London. Chapman & Hall. N.D. (1858).

As in the case of "The Story of Little Dombey," this collection was arranged by the author for his public readings. It is an 8vo book of 114 pp. in a green wrapper.

Value about £1 (original wrappers).

35. A Tale of Two Cities. By Charles Dickens. . . . London. Chapman & Hall, 193 Piccadilly. . . . MDCCCLIX.

Appeared originally in *All the Year Round* and in parts, issued simultaneously. The latter, eight in number, commencing in June 1859 and ending with the following December, are very scarce. They were issued, as usual, in green wrappers at 1s. each. The complete work, which was published at the close of the year 1859 in green cloth at 9s., contains pp. viii, 254, and 16 illustrations (inclusive of front and vignette) by "Phiz."

Value about £10 10s. (original eight parts, auction); £3 (original cloth, auction).

Another Edition, 1860, 8vo, Chapman & Hall. Issued in red cloth ; about 15s. (as issued, auction).

36. A Curious Dance Round a Curious Tree. By Charles Dickens. 1852. N.D. (but 1860).

Dickens had hardly anything to do with this pamphlet of 19 pp., which was written by W. H. Wills for the Committee of St. Luke's Hospital ; but as his name appears on the cover, it is mentioned here in its proper order. It is an 8vo, without any title-page, but lettered on a mauve wrapper. If the concluding lines on p. 19 are printed in *thick* type, the copy belongs to a late issue.

Value about £2 10s. (original wrappers, auction).

37. Great Expectations. By Charles Dickens. . . . London. Chapman & Hall, 193 Piccadilly. MDCCCLXI.

"Great Expectations" appeared originally in *All the Year Round*, and afterwards in 3 vols. post 8vo, blue or purple cloth, as above. There are no illustrations, but clean copies of the work are rare, as nearly all offered for sale have been very roughly used. Thus while some copies will bring no more than 25s. or 30s., others will realise £9 or £10 at auction, and occasionally even more.

Another Edition, in one vol. 8vo, Chapman & Hall, 1862, with frontispiece and vignette by Marcus Stone; about 12s. (original cloth).

Dickens prepared a "reading" from "Great Expectations," which was privately printed (without date, 8vo), for the use of a few friends. It is in "three stages." This pamphlet is exceedingly scarce. A copy once sold for £17 by auction (morocco extra, by Riviere).

The extra illustrations to "Great Expectations" include 21 etchings by Pailthorpe, published in 1885. A set of proofs on Japanese paper sell by auction for about £1 10s., or if coloured for £2 2s.

38. The Uncommercial Traveller. By Charles Dickens. London. Chapman & Hall. . . . MDCCCLXI.

This volume contains reprints of 17 articles which appeared in *All the Year Round*, constituting a first series. Other papers bearing the same chief title were arranged at a later date, and published in various collected editions of Dickens's works. The above book, published in magenta or green cloth, post 8vo, pp. viii, 264, is scarce, incomplete though it be.

Value about £2 5s. (original cloth, auction). Most copies of this book offered for sale are very dirty, and not worth a third of the above estimate.

Second Edition, 1861, 8vo, Chapman & Hall. About 8s. (original cloth).

39. Our Mutual Friend. By Charles Dickens. . . . London.   Chapman & Hall. . . . 1865.

Published originally in 20 monthly parts at 1s. each, in green wrappers. The series commenced in May 1864, the work being published in volume form at the latter end of 1865, in 2 vols. crown 8vo, green cloth. Vol. i. contains pp. xi, 320, and vol. ii. pp. vii, 306. There are 40 illustrations by Marcus Stone.

Value about 12s. (original cloth).   £1 5s. (in the original parts, clean and perfect).

40. Legends and Lyrics. By Adelaide Anne Procter. . . . Bell & Daldy, 186 Fleet Street. 1866.

This is a 4to book published at 21s., containing a number of illustrations by Tenniel, Millais, and others, and an introduction by Dickens, for which reason it is generally catalogued among his works. There are several prior editions without the introduction.

Good copies in the original cloth are scarce, realising as much as £2 10s. or £3 by auction. Inferior ones, especially if rebound, often sell for much less.

41. The Mystery of Edwin Drood.   By Charles
     Dickens. . . . .London.   Chapman & Hall. . . .
     1870.   . .

This was the work upon which Dickens was engaged at the time
of his death on the 9th of June 1870.   Only six monthly parts
appeared, and these were afterwards published in volume form as
above, 8vo, pp. viii, 190.   There are 12 illustrations by Fildes,
and a good engraved portrait of the author.

Value about 7s. 6d. (in parts).

A continuation of "Edwin Drood" was published in eight
monthly parts, demy 8vo, 1871–2, pictorial wrappers, under the
title of "John Jasper's Secret."   These parts are scarce, and sell
for about £1 15s. (auction).

42. Hunted Down : a Story.   By Charles Dickens.
     . . . London.   John Camden Hotten, 74 and
     75 Piccadilly.   N.D. (but 1870).

The story originally appeared in the *New York Ledger* during
the latter portion of the year 1859, and afterwards in *All the Year
Round*.   It was published in pamphlet form as above, in green
wrappers, at 6d.

Value about £1 1s. (original wrappers, auction).

43. The Lamplighter : a Farce.   1838.   Now
     First Published. . . . London.   1879.

This is a pamphlet of 45 pp. printed from the MS., bearing the
above title, now in the South Kensington Museum.   Only 250
copies were published.

Value about £1 1s. (original cover, auction).

44. The Mudfog Papers, &c. . . . Now First
Collected. . . . London.   Richard Bentley
& Sons. . . . 1880.

Reprinted from *Bentley's Miscellany*, and now published collectively for the first time at 2s. 6d.   It is a small book (12mo), containing pp. iv, 198, and is worth rather but not much more than
the published price.

———

The best Life of Dickens is that by Forster, published in 3 vols.
8vo, 1872-4, which is very frequently found extra illustrated with
autographs and additional portraits.   Theodore Taylor's "Story of
his Life," N.D. (J. C. Hotten), is also a useful book, full of interesting information.

His collected works are principally "The Library Edition," in
30 vols. 8vo, 1858–74; the "Charles Dickens Edition," 21 vols.
8vo, 1867–(74); the "Household Edition," 22 vols. 4to (1873–79),
originally published in parts; the "Illustrated Library Edition,"
30 vols. 8vo, 1876; and the *Edition de Luxe*, 30 vols. imperial 8vo,
1881–2.

An 8vo pamphlet by Charles Dickens, entitled "To be Read at
Dusk," reprinted from the *Keepsake* for 1852, sometimes appears
in the booksellers' catalogues at sums varying from £20 to £30.
In June 1893 a copy sold at Sotheby's for £8 15s. (morocco
extra, by Zaehnsdorf).

AUSTIN DOBSON.

IN addition to the works enumerated below, of which Mr. Austin Dobson is sole author, there are a considerable number of others which he either edited or annotated, or for which he wrote the introductory matter. Thus, he supplied the notes to the "Parchment Library" edition of Goldsmith's "Vicar of Wakefield," first published in 1883, and edited the same author's "Poems" for the "Clarendon Press" series, 1887, &c., and his "Poems and Plays," and "Citizen of the World," for the "Temple Library" series, 1888 and 1891. Mr. Dobson also edited Beaumarchais' "Le Barbier de Séville," and a selection from Steele's Essays in the *Tatler*, *Spectator*, and *Guardian* for the "Clarendon Press" series. He also wrote "Fielding," for Morley's "English Men of Letters," 1883; "Hogarth," for the "Illustrated Biographies of Great Artists," 1879; and "Richard Steele," 1886, for the "English Worthies" series. He also revised or edited selections from the works of Robert Herrick, N.D. (but 1883, Sampson Low & Co.), Matthew Prior, 1889, and Andrew Lang (see the article "Andrew Lang," No. 13), and has written the introduction to an edition of Gay's "Fables," 1882, Defoe's "Robinson Crusoe," 1883, and Fielding's "Voyage to Lisbon," 1892. The Memoir of Bewick affixed to the "Memorial Edition" of his works, 1885-7, was also prefaced and annotated by Mr. Dobson.

These and other books, touched upon but in some cases not entirely written by Mr. Dobson, do not come within our survey, and they are, moreover, mainly of small account from our special and extremely limited point of view, because they seem to have been published in large numbers, and are consequently comparatively easy to procure. This, however, is not always the case with the books mentioned in the following list. Many of these are scarce, very difficult to meet with, even in London, and often expensive when found. All Mr. Dobson's books have been growing in importance for some time, and their pecuniary value is noticeably increasing. For this and other reasons, it is necessary to describe them rather fully as follows :—

1. The Authentic History of Captain Castagnette, Nephew of the Man with the Wooden Head, from the French of Manuel. (By Austin Dobson.) . . . S. O. Beeton. N.D. (but 1866).

This work, which is in 4to, is illustrated with 43 engravings by Doré.

Value about £1 (pictorial cloth).

2. Vignettes in Rhyme and *Vers de Société* (now First Collected). By Austin Dobson. London. Henry S. King & Co. . . . 1873.

Published at 5s. in 12mo, in reddish-brown cloth, lettered in gilt on side and face. The work contains half-title, title as above, dedication to Anthony Trollope, one leaf with verses on reverse, contents (vii–viii), and text, pp. 1–220.

Value about £1 10s. (original cloth, auction).

Second Edition, 1874, Henry S. King & Co., 12mo, also published at 5s. Of little importance.

3. Proverbs in Porcelain, and other Verses. By
Austin Dobson. . . . Henry S. King & Co.
London. 1877.

This work is in post 8vo, and was published at 6s. in brown
cloth, lettered in gilt on side and face. It contains half-title,
title as above, dedication in verse to Frederick Locker (unpaged),
contents (vii–ix), and text, pp. 1–209.

Value about £1 10s. (original cloth, auction).

Second Edition, revised and enlarged, 1878, post 8vo, Kegan
Paul & Co. ; published at 6s. Present value about the same.

4. Eighteenth Century Essays. Selected and
Annotated by Austin Dobson. . . . London.
Kegan Paul, Trench & Co. MDCCCLXXXII.

Thick fcap. 8vo with rough edges, vellum, lettered in red on
side and red and black on face. Contains half-title with verses
on reverse, a woodcut of "The Tory Foxhunter," title as above,
dedication to Mrs. Ritchie (v–vi), contents (vii–ix), introduction
(xi–xxiii), and text, pp. 1–284. Fifty copies were printed on
large paper, 8vo, pp. xxiii, 284 as before.

Value from 8s. to 10s. (as issued), or on large paper from
17s. 6d. to £1 (*ibid.*).

5. Old-World Idylls, and other Verses. By Austin
Dobson. . . . London. Kegan Paul, Trench
& Co. . . . MDCCCLXXXIII.

Published in olive-green cloth, lettered in gilt on side and face,
fcap. 8vo. Contains half-title, title in red and black, leaf of verses
(unpaged), contents (vii–x), a second half-title, and text, pp. 3–246.
The published price of this book was 6s. Fifty copies were

printed on large paper, but these, having been struck off for the author, are extremely scarce.

Value about 10s. (as issued, auction).

Another Edition, 1883, fcap. 8vo, Kegan Paul, Trench & Co.; published at 6s.   Present value about the same.

6. Thomas Bewick and his Pupils.   By Austin Dobson. . . . London.   Chatto & Windus, Piccadilly.   1884.

This work was published in two sizes, both 4to, an ordinary edition at 10s. 6d., and what was called an "Édition de Luxe" in large 4to, half-vellum (250 copies printed).   The book is made up as follows:—Half-title, portrait of Bewick as front, title as above, dedication to W. J. Linton, preface (vii–x), contents (xi–xii), list of illustrations (xiii–xviii), and text, pp. 1–232, inclusive of index.   There are 95 illustrations, some whole-page and others in the text.

Value about £1 10s. (large paper, uncut, auction).   Copies on ordinary paper usually sell for 10s. or 12s.

Another Edition, post 8vo, 1889, Chatto & Windus, published at 6s.   Present value about the same sum.

7. At the Sign of the Lyre.   By Austin Dobson. . . . London.   Kegan Paul, Trench & Co. MDCCCLXXXV.

A thick fcap. 8vo book, bound in olive cloth and lettered in gilt on side and face.   It contains half-title, woodcut as front, title in red and black, dedication (unpaged), contents (vii–x), another half-title, and text, pp. 3–232.   An unpaged leaf on toned paper containing device and inscription ("Avtant icy qu'aillevrs"), should follow p. 232.   Half-titles follow pp. 94, 126, 156, 198, 210, and 224 respectively.

This work was published at 6s. ; the present value is about 10s. (cloth, uncut), or on large paper (of which there were seventy-five copies for England and America) about £1 10s. (as issued, auction).

Another Edition, 1887, fcap. 8vo, Kegan Paul & Co., published at 6s. Present value about the same amount.

Sixth Edition, revised and enlarged to pp. 252, 1889, 8vo, Kegan Paul & Co. Value about 10s. (as issued).

8. Life of Oliver Goldsmith. By Austin Dobson. London. Walter Scott, 24 Warwick Lane. . . . 1888.

This book was written for Walter Scott's "Great Writers" series, and published at 1s. 6d. Some large-paper copies were published in navy-blue cloth, lettered in gilt on face, at 2s. 6d. A half-title precedes, then follows title, contents (5–9), and text, pp. 11–214. A bibliography by J. P. Anderson, of the British Museum Library, completes the work. (Bibliography on pp. i–xxiv.)

The value of this book is small, owing to the large number of copies printed. The present prices do not exceed those at which the work was published.

9. Poems on Several Occasions. By Austin Dobson. New York. Dodd, Mead & Company. 1889.

This is a very beautiful book in 2 vols. crown 8vo, navy-blue cloth, most extensively and elaborately stamped in gilt on side and face.

Vol. i. has half-title, title, dedicatory rondeau (unpaged), contents (vii–x), half-title, and text, pp. 3–264.

Vol. ii. contains half-title, title, unnumbered page of verse, contents (vii–x), half-title, and text, pp. 1–277.

Value about 16s. (as issued, auction).

10. The Quiet Life : Certain Verses by Various Hands ; the Motive Set Forth in a Prologue and Epilogue by Austin Dobson. . . . London. Sampson Low, Marston, Searle & Rivington, Limited.   MDCCCXC.

In large 4to, brown cloth, stamped on both sides with numerous miniature roses in gilt, lettered in gilt on side and face, green end papers sprinkled with gilt, gilt edges.   This book contains blank leaf, half-title ("The Quiet Life "), on the reverse of which a woodcut of a rose in a pot, front, title as above, table of contents (unpaged), prologue (unpaged), and text, pp. 3–97.   Every page throughout the volume is adorned with drawings by Edwin A. Abbey or Alfred Parsons.   Though dated 1890, this work was actually published at the close of the preceding year.

Value about £1 5s. (in the original ornamented cloth, as issued).

11. Four Frenchwomen.   By Austin Dobson. London.   Chatto & Windus, Piccadilly.   1890.

The "Four Frenchwomen" referred to in this volume are Charlotte Corday, Madame Roland, the Princess de Lamballe, and Madame de Genlis.   The book is a fcap. 8vo, half-green cloth, the sides bright red.   It was published at 2s. 6d., and contains title as above, dedication to Brander Matthews (unpaged), prefatory note with contents on reverse (unpaged), half-title, and text, pp. 1–207.   A half-title precedes each biography.   There was a large-paper edition of fifty copies.

Value about 2s. 6d.

12. Horace Walpole : a Memoir.   By Austin Dobson.   With an Appendix of Books Printed at the Strawberry Hill Press.   New York. Dodd, Mead & Company.   1890.

Crown 8vo, pp. 370. Four copies were printed on vellum, and fifty on Japan paper. The work contains a number of etchings and other illustrations.

Value about £1 12s. (on Japan paper as issued, auction).

Second Edition, 1893, Osgood, M'Ilvaine & Co., published at 10s. 6d. Fifty copies were printed on hand-made paper at £1 1s. This new and revised edition is illustrated with portraits and views, printed on India paper and mounted, facsimile letters, &c.

13. William Hogarth. By Austin Dobson. . . . London. Sampson Low, Marston & Company, Limited. . . . 1891.

A demy 8vo book of which 150 copies were printed on large paper (4to) signed by the author. The latter are in half-vellum, with white label on face, green sides.

The work collates as follows :—Half-title, portrait of Hogarth, title, dedication to Cosmo Monkhouse, preface (vii–x), contents (xi–xiv), half-title ("Part I.—Memoir"), and text pp. 3–368. Numerous plates throughout the volume.

This work is yet in print, and can be obtained from the publishers (£1 4s. ; or £2 12s. 6d., large paper).

14. Eighteenth Century Vignettes. By Austin Dobson. . . . London. Chatto & Windus, Piccadilly. 1892.

This work, though published in London, was, to meet the requirements of the recent International Copyright Act, printed at Cambridge (Mass.). It is in crown 8vo, sage-green cloth, lettered on face in gilt. A portrait of Mr. Dobson precedes title, which is followed by dedication (unpaged), prefatory note (v–vi), contents (unpaged), and text, pp. 9–261. Only a very few copies of this edition are extant; probably not half a dozen.

English Edition, crown 8vo, navy blue cloth. A folding plan precedes, then follows title, dedication, preface (different from the American edition), contents (unpaged), and text pp. 9–261. Of this edition 250 copies were printed in crown 4to, half parchment, each copy signed by the author. There is a frontispiece portrait of Richard Steele, five other portraits, and at the end the folding plate which precedes in the case of the small-paper copies.

This edition is yet in print.

15. The Ballad of Beau Brocade, and other Poems of the Eighteenth Century. By Austin Dobson. . . . Kegan Paul, Trench, Trübner & Co. . . . MDCCCXCII.

A crown 8vo book in smooth dark red cloth, lettered (with scroll work) on side and face in gilt. A half-title precedes, then follows front, title, dedication in verse, prefatory note, and contents (all unpaged), list of illustrations (xi–xiii), half-title, and pp. 1–89. Half-titles precede each of the poems in the book. There are 50 illustrations by Hugh Thomson.

There are two issues of the first edition of the "Ballad of Beau Brocade." The first has "The long day lengthens" in line 6 of the Dedicatory Rondeau, instead of "Life's journey lengthens" in the second issue, and the Highwayman at p. 18 has a flap to his coat which is cut out in the second issue.

Of this work 450 copies were printed for England and America, in imperial 8vo, white cloth, plainly lettered in gilt on face. The illustrations are on India paper, and an impression of the design for the cover of the ordinary edition precedes.

Value about 7s. 6d. (as issued), or from £2 10s. to £2 15s. (large paper). Copies of the earlier issue are worth about 25 per cent. more.

PIERCE EGAN.

Pierce Egan, the elder, sporting journalist and historian of the prize-ring, is supposed to have been born in or near London in the year 1772. His early life was spent on the staff of the sporting newspapers, and it was not until 1814, when forty-two years of age, that he commenced to write the books which to this day make his name a household word among all who are in any degree interested in the now almost obsolete forms of sport which he particularly affected. His first book, "The Mistress of Royalty," 1814, was printed with his own hands; his second, "Boxiana: or Sketches of Modern Pugilism," firmly established his reputation, and paved the way for that still more noticeable work, " Life in London," which took the town by storm, and was provocative of plagiarisms and imitations innumerable.

Among these are "Carey's Life in Paris," 1821, with 21 coloured illustrations by George Cruikshank, a scarce work, which now sells by auction for as much as £6 or £7 when uncut. A catchpenny pamphlet published by Catnach of Monmouth Street in 1822, entitled " A New Song of Flash Fashion, Frolic and Fun," commanded an extensive circulation among the lower orders of the day, though clean and perfect copies are now but rarely met with.

Another book of the same, though a somewhat superior kind, is "Doings in London; or Day and Night Scenes of the Frauds, Frolics, Manners, and Depravities of the Metropolis," with 33 plates after R. Cruikshank, published by Hodgson, without date, but about 1840.

Numerous plays founded upon " Life in London " were produced at the theatres, and prints and broadsides flooded the streets.

In 1828 Egan published his " Finish to the Adventures of Tom, Jerry, and Logic," and enlisted the services of Robert Cruikshank to design the 36 plates it contains. This book is almost as well known as its predecessor, and enjoyed a very large circulation.

All Egan's books, particularly those with coloured plates, are very scarce when in anything like condition, a fact which is perhaps due to the numerous hands through which they passed, and the thumbing to which they were subjected, in most cases by persons whose love of literature extended no further than racy descriptions of prize-fights, cock-fights, and the career of men about town, in the elaboration of which Egan had no rival even in his own day.

Pierce Egan died at Pentonville, in August 1849.

1. Boxiana ; or Sketches of Ancient and Modern Pugilism. . . . By P. Egan. London. Published by G. Smeeton, 139 St. Martin's Lane, Charing Cross. 1812.

This work was published in parts, with a great variety of portraits and plates, some folding, but none coloured. The first and some of the other parts were published by Smeeton from July 1812 onward, but the entire work was published in volume form by Sherwood, Neely & Jones at different dates, viz. :—Vols. i. and ii. in 1818, vol. iii. in 1821, and vol. iv. (described as " The New Series ") in 1824. The complete work is nearly always found in four volumes, though a fifth, dated 1829, is frequently added. Smeeton's engraved title-page should be bound up with vol. i.

The value of this work varies very much, according to the character and quality of the binding. Thus the four volumes in the original grey pictorial boards sell by auction for about £5 10s., while the same set in calf would bring about £3 10s. Odd volumes in boards usually bring no more than 10s. or 12s. each.

Another Edition, 1829–30, 5 vols. 8vo, Virtue, published at £2 10s. Sound copies of this edition are, under similar circumstances, worth about the same as those of the earlier issue.

2. Life in London ; or, The Day and Night Scenes of Jerry Hawthorn, Esq., and his Elegant Friend, Corinthian Tom, accompanied by Bob Logic, the Oxonian, in their Rambles and Sprees through the Metropolis. By Pierce Egan. . . . London. Printed for Sherwood, Neely & Jones, Paternoster Row. 1821.

Published originally in parts, the first being dated the 15th of July 1821 ; afterwards in 1 vol. demy 8vo, pictorial boards, containing half-title, coloured front, title with woodcut vignette, dedication to George IV. (v–viii), contents (ix–xii), description of illustrations (xiii–xvi), and text pp. 1–376. Three folding sheets of music follow p. 118, and there are 36 coloured plates by J. R. and G. Cruikshank, with numerous designs on wood by the same artists. A few copies were printed on large paper.

Value about £10 in the original boards (auction), and about half that amount well bound in calf or half-calf (*ibid.*); £20 (large paper, boards).

Another Edition, 1823, demy 8vo, Sherwood, Jones & Co. This edition was also published in pictorial boards, and contains precisely the same matter, arranged similarly as the edition of 1821. The value is however considerably less, a clean copy in boards selling as a rule for no more than £3 or £3 10s. by auction, and a bound copy for about £2.

Another Edition, London, N.D. (but 1869), post 8vo. Hotten's reprint, with all the illustrations by J. R. and G. Cruikshank. Published at 7s. 6d., and now worth a little more.

3. Real Life in London ; or, The Rambles and
   Adventures of Bob Tallyho, Esq., and his
   Cousin the Hon. Tom Dashall, through the
   Metropolis. . . . By an Amateur. . . . London.
   Printed for Jones & Co., 3 Warwick Square.
   1821.

It is very doubtful whether this work, which is clearly an
imitation of the "Life in London," was written by Egan, but as
it is for convenience sake usually attributed to him, I have included it in the list.

The book was published originally in parts, in pink pictorial
wrappers ; afterwards in book form, pictorial boards, 2 vols. demy
8vo, 1821–22.   A few copies were printed on large paper.

Vol. i. contains coloured front, coloured pictorial title, plain
title, contents (iii–x), and text pp. 3–656.   There are 19 coloured
plates (inclusive of front and title).

Vol. ii. contains coloured front, coloured pictorial title, plain
title, contents (i–ix), and text pp. 3–668.   There are 13 coloured
plates (inclusive of front and title).

The following are average auction prices for copies in the condition named :—£7 or £8 (original parts), £6 (original boards),
£4 10s. (rebound, but uncut), £7 10s. (large paper, old calf).

Another Edition, 1822–23, 2 vols. demy 8vo.

Another Edition, 1829–30, 2 vols. demy 8vo.

The value of these two later editions varies but little from that
of the first, under similar conditions.

4. The Life of an Actor.   By Pierce Egan. . . .
   London.   Printed for C. S. Arnold, Tavistock
   Street, Covent Garden.   1825.

Demy 8vo, in pictorial white boards, with 27 coloured plates by
Theodore Lane, inclusive of front, and numerous designs on wood
by Thompson.

The volume contains coloured front, title as above with vignette, dedication to Edmund Kean (iii–vi), contents (vii–x), "Description of the Illustrations" (xi–xvi), and text pp. 1–272.

Good copies of this book are very scarce, and nearly all offered for sale have been rebound. A good bound copy, say in calf extra, sells by auction for about £6 10s. or £7.

Second Edition, 1892, 8vo, Pickering & Chatto, pp. xvi–257. The poetical descriptions are by T. Greenwood, and the plates by Lane. Published at 14s., and now worth a little more.

5. Pierce Egan's Anecdotes (Original and Selected) of the Turf, the Chase, the Ring, and the Stage. . . . London. Printed for Knight & Lacey, Paternoster Row, and Pierce Egan, 113 Strand. MDCCCXXVII.

A demy 8vo book, with 13 coloured plates designed and etched by Theodore Lane.

The volume contains coloured front, title with vignette, dedication to Sir Bellingham Graham, Bart. (iii–iv), contents (v–viii), and text pp. 1–304.

Value about £4 (calf extra, auction).

6. Finish to the Adventures of Tom, Jerry, and Logic, in their Pursuits through Life in and out of London. By Pierce Egan. London. G. Virtue. . . . 1830.

Published in demy 8vo, pictorial covers, with 36 full-page coloured engravings and many woodcuts by Robert Cruikshank. This work is a sequel to "Life in London," and, like that publication, is very scarce in the original boards.

Nearly all the copies offered for sale have been rebound, and the auction prices vary very much in consequence. A copy in the original boards sells for £10 or £12, while one that has been

rebound only brings about half the amount. Instances, however,
are not wanting of "Life in London" and the "Finish" selling
for £30 or £40 by auction (the two volumes rebound), though
under highly exceptional circumstances.

Another Edition, N.D. (but 1869), J. C. Hotten, demy 8vo, published at 21s. in red pictorial cloth, and now worth about the
same. This edition contains all the coloured plates.

Another Edition, 1887, demy 8vo, Reeves & Turner, published
at 16s. with coloured plates, or 10s. plain. This edition is scarce,
good coloured copies selling by auction at from £1 10s. to £2.

7. The Show Folks. . . . By Pierce Egan. . . .
    London. Printed for M. Arnold, Tavistock
    Street. . . . 1831.

This is a small-sized book in 12mo, containing nine designs in
wood by Theodore Lane. A woodcut of "The Stage-struck Hero"
faces title, after which follows dedication to Sir Martin Archer
Shee, Knight (5–8), and text pp. 9–59. A biographical sketch of
Theodore Lane occupies pp. 33–59.

Value about 5s. (in wrappers, as issued).

8. Pierce Egan's Book of Sports and Mirror of Life,
    embracing the Turf, the Chase, the Ring, and
    the Stage. . . . London. Printed for T. T. &
    J. Tegg, 73 Cheapside. . . . 1832.

The "Book of Sports" originally made its appearance in 25
weekly parts at 3d. each, the whole being subsequently bound in
boards, and issued with a pictorial title-page, inscribed as above,
demy 8vo, pictorial boards. A good index completes the volume,
and the front page of each part is embellished with a woodcut
representing some scene of the turf, the chase, or the road.

Value about 17s. 6d. (half calf, auction), £2 (original boards,
ibid.).

9. The Pilgrims of the Thames in Search of the
   National. By Pierce Egan. . . . London.
   W. Strange, 21 Paternoster Row, and all
   Booksellers. 1838.

Demy 8vo. Etched front faces title, after which follows a dedication to Queen Victoria (unpaged), contents (i–v), and text pp.
1–376.   In addition to the frontispiece, there are 23 full-page
etchings by Pierce Egan the younger.

Value about 10s. (half-bound, auction).

"GEORGE ELIOT."

Mary Ann Evans, better known under her pseudonym of "George Eliot," was born in Warwickshire in 1819. In 1846 she completed a translation of Strauss' "Life of Jesus," which had been partly made by another hand, and thus entered the literary world, five years later accepting the sub-editorship of the *Westminster Review*, and contributing to its pages from time to time many essays and articles. Her first venture in fiction was made with a short story which appeared in *Blackwood* in 1857, under the title of "Amos Barton." This forms one of the series known as "Scenes of Clerical Life," the last story in which, "Janet's Repentance," was published in the number of *Blackwood* for October 1857. These stories were afterwards reprinted in volume form, and achieved such a remarkable success, that the author was encouraged to publish a more ambitious novel in the orthodox three volumes, now known to all the world as "Adam Bede." These and all the other works separately published by the same authoress are described rather at length, on account of their importance, collectors having, of late years, taken a very great interest in them. As a consequence, the pecuniary value of many of these books is now high.

George Eliot married Mr. John Walter Cross in May 1880, but died in the December of the same year, and lies buried in Highgate Cemetery.

1. Scenes of Clerical Life.   By George Eliot. . . .
   William Blackwood & Sons. . . . MDCCCLVIII.

Published in 2 vols. post 8vo, reddish brown cloth, at 21s.

Vol. i. contains half-title, title, contents (unpaged), a second half-title, and text pp. 3–366. A third half-title follows p. 151.

Vol. ii. contains half-title, title, a second half-title, and text pp. 1–381. A third half-title follows p. 43.

Value from £2 15s. to £3 (original cloth, auction).

2. Adam Bede. By George Eliot, Author of “Scenes of Clerical Life.” . . . William Blackwood & Sons. . . . MDCCCLIX.

In 3 vols. post 8vo, orange cloth, lettered on face in gilt. Published at 31s. 6d.

Vol. i. contains half-title, title as above, contents (unpaged), second half-title, and text pp. 1–325.

Vol. ii. is made up in precisely the same way, but there are pp. 1–374.

Vol. iii. is also collated in the same manner, with pp. 3–333.

Value from £4 to £5, and even £6 if very clean (original cloth, auction).

3. The Mill on the Floss. By George Eliot, Author of “Scenes of Clerical Life” and “Adam Bede.” . . . William Blackwood & Sons. . . . MDCCCLX.

Also published at 31s. 6d. in 3 vols. post 8vo, orange cloth, lettered on face in gilt.

Vol. i. contains half-title, title, contents (v–vi), a second half-title, and text pp. 1–361.

Vol. ii. collates in the same manner, but has pp. 1–319.

Vol. iii. is also collated in the same manner, but has pp. 1–313.

Value about £1 5s. (original cloth, auction).

4. Silas Marner, the Weaver of Raveloe. By
George Eliot, Author of " Adam Bede," &c.
. . . William Blackwood & Sons. . . .
MDCCCLXI.

This story is complete in 1 vol. post 8vo, published at 12s.
No less than seven editions appeared before the close of the
year.

The original edition contains half-title, title, a second half-title
("Part I."), and text pp. 1–364.

Value about 10s. (original cloth, auction). Second and later
editions are not of the same value.

5. Romola. By George Eliot, Author of " Adam
Bede." . . . London. Smith, Elder & Co.,
65 Cornhill. MDCCCLXIII.

Published in 3 vols. post 8vo, bright green cloth, lettered in gilt
on face, at 31s. 6d.

Each volume contains title as above, and table of contents (iii–iv),
but no half-title or other preliminary matter.

Value about £2 10s. (original cloth, auction).

Edition de Luxe, 2 vols. 8vo, 1880, with illustrations by Sir
Frederick Leighton.

Value from 20s. to 25s. (in the original canvas boards, auction).

6. Felix Holt, the Radical. By George Eliot. . . .
William Blackwood & Sons. . . . MDCCCLXVI.

Published in 3 vols. post 8vo, red cloth, lettered in gilt on face,
at 31s. 6d.

Each volume contains half-title before title, but no other preliminary matter.

Value about £1 10s. (original cloth, auction).

7. The Spanish Gypsy : a Poem.   By George
   Eliot.   William Blackwood & Sons. . . .
   MDCCCLXVIII.

This work was originally written in the winter of 1864–5. After
a visit to Spain in 1867 it was rewritten and amplified.

It was published in bright blue cloth, demy 8vo, at 12s. 6d.
At least three editions appeared the same year.

The work contains half-title, title, note (unpaged), half-title,
and text pp. 3–358.

Value about 15s. (original cloth, auction).

8. Agatha.   By George Eliot.   London.   Trübner
   & Co., 60 Paternoster Row.   1869.

A fcap. 8vo book, published at 2s. 6d.   There is no half-title,
and the title is followed immediately by text pp. 3–16.

This is a very scarce work, rarely met with in any condition,
and more rarely still in the original paper covers.   Under such
circumstances, a copy would be worth some £10 or £12 at least,
and possibly more.

9. Brother and Sister : Sonnets.   By Marian Lewes.
   London.   For   Private   Circulation   only.
    1869.

This work is supposed to be a fictitious and ante-dated edition
reprinted from the "Legend of Jubal and Other Poems," 1874,
in which the Sonnets perhaps really first appeared.   (See p. 209
of the "Legend of Jubal," *post*, No. 11.)

The pamphlet is in post 8vo, wrappers, and contains half-title,
title as above, and text pp. 5–15, on thick toned paper.

Value about £3 3s. (original wrappers, auction).

10. Middlemarch.   By George Eliot. . . . William
     Blackwood & Sons, Edinburgh and London.
     . . . N.D. (but 1871–2).

Published in 8 parts, green pictorial wrappers, and often found
bound up in 8 vols. crown 8vo, cloth.

The collation of the bound volumes differs slightly.

Vol. i. has title, contents (unpaged), prelude (v–vii), and a
second half-title.
  Vol. ii. has two half-titles, but no title.
  Vol. iii. has half-title, title, contents, and a second half-title.
  Vol. iv. has half-title only.
  Vol. v. has half-title, title, contents, and a second half-title.
  Vol. vi. has half-title only.
  Vol. vii. has half-title, title, contents, and a second half-title.
  Vol. viii. has half-title only.

From this collation it is evident that it was the intention of the
publishers that the eight parts should, when complete, be bound
in four volumes, and this is often found to be the case, two parts
being comprised in one volume.

The value of original copies of " Middlemarch " is not great, an
enormous number of copies having been issued. Thus the four
volumes bound in eight, original cloth, may frequently be met
with in the auction room for about £1, while a clean set of the
parts sells for very little more.

11. The Legend of Jubal and Other Poems.   By
     George Eliot.   William Blackwood & Sons.
     . . . MDCCCLXXIV.

A fcap. 8vo book, published in cloth. A half-title precedes title
as above, and is followed by table of contents and leaf of errata,
both unpaged, then a second half title, and text pp. 3–242.

Value about 15s. (original cloth, auction).

12. Daniel Deronda. By George Eliot. . . . William Blackwood & Sons. . . . N.D. (but 1876).

As in the case of " Middlemarch," this work was originally published in eight parts or books, but in slate-coloured wrappers. The intention here also was to bind the parts, when completed, in four volumes, though they are frequently found in eight. Consequently title-pages were only added to Parts I., III., V., and VII., half-titles being substituted in the remaining parts.

A set of the parts in original wrappers, as issued, seldom sells by auction for more than 12s. or 15s., and the bound volumes are worth no more.

13. Impressions of Theophrastus Such. By George Eliot. William Blackwood & Sons. . . . MDCCCLXXIX.

This work was published in slate-coloured cloth, thick demy 8vo, lettered in gilt on face.

It contains half-title, title, contents (unpaged), half-title, and text pp. 3–357. Half-titles follow pp. 23, 52, 79, 97, 114, 129, 140, 155, 172, 186, 210, 222, 240, 258, 277, 296, and 309.

Value from 5s. to 6s. (original cloth).

A fourteenth work credited to George Eliot, but which was not published until after her death, is entitled " Essays and Leaves from a Note-Book," 8vo, 1884. This is not a very important book, and usually sells for no more than a few shillings in the original cloth.

EDMUND GOSSE.

In addition to the works described below, the rarity of which makes them interesting to collectors, the following may first be mentioned, although from our limited point of view they are of less importance. Mr. Edmund William Gosse is the author in verse of "On Viol and Flute," a volume of lyrical poems, 1873; "King Erik," a tragedy, 1876; "The Unknown Lover," a drama in verse, 1878; "New Poems," 1879. In prose he has published, besides what are mentioned below, the following original works:—"Northern Studies," 1879; a "Life of Gray," in the "English Men of Letters" Series, 1882; "Seventeenth Century Studies," 1883; "From Shakespere to Pope," 1885; a "Life of Sir Walter Raleigh," 1886; a "Life of Congreve," 1888; a "History of Eighteenth Century Literature," 1889; a "Personal Sketch of Robert Browning," 1890; a "Life of Philip Henry Gosse," 1890; "Gossip in a Library," 1891; "The Secret of Narcisse," a romance, 1892; and "Questions at Issue," a volume of critical essays, 1893.

He has also translated two plays of Ibsen, "Hedda Gabler" in 1891, and "The Master-Builder" (in conjunction with Mr. William Archer) in 1893, besides editing and introducing a considerable number of volumes. Among the latter may be mentioned his edition of the works of Gray, for the first time collected, in four volumes, in 1884; and of the poems of Beddoes, in two volumes, in 1888. Mr. Gosse is at the present time preparing for private circulation (65 copies only) an annotated catalogue of a portion of his library.

A scarce epistle (in verse) to Dr. Oliver Wendell Holmes on his seventy-fifth birthday is from the same hand. Only 40 copies of this poem were issued for private distribution.

1. Madrigals, Songs, and Sonnets. By John Arthur Blaikie and Edmund William Gosse. London. Longmans, Green & Co. 1870.

This is a foolscap 8vo book, bound in green cloth, lettered in gilt on face. There is no half-title, and title as above is followed by unpaged leaf, with inscription to Mrs. Henry Curtis, contents (v–viii), half-title ("Madrigals"), and text pp. 3–189. Half-titles face or precede pp. 28, 95, 133, and 174.

Not more than about 40 copies of this book can now be in existence, as very few were sold, and the remainder destroyed by the authors, whose first publication it was. The value of a stray copy would probably amount to £5 or near it.

2. English Odes, selected by Edmund W. Gosse. London. C. Kegan Paul & Co. . . . MDCCCLXXXI.

This is a post 8vo book in parchment, lettered on side and face in red and gilt. It contains half-title, frontispiece, title in red and black, contents (v–vii), introduction (viii–xxi), and text pp. 1–259. Fifty copies printed on large paper.

Value about £1 10s. (large paper, as issued).

3. Memoir of Thomas Lodge. Privately Printed. MDCCCLXXXII.

Only 10 copies of this book were printed. It is a medium-sized 4to in bright red cloth, lettered in gilt on face.

The contents comprise half-title, title, and text pp. 1–46.

Value from £2 10s. to £3 (as issued, auction).

4. A Critical Essay on the Life and Works of
   George Tinworth. By Edmund W. Gosse. . . .
   The Fine Art Society, Limited, 148 New
   Bond Street, London.   1883.

A small oblong folio in parchment binding. lettered in gilt on
face. A half-title precedes, then follows portrait of George Tinworth
as frontispiece, title as above, and text pp. 5–42. Next follows
a page on which is printed in large type "Works modelled by
George Tinworth," a catalogue pp. 47–81, another page lettered
"Plates," and then a collection of plates. Each printed page
throughout the work is enclosed within a pronounced Oxford
border in black.   The greater part of this edition was destroyed by
a fire which broke out in the warehouse of the Fine Art Society
a few days after publication.

Value about £1 (as issued, auction).

5. Cecil Lawson : a Memoir.   By Edmund W.
   Gosse.   With Illustrations by Hubert Her-
   komer, A.R.A., J. A. M'N. Whistler, and
   Cecil Lawson.   London.   The Fine Art
   Society, Limited. . . . 1883.

Crown 4to, blue cloth binding, lettered on side and face in
gilt. A half-title precedes, then follow portrait of Cecil Lawson
as frontispiece, title as above, prefatory note, list of illustrations,
and text pp. 1–38. There are seven full-page engravings, and 13
woodcuts in the text. The volume closes with a catalogue of the
pictures exhibited by Cecil Lawson at the Royal Academy, and

at the Grosvenor Gallery. About 30 copies were printed on large paper, and bound in parchment.

Value about £1 (large paper, auction).

6. Firdausi in Exile, and other Poems. By Edmund Gosse. London. Kegan Paul, Trench & Co. . . . MDCCCLXXXV.

This volume of poems was published in dark green cloth, lettered on side and face in gilt. A half-title precedes, then follow frontispiece, title as above in red and black, contents (v–vii), dedication to Austin Dobson (ix–x), a second half-title, and text pp. 3–218. The notes occupy pp. 221–224, and are preceded by a half-title ("Notes"). Fifty copies of this work were printed on large paper.

Value about £1 (large paper, as issued).

7. The Masque of Painters, as Performed by the Royal Institute of Painters in Water Colours, May 19, 1885, and Written by Edmund Gosse. Privately Printed. 1885.

This pamphlet was issued in a yellowish paper cover, lettered on the side somewhat, though not exactly, as above. A half-title precedes title, and there are pp. 3–12 of text. Fifty copies were printed on large paper.

Value from 12s. to 15s. (large paper, as issued).

8. On Viol and Flute. By Edmund Gosse. London. Kegan Paul, Trench, Trübner & Co., Ltd. . . . MDCCCXC.

A post 8vo book in brown cloth, lettered on side in gilt. A half-title precedes, then follows frontispiece, title in red and black, dedication, prefatory note, contents (ix–xi), and text pp. 1–212. Fifty copies were printed on large paper, demy 8vo.

With the exception of the dedicatory poem to Lady Wolseley, this was a reprint of portions of the "On Viol and Flute" of 1873, and the "New Poems" of 1879 rearranged, and with frontispiece by L. Alma Tadema, R.A., and tail-piece by Hamo Thornycroft, R.A., specially designed for this edition.

Value about £2 2s. (large paper, as issued).

LEIGH HUNT.

THE works of James Henry Leigh Hunt are very numerous. The following list contains a few that are especially sought after by collectors, with sufficient descriptive matter to enable them to be easily identified.

Leigh Hunt was one of those authors who begin life early, for in 1801, when only seventeen years of age, he published his " Juvenilia," a collection of poems which he himself, at a maturer age, described as a heap of imitations, all but absolutely worthless. The book sold, however, a second edition appearing the same year, and a third in 1802.

In 1808, Hunt became the editor of the *Examiner*, and while occupying that position wrote and published an article on " The First Gentleman in Europe," which was construed into a gross libel on the Prince Regent, whom he had described as " a corpulent man of fifty," " a libertine over head and ears in disgrace," " a companion of gamblers and demi-reps," and so on. This article cost the editor and his brother John, the proprietor of the journal in question, nearly £2000, and each suffered in addition two years' imprisonment. Leigh Hunt's literary reputation was, however, now firmly established, and he also acquired the invaluable friendship of Lord Brougham, Lord Byron, Tom Moore, Shelley, and others, who repeatedly came to see him in his misfortunes. While in prison, and afterwards on his release, he began to write the books which he produced from time to time to meet his necessities, for Leigh Hunt, though he frequently earned considerable sums by his pen, was always poor, and is said

to have had no idea of the value of money.   His best work
was undoubtedly composed during the declining period of
life, for he was then the recipient of a Civil Service pension,
and lived in comparative comfort, estranged from politics
and their distracting influences.

Leigh Hunt died at Putney in August 1859, and was
buried in Kensal Green cemetery.

   1. Juvenilia ; or a Collection of Poems written
      between the ages of twelve and sixteen.   By
      J. H. L. Hunt. . . . London.   J. Whiting.
      . . . 1801.

A small work in 12mo, containing frontispiece and pp. xxiii–
209.   The third edition of these poems, which was published in
1802, is important, as it contains several additions and also some
suppressions.   A second edition appeared in 1801.

Value from 15s. to £1 (original edition, auction).   A clean
copy of the third edition is worth a few shillings.

   2. Classic Tales ; Serious and Lively.   With Criti-
      cal Essays on the Merits and Reputation of
      the Authors.   London.   John Hunt and
      Carew Reynell. . . . MDCCCVI.

This work was published originally in 15 parts at 2s. 6d. each ;
afterwards in 5 vols. 12mo.   All the essays written by Hunt bear
his name.   The rest are supposed to have been written by Reynell.
The title-pages are engraved, and throughout there are 15 full-
page illustrations after Wilkie.

Value about £1 5s. (calf, auction), £1 15s. (*ibid.*).

3. The Reflector : a Collection of Essays on Miscel-
    laneous Subjects of Literature and Politics.
    . . . London.   N.D. (but 1810–12).

Only four numbers of this periodical were issued, and these are
frequently found bound up in two vols. 8vo. The magazine, a
quarterly one, was edited by Leigh Hunt, and contains many articles
by Lamb.   Byron, Hazlitt, and Shelley also contributed to its
pages.   It stopped for want of funds.

Value about £2 (original wrappers, auction).

4. The Feast of the Poets : with Notes and other
    Pieces in Verse.   By the Editor of the *Exa-
    miner*. . . . London.   James Cawthorn. . . .
    1814.

The "Feast of the Poets," which occupies the first 25 pp. of
this volume, originally appeared in the fourth and final number of
the *Reflector*.

The work is in 12mo, and contains pp. xiv–157.   It was published at 6s.

Value about 12s. (as issued, auction).

Another Edition, 1815, 12mo; a duplicate of the above with a
fresh title-page.

Value about 2s. 6d.

5. The Story of Rimini : a Poem.   By Leigh
    Hunt.   London. . . . Printed by T. Davison,
    Whitefriars.   1816.

Published in boards at 6s. 6d.   The work contains half-title,
title as above, dedication to Lord Byron (v–vi), preface (vii–xix),
a second half-title, and text pp. 3–111.   A half-title should precede
each of the four cantos.

Value about 15s. (original boards, auction).   Rebound and cut-
down copies are of trifling value.

6. Bacchus in Tuscany : a Dithyrambic Poem, from
    the Italian of Francesco Redi.   With Notes,
    Original and Select, by Leigh Hunt. . . . Lon-
    don.   Printed for John and H. L. Hunt. . . .
    1825.

A small book in 12mo, published at 7s.   A dedication to John
Hunt, dated from Florence, follows title, and there are pp. v–xix of
preface, text pp. 1–298.
Value about 15s. (as published, auction).

7. Lord Byron and some of his Contemporaries ;
    with Recollections of the Author's Life and
    of his Visit to Italy.   By Leigh Hunt. . . .
    London. . . . Henry Colburn. . . . MDCCCXXVIII.

This, the first edition of a book which is said to have almost
ruined the career of the author, was published in 4to.   A second
and better edition appeared the same year in 2 vols. 8vo.
The value of copies of the first edition in 4to is small, usually
not exceeding a few shillings, but good copies of the 2 vols. that
make up the second edition sell by auction for about 15s. (calf),
occasionally for a little more.

8. Captain Sword and Captain Pen : a Poem.   By
    Leigh Hunt.   With some Remarks on War and
    Military Statesmen.   London.   Charles Knight.
    . . . MDCCCXXXV.

A small book in 12mo, cloth, containing pp. viii–112, frontispiece, and seven plates.
It was published at 3s. 6d., and the average auction value is
about three times that amount (cloth, as issued).

9. The Palfrey, a Love Story of Old Times.   By
   Leigh Hunt. . . . London.   How & Parsons.
   1842.

This is a post 8vo book in pink paper covers, published at 5s.
It contains half-title, title as above, with vignette, "L'Envoy"
(unpaged), list of illustrations (unpaged), preface (9–19), another
half-title, and text pp. 23–80.   Most of the copies were issued
with cut yellow edges, but some of the earliest issue are uncut.
There are six woodcuts in the text.

The value of this book does not, as a rule, exceed a few shillings,
but uncut copies being very seldom seen and difficult to procure,
are worth much more.   About 35s. or 40s. seems to be a very
usual auction price under these circumstances.

10. Stories from the Italian Poets ; with Lives of
    the Writers.   By Leigh Hunt.   London :
    Chapman & Hall. . . . MDCCCXLVI.

Published in 2 vols. post 8vo at 24s.

Vol. i. contains half-title, title, dedication to Sir Percy Shelley
(unpaged), preface and contents (vii–xviii), a second half-title, and
text pp. 3–417.

Vol. ii. contains half-title, title, contents (v–vi), a second half-
title, and text pp. 3–515.   A half-title precedes the critical notice
of each poet.

Value about £1 7s. (uncut, auction).

11. Men, Women, and Books: a Selection of
    Sketches, Essays, and Critical Memoirs, from
    his uncollated Prose Writings.   By Leigh
    Hunt. . . . London.   Smith & Elder. . . .
    1847.

Published in 2 vols. post 8vo, cloth, at 21s. The first volume contains a portrait of the author.

Value about £1 10s. (original cloth, auction).

12. A Jar of Honey from Mount Hybla. By Leigh Hunt. . . . London. Smith & Elder. . . . 1847.

Published in 1 vol. post 8vo, fancy boards, designed by Owen Jones, at 14s. The 25 illustrations throughout the book are by Richard Doyle. The text is reprinted from *Ainsworth's Magazine*, in which "A Jar of Honey" originally appeared in 1844.

Some copies of this book were published, not in the fancy boards, but in cloth, and these are more difficult to meet with.

Value from 25s. to 30s., according to condition (fancy boards, auction). Copies in cloth are worth a little more.

13. The Town; its Memorable Characters and Events. By Leigh Hunt. .   . London. Smith & Elder. . . . 1848.

Published in 2 vols. post 8vo, cloth, with frontispieces and other illustrations, at £1 4s. These volumes contain an account of London, but chiefly a history of remarkable characters and events associated with its streets, between St. Paul's and St. James's.

Clean copies of this book are scarce, and sell by auction for about £2 (uncut). Occasionally, though rarely, this price is considerably exceeded.

Another Edition, 1878, 8vo, with 45 illustrations. The value of copies of this edition is small, rarely exceeding a few shillings.

14. A Book for a Corner : or, Selections in Prose
and Verse, from Authors the best suited to
that Mode of Enjoyment. . . . By Leigh
Hunt. . . . London.   Chapman & Hall. . . .
1849.

Published in 2 vols. post 8vo, cloth, at 12s.   The work contains
80 engravings.

The value of this book rarely exceeds 17s. by auction (original
cloth).   Sometimes, however, exceptionally clean copies produce
£1, or even a little more.

15. The Autobiography of Leigh Hunt ; with
Reminiscences of Friends and Contemporaries.
London.   Smith & Elder. . . . 1850.

In 3 vols. post 8vo, with portraits.

This work was published in cloth at £1 11s. 6d.   The present
auction value is, however, considerably less.

16. Table-Talk : to which are added Imaginary
Conversations of Pope and Swift.   By Leigh
Hunt.   London.   Smith & Elder. . . . 1850.

In post 8vo, cloth, published at 7s.   The matter of this book
consists partly of short pieces published under the head of "Table-
Talk" in the *Atlas* newspaper, and under that of "The Family
Journal" in the *New Monthly Magazine*.

Value from 8s. to 10s. (original cloth, auction).

Another Edition, 1882, 8vo, of trifling value.

17. The Old Court Suburb; or, Memorials of Kensington, Regal, Critical, and Anecdotical. By Leigh Hunt. . . . London. Hurst & Blackett. . . . 1855.

Published in 2 vols. post 8vo, cloth, at 21s. The work contains biographical references to celebrated persons who are identified with Kensington.

Two editions were published in 1855, of which the second is usually accounted the better. A good copy of this, in the original cloth and uncut, sells by auction for about £1 10s. Copies of the first edition are worth considerably less.

18. Stories in Verse. By Leigh Hunt. Now first collected. . . . London. George Routledge. . . . 1855.

A small book in 12mo, with illustrations, published at 3s. 6d.

The present value of this work is a little more than the published price.

19. A Saunter through the West End. By Leigh Hunt. . . . London. Hurst & Blackett. . . . 1861.

This work was published in post 8vo, cloth, at 10s. 6d. The papers which are comprised in the volume originally appeared in the *Atlas* newspaper.

Value about a guinea (original cloth, auction). Copies, however, more frequently sell for a little less.

RICHARD JEFFERIES.

RICHARD JEFFERIES, the novelist, was born at Coate Farm,
near Swindon, in 1848. He commenced his literary career
by writing rural sketches for the *North Wilts Herald*, of
which paper he was also a member of the staff for several
years. His first work in book form was a memoir of the
Goddard Family, which appeared in 1873, and his first novel,
"The Scarlet Shawl," 1874, but it was not until 1877, when
"The Gamekeeper at Home" appeared, that he took his
place among the popular authors of the day. Jefferies died
at Goring, in Sussex, in 1887, after a series of painful
illnesses, which, if they did not break his spirit, emptied his
purse, and seriously interfered with his only available means
of earning his living. After his death, a civil service pension
was bestowed on his widow, and there is a monument to his
memory in Salisbury Cathedral, and his bust is in the Shire-
Hall at Taunton.

In addition to the books mentioned below, Jefferies wrote
the preface to the 1887 edition of White's Selborne (one
of the Camelot Classics), a little book entitled "Reporting,
Editing, and Authorship, Practical Hints for Beginners in
Literature," Swindon (1873), which is now very scarce,
selling for a couple of guineas if clean, and a pamphlet
called "Suez-cide, or how Miss Britannia bought a dirty
puddle," 1876, which at the moment I am unable to meet
with. This last was published at 3d. in pink wrappers, and
sells by the booksellers at anything from £2 to £3. A very
indifferent imitation is said to have been recently thrown on

the market.　He also contributed a number of articles to various periodicals, including *Longman's Magazine*, all of which have been collected and published in a separate form, as mentioned later on.　The only memoir of Richard Jefferies is that by Mr. Walter Besant, under the title of "The Eulogy of Richard Jefferies," 1888.

1. A Memoir of the Goddards of North Wilts, Compiled from Ancient Records, Registers, and Family Papers.　By Richard Jefferies, Coate, Swindon.　N.D. (but 1873).

A small 4to book in blue cloth, lettered "Goddard" on the side in gilt, consisting of 56 pages.

Copies when met with sell for about 15s.

2. Jack Brass, Emperor of England.　By R. Jefferies. . . . London.　T. Pettitt & Co., 23 Frith Street, Soho, W.　1873.

This is an 8vo pamphlet of 12 pp., in yellow paper covers.　It contains sarcastic advice given to a fortunate litigant named John Brass, who, on the termination of a Chancery suit in his favour, came into a fortune of £10,000,000 sterling.

This pamphlet is probably worth 6s. or 8s. if clean.

3. The Scarlet Shawl : a Novel.　By Richard Jefferies.　London.　Tinsley Brothers, 8 Catherine Street, Strand.　1874.

In 1 vol. crown 8vo, red cloth, lettered in gilt on the back. Complete copies of this work have a half-title before the title as above. Then follows a dedication on an unpaged leaf, and text pp. 1–309.

Published at 10s. 6d. Value about £2 (original cloth). In 1887 Tinsley Brothers published a cheap reprint at 1s.

4. Restless Human Hearts : a Novel. By Richard Jefferies, Author of "The Scarlet Shawl." London. Tinsley Brothers. . . . 1875.

Three vols. post 8vo, in red cloth. Each contains half-title before title, as above. There is no dedication or other preliminary matter.

Value from £1 15s. to £2 (original cloth).

5. World's End : a Story in Three Books. By Richard Jefferies. . . . London. Tinsley Brothers. 1877.

The three volumes which make up this book are bound in slate-coloured cloth, figured on the sides in black, and lettered in gilt on the front. Each volume contains half-title before title, but there is no other preliminary matter.

Value about £2 10s. (original cloth).

6. The Gamekeeper at Home : Sketches of Natural History and Rural Life. . . . London. Smith, Elder & Co., 15 Waterloo Place. 1878.

Post 8vo, blue cloth, on the side a black pattern with a dead bird in gilt, lettered on the face in gilt. A half-title should precede title. There is a preface (v–vi), contents (unpaged), and text pp. 1–216.

Value about £1 10s. (original cloth).

Second Edition, 1878, post 8vo, Smith, Elder & Co., about 6s. (original cloth).

Third Edition, 1878, post 8vo, Smith, Elder & Co., about 3s. 6d. (original cloth).

Illustrated Edition, 1880, post 8vo, Smith, Elder & Co., containing 41 illustrations by Charles Whymper, pictorial drab (sometimes green) cloth.

The value of a good copy of this edition is from 17s. 6d. to £1.

7. Wild Life in a Southern County. By the Author of "The Gamekeeper at Home." London. Smith, Elder & Co. . . . 1879.

Bound in olive cloth, title in gilt. There should be half-title, title as above, inscription to Frederick Greenwood, preface (vii–viii), contents (ix–xii), and text pp. 1–387. This work is a reprint of articles which originally appeared in the *Pall Mall Gazette*.

Published at 6s. Value about 15s. (original cloth). Another edition appeared in 1889, post 8vo, 6s. cloth.

8. The Amateur Poacher. By the Author of "The Gamekeeper at Home." . . . London. Smith, Elder & Co. 1879.

Bound in brown cloth, gilt lettered, post 8vo. There should be half-title, title as above, preface, contents, and text pp. 1–240. None of the preliminary leaves are paged.

Value about 12s. (original cloth, auction).

9. Round About a Great Estate. By Richard Jefferies. . . . London. Smith, Elder & Co. 1880.

A post 8vo book published in blue cloth, gilt lettered. After the half-title comes title, preface, contents, and text of the novel pp. 1–201. The peculiarity about this book is that the reverse of p. 201 is blank, then follows two pages of " Notes," the last only being numbered (204).

Published at 5s. Present value, 10s. or 12s. (original cloth).

10. Hodge and his Masters. By Richard Jefferies. . . . London. Smith, Elder & Co. . . . 1880.

In 2 vols. post 8vo, dark green pictorial cloth. Vol. i. contains half-title, title, preface, contents, and text pp. 1–359. Vol. ii. the same, but no preface, and text pp. 1–312. The papers of which these volumes are composed originally appeared in *The Standard*.

Published at 12s., and now worth about the same (original cloth).

11. Greene Ferne Farm. By Richard Jefferies. . . . London. Smith, Elder & Co. 1880.

In 1 vol. post 8vo, yellow cloth, lettered on the side in black, and on the face in gilt. The book is made up as follows :—Half-title, title, inscription (" Inscribed to Jessie "), contents (vii–viii), and text pp. 1–290.

Published at 7s. 6d., and now worth about £1 (original cloth).

12. Wood Magic : a Fable. By Richard Jefferies. . . . Cassell, Peter, Galpin & Co. London, Paris and New York. 1881.

This work is complete in 2 vols. post 8vo, dark green cloth, figured on the sides in black, and lettered on the face in gilt. Vol.

i. contains half-title, title, inscription ("Inscribed to Harold"), contents, and text of novel pp. 1–235.   Vol. ii. the same, but there is no inscription, and text covers pp. 1–263.

Published at 21s.   Value about £1 10s. (original cloth).   In the same year a cheaper edition appeared in one volume at 6s.

13. Bevis: the Story of a Boy.   By Richard Jefferies. . . . London.   Sampson Low, Marston, Searle & Rivington. . . . 1882.

In 3 vols. post 8vo, brown cloth, lettered in gilt on sides and front.   Each volume contains title and table of contents.   In vol. i. an inscription to "Jessie, Harold and Phyllis" follows title, and a half-title precedes.   There is no half-title to vols. ii. and iii.

Published at £1 11s. 6d., and now worth about £2 (original cloth).

14. The Story of My Heart: My Autobiography. By Richard Jefferies. London. Longmans, Green & Co.   1883.

In 1 vol., bound in sage green cloth, gilt lettered on the face. A half-title precedes title as above, but there is no other preliminary matter.

Published at 5s.   Value about 15s. (original cloth).

Second Edition, 1891, 8vo.   Longmans, Green & Co., pp. xii–206.   Worth a few shillings.

15. Nature near London.   By Richard Jefferies. . . . London.   Chatto & Windus, Piccadilly. 1883.

In 1 vol. post 8vo, bound in pictorial cloth, gilt lettered on face. There is no half-title, but preface (iii–vi), contents (unpaged), and

text pp. 1–242. The sketches which comprise this book were originally published in *The Standard.* Published at 6s.
Value about 12s. (original cloth).
A new edition appeared in 1887, price 2s. 6d., 12mo.

16. Red Deer.   By Richard Jefferies. . . . London.   Longmans, Green & Co.   1884.

In 1 vol. post 8vo, green pictorial cloth, lettered in dark red on side and face.   A table of contents follows title.
Published at 4s. 6d., and now worth about 12s. (original cloth).
Second Edition, 1892, Longmans, Green & Co., post 8vo, red cloth, lettered in silver.   This edition contains 10 full-page illustrations (inclusive of front) and woodcuts.   A half-title precedes, and there is a table of contents.   Copies of this edition are worth about 3s. 6d.

17. The Life of the Fields.   By Richard Jefferies. . . . London.   Chatto & Windus, Piccadilly. 1884.

Bound in yellow pictorial cloth, gilt lettered on face, post 8vo. A half-title precedes, then follow title as above, "Note" (unpaged), contents, and text pp. 1–262.   The 23 articles contained in this book originally appeared in a number of London and country journals.
Published at 6s.   Value about 10s. or 12s. (original cloth).   A new edition appeared in 1888, price 2s. 6d., 12mo.

18. The Dewy Morn: a Novel.   By Richard Jefferies. . . . London.   Richard Bentley & Son. . . . 1884.

Published in 2 vols. post 8vo, green cloth. No preliminary matter in either volume, except title-page.

Published at 21s., and now worth a little more (original cloth).
Another Edition, 1891, post 8vo, pp. 396, Bentley & Son.
Value, a few shillings.

19. The Open Air. By Richard Jefferies. . . .
London. Chatto & Windus, Piccadilly. 1885.

Complete in 1 vol. post 8vo, yellow pictorial cloth, gilt lettered
on back. The book consists of half-title, title, "Note," contents,
and text pp. 1–270, comprising a collection of articles which
originally appeared in various periodicals.
Published at 6s. Value about 10s. (original cloth).
A new edition appeared in 1889, price 2s. 6d., 12mo.

20. After London; or Wild England. By Richard
Jefferies. . . . In Two Parts. I. The Relapse
into Barbarism. II. Wild England. Cassell
& Company, Limited. . . . 1885.

A thick post 8vo book, published at 10s. 6d., and bound in
yellowish brown cloth, lettered in black on the side and on the
face in gilt. A half-title precedes title, and a table of contents
follows; pp. 1–442. A new edition was published by Cassell & Co.
in 1886, at 3s. 6d.
Copies of the original edition, in cloth, as issued, sell by auction
for 10s. or 12s.

21. The Dove's Nest, and other Tales. By Joseph
Hatton and Richard Jefferies. . . . London.
Vizetelly & Co., 42 Catherine Street, Strand.
1886.

This is a post 8vo book, containing a series of 15 stories, of which
at least one ("Out of the Season") is by Jefferies. The work
contains 10 full-page illustrations and numerous cuts, some by
Randolph Caldecott.

A clean copy, in the original cloth, would be worth 5s. or 6s.

22. Amaryllis at the Fair : a Novel.   By Richard
    Jefferies. . . . London.   Sampson Low,
    Marston, Searle & Rivington. . . . 1887.

This was the last novel written by Jefferies before his untimely death.   It is in one volume, bound in dark green pictorial cloth, gilt lettered on face.   It contains blank preliminary leaf, half-title, title, dedication, and text pp. 1–260.
Published at 7s. 6d.   Present value about 12s. (original cloth).

23. Field and Hedgerow.   Being the last Essays
    of Richard Jefferies.   Collected by his Widow.
    London.   Longmans, Green & Co. . . . 1889.

This work, the title of which is sufficiently explanatory of the nature of the contents, consists of 29 essays contributed to various periodicals, and now collected for the first time.   The book consists of half-title, title, a short preface, contents, and text pp. 1–331, post 8vo.
Published at 6s.   The present value is about the same.
Of this book, 200 copies were published on large paper, thick imperial 8vo, with portrait of Jefferies by Strang, to face title. In these copies, curiously enough, pp. 330 and 331 are reversed.
Value from 15s. to £1.

24. The Toilers of the Field. . . . By Richard
    Jefferies. London. Longmans, Green & Co.
    . . . 1892.

A post 8vo book, consisting of a series of essays and sketches reprinted from *Fraser's*, *Longman's*, and other magazines.
This work contains pp. 330, and was published at 6s.

ANDREW LANG.

Mr. Andrew Lang's publications consist mainly of volumes of verse, translations, collections of articles which have appeared from time to time in the press, biographies, essays, folk stories and fairy tales, and to a limited extent, fiction. The whole of these books are now sought after by collectors of early editions, though as a rule it is only the large-paper copies that are in especial request, for these, as usual, were in every case issued in strictly limited numbers. This, of course, is so in most other cases when, speaking roughly, the importance of the larger sized volumes may be arithmetically put down as being equivalent to about two to one.

This seems to be the rule which collectors of original or early editions have formulated, but in Mr. Lang's case it is not always applicable, for the large-paper copies are, from a pecuniary point of view, frequently worth three or four times as much as their humbler prototypes, a fact which is perhaps explainable by reference to the great demand which has suddenly sprung up for them, the limited number published, limited, that is to say, in comparison with a very large edition on smaller sized paper which is invariably issued to meet the popular requirements, and to the further fact that the large-paper copies seldom get on the market at first-hand.

In this article most of the works accredited to Mr. Lang are (with the exception of " King Solomon's Wives," 1887, a skit on Mr. Rider Haggard's novel, not by Mr. Lang at all) described as shortly as possible. They are too widely known to need a very close collation, and it must be remembered also that copies are hardly ever found imperfect. They are too carefully preserved for that; the new school of collectors looks well to its own; if it has done nothing else, if some of the rules of the game it affects strike one as being arbitrary, irrational, or perhaps, in some instances, altogether absurd, there is no doubt that its ever-increasing roll of members protect where their forefathers mutilated, and treat every author admitted within their circle with a respect he might seek for in vain elsewhere.

In the case of contemporary authors who have the skill or good fortune to arrest the attention of the public, and through them that of the coterie which concerns itself chiefly with the history or description of books, the various editions through which they have passed, and, speaking generally, their *format* rather than their substance, there is not, therefore, quite the same need for a very minute collation, the only object of which is to enable the collector to guard against defects and omissions which, however unimportant in themselves, cannot fail to seriously affect the monetary value of any specimen in which they occur.

Mr. Lang's numerous contributions may be conveniently separated into two divisions, the one embracing those books edited by him, or for which he has written the preliminary matter, and the other, those for which he is responsible as joint or sole author, most of which will be found noted in their chronological order hereafter.

The books belonging to the former of these classes include "Aristotle's Politics," Books i., iii., iv. (vii.), with introductory essays, published in 1877. Another introductory essay, from Bolland and Lang's "Politics," appears in the edition of the "Politics of Aristotle" published by Longmans in 1886, and in 1879 Messrs. S. H. Butcher and Andrew Lang translated the "Odyssey," another edition of which appeared in 1887. A translation of "Theocritus,

Bion and Moschus" appeared in 1880 (for which see *post*, No. 3). All these books are in 8vo.

In 1881 Mr. Lang wrote an introductory essay on the Poems of Edgar Allan Poe, prefixed to the "Parchment Library" edition of his poems of that date. In 1883 he translated (in conjunction with other classical scholars) the "Iliad" into English prose, and in 1884 wrote an introduction to an edition of Grimm's "Household Tales." In the same year he edited Molière's "Les Précieuses Ridicules," with introduction and notes. The "English Worthies" series, under his editorship, began in 1885, and was completed two years later in eight octavo volumes.

Other volumes edited by the same author, or in which he was interested, include Lamb's "Beauty and the Beast," with introduction, N.D. (but 1887), 8vo; "A Discourse on the Fable," annexed to W. Adlington's "Most Pleasant and Delectable Tale of the Marriage of Cupid and Psyche," 1887, 8vo (only 60 copies on large paper were printed of this book); Perrault's "Popular Tales," with introduction, 1888, 8vo; the "Euterpe" of Herodotus, Englished by B. R. in 1584 and now edited, 1888, 8vo; Steel and Lyttleton's "Cricket," in the well-known "Badminton Library," 1888, 8vo; H. H. Romilly's "From my Verandah in New Guinea," with an introduction on "New Guinea Folk-Lore" (by Mr. Lang), 1889, 8vo; "The Strife of Love in a Dream," the Elizabethan version of the first book of the "Hypnerotomachia" of Columna, a new edition, 1890, 4to (one of the "Tudor Library" series); Lamb's "Adventures of Ulysses," with introduction, N.D. (but 1890); Longinus "On the Sublime," with an introduction, 1890; Burns' "Selected Poems," with introduction, 1891, 8vo (Parchment Library); E. H. Garrett's "Elizabethan Songs," with introduction, 1891, 8vo; and, up to the time of writing this article, H. G. Hutchinson's "Golf," in the "Badminton Library" series, 1890 and 1892, and a memoir of the late W. Y. Sellar, prefixed to that author's "The Roman Poets of the Augustan Age," Clarendon Press, Oxford, 1892.

Most of the above would be catalogued primarily under the names of their authors, and not under that of the editor or annotator, and accordingly we have little to do with them in this article. It may not be improper to mention, however, that the following prices have been realised at auction, for some of them, within a recent period :—

(*a.*) Euterpe ; being the Second Book of Herodotus. 1888. One of sixty copies on large paper, with the frontispiece in duplicate ; £1 7s. (uncut, in the parchment wrappers).

(*b.*) Marriage of Cupid and Psyche . . . with a Discourse on the Fable. . . . 1887. 8vo ; £1 (uncut, in the parchment wrappers).

(*c.*) Aristotle's Politics. Books i., iii., iv. (vii.). 1877. 8vo ; 9s. (original cloth).

(*d.*) E. H. Garrett's "Elizabethan Songs in Honour of Love and Beautie." . . . A large-paper copy, 1891, 8vo ; 16s. (uncut, as issued).

---

1. Ballads and Lyrics of Old France, with other Poems. By A. Lang. London. Longmans, Green & Co. 1872.

A crown 8vo book in cloth, containing pp. x, 164, bound in white parchment, with gilt lettering on side and face. The collation is :—Blank leaf, half-title, dedication to "E. M. S.," contents (viii–x), and text, pp. 1–164.

This work is scarce, good copies in the original cloth selling by auction for between £3 10s. and £4, and occasionally for a little more.

2. Oxford: Brief Historical and Descriptive Notes.
 . . . London.   Seeley & Co.   1880.

Folio.   This work contains ten etchings by Brunet-Debaines,
Toussaint, and Kent-Thomas, and woodcuts.   Some copies of this
work were printed on large paper.

Value about £4 (as issued, auction).

Second Edition.   Seeley & Co., 1882, folio, pp. 56.

Another Edition.   Seeley & Co., 1890, 8vo, pp. xvi, 282 ; published at 6s.

3. Theocritus, Bion and Moschus.   Rendered into
 English Prose, with an Introductory Essay
 by A. Lang, M.A.   London.   Macmillan & Co.
 1880.

Post 8vo, smooth navy blue cloth, lettered in gilt on face.

Value about 12s. (original cloth).

Another Edition, 1889, 8vo ; 6s. to 8s. (original cloth).

4. XXII. Ballades in Blue China. . . . C. Kegan
 Paul & Co.   1880.

This work was printed on hand-made paper, published in fcap.
8vo at 2s. 6d. in vellum wrapper, and contains 80 pages.   There is
a vignette on the title.   The real first edition has an accent on final
é of *Manque* and *passe*, in " Ballade of Roulette," lines 5 and 6.

Copies sell by auction for about £1 5s. (as issued), but, as
usual, prices vary considerably according to condition.   One of
these " Ballades " (the " Ode to Golf ") was published separately
in 1889, 8vo.   The large-paper copies are referred to in the next
entry.

5. XXXII. Ballades in Blue China. . . . C. Kegan
 Paul & Co.   1881.

In effect, this is an edition of "XXII Ballades" with ten additional poems, the whole complete in 112 pages 8vo. There is an etched frontispiece by Mr. Strang to this first edition, which is wanting in all the later issues.

Value from £1 10s. to £2 5s. (in the original vellum wrapper, auction).

So far as I know, no large-paper copies were issued at the time, but fifty copies of the kind were published in 1888, and these are generally described as belonging to the "first edition," presumably that of 1880 or 1881, though the whole work was recast.

Large-paper copies are scarce, selling for about £2 10s. by auction.

6. Notes on a Collection of Pictures by Mr. J. E. Millais. . . . 1881.

This is a pamphlet of 32 pages, published in 8vo by the Fine Art Society. A large number of copies were distributed, and the value is small.

7. The Library : with a Chapter on Modern English Illustrated Books by Austin Dobson. Macmillan & Co. 1881.

This book, which formed one of the "Art at Home" series, contains pp. xv, 184, with illustrations. Those of bindings are printed in colours in the large-paper copies (185 printed).

Value about 7s. (original cloth), or £1 10s. (large-paper, auction).

Another Edition, 1892, post 8vo, pp. 206 ; published at 4s. 6d.

8. Helen of Troy : her Life and Translation. Done into Rhyme from the Greek Books. . . . Bell & Sons. 1882.

A post 8vo book of 196 pages, published in vellum wrappers.

Value about £1 5s. (as issued).

Second Edition, Bell & Sons, 1883, 8vo, pp. 202.

Value about 15s. (as issued).

Another Edition, 1892, Bell & Sons, post 8vo, pp. 200 ; published at 2s. 6d. net.

9. The Black Thief; a New and Original Drama
    (adapted from the Irish).   In Four Acts. . . .
    London.   1882.

This book (privately printed for children to act) is described in Mr. C. I. Elton's catalogue as 12mo, published without any author's name.   I am not aware of any copy having been offered for sale, and it is therefore impossible to affix a value with any certainty. If, however, one should appear in the auction room, it might be expected to realise somewhere about £5.

10. The Princess Nobody : a Tale of Fairy-Land.
    . . . Longmans & Co.   N.D. (but 1884).

4to, pp. 56, with illustrations in colours after drawings by Richard Doyle.   These plates are the same as those which originally appeared in Allingham's "In Fairy-Land," a work published in 1870, for which the tale was written.

This book was published at 5s., the present value being somewhere about the same amount.

11. Custom and Myth : Studies of Early Usage
    and Belief. . . . Longmans & Co.   1884.

Published in cloth, post 8vo, pp. 312.

The auction value of this book is from 12s. to 15s. (cloth, as issued). A second edition appeared in 1885, with precisely the same number of pages. It cannot be mistaken for the original, as it is marked "Second Edition" on the title.

12. Ballades and Verses Vain. . . . New York. C. Scribner's Sons. 1884.

This book, which is in crown 8vo with pp. 3–165, blue cloth, contains a selection of poems made by Mr. Austin Dobson from "Ballades and Lyrics of Old France," "Ballades in Blue China," and from verses previously imprinted and not collated ; all by Mr. Lang. No half-title precedes in this case, but after title follows "Table of Contents" (on four unnumbered pages), a leaf containing two verses by "A(ustin) D "(obson), and half-title ("Ballades").

Value about 12s. (as issued). The published price was equivalent to 7s. 6d.

13. Rhymes à la Mode. . . . London. Kegan Paul & Co. 1885.

There is a frontispiece to this work, which was printed on ribbed paper and published in cloth in 1884, not 1885, as stated on the title. It is in 12mo, containing pp. x, 139, and scarce when in good condition.

Such a copy in the original cloth sells for about £1 5s. Large-paper copies, of which a few were printed, sell by auction for about £2.

14. Letters to Dead Authors. . . . Longmans & Co. 1886.

This is a post 8vo book, published at 6s. 6d., containing pp. x, 234. A new edition, containing pp. x, 194, was published in 1892 at 2s. 6d. net, and of this some copies were printed on large paper.

The values of the various copies of these two editions seem to

fluctuate very considerably, but the following approximate to the
medium.   For the first edition of 1886, about 10s. ; for the small-
paper copies of 1892, about 2s. ; and for the large-paper copies of
the same date, 10s. or 12s. (original bindings in each case).

15. The Mark of Cain. . . . Bristol.   J. W.
     Arrowsmith.   1886.

The "Mark of Cain" constitutes vol. xiii. of Arrowsmith's
"Bristol Library."   Like the rest of the works in that series, it
was published in 12mo, paper, at 1s., and contains pp. 198.   A
few copies were printed on large paper at 1s. 6d., 8vo.

Value on large paper 3s. 6d. (as issued).

16. Lines on the Inaugural Meeting of the Shelley
     Society.   London.   Printed for Private Dis-
     tribution only.   1886.

This pamphlet, in demy 8vo, is stitched in green paper wrappers.
Two blank leaves precede title, which is followed by a half-title,
a second half-title, prefatory note, pp. ix–x, a third half-title
("Lines"), and text of the poem on pp. 13–19.   A fourth half-
title ("Notes") and the notes referred to (pp. 23–25) complete
the work.   On the reverse of p. 25 appears Shelley's coat-of-
arms, with its heraldic quarterings.   The "Lines" were printed
as prose in the *Saturday Review* of March 13, 1886.   The author
had no concern with the republication.

Value about 12s. 6d. (as issued).

17. In the Wrong Paradise, and other Stories. . . .
     Kegan Paul & Co.   1886.

Post 8vo, pp. viii, 316.
Value about 9s. (original cloth, auction).

18. Books and Bookmen. . . . London.   Long-
      mans, Green & Co.   1887.

This work was published in narrow demy 8vo, sage-green cloth,
and is rather curiously made up.   A half-title precedes title as
above, which is followed by an inscription in verse, "To the
Viscountess Wolseley" (pp. v–vi), preface, contents, list of illustrations, a second half-title, and text, pp. 3–148.   There is no frontispiece, but there are ten full-page plates (those of bindings coloured),
and numerous woodcuts in the text.

Clean copies in the original cloth sell for about 10s. 6d.   100
large-paper copies (post 8vo, 1886, pp. vi, 148), were issued, and
these bring about £1 5s. by auction, if clean and in the original
covers.

Another Edition, 1892, 8vo, Longmans, Green & Co., pp. iv,
177 ; published at 2s. 6d.

"Books and Bookmen" was also issued in New York by C. J.
Coombes, 1886, 12mo, in the series known as "Books for the
Bibliophile."

19. Aucassin and Nicolete done into English.   By
      Andrew Lang. . . . David Nutt.   1887.

Of this book 550 copies were printed on Japan paper, and another
batch of 63 copies on Japan paper with the frontispiece in two
states.

A very ordinary auction price for one of the 550 copies is
£1 2s. (original wrappers), but one of the smaller issue cannot
be got for much less than £5 5s. retail.   The auction price
approaches £4.

"Aucassin and Nicolete" is a small book in 12mo, containing
half-title, full-page etching ("C'est D'Aucassin et de Nicolete")
by Jacomb Hood ; title, dedication, introduction (pp. v–xvi),
followed by the "Ballade of Aucassin" (xvii–xviii) and the
"Ballade of Nicolete" (xix–xx), half-title, text (pp. 3–66), "Notes
(pp. 67–70), followed by two leaves, the first having Whittingham's
device, and the other being blank.

20. Johnny Nut and the Golden Goose. . . . 1887.

This is a translation from the French of C. Deulin, and was published in royal 8vo, cloth.

Copies as issued sell for about 6s. The work is illustrated by A. Lynen. Copies on large-paper, of which 113 were printed, sell for about 12s.

21. Myth, Ritual, and Religion. . . . Longmans, Green & Co. 1887.

In 2 vols. post 8vo, published at 21s.

Value about £1 (original cloth, auction).

22. Perrault's Popular Tales. Edited from the Original Editions, with Introduction. By Andrew Lang. . . . Oxford. Clarendon Press. 1888.

Crown 8vo, large-paper copies on hand-made paper, half-vellum, gilt top, 4to.

Ordinary copies sell by auction for 5s. or 6s., large-paper copies for about 18s. (both as issued).

23. Grass of Parnassus; Rhymes Old and New. . . . Longmans, Green & Co. 1888.

Large as well as small-paper copies of this work were issued, the latter being in 18mo and the former in 8vo. There are in each pp. xii, 124.

Value about 6s. (small-paper, original cloth), or £1 (large-paper, half-Roxburghe, 113 copies issued).

New Edition, 1892, Longmans, 8vo, pp. xvi, 190; published at 2s. 6d. net.

24. The Gold of Fairnilee. . . . Bristol. J. W. Arrowsmith. N.D. (but 1888).

This is a 4to book containing a frontispiece by T. Scott, drawings by E. A. Lemann, and pp. 86.

Value about 5s. (as issued). Large-paper copies, of which a few were printed, realise about £1 at auction.

25. Ballads of Books. Edited by Andrew Lang. . . . Longmans, Green & Co. 1888.

A recast of "Ballads of Books," edited by Brander Matthews. The ordinary copies are in 12mo, pp. xx, 157, the large-paper copies in 8vo, half-Roxburghe (113 copies printed).

Value about 5s. (small paper), or 21s. (large paper, as issued).

26. Prince Prigio. . . . Bristol. J. W. Arrowsmith. 1889.

Pp. 144, 8vo, with 27 illustrations by Gordon Browne.
Value about 3s.
A few large-paper copies were published in half-parchment, 4to, which sell by auction for some 12s. or 13s.

27. Letters on Literature. . . . Longmans, Green & Co. 1889.

This is a small book in 16mo, pp. x, 200, but 113 copies were printed on large paper, 8vo, half-Roxburghe.
The value of the small-paper edition does not exceed a few shillings, but copies on large paper sell readily by auction for 20s., and sometimes bring more.
New Edition, 1892, post 8vo, Longmans, pp. viii, 171; published at 2s. 6d. net.

28. Lost Leaders. . . . Kegan Paul & Co.   1889.

The "Lost Leaders" consist of a number of articles which appeared originally in the *Daily News*, and were now collected and arranged in book form by Mr. P. Ridge.. The work is an 8vo, comprising pp. viii, 226.

Value about 5s. (original cloth).

A hundred copies were issued on large paper, and these sell by auction at sums varying from 15s. to £1 (half-Roxburghe, as published).

29. The Blue Fairy Book.   Edited by Andrew Lang. . . . Longmans, Green & Co.   1889.

The peculiarity about this book is that the large-paper copies contain Mr. Lang's introduction, which is not to be found in those on small paper.   The illustrations (8 plates and 130 illustrations in the text) are by H. J. Ford and G. P. Jacomb Hood ; pp. xxii (large-paper only), 390.

Both ordinary and large-paper copies are scarce, the former selling by the dealers for about 15s., more or less, and the latter bringing at auction as much as £3 3s., and sometimes more.

In 1890 Messrs. Longmans published a series of "Fairy Tale Books," seven in number, the stories in which are based on "The Blue Fairy Book."   Each of these was published at 1s., and now sells for a little more.   Five editions of the "Blue Fairy Book" have been issued up to the present time (April 1893).

30. The Dead Leman, and other Tales, from the French.   By Andrew Lang and Paul Sylvester. Swan, Sonnenschein & Co.   1889.

Pp. xvi, 336, crown 8vo, published in cloth extra at 6s.   Value about 6s. (as issued).   What is known as the "Stereotyped Edition" was published by Sonnenschein in 1890, pp. xvi, 336. This edition is of no consequence.

31. Life, Letters, and Diaries of Sir Stafford North-
cote, First Earl of Iddesleigh. . . . Blackwood
& Sons. 1890.

In 2 vols. 8vo, published at £1 11s. 6d.
New Edition, 1891, 8vo, Blackwood & Sons, pp. xxiii, 413;
published at 7s. 6d.

32. Old Friends : Essays in Epistolary Parody. . . .
Longmans, Green & Co. 1890.

The ordinary as well as large-paper copies of this book were
published, with frontispiece, in half-vellum, gilt top, pp. xiii, 205.
Of the large-paper copies, which are on Japanese paper, only 150
were issued.
Value about 5s. on small paper, and 21s. on large. The published price of the former was 6s. 6d.
New Edition, 1892, Longmans & Co., pp. xvi, 178; published
at 2s. 6d. net.

33. The World's Desire. By H. Rider Haggard
and Andrew Lang. . . . 1890.

Published in cloth, post 8vo, at 6s. Clean copies sell for a few
shillings each.

34. The Red Fairy Book. Edited by Andrew Lang.
. . . Longmans, Green & Co. 1890.

Post 8vo, pp. xvi, 367, with 4 plates and 96 illustrations in the
text by H. J. Ford and Lancelot Speed.
Value about 7s. 6d. (cloth gilt, as published). 113 copies were
issued on large paper, and these sell by auction at about £1, 10s.,
more or less. Three editions of the "Red Fairy Book" have been
issued up to the present (April 1893).

35. How to Fail in Literature. . . . Field & Tuer. Yᵒ Leadenhall Press. 1890.

A small book in square 12mo, pp. 95, wrappers, published at 1s. A published version of a lecture delivered by Mr. Lang under the above title.

Value 1s. or 1s. 6d. (as issued).

36. Angling Sketches. . . . Longmans, Green & Co. 1891.

This work contains 3 etchings and numerous woodcuts by W. G. Burn-Murdoch, also pp. xii, 176.

Small-paper copies in crown 8vo (cloth, as issued) sell for about 5s., those on large paper for 20s. or 25s.

"Angling Sketches" are mostly reprints from *Macmillan's Magazine*, the *Fishing Gazette*, and other journals.

37. Famous Golf Links. By Horace G. Hutchinson, Andrew Lang (and others). Longmans, Green & Co. . . . 1891.

The bulk of the articles which appear in this book were reprinted from the *Saturday Review*. The work contains 19 full-page illustrations (including front), and 13 woodcuts in the text. A half-title precedes title, and there are pp. 1–201, the whole being bound in pictorial slate-coloured cloth, and published at 6s.

38. Essays in Little. . . . Henry & Co. 1891.

The "Essays in Little" forms one of the series known as "The Whitefriars Library of Wit and Humour." It is a post 8vo book in cloth, with portrait and pp. 205.

Value about 5s., or on large paper (small 4to), 20s. (as published, auction).

39. The Blue Poetry Book. Edited by Andrew
       Lang. . . . Longmans, Green & Co.   1891.

Post 8vo, pp. xx, 351, with 12 plates and 88 illustrations in the text by H. J. Ford and Lancelot Speed.

Value about 5s., or on large paper, 15s. (as published, auction).

New Edition, with notes, 1892, Longmans, crown 8vo, pp. viii, 243, with a special issue printed on India paper, with notes and biographies but no illustrations; published at 7s. 6d.

An edition was also issued in 1892 at 2s. 6d., for the use of schools, with biographical notices by R. MacWilliams, pp. viii, 264.

Some copies of the original edition are bound in half-morocco extra, t.e.g., instead of the usual cloth. These copies are of slightly more importance than the ones usually seen, for only a very few examples were thus bound direct from the sheets.

40. A Batch of Golfing Papers.   By Andrew Lang.
        . . . Edited by R. Barclay. . . . Simpkin,
     Marshall & Co.   N.D. (but 1892).

A small 4to book in pink wrappers, published at 1s. It contains 18 essays on the game, six of which are by Mr. Lang. There is an etched front representing "Dr. Johnson on the Links," a preface by Mr. R. Barclay, the editor, and pp. 1–123.

The value is small.

41. The Green Fairy Book. . . . Longmans, Green
        & Co.   1892.

Crown 8vo, pp. 366, cloth, gilt edges, published at 6s., with 13 plates and 88 illustrations in the text by H. J. Ford.

Value about 8s. (small paper, as issued), large paper about 21s.

42. Homer and the Epic.   By Andrew Lang. . . .   Longmans, Green & Co.   1893.

A crown 8vo book, pp. 420, cloth, published at 9s. (net).   A few copies of this work were printed on large paper.

CHARLES LEVER.

CHARLES JAMES LEVER, the celebrated Irish novelist, was born at Dublin in 1806. Unlike most of the other authors whose works are noticed in these pages, he did not adopt a literary career until comparatively late in life, being some thirty-three years of age at the time of the publication of his first, and as many people think, his best work, "The Confessions of Harry Lorrequer."

Although Lever died so recently as 1872, his biography contains much that is doubtful or obscure; many works are credited, or perhaps debited to him, which probably never issued from his pen, and for this reason the compilation of a correct, and at the same time a complete bibliography, which has never yet been attempted, would be an exceptionally difficult task. Fitzpatrick, his biographer, who wrote in 1884, has recorded many incidents in the life of Lever which would by this time most certainly have been lost, but many obvious omissions yet remain to be supplied, and these in some cases materially weaken the evidence that is advanced to prove the authorship of several of the works, which, perhaps for the sake of convenience, are usually attributed to him.

It is probable that the following list includes the whole of Lever's novels, thirty-one in number, though there is one book which might perhaps have been added without any great appearance of credulity, viz., "The Maxims of Sir Morgan O'Doherty, Bart." For reasons which it is not necessary to explain here, I think the authorship of this work cannot reasonably be assigned to Lever. I dismiss it therefore with the remark that it is a small book in 16mo, pp. 138, published by Blackwood in 1849 at 2s. 6d. It is scarce, a clean copy in the original cloth selling readily enough at a guinea.

In March 1889 Messrs. Sotheby disposed of the collection of Lever's works formed by Mr. John Mansfield Mackenzie of Edinburgh, and it is worthy of note that the catalogue contained the items mentioned below, and no others. The collection realised £275, an exceptional price, for the books were uniformly bound in Rivière's best manner, and were often extra illustrated with Browne's original drawings and many extra plates. So far as I know, no other collection can claim to approach this in point of perfection and beauty of appearance, the cardinal points that regulate the course of every advanced collector of early editions.

Lever was for three years the editor of *The Dublin University Magazine*, in which many of his compositions will be found. He also contributed frequently to *Blackwood's Magazine* under the pseudonym of " Cornelius O'Dowd," and also to *All the Year Round*, in the pages of which " A Day's Ride, a Life's Romance," first appeared. Curiously enough, this story was not appreciated by the subscribers; it is even said to have temporarily injured the sale of the periodical. If so, Lever's reputation as a novelist suffered for the first and last time.

In estimating the pecuniary value of Lever's works, it must be remembered that the majority of copies offered for sale, or which appear in the market, are all more or less worn or otherwise out of condition, owing to their having passed through the circulating libraries. The question of condition is therefore, in this case, of the greatest possible importance.

1. The Confessions of Harry Lorrequer. . . .
    Dublin.   William Curry, Jun. and Company.
      . . . MDCCCXXXIX.

This, Lever's first novel, was originally published in 11 monthly
parts, 1838–9, with 22 full-page etchings by "Phiz," who also
designed the wrappers.   In 1839 it was issued in volume form,
demy 8vo, pictorial cloth, with the etchings as before, one consisting of frontispiece, and another of the vignette on title.

The make-up of the bound volume is as follows:—Front,
pictorial title, plain title, dedication, prefatory epistle (v–viii),
contents (ix–xv), list of plates (unpaged), a word of introduction
(3–4), and text pp. 5–344.

Value about £7 7s. (original parts, auction) ; £1 15s. (original
cloth, as issued, auction).

2. Charles O'Malley, the Irish Dragoon.   Edited
    by Harry Lorrequer. . . . Dublin.   William
    Curry, Jun. and Company. . . . 1841.

Published originally in 22 monthly parts, white wrappers, with
44 full-page etchings by "Phiz ;" afterwards in 2 vols. demy 8vo,
pictorial cloth, with the etchings as before.

Vol. i. consists of front, engraved title, plain title, dedication, contents (iii–ix), list of plates (22, including front and
vignette on title), a word of explanation (unpaged), and text pp.
3–348.

Vol. ii. contains front, engraved title, plain title, contents (iii–
vii), list of plates (as in vol. i.), and text pp. 1–336.

Value about £4 4s. (original parts) ; £1 10s. (original cloth, as
issued).

Another Edition, 2 vols. 8vo, Dublin, 1842, with 40 full-page
etchings by "Phiz :" £1 5s. (cloth, uncut, auction).

3. Our Mess. Edited by Charles Lever ("Harry Lorrequer"). Vol. I. Jack Hinton, the Guardsman. Vol. II. Tom Burke of "Ours." Vol. III. Tom Burke of "Ours." Vol. II. Dublin. William Curry, Jun. and Company. . . . MDCCCXLIII.

It will be seen that there are two distinct stories in "Our Mess," viz., "Jack Hinton" and "Tom Burke." Notwithstanding this, the whole publication appeared in 35 monthly parts, with portrait of the author, 69 full-page etchings, and several woodcuts by "Phiz," who also designed the pictorial pink (sometimes white) wrappers. "Our Mess" was, on completion of the parts, published in 3 vols. 8vo, with the etchings and woodcuts as before, as follows :—

Vol. i. (Jack Hinton), half-title, portrait of Lever, title, dedication, contents (v–x), list of illustrations (portrait, 25 plates, and 9 woodcuts in the text), leaf of verses (unpaged), notice (3–4), and text pp. 5–396.

Vol. ii. (Tom Burke), half-title, front, title, dedication, contents (vii–xi), illustrations (front, and 23 plates), leaf of verses (unpaged), prefatory epistle from Mr. Burke (unpaged), and text pp. 5–372.

Vol. iii. (Tom Burke, vol. ii.), half-title, front, title, contents (iii–x), list of illustrations (front, and 19 plates), and text pp. 1–294.

It occasionally happens that vol. i. is sold singly as constituting a complete novel in itself, and for a similar reason vols. ii. and iii. are also sold apart from vol. i. When this is the case the first volume realises about £1 at auction (original cloth, as issued), and vols. ii. and iii. about £2 (*ibid.*). The auction value of complete sets in parts or in volume form, as the case may be, is, however, about £8 8s. (original parts); £2 15s. (original cloth). The 20 numbers which correspond with vols. ii. and iii. of "Our Mess," sell by auction for about £2 5s.

4. Arthur O'Leary, his Wanderings and Ponder-
ings in Many Lands. Edited by his Friend
Harry Lorrequer. . . . London. Henry
Colburn. . . . 1844.

In 3 vols. post 8vo, with 10 full-page etchings by George
Cruikshank, comprising portrait of Arthur O'Leary and three
etchings in vol. i., three etchings in vol. ii., and a similar number
in vol. iii. Published at £1 11s. 6d.

Vol. i. consists of half-title, portrait, title, list of illustrations,
notice preliminary and explanatory (1–26), and text pp. 27–290.

Vol. ii., half-title, front, title, and text pp. 1–320.

Vol. iii., half-title, front, title, and text pp. 1–328. There is
a table of errata on an unpaged leaf at the end.

Value £5 to £6 by auction (original cloth, quite clean). Indifferent copies often sell for much less, even though in the original
binding.

First Demy 8vo Edition, 1845, published at 12s., with the portrait
and 9 full-page plates by Cruikshank, as before.

Value about £1 10s. (original cloth, auction).

5. Tales of the Trains, being some Chapters of
Railroad Romance. By Tilbury Tramp,
Queen's Messenger. . . . London. Wm. S.
Orr & Co. . . . 1845.

A small book in 16mo, fancy cloth, with gilt edges, published
at 2s. 6d. The illustrations are by "Phiz."

This work is very scarce, selling by auction for as much as
£4 4s. or £4 10s. (original cloth).

6. St. Patrick's Eve. By Charles Lever. London.
Chapman & Hall, 186 Strand. MDCCCXLV.

Small 4to, in fancy green cloth, gilt, published at 5s. The

illustrations, which are by "Phiz," comprise front, pictorial title, and full-page plates to face pp. 24, 82, and 186. There are numerous illustrations in the text, also by "Phiz," and the book collates as follows :—Front, illustrated title, dedication, and text pp. 1–203.

Value about £1 (original cloth, auction).

7. Nuts and Nut Crackers. London. Chapman & Hall, 186 Strand. MDCCCXLV.

A few copies of this book were dated 1844. It is in 12mo, cloth, with fanciful designs on face and side by "Phiz," and was published at 5s. A second edition also bears date 1845, and like the first, contains six full-page etchings and a number of woodcuts in the text by "Phiz."

A clean copy of the original edition is worth about £1 5s. (original cloth, auction), and of the second edition about 7s. 6d. (*ibid.*).

Third Edition, 1857, Chapman & Hall, small 8vo, pictorial cloth, with the etchings by "Phiz" as before.

The published price was 2s., and the present value is about 5s. (as issued). .

8. The O'Donoghue : a Tale of Ireland Fifty Years Ago. By Charles Lever, Esq. . . . Dublin. William Curry, Jun. & Company. . . . 1845.

Originally issued in 13 monthly parts at 1s. each, pink (some white) wrappers, commencing January 1844 ; afterwards in 1 vol. demy 8vo, 1845. Both parts and bound volume contain 26 full-page etchings by "Phiz." The demy 8vo volume comprises half-title, frontispiece, title, dedication, contents (vii–xi), list of illustrations, and text pp. 1–410. The published price was 14s.

Value about £2 2s. (original parts, auction) ; £1 5s. (original cloth, *ibid.*).

9. The Knight of Gwynne : a Tale of the Time of the Union. By Charles Lever. . . . London. Chapman & Hall, 186 Strand. MDCCCXLVII.

Published originally in 20 monthly parts at 1s. each, pink or white wrappers, with 40 full-page etchings by "Phiz" (inclusive of front and title). No. 1 is dated January (1846). Afterwards published in demy 8vo, 1847, cloth, at 21s. The bound volume consists of half-title, front, pictorial title, plain title, dedication, contents (vii–x), list of plates, and text pp. 1–628.

Value about £2 (original parts, auction), or £2 (original cloth, auction). In this case there is not much difference between the value of the parts and the bound volume.

Another Edition, 1847, in 1 vol. 8vo, with all the illustrations, published at 14s. ; present value about £1 (as issued).

Another Edition, 1852, in 2 vols. 8vo, with all the illustrations, about 10s. 6d. (as issued).

10. Diary and Notes of Horace Templeton, Esq., late Secretary of Legation at ———— . . . London. Chapman & Hall, 186 Strand. 1848.

Published in 2 vols. post 8vo, cloth, at 21s.

Present value about £2 (original cloth, auction).

Second Edition, 1849, 2 vols. post 8vo, Chapman & Hall, published at 21s. The present value is somewhere about the same amount.

Another Edition, 1852, 2 vols. post 8vo, Chapman & Hall. Value about 10s. 6d. (as issued).

A work bearing the title of "Horace Templeton, an Autobiography," was published by T. B. Peterson of Philadelphia, demy 8vo, without date (but probably 1840). It consists of title and pp. 7–212, and is very badly printed, though scarce.

11. Roland Cashel.   By Charles Lever. . . . London.   Chapman & Hall. . . . MDCCCL.

Originally published in 20 monthly parts at 1s. each. (1849–50), with 40 etchings by "Phiz," who also designed the wrappers. Afterwards in 1 vol. demy 8vo, as above, pictorial cloth. The collation of the bound volume is—Half-title, front, title with vignette, plain title, dedication, list of plates (40, including front and first title), and text pp. 1–627.   Published at 21s.

Value about £3 10s. (original parts, auction); £1 15s. to £2 (original cloth, *ibid.*).

Occasionally an edition in one, or sometimes two volumes, dated 1851, is described as the first.   This is not correct, for unless the book is dated 1850 in Roman figures, it does not belong to the first issue.   Another edition was published in 2 vols. 8vo, 1858, with all the illustrations, but it is of little importance.

12. The Confessions of Con Cregan, the Irish Gil Blas. . . . London.   William S. Orr & Co. . . . N.D. (1850).

Published in 14 monthly parts, with 28 full-page etchings and a number of woodcuts, all by "Phiz;" afterwards in 2 vols. post 8vo, pictorial cloth, designed by the same artist.

Vol. i. contains front, engraved title, plain title, undated and anonymous preface, contents (v–vi), list of illustrations (14, inclusive of front and title), and text pp. 1–336.

Vol. ii. contains half-title, engraved title, plain title, contents (v–vi), list of illustrations (15, including front and title according to the list, but as a matter of fact there is no front), and text pp. 1–305.

Value about £4 10s. (original parts, auction); £3 (original cloth, *ibid.*).

Another Edition, 1855, post 8vo, cloth, worth about 6s. or 8s. (as issued, auction).

13. The Daltons; or Three Roads in Life. By
Charles Lever. . . . London. Chapman &
Hall. . . . 1852.

Published in 24 monthly parts at 1s. each, with 48 full-page
etchings by " Phiz," and afterwards in 2 vols. 8vo, 1852, at 21s.

Vol. i. contains front, engraved title, half-title, plain title,
dedication, contents, list of plates (v–viii, 26 plates including front
and title), and text.

Vol. ii. contains half-title, plain title (no front or engraved title),
contents, list of plates (v–vii, 22 plates), and text.

Value about £4 4s. (original parts, auction), or from £1 10s.
to £2 (original cloth, *ibid.*).

Another Edition, 1852, crown 8vo, Chapman & Hall, published
at 14s., with all the plates.

Value about £1 (original cloth).

Proof impressions of the plates by "Phiz" are occasionally met
with in folio.   These are scarce.

14. The Dodd Family Abroad.   By Charles Lever.
. . . London.   Chapman & Hall. . . .
MDCCCLIV.

Published in 20 monthly parts, in pink or white pictorial
wrappers designed by " Phiz," at 1s. each, and afterwards in one
demy 8vo volume as above, at 21s.   In each case there are 40
illustrations (inclusive of front and engraved title) by " Phiz."
The bound volume has half-title, front, engraved title, plain title,
dedication, "A Word from the Editor" (vii–x), contents, and list
of plates (xi–xvi), and text pp. 1–624.

Value about £3 3s. (original parts, auction), or from £1 10s.
to £2 (original cloth, *ibid.*).

Another Edition, 1856, crown 8vo, Chapman & Hall, published
at 14s., with all the plates.

Value about a guinea (as issued).

15. Maurice Tiernay, the Soldier of Fortune. . . . London. Thomas Hodgson, 13 Paternoster Row. N.D. (1855).

A scarce little book (12mo), published in boards at 2s.

The present value is from 15s. to £1 (original boards, auction). This work forms one of the series known as the "Parlour Library."

16. Sir Jasper Carew: His Life and Experiences. By the Author of "Maurice Tiernay," &c., &c. London. Thomas Hodgson, 13 Paternoster Row. N.D. (1855).

Post 8vo, published at 2s. in boards. Title, dedication, notice (vii–viii), and text pp. 9–480. This work forms one of the series known as the "Parlour Library."

Value from 15s. to £1 (original boards, auction).

17. The Martins of Cro' Martin. By Charles Lever. . . . London. Chapman & Hall, 193 Piccadilly. MDCCCLVI.

This work was originally issued in 20 monthly parts at 1s. each, ommencing December 1854. The wrappers, which are sometimes white, sometimes pink, were designed by "Phiz," who also etched the 40 full-page plates (including front and vignette title).

On the completion of the novel in serial form, it was published in 1 vol. demy 8vo, at 14s. (cloth), which collates as follows :— Front, pictorial title, half-title, plain title, dedication, "Apology for a Preface" (vii–viii), contents (ix–xiii), list of illustrations, and text pp. 1–625.

Value about £3 3s. (original parts, auction), or from £2 to £2 10s. (original cloth, auction).

18. The Fortunes of Glencore. By Charles Lever. . . . London. Chapman & Hall, 193 Piccadilly. MDCCCLVII.

Published in 3 vols. post 8vo, green cloth, at 31s. 6d. There is no half-title to any of the volumes. Vol. i. contains title, notice (v-x), and text. Vols. ii. and iii. contain no preliminary matter except title. There are no illustrations.

Value about £2 (original cloth, auction).

19. Davenport Dunn ; or the Man of our Day. By Charles Lever. . . . Chapman & Hall. . . . MDCCCLIX.

Published in 22 monthly parts at 1s. each, pink wrappers, demy 8vo, from July 1857 to April 1859 ; afterwards in 1 vol. demy 8vo, as above, at 14s. Both parts and bound volume contain 44 full-page plates by "Phiz" (including front and engraved title). The collation is—Front, engraved title, plain title, dedication, contents, and list of plates (v-viii), and text pp. 1-695.

Value about £2 15s. (original parts, auction), or from 20s. to 25s. (original cloth, *ibid.*).

20. One of Them. By Charles Lever. . . . London. Chapman & Hall, 193 Piccadilly. MDCCCLXI.

Originally issued in 15 monthly parts at 1s. each, in white or pink wrappers designed by "Phiz." The first part appeared in December 1859. The work was next issued in 1 vol. demy 8vo, 1861, as above, and contains front, pictorial title, plain title, dedication, contents (v-vii), list of plates, and text. Both parts and bound volume have the same set of 30 full-page plates (including front and vignette on title) by "Phiz."

Value about £3 10s. (original parts, auction) ; £2 2s. (original cloth, *ibid.*).

Another Edition, 1861, 8vo, Chapman & Hall, reduced to 7s. ; the plates as before.

21. Barrington.   By Charles Lever. . . . London. Chapman & Hall, 193 Piccadilly.   1863.

Though dated 1863, this work was, in reality, published at the close of the preceding year, demy 8vo, cloth, with 26 full-page plates by "Phiz," price 14s.   It contains front, vignette title, plain title, dedication, contents (v–vi), list of illustrations (the list only mentions 25 plates, but the engraved title is omitted from the computation), and text pp. 1–411.

The 13 monthly parts in which the novel was originally issued, commence February 1862, and terminate with a double number in January 1863.   The wrappers, which are pink, were designed by "Phiz," whose 26 full-page etchings should also be found, two in each of the first 11 numbers, and four in the last.

Value about £3 10s. (original parts, auction) ; from £1 5s. to £1 15s. (original cloth, *ibid.*).

22. A Day's Ride : a Life's Romance.   By Charles Lever. . . . London.   Chapman & Hall, 193 Piccadilly.   1863.

"A Day's Ride" first appeared in the pages of *All the Year Round*, and was subsequently reprinted in 2 vols. post 8vo, 1863, at 21s.   A second edition followed the same year, but it cannot be mistaken for the first, as it is described as "Second Edition" on the title-page.   The first illustrated edition was published in 1864, at 3s. 6d.

Value of copies of the original edition of 1863, about £1 5s. (original cloth, auction).

23. Cornelius O'Dowd upon Men and Women and other Things in General. . . . . William Blackwood & Sons. . . . MDCCCLXIV–V.

Published, without illustrations, in 3 vols. post 8vo, cloth.

Vol. i. has half-title, title, dedication, notice (vii–ix), contents, and text pp. 1–299. It is dated MDCCCLXIV.

Vol. ii. (called "Second Series"), is dated MDCCCLXV, and has half-title, title, dedication, contents, and text pp. 1–322.

Vol. iii. (called "Third Series") is also dated MDCCCLXV, and has the same preliminary matter as vol. ii., and text pp. 1–287.

Value about £1 (original cloth, auction).

24. Luttrell of Arran. By Charles Lever. . . . London. Chapman & Hall, 193 Piccadilly. MDCCCLXV.

Originally published in 16 monthly parts, in pink wrappers, with 32 etchings by "Phiz," commencing December 1864. The front is included in this computation, but the vignette on title ("The Mock Marriage") is not, so that there are altogether 33 etchings. The edition in volume form, 1865, 8vo, comprises front, pictorial title, plain title, dedication, contents (v–vii), list of illustrations, and text pp. 1–503. Published at 17s. 6d.

Value about £3 (original parts, auction); £1 1s. (original cloth, *ibid.*).

25. A Rent in a Cloud. By Charles Lever. . . . William Blackwood & Sons. N.D. (but 1865).

This book was published in post 8vo, green cloth, at 5s.

The present value is about £1 (original cloth).

26. Tony Butler. . . . William Blackwood & Sons. . . . MDCCCLXV.

In 3 vols. post 8vo, green cloth. Each volume has half-title before title, but there is no dedication or other preliminary matter. "Tony Butler" was originally published in *Blackwood's Magazine*.

Value about £2 2s. (original cloth, auction).

27. Sir Brook Fossbrooke. By Charles Lever. . . . William Blackwood & Sons. . . . MDCCCLXVI.

In 3 vols. post 8vo, blue cloth. Vol. i. has half-title, title, and dedication. Vols. ii. and iii., half-title and title only. The three volumes were published at 24s. "Sir Robert Fossbrooke" first appeared as a serial in *Blackwood's Magazine*.

Value about £1 (original cloth, auction).

Another Edition, 1867, post 8vo, Blackwood & Sons, pp. 503, published at 6s. The present value is about the same.

28. The Bramleighs of Bishop's Folly. By Charles Lever. London. Smith, Elder & Co., 65 Cornhill. 1868.

In 3 vols. post 8vo, red cloth. There is a table of contents to each volume, and a dedication in vol. i., but no half-titles. Published at £1 11s. 6d., without illustrations.

Value about £1 10s. (original cloth, auction).

29. Paul Gosslett's Confessions on Love, Law, and the Civil Service. . . . London. Virtue & Co., 26 Ivy Lane. . . . 1868.

Post 8vo, blue pictorial cloth. The volume contains front by Marcus Stone, title, contents, and text pp. 1–152.

Value about £1 5s. (original cloth, auction).

30. That Boy of Norcott's. By Charles Lever.
London. Smith, Elder & Co., 15 Waterloo
Place. 1869.

Demy 8vo, green cloth, lettered in gilt on face, published at
12s. The book contains 5 full-page illustrations by Swain, half-
title, front, title, dedication, contents (vii–viii), and text pp.
1–274.

A good and fresh copy of this scarce book in the original cloth
sometimes sells by auction for as much as £4 4s., but prices vary
greatly according to the state of preservation in each particular
instance. The average auction value does not much exceed half
the amount stated.

31. Lord Kilgobbin: a Tale of Ireland in our
own Time. By Charles Lever. . . . London.
Smith, Elder & Co., 15 Waterloo Place. 1872.

This was the last work published by Lever, who died at Trieste
the same year. It is in 3 vols. post 8vo, green cloth.

Vol. i. has half-title before title, but there is no half-title to
vols. ii. and iii. Each volume, however, has a table of contents.

The published price was £1 11s. 6d., and the present value
averages £1 15s. by auction (original cloth).

———

The complete editions of Lever's works include that of 1872,
in 21 vols. 8vo, with illustrations by H. K. Browne, and an
edition published by Routledge, without date, which is complete
in 34 vols. 8vo.

FREDERICK LOCKER-LAMPSON.

SELECTIONS from the writings of Mr. Locker-Lampson have been made on several occasions, viz., in 1865, with illustrations by Doyle, and portrait by Millais (square post 8vo, light brown cloth), and again in 1868. Both these books were published by Moxon, and there is only a very slight difference between them. In 1881 Mr. Austin Dobson made another selection as mentioned below, and in 1892 prepared a similar work for Miles' "The Poets and the Poetry of the Century."

The works, properly so-called, credited to Mr. Locker-Lampson, consist of "London Lyrics," of which there are many editions, and "Patchwork," which was first and finally published in 1879. "Lyra Elegantiarum" (*post*, No. 2), though a compilation, is included here because it is very closely identified with the name of the editor, more so indeed than is usually the case under somewhat similar circumstances. Strictly speaking, works of this kind do not come within our scope.

Mr. Locker-Lampson is also known for his very important collection of Elizabethan and modern books, and of drawings by the old masters. A catalogue of the "Rowfant Library" was prepared by the owner himself and published by Quaritch in 1886, in a half roxburghe binding, demy 8vo, pp. xii, 232. It is an important volume not only on account of the large number of peculiar and exceptional works that are catalogued in it, copies frequently of unique interest by reason of autograph inscriptions by the authors or former owners which they contain, but also on account of Mr.

Locker-Lampson's notes appended to many of the entries. These are often based upon personal episodes, which otherwise would have been forgotten in the lapse of time. The Rowfant Library is divided into three sections. The first division contains books issued from 1480 to 1700; the second from 1700 to 1800; and the third is devoted to American literature.

In 1892 a society of American gentlemen obtained Mr. Locker's permission to use the title "Rowfant" in connection with a club established at Cleveland, Ohio. The "Rowfant Club" has so far (June 1893) printed one work—"The Culprit Fay" and other poems by Joseph Rodman Drake.

1. London Lyrics. By Frederick Locker. With an Illustration by George Cruikshank. London. Chapman & Hall, Piccadilly. 1857.

This is a square post 8vo book, bound in rough brown cloth, with device on side, lettered in gilt on face. There is no half-title. The frontispiece, etched by George Cruikshank, is entitled "Building Castles in the Air," then follow title as above, dedication (unpaged), note (unpaged), contents (vii–viii), and text pp. 1–90. A blank leaf with Whittingham's device follows p. 90.

Several of the pieces in this volume had previously appeared in a detached form, and were now collected for the first time.

The work was published at 3s. 6d. Good copies in the original cloth binding are very difficult to meet with, selling by auction for as much as 35s. or £2, and occasionally for more.

Second Edition, 1862, fcap. 8vo, Pickering. This edition is not illustrated. Most copies are lettered across the face in gilt, but a very few have the inscription lengthwise. Published at 4s. 6d., in cloth. Value about £1 1s. (original cloth, cross lettering, auction).

Another Edition, 1868, fcap. 8vo, J. Wilson. This edition was called "Locker's Poems," and was privately printed. It contains the impression in the first state of the etched portrait of the author, after Millais. The binding is half Roxburghe, with claret-coloured cloth sides. Only 120 copies were printed, 20 on hand-made paper. These have an etching by George Cruikshank, entitled "The Fairy Bootmakers." Of these 20 copies, six were coloured by hand by Mrs. Lionel Tennyson.

Value about £3 or £4 (original cloth, auction), or £7 or £8 on the large paper (*ibid.*).

About half of these 100 copies are called "London Lyrics." They are on ordinary, and are not large paper, and have no illustration. They sell for about £1 5s. They are in the same binding.

Another Edition, 1870, fcap. 8vo, Strahan & Co. Published at 6s. in green cloth. Value about the published price.

Another Edition, 1872, fcap. 8vo, Strahan & Co. Published at 6s., in green cloth. Value about the published price.

Later editions include the eighth, published in 1874 by Isbister & Co. in green cloth. Of this edition about 100 copies were made up in paper covers, with grey sides and white face and label, for presentation to the members of the Cosmopolitan Club. Two or three copies were also printed on larger sized paper and illustrated with Doyle's cuts on India paper. A later edition of 1876 in crown 8vo, said to be "enlarged and finally revised," is more noticeable as containing the portrait of the author after Millais (slightly altered). An edition of 1878 was published by Messrs. Kegan Paul & Co. without portrait at a cheaper rate, in light green cloth, and the same firm has since published editions of 1885 ("Elzevir Series," fcap. 8vo, green cloth, gilt-lettered on side and face ; 50 copies on large paper, white covers, crown 8vo, with Mr. Locker's portrait by Millais), 1891 and 1893.

In 1881 a privately printed edition appeared. A very few copies were printed on large paper, with an illustration by Kate Greenaway and another by Caldecott. These large-paper copies are exceedingly scarce, some £6 or £7 being a very ordinary auction price. A few copies contain Caldecott's illustration in two states. In 1882 another privately printed edition appeared, but only about 100 copies were issued. These two editions of 1881 and 1882 contain nearly everything Mr. Locker-Lampson has published and cares to keep. Mr. Austin Dobson made the selection for the prior edition, and the author embodied the remaining pieces in the edition of 1882.

Of the American editions of "London Lyrics," the first appeared at Boston in 1870 (Field, Osgood & Co.), in claret-coloured cloth, gilt. In 1883 a pirated edition was published at New York, by White, Stokes & Allen. The title-page in this instance varies, some being in red, others in blue. In 1884 another edition was issued by the same firm, but in this instance from the stereo plates of the English edition of 1881, which Mr. Locker-Lampson had forwarded to America. The title-page is in red, with the book-plate designed by Kate Greenaway as a vignette, and Du Maurier's full-length portrait as front. Another edition, also dated 1884, appears to have been published by the same firm on larger sized paper. This has an etching of part of Du Maurier's portrait (head and shoulders). The only copies that I have seen have the title-page reversed, the book-plate of the Jester which adorns it being upside down. Probably these are exceptional copies, purposely made by the publishers for the sake of distinction, though it is impossible to say what object they may have had in view.

Of the New York editions, the one printed for the "Book Fellows Club" is the most important. It contains a full-length portrait of the author by Du Maurier, device on title, and numerous illustrations throughout the text. Some of these etchings are by Caldecott, and appeared in this edition for the first time. A note states that 104 copies were printed for subscribers, of which 94 were on Holland paper, 6 on plated paper, and 4 on vellum. The work is bound in light yellow cloth, gilt-lettered on side and face, long fcap. 8vo.

2. Lyra Elegantiarum : a Collection of some of the Best Specimens of *Vers de Société* and *Vers d'Occasion* in the English Language by Deceased Authors. Edited by Frederick Locker. . . . London. Edward Moxon & Co., Dover Street. 1867.

Thick fcap. 8vo, bound in reddish brown cloth, stamped in gilt on side with the Tudor Rose and the Fleur de Lys, lettered on face with title in floriated design, gilt. The book contains half-title, title as above, quotation from Pliny the Elder (unpaged), dedication (unpaged), preface (ix–xx), and text pp. 1–360.

This edition was almost immediately suppressed on account of its containing poems by Landor, the copyright of which had not expired, and copies are consequently scarce. The auction value averages £2 (cloth, uncut), but occasionally this quotation is considerably exceeded.

A new and revised edition speedily took the place of the one above mentioned. It was published the same year by Moxon in 12mo, cloth gilt. The present auction value of copies of this edition averages 7s. 6d. (cloth, uncut). In 1884, White, Stokes & Allen published an edition in fcap. 8vo, New York, pp. xvi–360; and in 1891 a revised and enlarged edition was added to the "Minerva Library," published by Messrs. Ward, Lock & Co. This work contains pp. xx–425, post 8vo, though some copies were printed on large paper, 4to. On the preliminary leaf of one of these large-paper copies is the following verse, in Mr. Locker-Lampson's autograph : —

> "Verse of Society
> Filled with variety,
> Sentiment, Piety,
> Lark and 'Lurliety,'
> Strictest sobriety,
> No impropriety.
>
> Here Locker and Kernahan and Kernahan and Locker
> Tie a posy for Beauty.   That nothing should shock her
> THAT's their anxiety."

3. Patchwork.   By Frederick Locker.   London. Smith, Elder & Co., 15 Waterloo Place.   1879.

A post 8vo book, in dark green cloth, lettered in gilt on face. It contains half-title, title as above (with Mr. Locker's book-plate as vignette), dedication to Arthur Stanley, Dean of Westminster (though he is not mentioned by name) (unpaged), preface (vii–viii), and text pp. 1–234. "Patchwork" is a collection of prose and verse.

Value from £4 to £5 (hand-made paper, original cloth, auction); or from 6s. to 8s. (ordinary issue).

It is said that only 50 copies were printed on hand-made paper for members of the Philobiblon Society. These, like all the other publications of the Society, are bound in brown cloth.

GEORGE MEREDITH.

Mr. Meredith was born in Hampshire about the year 1828, and though educated for the bar, speedily relinquished the profession for literature. As in the case of many other successful prose writers, his first work consisted of a volume of poems, which was published by Parker & Son, of the Strand, in 1851. This was quickly followed by other poems, contributed to various periodicals, notably *Fraser's Magazine*, though it was not until 1856 that he appeared in his now familiar *rôle* of a novelist, with "The Shaving of Shagpat," a humorist composition written in the style of an Eastern tale. This was followed by "Farina, a Legend of Cologne," 1857, and "The Ordeal of Richard Feverel," Mr. Meredith's first long novel, which was published in the orthodox three volumes in 1859.

An unusually full and careful bibliography, by Mr. John Lane, was published in 1890, and to this the reader is referred for any general information he may require.

It will be as well to mention here that there are two collective editions of George Meredith's works, though neither is of course now complete. These were both published by Chapman & Hall in 10 vols. crown 8vo, 1885–87, and 10 vols. crown 8vo, 1889, respectively. The published price of the former was 6s. per volume, of the latter 3s. 6d.

On December 9, 1890, a complete set of the novels to date (not therefore including "One of our Conquerors"), in all 31 vols., first editions, and clean in the original cloth covers as issued, realised £12 by auction.

1. Poems. By George Meredith. . . . London. John W. Parker & Son, West Strand.

A fcap. 8vo book, published without date (but 1851). The work, which is now scarce, was issued in green cloth, lettered on the face. A half-title precedes title, which is followed by a dedication to Thomas Love Peacock, table of contents, and "Poems," pp. 1–160. Many of the leaves are not paged, notably pp. 22–26 inclusive, and care should be taken to see that the book is perfect in this respect.

Value about £7 10s. (original cloth, auction)..

2. The Shaving of Shagpat : an Arabian Entertainment. By George Meredith. London. Chapman & Hall, 193 Piccadilly. 1856.

This work was issued in crown 8vo, in red cloth, having title on the side and face. Mr. Lane says that a "remainder" of this edition was bound in red cloth, without lettering on the side, so that there are, in this case, two issues of the same edition. The original issue, which, following the general rule in such cases, is the more valuable of the two, contains half-title, title as above, a short prefatory note on an unpaged leaf, table of contents, and text, pp. 1–384.

Value about £1 (original cloth, first issue).

Second Edition, 1865, crown 8vo, Chapman & Hall, contains a frontispiece by Saddler, pp. 1–283, with a fresh prefatory note.

Published price 5s. Present value about 5s. (cloth, as issued).

Another Edition, 1872, post 8vo, published by Chapman & Hall at 2s., in boards. The present value is about the same.

"The Shaving of Shagpat," together with "Farina" (see *post*, No. 3), was reprinted in 1887 and at a later date by Chapman & Hall, crown 8vo.

3. Farina : a Legend of Cologne.   By George
    Meredith, author of "The Shaving of Shag-
    pat."   London.   Smith, Elder & Co., 65
    Cornhill.   1857.

Post 8vo, issued in emerald-green cloth, with gilt lettering on
face.   There is no half-title to this book, which is made up simply
of title as above, table of contents, and text, pp. 1–244.
    Value about £1 15s. (original cloth, auction).
Second Edition, 1865, crown 8vo, Smith, Elder & Co.   The title-
page to this edition is engraved.
    Value about 5s. (cloth, as issued).

4. The Ordeal of Richard Feverel : a History of
    Father and Son.   By George Meredith. . . .
    London.   Chapman & Hall, 193 Piccadilly.
    1859.

In 3 vols. crown 8vo, dark-green cloth, lettered on face in gilt.
There is no half-title to any of the volumes, but there should be a
table of contents in each.
    Value about £1 5s. (original cloth).
Second Edition, 1878, post 8vo, published in 1 vol. at 6s. by
Kegan Paul & Co.   There is, or should be, a frontispiece to this
edition.   Clean copies are worth some 5s. or 6s. each.

5. Evan Harrington.   By George Meredith, author
    of "The Ordeal of Richard Feverel." . . .
    London.   Bradbury & Evans, 11 Bouverie
    Street.   1861.

In 3 vols. crown 8vo, dark-red cloth, lettered on face in gilt.
Each volume contains a table of contents, but there is no half-
title.

Published at 31s. 6d., and now worth about 15s. (original cloth, auction).

Second Edition, 1866, in 1 vol. crown 8vo. Published at 6s. by Bradbury & Evans. This edition contains a frontispiece.

6. Modern Love, and Poems of the English Road-
    side ; with Poems and Ballads.   By George
    Meredith. . . . London.   Chapman & Hall,
    193 Piccadilly.   1862.

Published in green ribbed cloth, 12mo, at 6s. The book contains half-title, title, inscription to Captain Maxe, contents, and text, pp. 1–216.

Present value about £1 5s. (original cloth, auction).

In 1892 Messrs. Macmillan published a reprint of the first edition, but the two cannot be mistaken, as the title-page is dated 1892 and the work is specifically stated to be a reprint. It is bound in smooth navy-blue cloth.

7. Emilia in England.   By George Meredith. . . .
    London.   Chapman & Hall, 193 Piccadilly.
    1864.

In 3 vols. crown 8vo, purple cloth. Each volume contains title and table of contents, but no half-title.

Value about 17s. 6d. (original cloth).

See also "Sandra Belloni" (*post*, No. 9), under which title this novel was reprinted in 1889 by Chapman & Hall.

8. Rhoda Fleming : a Story.   By George Meredith,
    author of "The Ordeal of Richard Feverel."
    . . . London.   Tinsley Brothers, Catherine
    Street, Strand.   1865.

In 3 vols. crown 8vo, bright-green cloth.   Published at 31s. 6d.
In this instance there is a half-title to each volume, as well as title
and table of contents.

Value about 20s. (cloth, as issued).

9. Sandra Belloni, L'Anneau D'Amasis,—La Famille
   du Docteur. . . . Par E. D. Forgues.   Paris.
   Librairie de L. Hachette et Cie. . . . 1866.

This is not a reprint of "Emilia in England," but a study of
that novel, as well as of "Owen Meredith's" "Ring of Amasis,"
and the "Chronicles of Carlingford."   It is mentioned here because
it seems to have suggested the new title, "Sandra Belloni," under
which Messrs. Chapman & Hall reprinted "Emilia in England"
in 1889.   (See *ante*, No. 7.)

The value of this French work does not exceed two or three
shillings.

10. Vittoria.   By George Meredith. . . . London.
    Chapman & Hall, 193 Piccadilly.   MDCCCLXVII.

In 3 vols. post 8vo, blue cloth.   This story was now reprinted
from the *Fortnightly Review*, in which journal it had appeared
during the greater part of the previous year.   There is a table of
contents to each volume.   Another edition was published in 1889,
at 3s. 6d., in dark-blue cloth (same publishers).

Value of a clean copy of the original edition about 15s. (cloth,
as issued).

11. The Adventures of Harry Richmond.   By
    George Meredith. . . . London.   Smith, Elder
    & Co., 15 Waterloo Place.   1871.

In 3 vols. bright-red cloth, lettered in black on the side of each
volume, and on the face in gilt.   Each volume contains title and

table of contents, but there is no half-title. The published price
was 31s. 6d., and the present value is about 15s. (original cloth).
A second edition appeared the same year, but, being so described
on the title, there is no danger of mistaking the two. A copy
of this edition is worth about 5s. (cloth). "The Adventures of
Harry Richmond" was first published as a serial in vols. xxii. and
xxiii. of the *Cornhill Magazine.*

12. Beauchamp's Career. By George Meredith.
   . . . London. Chapman & Hall, 193 Piccadilly. 1876.

In 3 vols. crown 8vo, light-green cloth, lettered on the face in
gilt. Each volume contains half-title, title, and table of contents.
   The published price was, as usual, 31s. 6d., and the present
value is about 15s. (original cloth).
   This novel originally appeared in serial form in the *Fortnightly
Review*, vols. xxii., xxiii., and xxiv.

13. The Egoist: a Comedy in Narrative. By
   George Meredith. . . . London. C. Kegan
   Paul & Co., 1 Paternoster Square. 1879.

In 3 vols. crown 8vo, yellow cloth, gilt-lettered on face. Each
volume contains title and table of contents, but no half-title.
   Value about 17s. 6d. (original cloth).
   Second Edition, 1880, crown 8vo, C. Kegan Paul & Co., with
a frontispiece by Paget.
   Published at 6s., and now worth about the same.

14. The Tragic Comedians: a Study in a Well-
   known Story. . . . By George Meredith.
   London. Chapman & Hall, Limited, 193
   Piccadilly. 1880.

Published in 2 vols. post 8vo, olive-green cloth, at 12s. There
are two issues of this edition, exactly the same in every respect,
save that the second issue is dated 1881. In each case there
should be half-title and title, but no table of contents. This story
as separately published was enlarged from the *Fortnightly Review*,
vols. xxxiv. and xxxv., where it appears in serial form.

Value about 12s. (first issue, original cloth).

15. Poems and Lyrics of the Joy of Earth.   By
     George Meredith.   London.   Macmillan & Co.
     1883.

This is a small 4to book, bound in smooth navy-blue cloth, gilt-
lettered on face, and published at 6s. A perfect copy should
contain unpaged leaf giving a list of works by the same author,
half-title, title as above, inscription to James Cotter Morison,
contents, and poems, pp. 1–181. Care should be taken to see
that there is an unpaged leaf, containing a note about the metre
in which some of the poems are written. This leaf follows p. 181.

Value about 6s. (cloth, as issued).

16. Diana of the Crossways : a Novel.   By George
     Meredith. . . . London.   Chapman & Hall,
     Limited.   1885.

Published in 3 vols., smooth terra-cotta cloth, at 31s. 6d. Each
volume contains half-title, title, and table of contents.

Value about 12s. (original cloth).

This story was enlarged from the *Fortnightly Review*, where it
originally appeared as a serial. Several editions of the book
appeared in 1885, but all are appropriately described on their
respective title-pages.

17. Ballads and Poems of Tragic Life. By George Meredith. London. Macmillan & Co. And New York. 1887.

Published in fcap. 8vo, smooth navy-blue cloth, at 6s. The book contains unpaged leaf, which mentions other works by the same author, half-title, title, contents, and pp. 1–160; the last two pages containing notes on the metre.

Value about 5s. (as issued).

18. A Reading of Earth. By George Meredith. London. Macmillan & Co. And New York. 1888.

Published in fcap. 8vo, smooth navy-blue cloth, at 5s. The volume contains blank leaf, unpaged leaf with list of works by the same author, half-title, title, contents, and text, pp. 1–136.

Value about 4s. (as issued).

19. The Case of General Ople and Lady Camper. By George Meredith. . . . New York. John W. Lovell Company. N.D. (but 1890).

This book forms No. 3 of Lovell's "Westminster Series," and contains half-title, title, and text, pp. 5–126. It is not dated, but was published in 1890 at 25 cents. The story appeared in the *New Quarterly Magazine*, and was reprinted in a separate form for the first time as above. The value is trifling.

20. The Tale of Chloe : an Episode in the History of Beau Beamish. By George Meredith. . . . New York. John W. Lovell Company. N.D. (but 1890).

This is No. 6 of Lovell's "Westminster Series." It is in all respects like the previous volume (No. *20 supra*), but there are pages 5-144. The "Tale of Chloe" first appeared in the *New Quarterly Magazine*, and was printed in a separate form at New York as above. The value is trifling in this case also.

21. Jump-to-Glory Jane : a Poem.   By George Meredith.   Privately Printed. (?)   1889.

This is the extraordinary title of a poem which appeared originally in the *Universal Review* for October 1889, under the editorship of Mr. Harry Quilter. It is said by some that fifty copies of the poem were privately printed at the time for friends only, but this is denied by many experts, who assert that Mr. Quilter's reprint of 1892 is the only one that has legitimately appeared in the market. If this is so, the so-called reprint of 1889 is spurious. The following letter from a correspondent of the *Athenæum*, which appeared in the columns of that journal on the 3rd of December 1892, p. 780, will explain matters fully :—

"Your readers will do well to beware of a 'first and only edition' of Mr. George Meredith's poem 'Jump-to-glory Jane,' which is being offered for sale as an edition of 'fifty copies, privately printed for friends only.' This is nothing more nor less than untrue. The author has never seen a copy. 'Privately printed for friends only' is good. But I might ask, for whose friends? For those of the author, or for those of the printer? The poem appeared originally in the *Universal Review*, October 1889, and has been recently republished, with illustrations and by authority, under the auspices of Mr. Quilter. Therefore the private edition is neither the 'first' nor the 'only' one. The modest price asked for this production, a 'leaflet' of about four pages, varies from £5 to £15, according to the taste and fancy of the vendor."

The poem, as legitimately reprinted in 1892, pp. 25, 36, was printed on large as well as on small paper; the former on Van Gelder paper, bound in vellum and gilt (100 copies only). The book is embellished with 44 designs, drawn and engraved by

Laurence Housman.   750 copies were printed on small paper, with all the illustrations.

22. One of Our Conquerors.   By George Meredith. London.   Chapman & Hall, Limited.   1891.

Published in 3 vols. crown 8vo, in bright-blue cloth, gilt-lettered on face.   Each volume contains title and table of contents, but no half-title.
Value about 10s. (original cloth).

23. Poems: The Empty Purse; with Odes to the Comic Spirit, to Youth, on Memory, and Verses.   London.   Macmillan & Co. . . . 1892.

A post 8vo book in cloth, published in October 1892 at 5s. It contains pp. 136.
The present value does not exceed the published price.

WILLIAM MORRIS.

THE "Oxford and Cambridge Magazine, conducted by Members of the Two Universities," contains some of the earliest literary compositions of Mr. William Morris. This periodical was indeed founded by Mr. Morris himself, in 1856, when a graduate of Exeter College, Oxford, and many criticisms, stories and articles from his pen are scattered over its pages. The Magazine had a short life, for it lasted only a year; the twelve numbers which make up the complete set are scarce.

In addition to the more important and better known works of this author, which are catalogued in chronological order later on, there are a number of others with which his name is coupled, but which for various reasons are not of much interest to the collector. Among them are several volumes of the "Saga Library;" "The Decorative Arts and Modern Life and Progress," published by Ellis & White at 6d., without date (but 1878), 8vo; "Chants for Socialists," 1885, 8vo; "A Summary of the Principles of Socialism," by H. M. Hyndman and William Morris, 1884, 8vo; "The Manifesto of the Socialist League," annotated by William Morris, 1885, 8vo; "Useful Work and Useless Toil;" "A Short Account of the Commune of Paris;" and "True and False Society," forming Nos. 2, 4, and 6 respectively of a series known as "The Socialist Platform," 1885. A preface to Fairman's "Principles of Socialism," 1888, "An Address on the Collection of Paintings," &c., delivered and subsequently published at Birmingham in 1891, and a Preface to Mr. Ruskin's "Nature of Gothic" (1892).

Mr. Morris's greatest achievement, from one point of view, was perhaps the establishment at Hammersmith, in 1891, of the now world-famed "Kelmscott Press," from which such charming specimens of antique printing have issued. The first book—"The Story of the Glittering Plain"—appeared in April 1891, and from that date to the present, a considerable number of sumptuous and scholarly volumes have been published in rapid succession. Such of the books from this press as are credited to Mr. Morris's personal authorship will be found in their proper place in the list, a complete catalogue of the works issued from Hammersmith to date being added for convenience of reference.

1. The Defence of Guenevere, and other Poems. By William Morris. London. Bell & Daldy, 186 Fleet Street. 1858.

A post 8vo book, published at 6s. in cloth, containing half-title, title, dedication to Dante Gabriel Rossetti, contents (vii–viii), leaf of "Errata," and text, pp. 1–248.

Value about £1 1s. (as published, auction).

Another Edition, 1875, 8vo, published at 8s., a verbatim reprint of the first edition; about 10s. (as issued). Twenty-five copies of this edition were issued on large paper, and these sell by auction for about £2 15s. each (as issued). At the Buckley sale a copy brought £5 10s.

Another Edition, April 2, 1892, small 4to. The Kelmscott Press. Only 300 copies of this edition were printed (in golden type). Ten copies were printed on vellum.

Value about £2 10s. (one of 300 copies, auction).

2. The Life and Death of Jason: a Poem. By William Morris. London. Bell & Daldy, York Street, Covent Garden. 1867.

Post 8vo, published in cloth at 8s. Twenty-five copies were printed on large paper. Contents comprise half-title, title, leaf of "Errata," and text, pp. 1–363.

Value about £1 1s. (as issued, auction).

Another Edition (1869), post 8vo, Ellis & White, published at 8s., and now worth about the same amount. A few large paper copies of this edition were issued. These sell by auction for as much as £3 10s. (uncut, as issued).

3. The Earthly Paradise : a Poem. By William Morris, author of "The Life and Death of Jason." London. F. S. Ellis, 33 King Street, Covent Garden. MDCCCLXVIII.

The "Earthly Paradise" was originally published in four parts, of which the first and second were issued together, subsequently with a second title-page ("Parts I. and II. MDCCCLXX.").

Parts I. and II. collate as follows :—Half-title, first title as above, second title, dedication, contents (vii–viii), and text, pp. 1–676. A leaf with woodcut follows the last page.

Part III., dated MDCCCLXX., contains half-title, title, contents (unpaged), another half-title, and text, pp. 2–526. A leaf containing woodcut faces p. 526.

Part IV., dated MDCCCLXX., contains half-title, title, contents (unpaged), another half-title, and text, pp. 2–442. A leaf containing woodcut faces p. 442.

Twenty-five large-paper copies of this first edition were published, and these invariably command high prices.

Value about £1 16s. (in 6 vols., auction), £4 (in 3 vols., *ibid.*). The large-paper copies sell by auction at from £12 to £15, according to condition. At the Buckley sale one of these copies realised £23. The parts when offered for sale are often made up from various editions.

The Popular Edition, 1872, issued in 10 parts at 3s. 6d. each. Each part, containing two or more tales, is complete in itself.

Value about 21s. (as issued).

Another Edition, 1880, in 4 vols. 8vo, about £1 (as issued, auction).

Another Edition, 1886, in 5 vols. 12mo, published by Reeves & Turner at 5s. each, and now worth less.

Another Edition, 1890, 8vo, published in white cloth cover, designed by the author, at 7s. 6d. The present value is about 5s.

4. Grettis Saga : the Story of Grettir, the Strong. Translated from the Icelandic by Eiríkr Magnússon . . . and William Morris. . . . London. F. S. Ellis, King Street, Covent Garden. MDCCCLXIX.

Crown 8vo, in glazed navy-blue cloth with white label, containing half-title with sonnet by William Morris on reverse, title, preface (v–xvi), "Chronology of the Story" (xvii–xviii), contents (xix–xxiv), map of the west parts of Iceland, and text, pp. 1–306. Twenty-five copies were printed on large paper.

Value about 12s. (as issued, auction), £3 10s. (large paper, *ibid.*).

5. Volsunga Saga : the Story of the Volsungs and Niblungs, with certain Songs from the Elder Edda. Translated from the Icelandic by Eiríkr Magnússon . . . and William Morris. . . . London. F. S. Ellis, King Street, Covent Garden. MDCCCLXX.

Crown 8vo, published in ornamental binding, designed by the author, at 12s. The contents comprise half-title, title, preface (v–xi), contents (xiii–xvi), "The names of those who are most noteworthy in this story" (xvii–xviii), prologue in verse by William Morris (xix–xx), and text, pp. 1–275. A half-title follows p. 163. Twenty-five copies were printed on large paper.

Value about £1 10s. (as issued, auction), or £3 3s. (large paper, *ibid.*).

Another Edition, 1888, 8vo, worth a few shillings.

6. Love is Enough ; or the Freeing of Pharamond : a Morality. By William Morris. London. Ellis & White, 29 New Bond Street. 1873.

This work, though dated 1873, was published in 1872 in square crown 8vo, in navy-blue cloth, having short title in floriated device on side and on face in gilt. It contains half-title, title, "Dramatis Personæ" (unpaged), and text, pp. 1–134. Published at 7s. 6d.

Value about 10s. (as issued, auction), or £3 10s. (large paper, *ibid.*).

7. Three Northern Love Stories, and other Tales. Translated from the Icelandic by Eiríkr Magnússon and William Morris. London. Ellis & White, 29 New Bond Street. 1875.

Crown 8vo, published in cloth at 10s. 6d. Half-title, title, preface (v–vii), chronology (unpaged), contents (unpaged), half-title, and text, pp. 3–256. A "note to page 50, 26 ff." (unpaged), faces p. 246, and a half-title precedes each story throughout the book. A few copies were printed on large paper.

Value about 10s. (as issued, auction), £2 5s. (large paper, *ibid.*).

8. The Æneids of Virgil, Done into English Verse. By William Morris, author of "The Earthly Paradise." London. Ellis & White, New Bond Street. MDCCCLXXVI.

Though dated 1876, this book was published in the preceding

year, in glazed navy-blue cloth, with white label on face, at 14s.
It contains half-title, title, and text, pp. 1–382. No half-titles
before any of the twelve books into which the volume is divided.
Twenty-five copies were printed on large paper in 2 vols. 8vo.

.Value about 15s. (as issued, auction), £3 3s. (large paper, *ibid.*).

9. The Story of Sigurd the Volsung, and the Fall
of the Niblungs. By William Morris. . . .
London. Ellis & White, New Bond Street.
MDCCCLXXVII.

Though dated 1877, this work was published in 1876. It
contains half-title, title, contents (v–vii), and text, pp. 1–392.
The work is divided into four books, and it will be noted that pp.
165–167 are headed "Book III. Regin," instead of "Book II.
Regin." The published price was 12s., and twenty-five copies
were printed on large paper.

Value about £1 (as issued, auction), £3 10s. (large paper, *ibid.*).
At the recent Buckley sale a large-paper copy sold for £7 2s. 6d.

Another Edition, 1887, small 4to, published at 6s. by Reeves
& Turner. Value from 12s. to 15s. (as issued). A copy bound
in morocco extra, uncut, once realised £1 10s. at auction, but
this price is very unusual.

10. Hopes and Fears for Art: Five Lectures,
Delivered in Birmingham, London, and Not-
tingham, 1878–1881. By William Morris.
. . . London. Ellis & White. . . . 1882.

Post 8vo, published in navy-blue cloth, with white label, lettered
"Morris's Lectures on Art." The contents comprise half-title,
title, and text, pp. 1–217.

The published price of the book was 4s. 6d., and good copies,
as issued, sell by auction for close on £1 each, or if on large paper
for about £3.

11. The Odyssey of Homer, Done into English Verse. By William Morris, author of " The Earthly Paradise." . . . London. Reeves & Turner, 196 Strand. MDCCCLXXXVII.

Published in 2 vols. small 4to, and on large paper, in half-parchment binding.

Vol. i. contains half-title, title, contents (v–vii), and text, pp. 1–230. Vol. ii. is made up in precisely the same way, but with text, pp. 231–450.

Value about £1 5s. (large paper, as issued, auction).

12. Signs of Change: Seven Lectures, Delivered on Various Occasions. By William Morris. London. Reeves & Turner, 196 Strand. 1888.

Published in crown 8vo, cloth, at 4s. 6d.
Value, about the published price.

13. A Dream of John Ball, and a King's Lesson. . . . By William Morris. . . . London. Reeves & Turner, 196 Strand. MDCCCLXXXVIII.

Published in small 4to at 4s. 6d., and also on large paper. Both small and large-paper copies contain a frontispiece by E. Burne-Jones, and collate as follows :—Half-title, title, contents (vii–viii), front, and text, pp. 1–143. There is a separate half-title to "A King's Lesson," following p. 129. The large-paper copies are bound in half-vellum, with white label on face. The "Dream of John Ball," and "The King's Lesson," were reprinted from the *Commonweal.*

Value about 5s. (in cloth, as issued), or on large paper from 15s. to 20s. (as issued).

Another Edition, 1892, small 4to, the Kelmscott Press. Published by Reeves & Turner on May 13, in vellum covers with green strings, lettered on face in gilt, "John Ball." There are five preliminary blank leaves, half-title, frontispiece by E. Burne-Jones, and text, pp. 1–123, the last containing the colophon. This edition contains "The Dream of John Ball" only. The text is in the "golden type," printed in black and red. Only 300 copies were printed, and an additional 11 on vellum.

Value about £2 (one of 300 copies, as issued).

"A King's Lesson" was separately published at Aberdeen in 1891, 8vo. This reprint is of trifling value.

14. A Tale of the House of the Wolfings and all the Kindreds of the Mark : Written in Prose and in Verse. By William Morris. London. 1889. Reeves & Turner, 196 Strand.

Published in crown 8vo at 6s., 100 copies were printed on large paper (large 4to), bound in bright red cloth, with white label on face. The contents comprise half-title, title, contents (one leaf, reverse blank), and text, pp. 1–199.

Value 5s. or 6s. (as issued), or £1 5s. (large paper, original binding, auction).

15. The Roots of the Mountains : Wherein is Told Somewhat of the Lives of the Men of Burgdale. . . . By William Morris. London. MDCCCXC. Reeves & Turner, CXCVI. Strand.

Published in post 8vo at 8s., or on large paper in 4to (250 copies printed) at 21s., with fancy covers designed by Mr. Morris. Though dated 1890, the book was published towards the end of the previous year. It consists of half-title, title, contents, and text, pp. 1–424.

Value about 6s. (as issued, auction), or £1 (large paper, *ibid.*).

16. News from Nowhere ; or an Epoch of Rest :
being Some Chapters from a Utopian Romance.
By William Morris. London. Reeves &
Turner. . . . 1891.

250 copies were printed on large paper (demy 8vo) and bound
in half-vellum, blue boards, with white label on face. There is
no half-title, merely title, and text, pp. 1–238. The small-paper
copies were published at 1s. 6d. each.

Value about 10s. (large paper, auction).

Another Edition, 1893, the Kelmscott Press ; woodcut designed
by C. M. Gere. Only 300 copies printed in black and red, and 10
copies on vellum, "golden type."

17. The Story of the Glittering Plain : which has
been also called the Land of Living Men, or
the Acre of the Undying. Written by William
Morris. N.D. (but 1891).

Printed at the Kelmscott Press, April 4, 1891, and published
by Reeves & Turner. 200 copies were printed in small 4to, and
six copies on vellum, in the "golden type." Two blank leaves
precede title as above, which has on the reverse "A Table of the
Chapters of this Book," text, pp. 1–188, with colophon on last
leaf, three blank end leaves. The book is bound in white vellum,
lettered in gilt on face, with leather strings.

Value about £4 (in the original vellum binding, auction).

A second edition of this work is in preparation at the Kelmscott Press, large 4to, with twenty-three woodcuts designed by
Walter Crane.

18. Poems by the Way. Written by William
Morris. London. Reeves & Turner. 1891.

There are two issues of this book, one printed at the Kelmscott

Press in September 1891, and the other in the previous March of the same year. Of the Kelmscott Press issue 300 copies were printed in "golden type," small 4to, and thirteen extra copies on vellum. The earlier edition was published in 16mo at 6s., 100 copies on large paper, 4to.

The collation of the Kelmscott Press issue is as follows :—Three blank leaves, title ("Poems by the Way: written by William Morris"), contents (unpaged), and text, pp. 1–197, the last page containing the colophon, with device. Binding, vellum, lettered in gilt on face, sage-green strings.

Value about £3 10s. to £4 (one of 300 copies, Kelmscott Press, auction), from 5s. to 6s. (edition of March, 1891, small paper, or large paper about three times as much).

———

Works Printed at Mr. William Morris's Private Press at the Upper Mall, Hammersmith, known as the "Kelmscott Press." (*This list is brought down to May* 1893.)

Three kinds of type are in use at this Press, viz. :—

The Golden Type.
The Troy Type.
The Chaucer Type.

(*a.*) The Story of the Glittering Plain. April 4, 1891. See *ante*, No. 17.

(*b.*) Poems by the Way. Sept. 24, 1891. See *ante*, No. 18.

(*c.*) Love-Lyrics and Songs of Proteus, and other Poems. By Wilfrid Blunt. January 26, 1892. Small 4to, in black and red. 300 printed. Published by Reeves & Turner, 196 Strand. Golden type.

(*d.*) Of the Nature of Gothic. By John Ruskin. February 15, 1892. Small 4to. 500 printed. Published by George Allen, 8 Bell Yard, Temple Bar. Golden type. About 25s. (as issued, auction).

(*e.*) The Defence of Guenevere, and other Poems. April 2, 1892. See *ante*, No. 1.

(*f.*) A Dream of John Ball. May 13, 1892. See *ante*, No. 13.

(*g.*) The Golden Legend. Translated by William Caxton. Sept. 12, 1892. 3 vols. large 4to. 500 copies printed, with two woodcuts designed by E. Burne-Jones. The Golden type. Published by Bernard Quaritch, 15 Piccadilly. About £7 10s. (as issued, auction).

(*h.*) The Recuyell of the Histories of Troye. Translated by William Caxton. A Reprint of the First Book printed in English. October 14, 1892. In 2 vols. large 4to, in black and red, Troy type. 300 copies printed, five copies on vellum. Published by Bernard Quaritch, 15 Piccadilly. About £7 10s. (as issued, auction).

(*i.*) Biblia Innocentium. By J. W. Mackail. 8vo. 200 copies printed. November 6, 1892. Published by Reeves & Turner, 196 Strand. Golden type. About £1 10s. (as issued, auction).

(*k.*) News from Nowhere. See *ante*, No. 16.

(*l.*) The Historye of Reynard the Foxe. Translated from the Dutch by William Caxton. Reprinted from the edition of 1481. December 15, 1892. 300 copies printed on ordinary paper, and 10 on vellum. Troy type. Published by Quaritch.

(*m.*) Shakespeare's Poems and Sonnets. Reprinted from the first editions, January 17, 1893. 500 copies printed on ordinary paper, and 10 copies on vellum, 8vo. Published by Reeves & Turner, at 25s. Golden type.

(*n.*) The Order of Chivalry. Reprinted from Caxton's edition of 1484, with L'Ordene de Chevalerie, a French poem of the thirteenth century, translated by William Morris. Small 4to, with woodcut designed by E. Burne-Jones. February 24, 1893. 225 copies printed, with 10 copies on vellum. Published by Reeves & Turner.

(*o.*) Godefrey of Boloyne. Reprinted from Caxton's edition of 1481, in large 4to. Troy type. 300 copies published at £6 6s., and 6 copies on vellum at £21 each.

(*p.*) Cavendish's Life of Wolsey. Reprinted from the author's M.S. 8vo. 30th March 1893. Golden type. 250 copies printed, with 6 copies on vellum. Published by Reeves & Turner, 196 Strand.

"NIMROD."

" Nimrod " was the pseudonym adopted by Charles James Apperley, a well-known sporting author of fifty years ago and more. Apperley was born in 1778, and when twenty years of age served against the Irish rebels, afterwards settling down in Leicestershire, then, as now, the foremost hunting county in England. In 1822 he commenced to write on his favourite subject, and from then to the time of his death in 1843, articles and works flowed from his pen in quick succession.

"Nimrod's" best known book is the "Life of Mytton," which details the Quixotic behaviour of a Shropshire squire, whose reckless acts are even yet a frequent topic of conversation in the Midlands. The success of this book was no doubt materially enhanced by Alken's coloured and highly characteristic plates with which it is embellished.

All "Nimrod's" works are given below. They rank, with those of Pierce Egan and Surtees, as the best on the particular branch of sport to which they relate, and, like them, are highly esteemed by collectors of English printed books throughout the world.

1. Remarks on the Condition of Hunters, the Choice of Horses, and their Management. . . . By Nimrod. . . . London. Printed and Published by M. A. Pittman, 18 Warwick Square. . . . 1831.

O

Demy 8vo, published at 15s. The book contains title as above,
advertisement on one leaf (unpaged), contents (v–vii), and text
pp. 1–503. There are no illustrations, though Turner's twelve
plates are often found inserted.

The series of articles reprinted in this volume, appeared originally in the *Sporting Magazine* at intervals between 1822 and
1828.

Value about £1 5s. (original cloth, with Turner's plates inserted,
auction), or about 10s. or 12s. (without the plates, *ibid.*).

Fourth Edition, London, 1855, 8vo. This and the two prior
editions are of little consequence.

2. Nimrod's Hunting Tours, interspersed with
   Characteristic Anecdotes, Sayings, and Doings
   of Sporting Men . . . to which are added
   Nimrod's Letters on Riding to Hounds. . . .
   London. M. A. Pittman, Warwick Square.
   1835.

Published in demy 8vo at 15s. The book contains title as
above, advertisement (iii–v), analytical contents (vii–xvi), and
text pp. 1–598. There are no illustrations.

The "Hunting Tours" originally appeared, in the form of a
series of articles entitled "Letters on Hunting," in the pages of
the *Sporting Magazine*, and were now reprinted for the first time,
without any addition, but with the omission of all extraneous
matter not connected with fox-hunting.

Value about 10s. (original cloth, auction).

In 1838 a new work appeared under the title of "Nimrod's
Northern Tour, descriptive of the Principal Hunts in Scotland
and the North of England." The book was published by Walter
Spiers at the *New Sporting Magazine* office, demy 8vo.

It contains title as above, preface on an unpaged leaf, and text
pp. 1–427, with 4 pp. of index, not numbered. There are no
illustrations in this work.

The "Northern Tour" appeared in the *New Sporting Magazine*, but was greatly delayed at times, so that its continuity was often broken. Anticipating considerable inconvenience by reason of this, the proprietors took off a limited impression, as the work passed through the pages of the magazine, in order that purchasers might have it in a connected form, without searching through the various volumes in which it lies scattered.

Value about £1 (original pictorial cloth, auction).

3. The Chace, the Turf, and the Road. By Nimrod. . . . London. John Murray, Albemarle Street. MDCCCXXXVII.

Published in demy 8vo, with portrait of " Nimrod " by Maclise and 13 full-page plates (uncoloured) by H. Alken.

The book contains the portrait as front, title as above, preface (unpaged), contents (unpaged), alphabetical table of contents (v–xvii), list of plates (xix–xx), half-title, and text pp. 3–301.

The papers here reprinted appeared originally in the *Quarterly Review.*

Value from 25s. to 30s. (original cloth, auction).

There are other editions of 1843, 12mo; 1852, 8vo (forming one of a series known as " Murray's Reading for the Rail ") ; and 1870, 8vo. Each essay has also been published separately. None of these issues are of much consequence with the exception of the edition of 1870, which has the plates coloured. Good copies of this sell for about £1 5s. (original cloth, auction).

4. Memoirs of the Life of the Late John Mytton, Esq. of Halston, Shropshire. . . . By Nimrod. . . . London. Rudolph Ackermann. . . . 191 Regent Street. 1837.

This well-known work was published in demy 8vo at 25s., and contains engraved title, title as above, preface (iii–v), contents (vii–ix), list of plates (unpaged), and text pp. 1–206. The engraved title is sometimes found coloured, but more often not.   There are 18 highly coloured full-page plates by Alken and Rawlins.

Value about £5 (original cloth, auction).

Second Edition, demy 8vo, 1837, made up in precisely the same manner as above, but lettered "Second Edition" on the title-page. Value about £5 (original cloth, auction).

Another Edition, demy 8vo, 1869, Routledge, with all the coloured plates, about 17s. (original cloth, auction).

Another Edition, demy 8vo, 1851, R. Ackermann, with all the coloured plates, about £3 10s. (original cloth).

Another Edition, with a Memoir of Nimrod, Routledge, 1892, pp. xi, 235.

5. Sporting, Embellished by Large Engravings and Vignettes Illustrative of British Field Sports. . . . Edited by Nimrod. . . . London.   A. H. Baily & Co., 83 Cornhill.   MDCCCXXXVIII.

An imperial 4to book containing front, engraved title, plain title, dedication (unpaged), introduction (i–viii), contents (unpaged), "List of Embellishments" (unpaged), and text pp. 1–144.   It was published at £2 2s.

The steel plates and woodcuts (38 in number) are after Gainsborough, Landseer, Cooper, and other well-known artists ; the text by Tom Hood and other contributors.

Value about £1 5s. (original cloth).

6. Nimrod's Northern Tour, 1838.   See *ante*, No. 2.

7. Nimrod Abroad.   By C. J. Apperley, Esq., Author of "The Chase, the Turf, and the Road," etc., etc.   London.   Henry Colburn, Publisher, Great Marlborough Street.   1842.

This work was published in 2 vols. post 8vo, cloth, at 12s.

Vol. i. contains title, contents (iii–ix), and text pp. 1–285.
Vol. ii. contains title, contents (iii–viii), and text pp. 1–306.
Value about 12s. (original cloth, auction).

8. The Horse and the Hound : their Various Uses
   and Treatment. . . . By Nimrod.   Adam &
   Charles Black, Edinburgh.   1842.

Published in crown 8vo, cloth, at 10s. 6d.   An engraved front
by Dobbie faces title as above, and there are pp. iii–viii, 524,
eight full-page plates (inclusive of front), vignette on title, and
woodcuts.

Value, the published price or near it.

Another Edition, Black, 1858, 8vo, of little importance.

9. The Life of a Sportsman.   By Nimrod.   London.
   Rudolph Ackermann. . . . MDCCCXLII.

Demy 8vo, published at 42s., with 36 highly coloured plates by
Alken.

The work is made up as follows :—Coloured front, coloured title,
plain title, preface (iii–vi), contents with list of illustrations on the
reverse, and text pp. 1–402.

This work is very scarce, especially when clean and otherwise
in good condition.   Under these circumstances a copy would sell
by auction at from £6 to £7.

Another Edition, 1874, demy 8vo, Routledge, with all the
coloured plates.   Good copies of this edition, in the original cloth,
sell for about £1 (auction).

10. Hunting Reminiscences : comprising Memoirs
    of Masters of Hounds ; Notices of the Crack
    Riders. . . . By Nimrod. London. Rudolph
    Ackermann. . . . 1843.

Demy 8vo, published at 16s., containing engraved front, engraved title, plain title, preface (iii–iv), contents (v–ix), with list of illustrations on the reverse, and text pp. 1–332. There are 32 full-page plates and maps by Wildrake, Alken, and Henderson, not coloured.

Value from £3 to £3 10s. (original cloth, auction).

———

In Captain Malet's well-known "Annals of the Road," published by Longmans, Green & Co. in 1876, certain "Essays on the Road," by "Nimrod," are to be found at p. 177. These essays first appeared in the form of letters to the *Sporting Magazine*, and were now reprinted in this volume.

Captain Malet's work above referred to is a thick 4to, bound in bright red pictorial cloth. It contains 10 full-page coloured plates, and 3 woodcuts. A good copy of this book sells by auction for about £1 5s. (original cloth).

D. G. ROSSETTI.

THE published works in volume form attributed to Rossetti
number but four, though to this computation may perhaps
be added the collected edition of his works published in two
vols. 8vo, 1886, since this contains several pieces, in poetry
or prose, which then saw the light for the first time.

The Painter-Poet commenced his literary career when a
schoolboy, with a privately printed "Legendary Tale" in
verse, called "Sir Hugh the Heron." This has not been
reprinted, though Mr. Joseph Knight's assertion that it "has
hitherto escaped the attention of the grubbers after early
productions of genius" is inaccurate. "Sir Hugh the
Heron" was perfectly well known in 1887, the date of
Mr. Knight's monograph in the "Great Writer" series, and
copies, though rarely met with, are not by any means unprocurable. Moreover, it bears its author's name on the
title, and could not therefore be universally overlooked, like
so many anonymous publications have been and are.

In 1850 the *Germ* appeared under the editorship of
William Rossetti. This periodical, which expired with its
fourth number, is remarkable for the high quality of its
contents. William and Christina Rossetti, Ford Madox
Brown, Coventry Patmore, Arthur Hugh Clough, Woolner,
and Dante Rossetti, all contributed to its pages, though
even their combined efforts failed to keep it alive. It was
essentially the organ of a cult, afterwards of world-wide
fame, but then perhaps misunderstood or altogether ignored.
The four numbers of the *Germ* are very scarce, selling by
auction for as much as £6 to £8. They were published in

January, February, March, and May 1850 respectively, in pale pink wrappers.　No number appeared in April, though some copies of the fourth number have the word "April" pasted over "May."

The prose allegory by Dante Rossetti, which appeared in the *Germ*, entitled "Hand and Soul," was afterwards privately reprinted.　Only a few copies of this pamphlet were circulated among friends.　One sold by auction in June 1891 for £1 18s.

Another work with which the name of Rossetti is intimately connected, is Gilchrist's "Life of Blake," 2 vols. 8vo, 1863, vol. i. containing certain additions from his pen, and vol. ii. being edited throughout by him.　With these exceptions, most of the literary compositions attributed to Rossetti will be found in the works subsequently described and in the collective editions of his works published in 1886 and 1891, though it may be mentioned that in conjunction with William Morris, E. Burne Jones, and others, he contributed to the *Oxford and Cambridge Magazine*, which had a short life in 1856 (*see* introductory notes to the Bibliography of William Morris), as well as to several other periodicals.

1. Sir Hugh the Heron : a Legendary Tale, in Four Parts.　By Gabriel Rossetti, Junior. . . . London.　MDCCCXLIII.　G. Polidori's Private Press, 15 Park Village East, Regent's Park. (For Private Circulation only.)

This scarce pamphlet was privately printed in 4to wrappers. There is no half-title, and after title as above follows text of the poem, pp. 3–24.　Rossetti is said to have been thirteen years old when he composed these lines, and was but fifteen when they were printed.

"Sir Hugh the Heron" is met with occasionally in the auction room. A copy in the original covers, as issued, sold at Sotheby's in December 1890 for £16. It would probably bring more now.

2. The Early Italian Poets from Ciullo D'Alcamo to Dante Alighieri (1100–1200–1300) in the Original Metres, together with Dante's Vita Nuova. Translated by D. G. Rossetti. . . . London. Smith, Elder & Co., 65 Cornhill. 1861.

Post 8vo, published in cloth at 12s. The work contains half-title, title as above, inscription (unpaged), preface (vii–xii), contents (xiii–xx), a second half-title ("Part i., Poets chiefly before Dante"), table of poets in part i. (xxiii–xxxvi), and text, pp. 1–464. An unpaged leaf of "Errata" follows the last page. The second part of this volume is entitled "Dante and his Circle," and consists of a lengthy introduction (pp. 189–222), "La Vita Nuova" of Dante, and "Dante and his Circle" (pp. 310–436). A revised and re-arranged edition of this second part appeared in 1874 (Ellis & White, pp. xxii, 468), and again in 1892 (pp. xl, 403).

Rossetti's translation of "La Vita Nuova" as it appears in this work was, with the omission of some of the notes, published at New York in 1866 by James Miller. The book, which is des-cribed as, "By the Author of Remarks on the Sonnets of Shakes-peare," contains many of Dante's Sonnets as translated by Rossetti, as well as numerous other pieces. "Notes on Pythagoras," &c., &c.

The value of a good copy of the "Early Italian Poets" is about £3 by auction. The author etched a plate for the work, which, after one or two impressions had been struck off, was cancelled. Copies containing it are worth three or four times the sum quoted. One was in the library of the late William Bell Scott. "Dante and his Circle," 1874, in the original cloth gilt, is worth from 20s. to 25s. by auction.

3. Poems. By Dante Gabriel Rossetti. London. F. S. Ellis, 33 King Street, Covent Garden. 1870.

Post 8vo, bound in navy-blue cloth, with gilt design of roses and trellis-work on side, lettered on face in gilt. Twenty-four copies were printed on large paper.

The work contains half-title, title, dedication to W. M. Rossetti, contents (vii–xi), and text (pp. 1–282). A second edition of this work was published the same year, but it cannot be mistaken for the first, as it is lettered "Second Edition" on the title-page. A pirated edition was also published at Boston in 1870. In 1881 a third edition of these poems appeared, the contents being almost, though not quite, the same as those of the edition of 1870. A few pieces were omitted, and one or two others added. An edition of 1882, published by Roberts Brothers of Boston, contains a very extensive collection of Rossetti's poems, including all those which appeared in the English editions of 1870 and 1881. A portrait of Rossetti faces the title.

A good copy of the first edition of 1870 sells by auction for about £3 3s., or, if on large paper, for about £10 10s.

4. **Ballads and Sonnets. By Dante Gabriel Rossetti. London. Ellis & White, 29 New Bond Street, W. 1881.**

A post 8vo book, containing half-title, title as above, dedication to Theodore Watts, contents (v–xii), and text (pp. 3–335). Of the poems appearing in this volume, fifty-four had been previously published, the rest were new. Twenty-four copies of this work were published on large paper.

Value about £2 (original cloth, auction), or £7 7s. (large paper, *ibid.*).

An edition of the entire "Poetical Works of Dante Gabriel Rossetti," with etched portrait and preface by W. M. Rossetti, was published in 1891 on large as well as on small paper. The large-paper copies are worth about £1, selling as a rule for something less at auction.

JOHN RUSKIN.

In addition to the works mentioned in chronological order
below, reference may conveniently be made to a few other
publications which for one reason or another it has been
thought undesirable to describe in full. The ground of the
omission is generally the unimportance of the items from
the collector's standpoint, or the fact that in some cases
Mr. Ruskin merely contributed an introduction or notes,
and had no hand in the work itself.

The omissions include "The Opening of the Crystal
Palace, considered in some of its Relations to the Prospects
of Art," a shilling pamphlet published in a buff-coloured
wrapper, 1854; "Catalogue of the Sketches and Drawings
by J. M. W. Turner, R.A., exhibited in Marlborough House
in the years 1856-7-8" (two pamphlets); "Catalogue of
the Turner Sketches in the National Gallery," printed by
Spottiswoode & Co. for private circulation in 1857. This
pamphlet is not complete, for which reason the second and
enlarged edition, also published in 1857, is preferable, especially as only a very small number of copies were circulated
"The Unity of Art," a lecture delivered at the Manchester
School of Art on Feb. 22, 1859. A few copies of this pamphlet
are believed to have been printed on larger sized paper
(imperial), and these doubtless are scarce enough. "Leoni,
a Legend of Italy," 1868, a rare pamphlet of 16 pp., which
sells readily for £5. This I have not been able to meet
with, and the same remark applies to "The Sepulchral
Monuments of Italy," printed for the Arundel Society in

1872, and now worth about 17s. 6d. "The Nature and Authority of Miracle," 1873, is a privately printed pamphlet of 16 pp. of some little importance. "Frondes Agrestes; Readings in 'Modern Painters,'" a work published at 3s. 6d. in 1875, and now worth a little, but not much, more.

In like manner, passing notice may be taken of "Yewdale and its Streamlets," a pamphlet published at 3d. in 1877; "The Pleasures of England," published in (four) shilling parts in 1884; "The Storm Cloud of the Nineteenth Century," 1884; "Dilecta: Correspondence, Diary Notes, and Extracts from Books," of which two parts only have so far appeared (1886–87); "Cœli Enarrant, Studies of Cloud Form," 1885 (one part, 4to, at 1s. 6d.); "In Montibus Sanctis, Studies of Mountain Form," 1885 (two parts, at 1s. 6d.); and "Letters upon Subjects of General Interest," privately printed in 8vo, pp. xii, 101, 1892.

In 1868 Mr. Ruskin wrote the introduction to "German Popular Stories," published by Hotten in the same year, and in 1874 the introduction and notes to the "Catalogue of the Plates of Turner's Liber Studiorum," a 4to book containing facsimiles of three etchings. Introductions from the same pen precede T. C. Horsfall's "The Study of Beauty and Art," 1883; W. G. Collingwood's "The Limestone Alps of Savoy," 1884; and Turner's "Rivers of France," 1887. None of these books can be consistently described in full here.

The works edited by Mr. Ruskin are of greater interest, and some of them are moreover usually catalogued under his name. These include, for example, Mrs. Francesca Alexander's "The Story of Ida," a pamphlet published at 1s. 6d. in 1883; and the same authoress's "Roadside Songs of Tuscany," George Allen, 1885, crown 4to, pp. vii, 340, with 20 illustrations. This work, which is important,

appeared originally in 10 parts, and was afterwards published at £3 10s. in cloth. The present value of a clean
copy as issued is about two guineas by auction. A third
book of Mrs. Alexander's was also edited by Mr. Ruskin,
viz., "Christ's Folk in the Apennines," 1887 ; and see also
Gotthelf's "Ulric the Farm Servant," a translation published
at 10s. in 8vo.

In 1885, "Dame Wiggins of Lee and her Seven Wonderful Cats" appeared in a new guise, with 4 illustrations by
Kate Greenaway, and 22 woodcuts. To this book Mr.
Ruskin contributed the preface and four new verses (3, 4,
8 and 9). An interesting note on the authorship of the
original rhyme will be found in the "Literary Gossip" of
the *Athenæum* for September 24, 1887, p. 409.

One point may be referred to in conclusion, and that is
the very great difficulty that has been experienced in pro-
curing good copies of many of Mr. Ruskin's works for comparison or collation. Some books, not particularly scarce in
themselves, have proved to be so under special circumstances, and when this is the case the most I could do was
to describe them as fully as possible from the copy before
me, and what I remember of better ones in times past.
Much further and far more minute information can readily
be obtained from Mr. T. J. Wise's "Bibliography of
Ruskin," without exaggeration a splendid monument of
industry and research, and one that is never likely to lose
its place in the esteem of those who have occasion to
consult it.

1. Salsette and Elephanta : a Prize Poem, Recited
   in the Theatre, Oxford, June 12, 1839, by
   John Ruskin, Christ Church, Oxford. Printed
   and Published by J. Vincent. MDCCCXXXIX.

This is a foolscap 8vo pamphlet of 19 pp. in a blue wrapper, lettered in the precise words of the title. The poem commences on p. 3.

The pamphlet is scarce, though copies are occasionally to be met with for some two or three guineas.

Another Edition, 1879, Allen, fcap. 8vo, published at 1s.

2. Modern Painters : their Superiority in the Art of Landscape Painting to all the Ancient Masters proved by Examples of the True, the Beautiful, and the Intellectual, from the Works of Modern Artists, especially from those of J. M. W. Turner, Esq., R.A.   By a Graduate of Oxford. . . . London.   Smith, Elder & Co., 65 Cornhill.   1843.

The first volume of this work was published at 18s. in 1843, under the above title. It is a royal 8vo book in green (other colours are met with) cloth, lettered on face in gilt. There are no illustrations.

A second edition of this first volume appeared in 1844. It cannot be mistaken for the first, as the date is different, and the title is lettered "Second Edition." This book is also in royal 8vo.

A third edition of the first volume was published in 1846, but this time in imperial 8vo, in order to match the first edition of vol. ii., which had just been issued. This third edition contains pp. lxiii, 422, and was published in a green cloth binding. The prefaces are those to the first and second editions. A clean uncut copy is worth about 15s.

A fourth edition of the first volume was issued in 1848, imperial 8vo, and the fifth, sixth, and seventh editions in 1851, 1857, and 1867 respectively, all in imperial 8vo.

. The second volume of "Modern Painters" was published in

imperial 8vo, 1846, and contains pp. xvi, 217. The binding is uniform with copies of the third edition of vol i. above mentioned.

A second edition of vol. ii. appeared in 1848, in a green cloth binding as before, and the third, fourth, and fifth editions in 1851, 1856, and 1869 respectively; the last two editions being reprints of the third, which, like all the other editions of this second volume, was published in imperial 8vo, green cloth.

It is worthy of note that a revised issue of this second volume appeared in 1883 and later, in a rearranged form, in 2 vols. crown 8vo, price 10s.

The third volume of " Modern Painters " was published in 1856 by Smith, Elder & Co., in imperial 8vo, green cloth, pp. xix, 348. It contains a frontispiece entitled " Lake, Land, and Cloud," engraved by Armytage after a drawing by Mr. Ruskin, 17 whole-page plates (that to face p. 208 coloured) by various artists, and numerous woodcuts in the text.

A second edition of this third volume appeared in 1867 in the usual green cloth, with all the illustrations.

The fourth volume of " Modern Painters " was also published in 1856 by the same firm. It is an imperial 8vo book, bound in green cloth as before, and containing pp. xii, 411. The illustrations, engraved or etched by different artists, include a frontispiece (" The Gates of the Hills," after Turner) and 34 full-page plates, besides numerous woodcuts, in the text.

A second edition of this fourth volume appeared in 1867 (1868?) in the usual green cloth, with all the illustrations.

The fifth and concluding volume of " Modern Painters " was published in 1860, imperial 8vo, pp. xvi, 384, in the customary green cloth. This volume contains, inclusive of frontispiece, 34 steel engravings (one unnumbered), and 8 separate engravings on wood.

No second edition was separately published at any time, but complete editions of the whole work appeared in 1873 (five volumes), and 1888 (six volumes, including index), imperial 8vo, green cloth, published at £6 6s. The edition of 1888 is uniform with the larger (imperial 8vo) editions of the "Stones of Venice," and "The Seven Lamps," and contains all the woodcuts, one lithograph, and the 86 full-page steel engravings, besides three hitherto unpublished ("The Lake of Zug," "Dawn after the Wreck," and "Chateau de Blois"), mezzotinted by Lupton after drawings by Mr. Ruskin. These three extra plates were originally intended for the fifth volume.

Each copy of the edition of 1873 contains Mr. Ruskin's signature at the end of the preface, from which cause it is often called the "Autograph Edition."

A complete index and collation of the different editions was published in 1888 at 14s.

It will be evident that a set of the earliest editions of "Modern Painters," *to match*, so far as size is concerned, would be the third edition of the first volume, 1846, and the original edition of each of the remaining four volumes published respectively in 1846–56, 1856–60. Mr. Ruskin enlarged the size from crown to imperial 8vo, with a view to having plates in the three last volumes, and as there are no plates in vols. i. and ii., later editions of these are considered the most important, as they contain corrections and additions by the author.

Good and clean copies of the early editions of "Modern Painters" in the original binding are exceedingly scarce. As a rule, sets offered for sale are "made up" from different editions, so that the valuation often becomes a rather complicated process.

A convenient set in the original cloth made up by vol. i. (fourth edition, 1848), vol. ii. (second edition, 1848), and vols. iii., iv., and v. (first editions of 1856, 1856 and 1860), realises from £15 to £20 by auction, according to condition and the freshness of the binding. A very bright set once brought £25. So long as the last three volumes belong to the first edition, the issue of the first and second volumes is not very material, from £15 to £20 being a very usual auction price (original cloth) in any case. Neither the first nor the second volume (original editions) is worth much more than about £1 10s. by auction, but original copies

of the three remaining volumes frequently bring as much as £5
and even £6 each (original cloth).

The edition of 1873, in 5 vols. imperial 8vo, sells for about
£10 10s. (original cloth), that of 1888, in 6 vols. imperial 8vo,
for about £12 (large paper, as issued), or for about £3 10s. to
£4 (small paper, *ibid.*).

3. The Seven Lamps of Architecture.   By John
   Ruskin, Author of "Modern Painters."   With
   Illustrations Drawn and Etched by the
   Author.   London.   Smith, Elder & Co., 65
   Cornhill.   1849.

Imperial 8vo, published in purple figured cloth, the edges gilt
at the top, lettered on face in gilt.   A half-title precedes title as
above, preface (v–viii), contents (ix–x), list of plates (xi), and text
pp. 1–205.   The plates, fourteen in number, were etched by the
author after his own designs.

Value about £4 (original cloth, auction).

Second Edition, 1855, imperial 8vo, pp. xx, 205, Smith, Elder
& Co.   This edition contains a new preface, in addition to that
which appeared to the first edition, and a fresh set of fourteen
plates after the same designs, by R. P. Cuff.   The frontispiece
was etched from a new drawing by Mr. Ruskin.   In other respects
the second edition does not materially differ from the first, though,
by reason of the additions mentioned above, it is usually called
"the best."

Value about £4 10s. (original cloth, auction).

Third Edition, 1880, imperial 8vo, pp. xvi, 222, George Allen.
Contains a fresh preface dated "Brantwood, February 25th, 1880."
The plates are the same as those in the second edition, but there
are some fresh notes, and the text is not always in the same
sized type as before.

Of this, the third edition, 75 copies were printed on larger
paper at £4 4s. each, the published price of the ordinary edition
being half that amount.

Value about £1 7s. (original cloth, auction); or £2 (large paper, *ibid.*).

Other Editions, 1883 and 1886, each in imperial 8vo, George Allen.

The published price of each of these editions was a guinea, and the present value is about one third less. A few copies of the edition of 1883 were printed on large paper, and bound in cloth.

4. Poems. J. R. Collected. 1850.

This extraordinarily scarce little book was issued for private circulation only. It is a fcap. 8vo, and contains half-title, and text pp. 3–283. Mr. Wise says that the book was published in green, or in some cases purple cloth, and that in most cases the edges of the leaves were "cut" and gilt. His own copy, which is quite "uncut," measures $7\frac{1}{4} \times 4\frac{1}{2}$ inches. Mr. Locker-Lampson's is in green cloth, with a device in gilt on the side, and gilt edges.

The work contains 51 distinct poems, of which 10 were now printed for the first time. The others had already appeared in the pages of *Friendship's Offering*, the *London Monthly Miscellany*, the *Amaranth*, and other periodicals.

No copy of this work has appeared in the market for a long time. There is, however, very little doubt that a stray copy in the original cloth would realise £50 or £60, or even more, if quite clean.

5. The King of the Golden River; or, the Black Brothers. A Legend of Stiria. Illustrated by Richard Doyle. London. Smith, Elder & Co., 65 Cornhill. MDCCCLI.

This is a small 4to book in glazed yellow boards. It contains frontispiece, pictorial title, title as above, advertisement (v), table of contents (vii), list of illustrations (viii), and text pp. 1–56. Though the title-page is dated 1851, the book was published about the end of the previous year. The illustrations by Doyle are 22 in number (inclusive of front and engraved title). The published price was 6s.

Value from £3 10 to £4 (original boards, auction).

Second Edition, 1851, small 4to, pp. viii, 56, Smith, Elder & Co. This edition is identical with the last, but the two cannot be mistaken, as the title-page is lettered "Second Edition."

Value about 10s. (as issued, auction).

Other Editions of less importance were published at later dates, generally at half-a-crown each.

The value does not much exceed the published price in any of these cases.

6. Pre-Raphaelitism. By the Author of "Modern Painters." London. Smith, Elder & Co., 65 Cornhill. 1851.

This pamphlet consists of title as above, dedication (iii–iv), preface (v–vi), and text pp. 7–68. It was published at 2s. in a wrapper. A "new edition" appeared in 1862.

Value of a clean copy of the original edition in boards as issued, about 12s.; of the reprint, about 4s.

7. The Stones of Venice. . . . By John Ruskin. . . . With Illustrations Drawn by the Author. London. Smith, Elder & Co., 65 Cornhill. 1851.

This work is complete in 3 vols. imperial 8vo, the first published in 1851 as above, and the other two in 1853. As different editions of the three volumes were published independently, at different times, it is necessary to deal with each volume separately.

The first edition of the first volume, the title-page of which is partly transcribed above, appeared in 1851, imperial 8vo. The book has half-title before title, after which follows preface (v–xii), contents (xiii–xv), list of plates (xvi), text pp. 1–413, and a slip

of "Errata." It was published in cloth at £2 2s. There are
21 full-page plates engraved by different artists, after drawings by
Mr. Ruskin.

A second edition of this first volume appeared in 1858 in
imperial 8vo, pp. xvi, 400. There is practically no difference
between this edition and the last.

The second volume of the "Stones of Venice" was published
at £2 2s. in 1853 by Smith, Elder & Co., in imperial 8vo, cloth.
It contains title, advertisement, contents (v–vi), list of plates (vii),
and text pp. 1–394. There are 20 full-page plates (Nos. iii. and v.
coloured), and two wood engravings on one leaf, facing p. 282.

A second edition of this second volume appeared in 1867. It
resembles the prior edition, save that the title-page is altered to
suit the exigencies of the case.

The third volume of the "Stones of Venice" was also published
in 1853 by the same firm, in imperial 8vo, cloth. The volume
contains title, contents, list of plates (iv), and text pp. 1–362. It
contains twelve plates by different engravers, after drawings by
Mr. Ruskin, and a few woodcuts.

A second edition of the third volume was published in 1867.
It resembles the first edition.

A complete issue of the "Stones of Venice" appeared in 1873–4,
in 3 vols., cloth, with top edges gilt, imperial 8vo, which, from
the circumstance of the preface in every copy being signed by the
author, is sometimes called the "Autograph Edition." Another
complete edition (called the fourth) was published in 3 vols.,
imperial 8vo, 1886, at £4 9s. (inclusive of new index), and of
this there was a special issue on hand-made paper, plates on India
paper, green cloth. Wedderburn's "Index" (1886) should be
bound up with the third volume.

In 1879–81 Mr. Ruskin published the introductory chapters
and local indices contained in the "Stones of Venice," for the

use of travellers while staying in Venice and Verona. This abridgment is complete in two small 8vo volumes, published at 5s. each. Three other editions have appeared at intervals, but, as in the case of other works by Mr. Ruskin, each volume seems to have been regarded in the light of a separate publication, and was issued quite independently of the other.

The average auction value of the 3 vols., 1851–53–53, which constitute the original edition, is from £12 to £15 according to condition (original cloth). A set of second editions of each volume, 1858–67–67, brings from £3 10s. to £4 (*ibid.*). The "Autograph Edition," 3 vols., imperial 8vo, 1873–74, sells readily enough at sums varying from £4 10s. to £5 (original cloth, auction), and the edition of 1886, also in 3 vols., imperial 8vo, for about £3 (*ibid.*). If any copy offered for sale is "made up" of two or more editions, the value will have to be estimated by reference to the proportionate worth of each volume, less a reasonable sum for want of uniformity in the series.

8. Examples of the Architecture of Venice. Selected and Drawn to Measurement from the Edifices. By John Ruskin. . . . London. Smith, Elder & Co., 65 Cornhill; and Paul and Dominic Colnaghi & Co., Pall Mall East. MDCCCLI.

This work was originally intended to consist of a dozen parts, but only three appeared, the undertaking being then discontinued. These parts were enclosed in greyish paper wrappers (atlas folio), and published at a guinea, though fifty copies of each with India proof plates were issued at double the price to subscribers only. No doubt an appropriate title-page would have been published with the last part. The first number contains six plates, and the second and third five each, making 16 plates in all, engraved by different artists, after drawings by Mr. Ruskin.

A set of the three parts as published, with India proof plates, was worth about 50 guineas by auction; a set of the proof plates, mounted on cardboard, in a portfolio, about £5. An odd part with plates in the ordinary state sells for about £2 10s.; a set of the parts in like condition for about £8 8s.

Second Edition, 1887, atlas folio, George Allen, published at £3 3s., or with India proofs at double that amount. It will be noticed that only the first edition was published in distinct parts at different periods, and that this second edition, whether on large or small paper, was issued complete in cases. Each plate has its appropriate description on a leaf facing it, and both plates and letterpress are loose.

Value from £3 to £4 (India proofs, in a case as issued), or about £1 15s. (ordinary impressions, *ibid.*).

9. Notes on the Construction of Sheepfolds. By John Ruskin. . . . London. Smith, Elder & Co. . . . 1851.

There are two editions of this date, but they cannot be mistaken, as the second is properly described on the title. The third edition of 1875 is erroneously described as "Second Edition," though the mistake appears to have been subsequently discovered, for the fourth edition of 1879 has the proper reference. All four editions of this pamphlet were published at 1s., post 8vo.

In 1890, a pamphlet containing two of Mr. Ruskin's letters on the subject of "Notes on the Construction of Sheepfolds" was printed for private distribution. This pamphlet is scarce, as a very small number of copies were distributed, but there is nothing very important about the "Notes" themselves.

10. Giotto and his Works in Padua : being an Explanatory Notice of the Series of Woodcuts Executed for the Arundel Society after the Frescoes in the Arena Chapel. By John Ruskin. Printed for the Arundel Society. 1854.

A square royal 8vo book in a yellow paper wrapper, containing pp. 7–96 (two parts only). A half-title precedes, then follows title as above, and "Advertisement" (unpaged). This work was printed in three parts, primarily for members of the Arundel Society, but a few copies were supplied to non-members at a higher price. The earliest issue has the imprint of Levey, Robson, and Franklyn on the reverse of half-title.

The series of woodcuts seems to have been published separately, and are occasionally met with in that state.

Value about 17s. 6d. (the three parts, in a wrapper).

11. Lectures on Architecture and Painting, Delivered at Edinburgh in November 1853. By John Ruskin. London. Smith, Elder & Co. . . . 1854.

A crown 8vo book published in cloth at 8s. 6d., containing viii pages of preliminary matter, and 239 pages of text. There are also 14 plates (exclusive of frontispiece), by the author, which are often placed together at the end of the volume.

Value about the published price (as issued, auction).

Second Edition, 1855, Smith, Elder & Co., published at 8s. 6d. This edition is a close reprint of the first.

The value of a clean copy of this edition does not exceed 5s. or 6s.

12. Notes on Some of the Principal Pictures Exhibited in the Rooms of the Royal Academy, 1855. By the Author of "Modern Painters." London. Smith, Elder & Co. . . . 1855.

This is the first of a series of "Notes" by Mr. Ruskin on the chief Academy pictures of 1855, 1856, 1857, 1858, 1859, and 1875.

Each of these pamphlets went through several editions, but all the examples I have seen have the number of the edition stated on the title-page. Copies of the original edition of the Academy Notes for 1855 are not often seen now.

Value about £1 10s. (the six parts as issued, auction).

13. The Harbours of England. Engraved by Thomas Lupton from Original Drawings Made Expressly for the Work by J. M. W. Turner, R.A.; with Illustrative Text by J. Ruskin, Author of "Modern Painters." London. Published by E. Gambart & Co. . . . 1856.

This is a royal 4to book containing pp. vii–53. There are 12 plates in mezzotint by Lupton, a limited number of which were impressed on India paper.

Value about £1 10s. (original cloth, auction).

Second Edition, N.D. (but about 1856), Gambart & Co., royal 4to, published in cloth, lettered in gilt on side and face.

Value about £1 (original cloth, auction).

There are altogether five editions of the "Harbours of England," the two above mentioned and three others, which are made up in precisely the same way as the second, and are found in different coloured cloths.

The value of clean copies of these editions averages from 15s. to £1 (original cloth).

14. The Political Economy of Art: being the Substance (with Additions) of Two Lectures Delivered at Manchester, July 10th and 13th, 1857. By John Ruskin, M.A. . . . London. Smith, Elder & Co. . . . 1857.

This is a small book in 12mo, green cloth, published at half-a-crown. A later edition, under the title of "A Joy for Ever (and its price in the market)," appeared in 1880 at 18s. (dark blue calf antique, with gilt edges), and on subsequent occasions.

The value of a clean copy of the original edition of "The Political Economy of Art" does not exceed a few shillings.

15. The Elements of Drawing: in Three Letters to Beginners. By John Ruskin, M.A. . . . With Illustrations Drawn by the Author. London. Smith, Elder & Co. . . . 1857.

A crown 8vo book in green cloth, containing half-title, title, preface (v–xxii), contents (unpaged), text pp. 1–350, and a number of woodcuts in the text after Mr. Ruskin's drawings. A second edition appeared in 1857, and a third in 1859, though some copies of the last edition are dated 1860, and others 1861. The published price of each of these editions was 7s. 6d., and there is very little variation between them.

Value about 15s. (original edition. cloth as issued). Copies of the second edition sell almost as well as the first.

16. The Elements of Perspective: Arranged for the Use of Schools, and Intended to be Read in Connexion with the First Three Books of Euclid. By John Ruskin, M.A. . . . London. Smith, Elder & Co. . . . 1859.

Published in green cloth, post 8vo, at 3s. 6d., containing pp. xii, 144. A half-title precedes title, and there are numerous geometrical figures in the text.

Value about 7s. 6d. (original cloth).

17. The Two Paths: being Lectures on Art, and its Application to Decoration and Manufacture, Delivered in 1858–9. By John Ruskin, M.A. . . . London. Smith, Elder & Co. . . . 1859.

A crown 8vo book in ornamental cloth. A half-title should precede title, and there are pp. xi, 271, and two full-page illustrations (one frontispiece), besides woodcuts in the text. The book was published at 7s. 6d. It was reprinted in 1878 in the 10th volume of Mr. Ruskin's "Collected Works," published by George Allen, and there are several later editions.

The value of a clean copy of the original edition is about 12s. (cloth, as issued).

18. "Unto this Last:" Four Essays on the First Principles of Political Economy. By John Ruskin. London. Smith, Elder & Co. . . . 1862.

A book in 12mo, published at 3s. 6d. in green cloth. It contains pp. xix, 174. Many later editions have appeared, the eighth being now in print, and to be had from the publishers for 3s.

Value about 5s. (original edition, cloth as issued).

19. Sesame and Lilies: Two Lectures Delivered at Manchester in 1864. By John Ruskin, M.A. I. Of Kings' Treasuries. II. Of Queens' Gardens. . . . London. Smith, Elder & Co. . . . 1865.

This book is a fcap. 8vo. It contains half-title, title, and pp.

196. A second edition was published the same year, and there are several later ones, notably what was called a "Revised and Enlarged Edition," constituting the first volume of Mr. Ruskin's "Collected Works," published in 1871 &c. at 7s.

Value about 10s. (original edition, cloth). Copies of the later editions sell for about 5s. each.

20. The Ethics of the Dust : Ten Lectures to Little Housewives on the Elements of Crystallisation. By John Ruskin, M.A. London. Smith, Elder & Co. . . . 1866.

A crown 8vo book in brown cloth, lettered in gilt on face and side. It contains half-title, title, dedication (v), preface (vii–ix), contents (xi), "Personæ" (xiii), and text pp. 1–244. A second edition with an additional preface appeared in 1877, and there are several of later date, notably a third edition of 1883.

The value of a clean copy of the original edition is some 5s. or 6s. ; of the others, less.

21. The Crown of Wild Olive : Three Lectures on Work, Traffic, and War. By John Ruskin, M.A. . . . London. Smith, Elder & Co. . . . 1866.

This is a fcap. 8vo book containing title, preface (xxxiv), contents (xxxv), half-title, and text pp. 1–219. Second and third editions the same in all respects as the first, and published at the same price (5s.), appeared in 1866 and 1867 respectively, and then the text was reprinted as vol. vi. of Mr. Ruskin's "Collected Works," 1871 &c., and at later dates.

The present value of a clean copy of the original edition of 1866 is a little more than the published price.

22. Time and Tide, by Weare and Tyne : Twenty-Five Letters to a Working Man of Sunderland on the Laws of Work. By John Ruskin, LL.D. . . . London. . . . Smith, Elder & Co. . . . 1867.

A fcap. 8vo book in dark reddish-brown cloth, published at 1s. 6d. It contains viii pp. of preliminary matter, and pp. 1–199 of text. A second and precisely similar edition appeared in 1868, and then the book was reprinted as vol. v. of Mr. Ruskin's "Collected Works," 1871 &c.

A clean copy of the edition of 1867 sells for about 7s. 6d. ; of the second edition for about 2s. 6d.

23. The Queen of the Air : being a Study of the Greek Myths of Cloud and Storm. By John Ruskin, LL.D. London. Smith, Elder & Co. . . . 1869.

This first edition of "The Queen of the Air" was published in green cloth at 6s. There is no half-title, but after title follows preface (iii–viii), and text pp. 1–199. A second edition precisely similar in every respect to the first was published later in the same year, and then the book was reprinted as vol. ix. of Mr. Ruskin's "Collected Works," 1871 &c. "The Queen of the Air" was also published separately on several later occasions. There is a New York edition of 1885, pp. 130, fcap. 8vo, J. B. Alden.

Value of an original copy about 10s. (cloth, as issued).

24. Lectures on Art : Delivered before the University of Oxford, in Hilary Term, 1870. By John Ruskin, M.A. . . . Oxford. At the Clarendon Press. MDCCCLXX.

Published at 6s. A half-title precedes title, after which follow contents (unpaged), note (unpaged), and text pp. 1–189. A second edition appeared in 1875, and a fourth in 1887 (1888?) There is no material difference between any of these editions.

Value of a copy of the original edition about 8s. (original cloth). Copies of the later editions are worth less.

25. Fors Clavigera : Letters to the Workmen and Labourers of Great Britain. By John Ruskin, LL.D. . . . London. Smith, Elder & Co., 15 Waterloo Place. N.D. (but 1871).

The 96 letters forming the complete series of "Fors Clavigera" are met with in 8 volumes, grey boards, crown 8vo, 1882–84. The letters were in the first instance issued quite independently of one another, and at different times, No. 1 appearing on the 1st of January 1871, and the remainder at intervals of one month, to the end of the series (vol. viii., 1884). Each number was published at 7d. or 10d., in a wrapper which was light grey in some cases, and light yellow in others. Indices to portions of "Fors Clavigera" have been published on different occasions, but the first complete index was published by George Allen in 1887, pp. xv, 503. It must be remembered that subsequent editions of many of these single letters were published, and as Mr. Ruskin made many alterations and additions in the later issues, an ideal set would comprise a copy of each.

A set of the 96 parts, original issue, in the wrappers, with the index of 1887 in boards as issued, sells by auction for about £4. Bound copies rarely bring more than about £3 ; frequently not so much.

26. Munera Pulveris : Six Essays on the Elements of Political Economy. By John Ruskin. . . . London. . . . Smith, Elder & Co. . . . And Mr. G. Allen, Heathfield Cottage, Keston, Kent. 1872.

This work is mentioned here although it forms vol. ii. of Mr.
Ruskin's "Collected Works," 1871 &c., because that is the earliest
form in which it can be obtained.   The essays originally appeared
in *Fraser's Magazine*, and were finally collected and published in
separate form as above stated.   "Munera Pulveris" is in effect a
sequel to "Unto this Last" (see *ante*, No. 18).   Like all the other
volumes in the "Collected Edition" of 1871, it was published in
dark blue calf antique, with gilt edges, and lettered in gilt on
the face.

Value from 8s. to 10s. (as issued).

27.　Aratra Pentelici : Six Lectures on the Elements
　　　　of Sculpture, given before the University of
　　　　Oxford, in Michaelmas Term, 1870.   By John
　　　　Ruskin. . . . London. . . . Smith, Elder &
　　　　Co. . . . And sold by Mr. G. Allen. . . .
　　　　1872.

As in the case of "Munera Pulveris" (see No. 26), this work
forms one of the volumes (vol. iii.) of Mr. Ruskin's "Collected
Works," 1871 &c.   There are, as usual, two title-pages, after which
follow contents (unpaged), preface (vii–xii), and text pp. 1–207.
A second edition appeared in 1879, and a cheaper edition in 1890.
Each contains coloured and other illustrations.

28. The Eagle's Nest : Ten Lectures on the Re-
　　　　lation of Natural Science to Art, given before
　　　　the University of Oxford, in Lent Term,
　　　　1872.   By John Ruskin. . . . London. . . .
　　　　Smith, Elder & Co., . . . And sold by Mr.
　　　　G. Allen. . . . 1872.

This volume is the fourth in Mr. Ruskin's "Collected Works,"
1871 &c.   It is bound as usual in dark blue calf antique, with

gilt edges, lettered on face, and contains pp. viii–232.   A second edition was published without alteration (except that the title is marked "Second Thousand") in 1880, at 18s., and a cheap edition appeared in 1887.

29. Ariadne Florentina : Six Lectures on Wood and Metal Engraving. . . . given before the University of Oxford, in Michaelmas Term, 1872.   By John Ruskin, LL.D. . . . George Allen, Sunnyside, Orpington, Kent.   1876.

This work forms the seventh volume of Mr. Ruskin's "Collected Works," 1871 &c., and, like the rest in the series, was published in dark blue calf antique, with gilt edges, lettered on face.   Some copies are met with in boards.

The volume contains the two titles, contents (v–vi), half-title, a third title, "Advice," and text pp. 1–266.   There are four engravings on wood from Holbein's "Dance of Death," and a number of autotype plates and woodcuts.   A second and cheaper edition appeared in 1890 at 7s. 6d.

"Ariadne Florentina" was originally published in two parts, consisting of "Definition of the Art of Engraving," 1873, price 1s., and "Appendix," 1876, price 2s. 6d.   Each part was published in a slate-coloured wrapper.

A clean copy of the first edition sells by auction for 5s. or 6s. ; of the later edition for considerably less.

30. Val D'Arno : Ten Lectures on the Tuscan Art, Directly Antecedent to the Florentine Year of Victories, given before the University of Oxford, in Michaelmas Term, 1873.   By John Ruskin. . . . George Allen, Sunnyside, Orpington, Kent.   1874.

This work forms the eighth volume of Mr. Ruskin's "Collected

Works," 1871 &c. It is bound in the usual dark blue calf antique.
After the two title-pages there are pp. 230 of text, with thirteen
full-page plates, inclusive of front. A second edition appeared in
1882 in boards, and a cheaper edition at 7s. 6d. in 1890.

31. Mornings in Florence : being Simple Studies
    of Christian Art for English Travellers. By
    John Ruskin, LL.D. . . . George Allen. . . .
    1875.

The six parts in which this work was originally published,
appeared in stiff reddish-brown wrappers, gilt lettered on the side,
post 8vo, between the years 1875 and 1877. The pagination,
commencing with page 1 of the first part, ends with page 187
in part six. After the publication of the final part, the series was
bound up with all the titles and half-titles. There is no half-
title to the first part. A second edition, also in parts, was commenced in 1881, but is lettered " Second Edition " on the title,
so that there can be no chance of any mistake arising.

A clean copy of the original edition, whether in parts or bound,
is worth about 8s. The edition now in print is the third (4s.
cloth).

32. Proserpina : Studies of Wayside Flowers, while
    the Air was yet Pure among the Alps, and in
    the Scotland and England which my Father
    knew. By John Ruskin, LL.D. . . . George
    Allen. . . . 1875.

" Proserpina " is in two series, post 8vo, the first containing six
parts, and the second four (the last dated 1885). The first six
parts are also found in volume form (dated 1879), with half-title,
title, contents, a second title, and pp. 287. The volume contains
13 full-page plates, and a number of woodcuts in the text.

The four parts that form the second series were issued in buff-
coloured wrappers, and have never been published in volume

form, being as yet incomplete. They contain seven engravings inclusive of fronts, and a number of woodcuts in the text.

A second edition of vol. i. was published in 1882 in boards at 10s., but is so dated on the title-page. It must also be remembered that there is more than one edition of the first six parts. No mistake can however arise, as each new edition was properly described as such on the title of each part as issued. The first four parts of the second series are still in print, and can be had from the publisher for 1s. 8d. each.

Value 6s. or 8s. (the first six parts, as issued).

33. Deucalion : Collected Studies of the Lapse of
    Waves, and Life of Stones. By John Ruskin,
    LL.D. . . . George Allen. . . . 1875.

As in the case of "Proserpina" (see *ante*, No. 32), this work appeared originally in parts, six being allotted to the first series. The second series is incomplete, only two parts having as yet appeared.

The first part "Deucalion" was published in 1875, and the sixth in 1879, in which year the series was bound up and published in volume form at 15s. The book is a large 8vo, and contains six pages of preliminary matter, and pp. 1–290 of text. In addition to the frontispiece there are, or should be, six full-page plates (some coloured).

The two parts which are all that have, so far, appeared in the second series, were published in 1880 and 1883 respectively, at 2s. 6d. Each part contains two plates inclusive of front, and was issued in buff-coloured paper wrappers.

Value 6s. or 8s. (the first six parts, as issued).

34. Bibliotheca Pastorum. Edited by John Ruskin.
    . . . Ellis & White, 29 New Bond Street.
    London. And George Allen. . . . 1876.

This work should be complete in four parts, royal 8vo, but curiously enough the third part, though frequently announced, has not yet appeared. Each of the published parts was issued in stiff yellow boards at 7s. 6d., 1876 (part i.), 1877 (part ii.), and 1885 (part iv.) respectively. Only the first part has half-title, and there are no illustrations to any of the volumes. In part i. is, or should be, a slip dated "Brantwood, Longest day, 1876," in which Mr. Ruskin states that he has spoiled the engraving of Mr. Jones's design by his interference with it, and that he had ordered the old stamp of Fors to be employed instead. It never appeared, however.

Another peculiarity about this book is that the fourth volume (only) was published in parts (three).

Value about 10s. (the three parts, as issued).

35. St. Mark's Rest : The History of Venice, Written for the Help of the Few Travellers who still Care for her Monuments. By John Ruskin, LL.D. . . . George Allen, Sunnyside, Orpington, Kent. 1877.

This work was published in six parts, consisting of three parts properly so-called (1877, 1877 and 1879), an appendix (1884), and two supplements (1877 and 1879). Each part was issued in a stiff dark red wrapper, lettered on face in gilt, price 1s., and in 1884, when the series was complete, the whole was bound up into volume form and published in green cloth at 6s., post 8vo.

The present value of this book, in parts, is a little more than the published price. The bound volume can still be got from the publisher.

36. The Laws of Fésole : a Familiar Treatise on the Elementary Principles and Practice of Drawing and Painting, as Determined by the Tuscan Masters. Arranged for the Use of Schools. By John Ruskin, LL.D. . . . George Allen. 1877.

This work is described as "Volume I." on the first title, but volume ii. has, so far, not appeared. The work was originally published in parts, in paper wrappers, which parts were on their completion in 1879 bound up in volume form in boards, price 10s. A half-title should precede title as above, then follow contents (iii–iv), preface (v–xvi), text pp. 1–208, and twelve full-page steel plates (including front).

Value about the published price, in parts, but the bound volume is still in print, and the price appears to have been reduced by the publisher to 8s.

37. Notes by Mr. Ruskin on his Collection of Drawings. By the Late J. M. W. Turner, R.A. Exhibited at the Fine Art Society's Galleries. . . . London. Printed at the Chiswick Press, for the Fine Art Society, 148 New Bond Street. 1878.

The original edition of these notes took the form of a post 8vo guide of 101 pp., in wrappers.

No less than thirteen editions appeared in 1878, one of them (that described above) being illustrated with 35 steel plates and a map. This edition is in 4to, and was published in half Roxburghe at £1 11s. 6d., a hundred copies with India proof plates being issued in cloth at £2 12s. 6d. The work contains eleven pages of preliminary matter, and pp. 13–188.

Copies of the pamphlet sell for a few shillings each (any edition), but the illustrated edition of 1878 brings much more. A very usual price is from £1 10s. to £2 (half Roxburghe, as issued); or £4 (large paper, cloth, as issued).

38. Notes by Mr. Ruskin on Samuel Prout and William Hunt. Illustrated by a Loan Collection of Drawings Exhibited at the Fine Art Society's Galleries, 148 New Bond Street. 1879–80.

This work is a crown 8vo, pp. 108 (in slate-coloured wrappers), inclusive of appendices, catalogue, and list of contributors to the collection. It was published at 1s. 6d., as also were three other editions issued the same year.

In 1880 a very important illustrated edition in royal 4to appeared. It was printed on thick hand-made paper, and issued in half Roxburghe, with a frontispiece and 19 autotype plates.

The pamphlet of 1879 is not worth more than two or three shillings, but an uncut copy of the edition of 1880 would sell by auction for about £1 5s., more or less.

39. Arrows of the Chace : being a Collection of Scattered Letters, Published Chiefly in the Daily Newspapers, 1840–1880. By John Ruskin, LL.D. . . . George Allen, Sunnyside, Orpington, Kent.   1880.

This work was published in 2 vols., royal 8vo, boards, at £1 10s., or on large paper (4to) at £3. Only 110 copies were printed on large paper.

Vol. i. contains half-title, title as above, contents (v–viii), prefaces (ix–xxi), list of letters (xxii–xxv), another half-title, and text pp. 3–306.

Vol. ii. has half-title, title, contents (v–ix), list of letters (x–xv), half-title, and text, including index, pp. 3–348. The large-paper copies contain a frontispiece ("British Ferns") to vol. i.

Value about £1 15s. (large paper). Copies of the ordinary edition appear to be still procurable from the publisher.

40. "Our Fathers have Told Us :" Sketches of the History of Christendom for Boys and Girls who have been Held at its Fonts. By John Ruskin. . . . Part I.—The Bible of Amiens. . . . George Allen, Sunnyside, Orpington, Kent.   1880.

This work consists of "The Bible of Amiens," and was published originally in four parts, in yellow wrappers. The last part appeared in 1885, and the same year the series was bound up in volume form and sold at 6s. in cloth. A half-title should precede title, and there are 263 pp. of text. The five engravings (inclusive of front) are after drawings by the author.

Value about 5s. (original edition, cloth, as issued). The volume appears to be yet in print.

41. Love's Meinie : Lectures on Greek and English Birds. . . . By John Ruskin, LL.D. . . . George Allen. . . . 1881.

This work originally appeared in three parts (the third issued in 1881, "The Dabchicks, Preface and Appendix"), each embodying the contents of a separate lecture delivered during the year 1873, and made up in yellow wrappers. Afterwards, in 1881, the entire work was issued as above in stiff boards at 4s. 6d., the collective price of the parts.

Value about 5s. (in parts). The bound volume of 1881 is still in print.

42. The Art of England : Lectures Given in Oxford. By John Ruskin, D.C.L. . . . George Allen. . . . 1883.

A crown 4to book containing half-title, title as above, contents, a second title, half-title, and text pp. 1–292. It was published at 8s. in volume form, with title as above, though the lectures had previously appeared in seven shilling parts, the last containing appendix and index. A second edition of the work was published in 1887, and each of the parts passed through several editions.

Value about 10s. (original cloth or parts). Copies of the second edition are worth considerably less.

43. On the Old Road : a Collection of Miscellaneous Essays, Pamphlets, &c., &c. Published 1834–1885. By John Ruskin, LL.D. . . . George Allen . . . 1885.]

"On the Old Road" was published in 3 vols., crown 8vo, at £1 10s. (boards), or on large paper (4to). A half-title should precede title to each volume.

Value about £2 10s. (large paper, *ibid.*). The edition on ordinary paper is still in print.

44. Præterita : Outlines of Scenes and Thoughts perhaps Worthy of Memory in my Past Life. By John Ruskin, LL.D. . . George Allen. . . . 1885.

" Præterita " was originally published in shilling parts (or on large paper at 2s.), with greyish wrappers, every twelve of these parts being subsequently issued together in volume form. A first volume so made up appeared in 1885–86, a second in 1887, and a third is so far complete that four parts appear to have been issued (the first two dated 1888, and the last two 1889). Vol. i. contains a frontispiece (" My two Aunts "). A steel plate (" The Old Dover Packet's Jib ") also appears in vol. ii. In the large-paper copies, of which a few were published in 4to, both these plates are on India paper, and there is an additional plate (an etching of " The Castle of Annecy ") in vol. iii., chapter i., which does not appear in the ordinary copies.

Value from £1 15s. to £2 (vols. i. and ii., with the four parts of vol. iii. as issued, auction, large paper). Copies on ordinary paper are worth considerably less.

45. Hortus Inclusus : Messages from the Wood to the Garden, Sent in Happy Days to the Sister Ladies of the Thwaite, Coniston. By their Thankful Friend John Ruskin, LL.D. George Allen. . . . 1887.

This is a crown 8vo book in dark green cloth, containing pp. xiii, 172. The published price was 4s., but a small number of large-paper (demy 8vo) copies were issued at 10s. 6d.

Small-paper copies are worth about the published price, those on large paper from 12s. to 15s.

46. The Poems of John Ruskin : now First Collected from Original Manuscript and Printed Sources ; and Edited . . . by W. G. Collingwood. . . . George Allen, Sunnyside, Orpington, and Bell Yard, Temple Bar, London. 1891.

These collected poems are in two volumes, the first devoted to "Poems written in Boyhood, 1826–1835," and the second to "Poems written in Youth, 1836–1845, and later poems."

Vol. i. contains half-title, front, title as above, prefatory notes on the plates (v–xi), contents (xiii–xvi), list of illustrations (unpaged), editor's introduction (xix–xxviii), and text pp. 3–289. There are 14 plates inclusive of front.

Vol. ii. contains half-title, front, title, contents (v–viii), list of illustrations (unpaged), and text pp. 3–360. This volume contains 12 full-page plates inclusive of front.

The above collation has reference to the large-paper edition issued in 2 vols. (4to), half bound in vellum, with dark green cloth sides.

Value from £1 to £1 10s. (the two volumes as issued, auction).

47. The Poetry of Architecture ; or, The Architecture of the Nations of Europe Considered in its Association with Natural Scenery and National Character. . . . George Allen. . . . 1893.

Published in 1 vol. 4to, cloth, at £1 1s., with chromolithograph frontispiece, 14 plates in photogravure from unpublished drawings by the author, and 9 full-page and other new woodcuts, pp. 280.

This work was now reprinted in book form for the first time from the pages of *Loudon's Magazine*.

PERCY BYSSHE SHELLEY.

Mr. Buxton Forman, in his "Shelley Library" published at London in 1886, gives a complete descriptive list of the works of Shelley, from which it appears that there are several of this great poet's earlier productions that cannot now be traced. Although mentioned in advertisements of the period, in correspondence, reviews, and elsewhere, they have as completely disappeared as though they had never been written. These lost works consist of pamphlets like "Original Poetry. By Victor and Cazire," which seems to have been published in 1810, but of which no copy is now known to exist.

All Shelley's early publications were in pamphlet form, and particularly liable to be destroyed or lost, for people cared as little for pamphlets at the beginning of the century as they do now at the close of it, and for the most part treated them with scant courtesy. As a rule they were safe in so doing, for not one pamphlet out of many thousands has more than a passing interest, unless, indeed, it be the known production of some man already famous in the literary world. Shelley made his reputation with "Queen Mab," printed in 1813, and most of these vanished pamphlets were published before that date, when his name had not yet begun to be whispered abroad, and when whatever he wrote had to take its chance with the countless other publications of the day.

Every age furnishes similar examples of lost and forgotten works written by men who subsequently became famous; forgotten, that is to say, by every one but a few specialists, and lost for the time being, or for ever, to all. It is extremely probable that copies of these Shelley pamphlets are in existence somewhere, but being published anonymously or under an assumed name, and of mean exterior, they might pass through fifty hands and yet preserve their secret.

In July last a very interesting exhibition of Shelley relics was open to the public at the Guildhall. Among the books and pamphlets were the following rarities :—

(*a.*) "A Vindication of Natural Diet. Being One in a Series of Notes to 'Queen Mab.' A Philosophical Poem. . . . London. Printed for J. Callow, Medical Bookseller, Crown Court, Princes Street, Soho. . . . 1813." A foolscap 8vo pamphlet in a slate-coloured wrapper; only two perfect copies known. There is a reprint of 1884 (London, F. Pitman; Manchester, John Heywood) in light green paper covers.

(*b.*) A variation of "Hellas," 1882 (see *post*, No. 19), which contains some lines deleted from ordinary copies of the book. A second copy of this variety is in America.

(*c.*) "We Pity the Plumage but Forget the Dying Bird. An Address to the People on the Death of the Princess Charlotte. By the Hermit of Marlow." This is a reprint (executed by Thomas Rodd) of a pamphlet now lost. It is in a white paper cover, lettered as above, stitched.

Mr. Buxton Forman's Bibliography of Shelley, as given in his "Shelley Library," is a work of art. It is not merely a dry catalogue of his writings, but an extremely interesting and carefully constructed record of his literary life, compiled from sources frequently the most unlikely or obscure; a high tribute to the deep research and industry of its author.

The following list contains nearly all the published works of Shelley that are available to collectors. I have purposely omitted his lost writings, partly because it would be impossible to describe them, and also because Mr. Forman's work, which should be in the hands of every collector who includes Shelley in his repertory, is the proper authority to refer to.

For the recent publications of the "Shelley Society," consisting of facsimile reprints, reproductions of MSS., and much other useful matter, see their catalogue.

1. Zastrozzi, a Romance. By P. B. S. . . . London. Printed for G. Wilkie & J. Robinson, 57 Paternoster Row. 1810.

Published in 12mo, boards, at 5s.
The work contains half-title before title as above, and text pp. 252.
This is an excessively scarce little book, which might be expected to sell for about £25 in the original cover. In 1888 two copies made their appearance in the auction room, realising respectively £10 5s. (calf extra, by Bedford) and £5 15s. (morocco extra, by Pratt). In April 1890, an uncut copy in calf sold for £12 5s.

2. Posthumous Fragments of Margaret Nicholson ; being Poems found among the Papers of that Noted Female. . . . Edited by John Fitz-Victor. Oxford. Printed and Sold by J. Munday. 1810.

A 4to book containing half-title, title, advertisement (unpaged), and text pp. 7–29. Most, if not all, of the poems were written by Shelley.
There is a dangerous reprint of this book, which was published some twelve or fifteen years ago by R. H. Shepherd. It can be detected by reference to page 8, line 12, where the word "baleful" is printed "hateful."
In 1877 Mr. Buxton Forman privately reprinted the "Posthumous Fragments." A few copies were printed on vellum.

Mr. Forman's private reprint on vellum sells for about £4 (uncut).   The original is very rare (about £20 stitched).

3. St. Irvyne ; or the Rosicrucian : a Romance. By a Gentleman of the University of Oxford. London.   Printed for J. J. Stockdale, 41 Pall Mall.   1811.

A small but scarce book in 12mo, containing half-title, title, and text pp. 1–236.

This work did not sell at the time of its publication, and there was a very considerable remainder.   In 1822 the holders of the original sheets bound them up in brown boards with white label on the side, and published a number of copies with a fresh title-page (dated 1822).   This re-issue differs in no way from the original edition, except in the title.

Uncut copies of the first issue are very rare, selling readily enough by auction for £12 or £15, or more in the original boards. Copies of the re-issue are worth considerably less.

4. The Necessity of Atheism. . . . Worthing. Printed by E. & W. Phillips.   Sold in London and Oxford.   N.D. (but 1811).

This is a foolscap 8vo pamphlet, containing half-title, title, advertisement (unpaged), and text pp. 7–13.

For writing this defence of atheism, Shelley was sent down from his College for good.   Nearly all the copies were destroyed by the printers when attention was drawn to the noxious opinions of the author, and the few that escaped are very rarely seen.   I should assess the value of a clean copy of this pamphlet at somewhere about £20.

5. An Address to the Irish People.   By Percy Bysshe Shelley. . . . Dublin.   1812.

A demy 8vo pamphlet, containing title as above, and text pp. 22.

This miserable-looking print was published at 5d., on very bad paper, and with worn-out type.   The present value is nevertheless more than 350 times the published price, or about £8 by auction (cut), or £12 with the postscript (cut).

6.   Queen Mab : a Philosophical Poem ; with Notes. By Percy Bysshe Shelley. . . . London. Printed by P. B. Shelley, 23 Chapel Street, Grosvenor Square.   1813.

Crown 8vo, with title-page, dedication to Harriet * * * * * and pp. 1–240 of text.   A half-title follows p. 122.

Copies of the earliest issue have title as above, and on page 240 the same imprint, which was afterwards suppressed.

In 1891 a copy of the earliest issue, uncut, in the original brown boards, sold by auction for £22 10s., which would appear to be a good but not unusual price for uncut copies.   As usual, however, a great deal depends on the condition, and sometimes the work will not realise a fifth part of the amount stated.

Other editions of "Queen Mab" are often met with, notably W. Clarke's edition of 1821 (the first *published* edition) ; Carlyle's editions of 1822, 1823, and 1826 ; a New York edition of 1821 ; and Brooks' edition of 1829.

The value of each of these editions is about the same, viz., 15s. by auction (original boards).

7.   A Vindication of Natural Diet. . . . London. . . . Smith and Davy, Queen Street, Seven Dials.   1813.

Published in 12mo, in slate-coloured wrappers, at 1s. 6d.   The pamphlet contains half-title, title, and text pp. 1–43.

This is a scarce piece, which would probably sell for £50 or £60 in the original wrappers, as issued.   See *ante*, p. 250 (*a*).

8. A Refutation of Deism in a Dialogue. . . .
London. Printed by Schulze & Dean, 13
Poland Street. 1814.

Fcap. 8vo, with title-page, preface (iii–v), leaf of "Errata"
(unpaged), and text pp. 1–102.

This work was published in a slate-coloured wrapper, with white
label on the side, and is under these circumstances excessively
rare. In 1891 a copy in this condition sold by auction for £33
(damaged). It is said that only three perfect copies are known.

9. Alastor ; or, the Spirit of Solitude, and other
Poems. By Percy Bysshe Shelley. London.
Printed for Baldwin, Cradock & Joy, Pater-
noster Row. . . . 1816.

Fcap. 8vo, containing title-page, preface (iii–vi), half-title, and
text pp. 1–101.

Value about £15 in the original boards as issued (auction).
Cut copies in calf are worth no more than a fifth or sixth of that
amount.

In 1876 Mr. Buxton Forman privately reprinted this work (50
copies on ordinary paper, 25 on Whatman's, and 5 on vellum).

10. A Proposal for Putting Reform to the Vote
throughout the Kingdom. By the Hermit of
Marlow. London. Printed for C. & J. Ollier,
3 Welbeck Street, Cavendish Square. . . .
1817.

This pamphlet was published in March 1817, and in addition
to the title contains pp. 1–14, fcap. 8vo. There are no wrappers.

The work should not be particularly scarce, as more than 100
copies are known to have been distributed, and the total issue

probably amounted to considerably more. It seems, however, that no copies are now forthcoming (not one has been sold by auction for many years), and that only a very few (four at the most) are known to be in existence.

A facsimile of the original MS. in Shelley's handwriting, now in the possession of Mr. Thomas J. Wise, was published by the Shelley Society in 1887.

The value of a copy of the pamphlet would probably amount to £30 or £40.

11. Laon and Cythna; or, the Revolution of the Golden City. . . . By Percy B. Shelley. . . . London. Printed for Sherwood, Neely & Jones, Paternoster Row. . . . 1818.

Published at 10s. 6d., demy 8vo. Though dated 1818, this work appeared the previous year.

It contains title as above, preface (v–xxii), dedication (xxiii–xxxii), a second half-title, and text pp. 1–270. There should be a leaf containing an advertisement by C. and J. Ollier, and also a leaf of "Errata," both at the end.

Perfect and uncut copies of this work are worth about £12 by auction (original boards).

12. The Revolt of Islam: a Poem, in Twelve Cantos. By Percy Bysshe Shelley. London. Printed for C. & J. Ollier, Welbeck Street. . . . 1817.

This is the same book as the last described, with alterations and a fresh title-page. The collation is almost the same, though Shelley made many revisions in the text.

The explanation of this duplicate issue probably is, that a large remainder of " Laon and Cythna" remained on Sherwood's hands, and that Shelley altered the title and put the work in the hands of a new publisher.

"The Revolt of Islam" is a comparatively common book, copies selling on the average for about £2 10s. or £3 by auction (original boards).

Another Edition. John Brooks. 1829. Demy 8vo, brown boards.

13. Rosalind and Helen : a Modern Eclogue, with Other Poems. By Percy Bysshe Shelley. London. Printed for C. & J. Ollier. . . . 1819.

Published in slate-coloured wrappers with white label on side. The book contains half-title, title, "advertisement" (one leaf), contents, a second half-title, and text pp. 3–92.

Value about £3 3s. (original wrappers, auction).

The poem was privately reprinted in 1876 by Mr. Buxton Forman.

14. The Cenci : a Tragedy, in Five Acts. By Percy B. Shelley. Italy. Printed for C. and J. Ollier. . . . 1819.

Published in 8vo, boards, with label on side, at 4s. 6d.

The book contains title, dedication (iii–v), preface (vii–xiv), half-title, and text pp. 3–104. No half-title precedes title.

Value from £5 to £6 (original boards). When rebound, this work sells for much less.

Second Edition, 1821, C. and J. Ollier. The value of copies of this edition is from 12s. to 15s.

15. Prometheus Unbound : a Lyrical Drama in Four Acts, with other Poems. By Percy Bysshe Shelley. . . . London. C. and J. Ollier, Vere Street, Bond Street. 1820.

Published in demy 8vo, at 9s., in slate-coloured boards. The work contains half-title, title, preface (vii–xv), a second half-title, and text pp. 19–222.

Value about £2 5s. (original boards, auction).

16. Œdipus Tyrannus ; or, Swellfoot the Tyrant : a Tragedy, in Two Acts. . . . London. Published for the Author by J. Johnston, 98 Cheapside. . . . 1820.

An 8vo pamphlet without wrappers, containing title as above, "advertisement" (one leaf), and text pp. 5–39.

A reprint of this excessively scarce publication was privately printed on vellum by Mr. Buxton Forman in 1876.

As to the value of the original edition of "Œdipus Tyrannus" I can say nothing, as only five copies are known. One of these is in the South Kensington Museum. Mr. Forman's reprint has sold for £1 10s. by auction.

17. Epipsychidion. Verses addressed to the Noble and Unfortunate Lady Emilia V——, now imprisoned in the Convent of —— . . . London. C. & J. Ollier, Vere Street, Bond Street. MDCCCXXI.

An 8vo pamphlet published at 2s. without wrapper, and containing half-title, title, "advertisement" (one leaf), and text pp. 7–31.

This work was privately reprinted by Mr. Buxton Forman, without date.

R

The original is very scarce, selling by auction whenever it occurs
for as much as £20. Mr. Forman's reprint (on vellum) brings
about £2.

18. Adonais : an Elegy on the Death of John
　　Keats, author of Endymion, Hyperion, etc.
　　By Percy B. Shelley. . . . Pisa, with the
　　types of Didot. MDCCCXXI.

Large 4to, in blue wrapper with black device on sides, containing title as above, preface (3–5), and text pp. 7–25.

In 1876 Mr. Buxton Forman issued a private reprint of this
work on Whatman's hand-made paper.

Value about £40 (original wrapper, auction); £1 5s. (Mr.
Forman's reprint, *ibid.*). Rebound copies of the original edition
seldom bring more than about £12 by auction.

Another Edition, Cambridge, 1829, edited by Arthur Henry
Hallam, from 12s. to 15s. (uncut, auction).

19. Hellas : a Lyrical Drama. By Percy B. Shelley.
　　. . . London. Charles and James Ollier. . . .
　　MDCCCXXII.

Demy 8vo, brown wrappers with white label on side. The
work contains preliminary leaf (blank), half-title, title, dedication
(unpaged), preface (vii–xi), a second half-title, and text pp. 3–60.
The last two pages contain five verses " Written on Hearing the
News of the Death of Napoleon."

In 1876 Mr. Buxton Forman privately reprinted this work on
vellum, with notes.

A good copy of " Hellas " in the original wrappers sells by auction for about £5 ; of Mr. Forman's reprint for about £2.

20. The Masque of Anarchy : a Poem. By Percy
Bysshe Shelley. Now first published, with a
Preface by Leigh Hunt. . . . London. Ed-
ward Moxon, 64 New Bond Street. 1832.

In 1819, when Leigh Hunt was editor of the *Examiner*, he
received the MS. of "The Masque of Anarchy" from Shelley.
The poem was written to denounce the state of things that occa-
sioned the "Peterloo Massacre" at Manchester. Hunt did not
use the MS. at the time, but printed it as above in 1832. A
later edition was published by J. Watson in 1842.

This book is a foolscap 8vo, containing title, preface (v–xxx),
and text 1–47.

Value about £2 (original boards, auction).

———

Another work published after the death of Shelley must here
be referred to, as it is of considerable importance. This is the
"Posthumous Poems," edited by Mary Wollstonecraft Shelley
and published by J. and H. L. Hunt in 1824, 8vo. An average copy
of this is worth from 25s. to 30s.

What purported to be a collection of "Letters" by Shelley
was published by Moxon in 1852, with an introductory essay by
Robert Browning. It turned out that the "Letters" were spurious,
and the edition was thereupon suppressed.

Good copies, which are now scarce, sell by auction for about
£4 (original cloth), though rebound copies may frequently be met
with for much less.

ALBERT SMITH.

ALBERT RICHARD SMITH (born 1816, died 1860) was a native
of Chertsey, where his father had a medical practice. It is
said that he too was destined for the same profession, and
that he actually passed the necessary examinations, though it
seems he could not have practised much if at all, for in 1839
he delivered a lecture on the subject of Alpine scenery, which
was so favourably received, that he determined to direct his
exclusive attention to lecturing and authorship. The lecture
on Alpine scenery was repeated at short intervals throughout the years 1839 and 1840, and in 1841 he commenced to
write for the periodicals. His well-known fictional works
"The Marchioness of Brinvilliers" and "The Adventures
of Mr. Ledbury" appeared in serial form before they were
separately published, and from that time his success as an
author as well as a lecturer was virtually assured. From
the first he obtained the inestimable services of John
Leech and "Crowquill," and subsequently of Kenny Meadows,
Gavarni, H. K. Browne, and other artists whose illustrations
were of themselves almost sufficient to ensure the sale of any
book in which they appeared. As a lecturer in monologue
Albert Smith had very few equals; all his subjects were prepared on the basis of practical experience, and extensively
illustrated by means of set scenes, drawings, the production
of objects of interest acquired during his extensive travels
through Europe and the East, and in many other ways, so
that his lectures speedily came to be looked upon as particularly instructive, and perhaps indispensable to those who

had not the opportunity or the means of viewing for themselves the scenes he so graphically described.

Albert Smith's literary performances consist of many contributions to the *Comic Almanack* and other light periodicals of a similar kind. He was at one time the editor of *Bentley's Miscellany*, *The Town and Country Miscellany*, and *The Squib*, a folio magazine first published in 1842, which ran through thirty numbers. He is also credited with several dramas, notably one in three acts, prose and verse, founded upon Charles Dickens's " Battle of Life," which, like that successful Christmas story, appeared in 1846.

In this article a list is given of all Albert Smith's more noticeable books, though there are a considerable number of others which, being published for the most part in large quantities at a very low price, are not of sufficient importance to merit more than a passing reference. These minor productions comprise the following :—

(1.) The Marchioness of Brinvilliers, fcap. 8vo, 1846 ; published at 5s.

(2.) The Physiology of Evening Parties, fcap. 8vo, Bentley, 1846 ; published at 2s. 6d. The best edition of this book is a later one published in white boards, and worth some 6s. or 8s. Like the first edition, it is dated 1846.

(3.) Natural History of Stuck Up People. D. Bogue, 1847, 16mo ; published at 1s.

(4.) Natural History of the Gent. D. Bogue, 1847, 16mo ; published at 1s.

(5.) Natural History of the Ballet Girl. D. Bogue, 1847, 16mo ; published at 1s.

(6.) Natural History of the Idler upon Town. D. Bogue, 1848, 16mo ; published at 1s.

(7.) Natural History of the Flirt. D. Bogue, 1848, 16mo ; published at 1s.

(8.) A Pottle of Strawberries to beguile a Short Journey. 1848, 16mo ; published at 1s.

(9.) A Bowl of Punch. 1848, 16mo ; published at 1s.

(10.) Natural History of Evening Parties.   1849, 16mo; published at 1s.

(11.) A Month at Constantinople, post 8vo.   D. Bogue, 1850; published at 10s. 6d.

(12.) The Miscellany : a Book for the Field and Fireside.   D. Bogue, 16mo, 1850; published at 1s.

(13.) Comic Tales and Sketches, post 8vo, 1852 ; published at 2s.

(14.) Pictures of Life at Home and Abroad, post 8vo, 1852 ; published at 1s.

(15.) The English Hotel Nuisance, post 8vo, 1855 ; published at 1s.

(16.) To China and Back, being a Diary kept out and home, post 8vo, 1859 ; published at 1s.

(17.) Sketches of London Life, 12mo, 1859 ; published at 2s.

(18.) The London Medical Student, post 8vo, 1861 ; published at 1s. (a posthumous work).

It may be mentioned that these trifles sell, with the exception of Nos. 2, 8, and 9, which are worth a little more if quite clean, for about 5s. each, if in the original covers, as issued.   There are several editions of each, but subject to the remarks appended to No. 2, only the first is of any material importance or value. The following books by Albert Smith are, however, in a different position, and with regard to them it must be observed that the value of copies in the original binding, as issued, have greatly increased in value during the last five years.

1. Beauty and the Beast.   By Albert Smith.   With
    Illustrations by Alfred Crowquill.   London.
    Wm. S. Orr & Co., Amen Corner, Pater-
    noster Row.   N.D. (but 1843).

A small quarto book in pictorial paper cover.   A yellow blank leaf precedes, then follows tinted frontispiece, title with coloured cut of Cupid, and text, in verse, pp. 1–51.   There are 12 full-page tinted plates (inclusive of front) and several woodcuts in the text.

A good and clean copy of this little work is worth some 10s. or 12s. (original paper wrappers).

2. The Wassail Bowl.   By Albert Smith. . . .
London.   Richard Bentley, New Burlington
Street.   1843.

In 2 vols. post 8vo, each containing a frontispiece and numerous
woodcuts in the text by Leech.   Published at 10s. 6d.

Vol. i. consists of half-title, frontispiece, title, preface (unpaged),
the prologue (unpaged), and text pp. 1–252.

Vol. ii. comprises half-title, frontispiece, title, half-title (unpaged), advertisement (unpaged), and text pp. 5–249.

These volumes consist of a number of short stories, before some,
but not all, of which half-titles appear.   The first volume has a
half-title before the front, but in the second volume half-titles
precede front, and follow the title and pp. 85 and 207.

In 1848 a small book entitled "Comic Sketches from the
Wassail Bowl" was published in 16mo.   This is only of trifling
importance.

A clean and perfect copy of "The Wassail Bowl," in the original
cloth, as issued, sells by auction on the average for about £2.
Occasionally, however, an unusually bright copy will bring
more.

3. The Adventures of Mr. Ledbury and his Friend,
Jack Johnson.   By Albert Smith, Esq. . . .
London.   Richard Bentley, New Burlington
Street.   1844.

Published in 3 vols. post 8vo, at £1 11s. 6d., in cloth.   There
are, or should be, 18 full-page illustrations by Leech, viz., 6 in
vol. i., 5 in vol. ii., and 7 in vol. iii., inclusive of frontispiece in
each case.

Vol. i. contains front, title, dedication (unpaged), preface
(iii–iv), contents (v–vi), list of illustrations (unpaged), and text
pp. 1–292.

Vol. ii. has front, title, contents (iii–iv), and text pp. 1–292.

Vol. iii. has front, title, contents (iii–iv), and text pp. 1–297.

Uncut copies of this book are very seldom met with, though they are not so hopelessly rare as some would have us believe. In June 1890, an entirely uncut, but rebound example, sold by auction for £6 15s., and a copy in the original pictorial cloth would not be likely to produce much more, for in the case mentioned the work had been rebound by Bedford in accordance with all the arbitrary rules in vogue among bibliophiles. Inferior and cut-down copies of the work are common enough, and as a rule realise considerably less than £1 at auction. It may be said that only two copies of the work have sold publicly for more than £1 during the past six years. One of these is mentioned above ; the other was also uncut, and had been bound in morocco extra by Rivière. This book, which sold for £3 3s. in April 1889. is good evidence of the advance which has taken place in the values of works of a certain class, for the present auction price would be some 40 or 50 per cent. higher at least than it was four years ago.

Another Edition, 1846, 3 vols. post 8vo, with the 18 full-page plates by Leech. The plates are worn, and the edition itself in little repute. Uncut copies in the original cloth are, however, very unusual.

Value of the edition of 1846 from £2 to £3 (original cloth, uncut), or about 15s. (rebound, cut).

4. The Fortunes of the Scattergood Family. By
   Albert Smith, Author of "The Adventures
   of Mr. Ledbury." . . . London.   Richard
   Bentley, New Burlington Street.   1845.

In 3 vols. crown 8vo, with 14 plates by Leech, published at 31s. 6d.

Vol. i. contains front, title, dedication (unpaged), text pp. 1–291, and 7 plates inclusive of front.

Vol. ii. contains front, title, text pp. 1–320, and 6 plates inclusive of front.

Vol. iii. has front, title, and text pp. 1–332. With the exception of the frontispiece, this volume is not illustrated. In addition

to the closing chapters of the "Scattergood Family," the third
volume contains "Marguerite de Bourgogne, a Tradition of Ancient
Paris," pp. 61–175, and "The Armourer of Paris, a Romance of
the Fifteenth Century," pp. 179–332. Half-titles follow pp. 58
and 175.

Value about £7 7s. (original cloth, auction). If rebound and
cut down, much less.

5. The Man in the Moon. Edited by Albert Smith
  and Angus B. Reach. With Illustrations by
  "Phiz," Kenny Meadows, Hine. . . . London. Clarke, Warwick Lane, and all Booksellers. . . . N.D. (but 1847, &c.).

This monthly periodical ran to 30 numbers, 12mo, each of which,
up to and inclusive of No. 20, contains a folding plate. From
No. 21 to No. 30 this folding plate was discontinued, on account
of its liability to injury, the text being more extensively illustrated
with woodcuts to compensate for the omission.

The periodical is seldom found complete in the original parts,
but bound sets (always in 5 vols. 12mo) are comparatively
common. Each volume should contain title and general table of
contents, in addition to the table of contents that precedes each
number. The volumes were of course bound up from the
numbers.

Nos. 4 to 12 inclusive contain a series of 9 folding plates illustrative of a story entitled "Mr. Crindle's Rapid Career upon
Town." Subsequently, when the series was complete, the illustrations (of which there are many on each plate) were worked off
separately, and published in a paper wrapper at 2s. The present
value is three or four times that amount.

An average set of the five volumes, bound say in half calf,
sells by auction for about £1 10s., or if in the original cloth, for
about £2 10s., or sometimes £3. A clean and perfect set of the
numbers with all the wrappers and folding plates has sold for as
much as £9, but £5 or £6 would appear to be more usual.

6. The Struggles and Adventures of Christopher
   Tadpole at Home and Abroad.   By Albert
   Smith. . . . London.   Richard Bentley. . . .
   1848.

"Christopher Tadpole," which is undoubtedly Albert Smith's masterpiece, was published at 16s. in 1847, though the date on the title-page is as above stated. The book, a demy 8vo, in pictorial cloth covers, contains the portrait of the author, and 32 full-page plates by Leech. It collates as follows :—Portrait of Albert Smith, title as above, dedication to Serjeant Talford (unpaged), list of illustrations (v–vi), table of contents (vii–xi), and text pp. 1–512.

It must be remembered that "Christopher Tadpole" originally made its appearance in 16 monthly parts, which, when clean and perfect, used to sell by auction some four or five years ago for about £2 10s., while copies in the original cloth brought a little less. The present value in each case is at least a hundred per cent. higher. Rebound and cut-down copies seldom sell for as much as £1 by auction.

The editions of 1853 and N.D. (published by Willoughby) are quite unimportant.

7. Gavarni in London : Sketches of Life and
   Character.   With Illustrative Essays by
   Popular Writers.   Edited by Albert Smith.
   London.   David Bogue, 86 Fleet Street.
   MDCCCXLIX.

The Essays in this volume are by Albert Smith and several other popular writers of the day. The work was published at 10s. 6d., cloth gilt, imperial 8vo, and contains 24 full-page tinted engravings by Gavarni, which computation includes the portrait of the artist on the illustrated title.

The work contains tinted frontispiece, title with large tinted portrait, plain title, contents (unpaged) and text, consisting of two unnumbered leaves, and then pp. 1–115.

Value, about the published price (original cloth, auction).

8. The Pottleton Legacy : a Story of Town and
    Country Life. By Albert Smith. . . . London.
    David Bogue. . . . MDCCCXLIX.

Published originally in 10 monthly parts, each containing two full-page plates by "Phiz," who also designed the wrappers ; afterwards in post 8vo, cloth, at 10s. 6d., as above.

The work contains front, title, dedication, with list of plates on reverse (unpaged), contents (v–viii), " To My Readers " (1–3), and text pp. 1–472.

Value about £1 15s. (original cloth, auction), though very clean and bright copies often sell for considerably more. A complete set of the parts would bring about £3 3s.

Another Edition, 1854, post 8vo, with the plates by "Phiz."

Value about 10s. (original cloth).

9. The Month : a View of Passing Subjects and
    Manners, Home and Foreign, Social and
    General. By Albert Smith and John Leech.
    . . . Published at the office of " The Month,"
    No. 3 Whitefriars Street. July 1851.

This periodical was discontinued after six numbers (July to December 1851) had been published. Square post 8vo, at 1s. 6d. each. The numbers were afterwards bound together in drab pictorial boards, in which state they are generally met with.

All the illustrations in the volume are by Leech in his familiar *Punch* style. To face p. 216 there is a full-page humorous plate of Cleopatra's Needle "as it will appear in England, A.D. 1851," and opposite p. 48 a caricature of Thackeray "as he appeared at Willis's Rooms." The pagination (3–480) is continuous throughout, and each *Month* has a separate title-page and frontis-piece.

Value about £1 15s. (original parts, auction), or 15s. (bound copy, original drab boards).

10. The Story of Mount Blanc.   By Albert Smith.
     . . . London.   David Bogue. . . . MDCCCLIII.

Post 8vo, published at 10s. 6d., in orange cloth. The work contains a coloured frontispiece, and has numerous cuts in the text. It collates as follows :—

Coloured front, title with vignette, dedication (unpaged), notice (v–x), contents (xi–xii), and text pp. 1–219.

Value about 10s. (original cloth).

There is a work known as " A Handbook of Mr. Smith's Ascent of Mount Blanc," which was published at London without date (but 1852), 8vo.   It is only of trifling value.

11. Wild Oats and Dead Leaves.   By Albert
     Smith.   London.   Chapman & Hall, 193
     Piccadilly.   MDCCCLX.

A post 8vo book bound in drab cloth, and lettered in black on the side and face.   Published at 5s.

The work contains title, preface (iii–iv), contents (v–vi), and text pp. 1–359.

Value, the published price or near it.

ROBERT LOUIS STEVENSON.

Mr. Robert Louis Balfour Stevenson was thirty-three years of age when his reputation as a novelist was firmly established by the publication of "Treasure Island." Since 1883 Mr. Stevenson has never lacked readers, and his works have followed one another in rapid succession. It may be stated that collectors of Stevenson's works are more than usually punctilious in the matter of condition and binding.

Mr. Stevenson has written much in the periodicals, notably the *Cornhill Magazine*; but as these scattered articles do not come within the scope of this work, they must be passed over as heretofore in favour of volumes separately published. It will be noticed that so far as these are concerned, those published prior to 1884 are the most difficult to procure. Special reference should also be made to the following pamphlets :—

(*a.*) The Pentland Rising. A Page of History. 1666. . . . Edinburgh, Andrew Elliot, 17 Princes Street. 1866.

A post 8vo pamphlet in a green cover, lettered as above. No title, pp. 3–22.

(*b.*) The Charity Bazaar: an Allegorical Dialogue.

No title-page ; a 4to pamphlet of pp. 1–4 on ribbed paper.

(*c.*) An Appeal to the Clergy of the Church of Scotland, with a Note for the Laity. . . . William Blackwood & Sons, Edinburgh and London. Price 3d. 1875.

Post 8vo, no wrapper, pp. 3–11.

(*d.*) Deacon Brodie ; or, the Double Life. A Melodrama, founded on facts, in four acts and ten tableaux. By Robert Louis Stevenson and William Ernest Henley. MDCCCLXXX.

A post 8vo pamphlet in a slate-coloured paper wrapper, lettered as above. Then follows title-page as above, and text pp. 3–97.

Second Edition. White wrappers, lettered "Deacon Brodie, or the Double Life, for private circulation only;" then follows leaf with "Personages and Synopsis of Acts and Tableaux" on reverse; title, "Deacon Brodie, or the Double Life, a Melodrama in four acts and eight tableaux. By William Ernest Henley and Robert Louis Stevenson. Edinburgh University Press. T. & A. Constable, Printers to her Majesty." MDCCCLXXXVIII.

Text 1–88.

(*e.*) With Mr. R. L. Stevenson's compliments. Father Damien; an open letter to the Reverend Dr. Hyde of Honolulu from Robert Louis Stevenson. Sydney, 1890.

Post 8vo, pp. 3–32. No wrapper. This is the first issue, of which only 25 copies were printed. Subsequently the letter was sent to the *National Observer*, and then brought out in pamphlet form in chocolate-coloured paper covers. This, the booksellers are in the habit of saying, is the first edition, though such is not the case.

All the above pamphlets are rare, and when met with invariably command substantial prices. Some £3 or £4, or possibly more, would be asked in most cases. Care must be taken to distinguish between the genuine first issue of the letter to Dr. Hyde, and the comparatively common edition in paper covers.

About the years 1884–85, Mr. Stevenson printed four or five little volumes of prose and verse, which are now, and have always been, exceedingly scarce. They were issued from the press of Lloyd Osbourne, at Davoz Platz.

1. An Inland Voyage.   By Robert Louis Steven-
    son. . . . London.   C. Kegan Paul & Co.,
    1 Paternoster Square.   1878.

This is a crown 8vo book, in pictorial slate-coloured cloth. It consists of half-title, followed by pictorial title, then a plain title, preface (v–viii), contents (ix–x), and text pp. 1–237.

Value about £1 15s. (original cloth, auction); £2 (*ibid.*).

2. Edinburgh : Picturesque Notes. By Robert Louis Stevenson. . . . Seeley, Jackson & Halliday, 56 Fleet Street, London. MDCCCLXXIX.

Though dated as above, this work was actually published in 1878. It is a folio book, in blue cloth, gilt edges, with the arms of the City of Edinburgh on the side. There should be a frontispiece and four full-page etchings by W. E. Lockhart, one full-page etching by Sam Bough, and twelve vignettes. A half-title precedes. This work is a reprint from the *Portfolio*.

A good copy of this book in the original cloth sells by auction for about £3.

Another Edition, 8vo, 1888, Seeley & Co., bound in boards, with cloth face, top edges gilt. A half-title precedes, there is a view of Princes Street, Edinburgh, on the title, and there should be 27 illustrations, many of them full-page.

A clean copy is worth some 4s. or 5s.

3. Travels with a Donkey in the Cevennes. By Robert Louis Stevenson. London. C. Kegan Paul & Co., 1 Paternoster Square. 1879.

Post 8vo, in green pictorial cloth, gilt title on face. A complete copy of this work should have a blank leaf, then an advertisement of "An Inland Voyage" on an unpaged leaf, half-title followed by frontispiece by Walter Crane, title as above, letter addressed to "My Dear Sidney Colvin," contents, half-title ("Velay"), and text pp. 3–227. The work is divided into five sections, each of which should be preceded by a half-title.

Value about £1 10s. (original cloth).

4. Virginibus Puerisque, and other Papers. By Robert Louis Stevenson. . . . London. C. Kegan Paul & Co., 1 Paternoster Square. 1881.

A crown 8vo book of 296 pp., in orange cloth, gilt lettered on face.   There should be a half-title, a dedication to W. E. Henley, and table of contents.

Value about £1 10s. (original cloth).

5. Familiar Studies of Men and Books.   By Robert Louis Stevenson.   London.   Chatto & Windus, Piccadilly.   1882.

This is a thick 8vo of 397 pp., bound in a light olive cloth, with scrollwork on the sides, and gilt inscription on face.   It should have a half-title, and following title there is a dedication to Thomas Stevenson, the father of the author, a preface on pp. vii–xxviii, and table of contents.

Value about 12s. (original cloth, auction).

An edition was issued in 1888 which is noticeable on account of the large-paper copies, a limited number of which were issued in 4to, boards.   These sell for about a guinea each, more or less.

6. New Arabian Nights.   By Robert Louis Stevenson.   London.   Chatto & Windus, Piccadilly. 1882.

This work was first published as above in 2 vols., square 8vo, in greenish boards, with Moorish figuring on the sides, and gilt inscription on the face.   Vol. i., which is made up rather irregularly, should contain "Note" signed R. L. S., contents, a blank leaf, half-title, title as above, dedication to Robert Alan Mowbray Stevenson, another half-title ("The Suicide Club"), and text pp. 3–269.   A half-title faces p. 134.   Vol. ii. contains blank leaf, half-title, title, contents, and another half-title ("The Pavilion on the Links").   After p. 101 there is a half-title, and other half-titles to face p. 140 and to follow p. 179.

Value about £1 (original cloth, auction).

A *Second Edition* appeared in 1882, crown 8vo, Chatto & Windus, a clean copy of which sells by auction for 10s. or 12s.

7. Treasure Island. By Robert Louis Stevenson. Cassell & Company, Limited. . . . 1883.

Crown 8vo, in blue cloth, lettered in gilt on the face. There is a half-title and a frontispiece ("Facsimile of Chart"), title, dedication with some verses on the reverse "To the Hesitating Purchaser," contents, and text pp. 1–292.

Value about £1 (original cloth, auction).

Another Edition, 1885, 8vo, Cassell & Co., the first illustrated edition. A half-title precedes, then follows "Facsimile of Chart" as in the first edition, pictorial half-title, illustrated title with the verses on the reverse, dedication with list of illustrations on the reverse, contents, and text pp. 1–292. The illustrations number 27, inclusive of front and cut on title. The "thirty-sixth thousand" issue of "Treasure Island" appeared in 1891. Good copies of the illustrated edition of 1885 are worth some 6s. or 8s. each, but none of the other editions, except the first, are of any importance.

8. The Silverado Squatters. By Robert Louis Stevenson. London. Chatto & Windus, Piccadilly. 1883.

A crown 8vo book, published in greenish pictorial cloth, with gilt lettering on the face. After half-title follows frontispiece to face title, a dedication, contents, and text pp. 1–254. It should be specially noted that half-titles face pp. 10, 56, 102, 126, 184, 196, and 222, and follow pp. 151 and 169. Prior to the publication of this book, portions were collected and issued by Chatto & Windus in a green wrapper bearing the title "The Silverado Squatters, Sketches from a Californian Mountain," price sixpence. This was done, no doubt, to preserve the copyright in the title.

A clean copy of the pamphlet (only 10 copies issued), which is a mere curiosity, would, however, sell for more than the work itself, which usually brings about 17s. 6d. in the original cloth.

9. A Child's Garden of Verses. By Robert Louis
Stevenson. London. Longmans, Green &
Co. 1885.

This is a small book in 12mo, published in blue cloth, with
Longmans device on the side, and gilt lettering on the face. It
consists of 101 pp. on thick paper, and is made up as follows:—
Blank page containing on the reverse list of works by the same
author, half-title, title, dedication in verse to Alison Cunningham,
contents, another half-title, then the first poem, "Bed in Summer,"
on p. 3.
Value about £2 2s. (original cloth, auction).
Second Edition, 1885, 12mo, Longmans, about 5s. (original
cloth).

10. More New Arabian Nights: The Dynamiter.
By R. L. and F. Stevenson. London. Longmans, Green & Co. Price One Shilling.

This was published in pictorial paper covers, at the price named,
without date, but in 1885. Half-title precedes title, and there are
207 pp. Some copies appear to have been issued in red cloth
at 1s. 6d.
Value about 5s. (original wrapper).

11. Prince Otto: a Romance. By Robert Louis
Stevenson. London. Chatto & Windus,
Piccadilly. 1885.

Published in greenish cloth, floriated on the sides in red, and
lettered in gilt on the face, crown 8vo, pp. 3–300. The work is
divided into three books, and a half-title precedes each. A half-
title also precedes title.
Value about 5s. (original cloth), as a rule, though very clean
copies often sell for 8s. or 10s.

12. Kidnapped : being Memoirs of the Adventures of David Balfour in the Year 1751. . . . By Robert Louis Stevenson.   Cassell & Company, Limited.   MDCCCLXXXVI.

A crown 8vo book in green, red, blue, or brown cloth.   After half-title there is a folding map giving a "Sketch of the Cruise of the Brig Covenant."   Possibly for the purpose of preserving the copyright in the title, Mr. Stevenson had previously published the first ten chapters in yellow wrappers 4to, pp. 3–27.   This advance issue was printed and published for the author by James Henderson, Red Lion House, &c., without date.

Many editions of "Kidnapped" have appeared, notably the illustrated edition of 1887, Cassell & Co., 8vo, pp. vi–311, about 7s. 6d., and an edition of 1892, about 4s. 6d.

A good copy of the original edition of 1886 is worth about 10s. (cloth, as issued).

13. Strange Case of Dr. Jekyll and Mr. Hyde. By Robert Louis Stevenson.   London.   Longmans, Green & Co.   1886.

The original edition of this well-known little book is bound in orange cloth, with lettering and Longmans device in black on the side, post 8vo.   A half-title precedes title, which should be followed by a dedication in verse to Katharine de Mattos.   There are 141 pages.   There was a simultaneous issue in paper covers.

Value about 7s. (original cloth, or paper).

14. Memories and Portraits.   By Robert Louis Stevenson.   London.   Chatto & Windus, Piccadilly.   1887.

A post 8vo book, bound in dark blue cloth.   A half-title precedes title as above, and is followed by dedication, note, contents, and text pp. 1–299.

Value about 5s. (original cloth).

15. Underwoods.   By Robert Louis Stevenson. London.   Chatto & Windus, Piccadilly.   1887.

Post 8vo, bound in dark cloth, lettered in gilt on the face. The work consists of a series of poems in two books, the first containing 38, and the second 16.   A half-title precedes, as usual, then title, then follow dedication, note, contents, and poems pp. 1–138.

Value about 7s. 6d. (original cloth, auction).   Fifty copies of this work were printed on large paper, in 4to.   These are scarce, selling at auction for as much as £1 15s. (uncut).

16. The Merry Men, and other Tales and Fables. By Robert Louis Stevenson.   London.   Chatto & Windus, Piccadilly.   1887.

Published in dark green or light blue cloth, post 8vo, with device composed of 5 silver stars on the side, and gilt letters on face.   A half-title precedes title and each of the stories throughout the book.

Value about 7s. (original cloth).

17. Papers, Literary, Scientific, &c.   By the late Fleeming Jenkin, F.R.S., LL.D. . . . . London. Longmans, Green & Co.   1887.

This work appeared in 2 vols. demy 8vo, red cloth, and was published at £1 12s.   The memoir, comprising pp. xi–cliv of vol. i., was written by Mr. Stevenson.

18. Ticonderoga. By Robert Louis Stevenson. Printed for the Author by R. & R. Clark, Edinburgh. 1887.

"Ticonderoga" is a poem in 2 parts or cantos. The work was privately printed in large 4to, vellum binding; the paging begins on p. 10. There should be two blank leaves, followed by half-title, then another leaf ("only fifty copies of this book have been printed"), title, inscription in verse, and the poem pp. 9–27.

No copy of this book has as yet been offered for sale in the open market, and it is difficult to assess the value. About £5 would be a probable amount.

19. The Black Arrow: a Tale of the Two Roses. By Robert Louis Stevenson. . . . Cassell & Company, Limited. . . . 1888.

Crown 8vo, red cloth, with title and an arrow, in black, on side. A half-title precedes, and there is an address to the "Critic on the Hearth," contents, and pp. 1–324. Published at 5s. The seventeenth thousand of this story appeared in 1891. Present value about 6s. (cloth, as issued).

20. The Wrong Box. By Robert Louis Stevenson . . . and Lloyd Osbourne. London. Longmans, Green & Co. 1889.

Published in slate-coloured cloth, crown 8vo, lettered in gilt on face. No half-title precedes title, but a preface on one page follows. There are 283 pages. A new edition was published by Cassell & Co. in 1892, 8vo, pp. 283.
Value about 5s. (cloth, as issued).

21. Ballads. By Robert Louis Stevenson. London. Chatto & Windus, Piccadilly. 1890.

A fcap. 8vo book in smooth navy blue cloth, gilt lettered on the face. Half-title precedes title, and each of the complete poems, five in number. There are 137 pp. This work contains a reprint of "Ticonderoga."

Value about 6s. (cloth, as issued).

22. The South Seas : a Record of Three Cruises. By Robert Louis Stevenson. Cassell & Company, Limited. 1890.

Published in scarlet cloth, pp. 123. This is by far the rarest of Stevenson's published books. Only 22 copies were printed to secure copyright, and of these about 15 were cut up for serial use. Mr. Stevenson afterwards determined to suppress the work entirely, so that it is not likely ever to be reprinted. No copy has yet been offered for sale.

23. The Master of Ballantrae : a Winter's Tale. By Robert Louis Stevenson. . . . Cassell & Company, Limited. . . . 1891.

Published in various coloured cloths, lettered in gilt on the face. A half-title precedes, and there are 10 full-page illustrations (inclusive of front) by W. Hole, pp. 1–332.

Value about 5s. (cloth, as issued).

24. The Wrecker. By Robert Louis Stevenson and Lloyd Osbourne. . . . Cassell & Company, Limited. . . . 1892.

Published in blue cloth, with 12 illustrations (including front) by William Hole and W. L. Metcalfe, pp. 1–427.

Value about 4s. (cloth, as issued).

Several other editions of this book appeared in 1892.

25. A Footnote to History : Eight Years of Trouble
in Samoa.   By Robert Louis Stevenson. . . .
Cassell & Company, Limited. . . . 1892.

Published in dark green cloth, crown 8vo.   On the back of the half-title is a sketch map of part of the north coast of Upolu. After title comes preface (v–vi), contents, and text pp. 1–322.
Value about 6s. (cloth, as issued).

26. Across the Plains : with other Memories and
Essays. By Robert Louis Stevenson. London.
Chatto & Windus, Piccadilly.   1892.

Published in dark purple cloth, crown 8vo, gilt lettered on face. Half-title, title as above, dedication, letter to the author, contents, and text pp. 1–317.
Value about 6s. (cloth, as issued).

27. Island Nights' Entertainments. . . . By Robert
Louis Stevenson. . . . London.   Cassell &
Company, Limited. . . . 1893.

A post 8vo book consisting of "The Beach of Falesa," "The Bottle Imp," and "The Isle of Voices," pp. 276, with illustrations by Gordon Browne and W. Hatherill.
It was published at 6s. in April last.

R. S. SURTEES.

Robert Smith Surtees, of Hamsterley, in Durham, was born about the year 1803. He was educated for the law, and actually practised for a short time in London, subsequently, however, abandoning that profession for literature. He made his *début* in the pages of the old *Sporting Magazine*, and in 1831 published a work called "The Horseman's Manual," consisting of a digest of cases collected from the Law Reports of the day. This work is now forgotten and of no importance. In 1831, Surtees started the *New Sporting Magazine*, and acted as its editor for nearly five years. It was in the pages of this journal that he first attracted public attention with a series of papers in which the vagaries of Mr. John Jorrocks, "a fox-hunter—a shooter—and a grocer," are detailed with a vigour and humour that have made the character a typical one in the annals of Sporting literature. Not only in "Jorrocks's Jaunts and Jollities," under which title the papers were afterwards collected and published, is the Cockney Sportsman the principal actor; he appears again in "Hillingdon Hall," and "Handley Cross," and makes his mark at intervals in the pages of *Bell's Life* and other sporting journals.

Surtees had more wit and less vulgarity than Egan, and in his hands "John Jorrocks," the plain citizen, acquires at least as much fame, and will be remembered as long as the fashionable "Corinthian Tom," who after all is but a stage character, and would be as dead, but for the accessories by which he was, perforce, surrounded on all sides. The details

of sporting life had undergone a radical change by the time
Surtees constituted himself the historian of the hour. If he
had less available material than Egan, he knew better how
to make the most of what he had.

Surtees died in 1864.

1. Jorrocks's Jaunts and Jollities ; or, The Hunting,
    Shooting, Racing, Driving, Sailing, Eating,
    Eccentric, and Extravagant Exploits of that
    Renowned Sporting Citizen, Mr. John Jorrocks.
    . . . London.   Walter Spiers, . . . 399 Oxford
    Street.   1838.

This work was originally published in serial form, in the pages
of the *New Sporting Magazine*, between the months of July 1831
and September 1834 ; afterwards in one volume with the above
title, demy 8vo, pictorial cloth.

The work contains 12 full-page illustrations by H. K. Browne,
and is collated as follows :—

Half-title, front, title as above, preface (unpaged), contents (unpaged), half-title, and text pp. 3–358. The book consists of 10
papers or articles reprinted as aforesaid from the *New Sporting
Magazine*, and a half-title should precede each.

Value from £8 to £9 (original cloth, auction).

Another Edition, 1839, 8vo. There is no difference between
this edition and the last, except the title-page, which is altered to
suit the circumstances.

Value about £2 2s. (original cloth, auction).

Another Edition, 1843, 8vo, R. Ackermann, with 15 full-page
coloured plates (inclusive of title) by Henry Alken.

Value from £6 to £8 (original pictorial cloth, auction).

Another Edition, 1869, 8vo, Routledge, with 15 coloured illustrations by Henry Alken. This edition contains three additional
papers, viz., " A Week at Cheltenham," " A Ride to Brighton,"
and " The Day after the Feast."

Value about 15s. (original cloth).

Another Edition, 1874, 8vo, with 16 coloured illustrations by
Alken.

Value about 12s. (original cloth).

2. Handley Cross ; or, The Spa Hunt : a Sporting
   Tale. By the Author of "Jorrocks's Jaunts
   and Jollities," &c. . . . London. Henry
   Colburn. . . . 1843.

In 3 vols. post 8vo, each dated 1843. The first volume contains
dedication "to sportsmen and would-be sportsmen," and preface
(v–viii), and in vols. ii. and iii. a half-title precedes title. No
other preliminary matter except the usual title-page. These
volumes are not illustrated.

Value about £1 6s. (original cloth, auction), or from that sum
to £1 15s., according to the condition of the binding. This is a
library book, which is not often met with in a clean state.

3. Hillingdon Hall ; or, The Cockney Squire : a
   Tale of London Life. By the Author of
   "Handley Cross," &c. . . . London. Henry
   Colburn, Publisher, Great Marlborough Street.
   1845.

In 3 vols. post 8vo, each dated 1845. The first volume contains,
after title, a dedication to the Royal Agricultural Society, and a
preface, but the other two have no preliminary matter except
title-page. These volumes are not illustrated.

Value about £2 5s. (original cloth, auction), or less if rebound.
Clean copies in the original cloth are, as in the case of most library
books, very difficult to meet with.

Another Edition, 1888, thick 8vo, Bradbury, Agnew & Co., with
12 coloured plates by Wildrake, Heath, and Jellicoe.

Value from 7s. 6d. to 10s. (cloth, as issued).

4. The Analysis of the Hunting Field : being a
   Series of Sketches of the Principal Characters
   that Compose One; the whole forming a Slight
   Souvenir of the Season 1845-6.   London.
   Published by Rudolph Ackermann, 191 Regent
   Street.   MDCCCXLVI.

The papers reprinted in this volume appeared in *Bell's Life*
during the hunting season 1845–6.

The work in volume form is an oblong 8vo, with coloured title,
6 coloured plates, and numerous woodcuts in the text, all by H.
Alken.   It contains half-title, coloured pictorial title, plain title,
preface (v–vi), contents, and on the reverse "List of Plates," text
pp. 1–326.   The six coloured plates are generally found together at
the end of the volume.

Value from £3 to £4 10s., in the original cloth, with gilt edges
as published (auction).

5. Hawbuck Grange ; or, The Sporting Adventures
   of Thomas Scott, Esq.   By the Author of
   "Handley Cross ; or, The Spa Hunt." . . .
   London.   Printed for Longman, Brown,
   Green & Longmans. . . . 1847.

A work in demy 8vo, scarlet cloth, with 8 full-page etchings by
" Phiz."

After half-title follows front ("Hawbuck Grange as seen from
the South "), title, preface (unpaged), contents (unpaged), and
text pp. 1–329.

This series of sketches appeared in the columns of *Bell's Life*
during the winter of 1646–7.

Value about £4 10s. (original cloth, auction), or from £3 to
£3 10s. (half calf, uncut, *ibid.*).

A reprint of this work, with coloured plates by Wildrake, Heath,

and Jellicoe, was published by Bradbury, Agnew & Co., without
date (but 1888).   The value of this reprint does not exceed 8s.
or 10s.

6. Mr. Sponge's Sporting Tour.   By the Author of " Handley Cross." . . . London.   Bradbury & Evans, 11 Bouverie Street.   1853.

This work was originally published in 13 monthly parts, in red
wrappers designed by Leech, who also engraved the 13 full-page
illustrations (coloured), and numerous woodcuts which are found
in the text.

When the parts were complete the novel was issued in volume
form, with the above title-page and all the illustrations, demy 8vo,
pictorial cloth, also designed by Leech.   A half-title precedes title,
then follow dedication and preface (both unpaged), contents
(ix–x), list of the 13 engravings on steel, and on the reverse a
"List of Engravings on Wood" (which number 84), text pp.
1–408.

Value about £8 (original parts, auction), or from £3 to £4
(original cloth, *ibid.*).

A reprint of this work, with coloured plates by Wildrake, Heath,
and Jellicoe, was published by Bradbury, Agnew & Co., without
date (but 1888).   The value does not exceed 8s. or 10s.

7. Handley Cross; or, Mr. Jorrocks's Hunt.   By the Author of " Mr. Sponge's Sporting Tour. . . . London.   Bradbury & Evans, 11 Bouverie Street.   N.D. (but 1854).

Published originally in 17 monthly parts (March 1853–October
1854), in red wrappers designed by Leech.   There are 17 engravings in steel (coloured) and 84 woodcuts in the text by the same
artist.

The work was published in volume form on the completion of the parts, demy 8vo, fancy red cloth, with sporting device on side and face. This book contains half-title, title, dedication to Lord John Scott, preface (unpaged), contents (vii–viii), "List of Engravings on Steel," and on the reverse "Engravings on Wood" (unpaged), coloured front, and text pp. 1–550.

A complete set of the parts is seldom met with, though odd parts are, comparatively speaking, common enough. A full set would probably sell by auction for about £9 if clean, with all the advertisements as issued. Copies of the bound volume sell on the average for about £2 or £2·10s. (original cloth).

A reprint of this book, with coloured plates by Wildrake, Heath, and Jellicoe, was published by Bradbury, Agnew & Co., without date (but 1888). The value does not exceed 8s. or 10s.

8. "Ask Mamma"; or, The Richest Commoner in England. By the Author of "Handley Cross." . . . London. Bradbury & Evans, 11 Bouverie Street. 1858.

Published originally in 13 monthly parts, in red pictorial wrappers designed by Leech, afterwards in volume form with the above title, demy 8vo.

The bound volume contains half-title, coloured front, title, dedication (unpaged), preface (unpaged), contents (vii–x), leaf of "Engravings on Steel" and "Engravings on Wood," and text pp. 1–412. There are 13 coloured plates (inclusive of front) and 69 woodcuts in the text, all by Leech.

Value about £4 (original wrappers, auction), or £2 10s. (original cloth, *ibid.*).

Another Edition, being a reprint in royal 8vo, Bradbury, Agnew & Co., N.D. (but 1888), with coloured plates by Leech. This reprint is worth about 7s. 6d. in the original cloth, as issued.

9. Plain or Ringlets? By the Author of " Handley Cross." . . . London. Bradbury & Evans, 11 Bouverie Street.   1860.

This work was published originally in 13 monthly parts, in red pictorial wrappers designed by Leech, and afterwards in volume form, demy 8vo, in red cloth, with sporting designs on sides and face.

The bound volume contains half-title, coloured pictorial title, title as above (with vignette), dedication (unpaged), contents (v–viii), and text pp. 1–406.   There should be a leaf giving list of illustrations, and this is bound up, sometimes after table of contents, and sometimes at the end of the volume.   The illustrations, all by Leech, consist of 13 coloured plates, inclusive of first title and 44 woodcuts in the text.

Original copies of this work, bound or in parts, are scarce, and sell at prices which vary with the condition.   The parts will often bring as much as £5 or £6 at auction, and a good copy in the original cloth from £3 3s. to £5.

The reprint issued by Bradbury, Agnew & Co., without date (but 1888), with Leech's illustrations, is worth about 7s. 6d.

10. Mr. Facey Romford's Hounds.   By the Author of " Handley Cross." . . . London. Bradbury & Evans, 11 Bouverie Street.   1865.

As in the four preceding instances, this novel appeared in parts, in red pictorial wrappers designed by Leech.   The work, though written throughout by Surtees, was practically posthumous, as the author died immediately after the publication of the first number. Curiously enough, Leech also died before the work had made much progress, and the task of designing the further illustrations was entrusted to " Phiz."   These illustrations consist of twenty-four engravings on steel (coloured), of which the first fourteen (inclusive of front) were designed by Leech, and the remainder by Browne.

Collation :—Half-title, coloured front, title as above (with vignette), contents (v–vi), list of engravings (unpaged), and text pp. 1–391.

Copies of " Romford's Hounds " in the 12 parts sell by auction at from £3 3s. to £4 10s., according to condition. Bound copies bring from £2 to £2 10s. (original fancy cloth, with sporting designs on side and face).

ALGERNON CHARLES SWINBURNE.

Mr. A. C. Swinburne commenced his literary career when at Balliol College, Oxford, as a contributor to a periodical entitled *Undergraduate Papers*, published by W. Mansell of the High Street in that city, and edited by Professor John Nichol.

Of this journal only some three or four copies are known, and one of these was sold a few years ago for £16. It appeared during 1857 and 1858, and is complete in four numbers 8vo, pp. 186. As the title implies, the periodical was only of local interest, though it is now noticeable by reason of its extreme scarcity, and the personality of some of the contributors who have since attained a very high position in the literary world.

Mr. Swinburne's first personal work was, however, "The Queen-Mother: Rosamond," two separate and distinct plays published in one volume by Pickering in 1860. Since that date he has been remarkably active, his letters, articles, and poems in the pages of the periodicals being continuous, and his works in volume form more numerous than in the case of the majority of authors.

Mr. Swinburne's detached pieces are given with great fidelity in Mr. R. H. Shepherd's "Bibliography," the last edition of which appeared in 1887, and most of his separately published works will be found fully described below.

It must be remembered, however, that Mr. Swinburne has edited or annotated many works which do not come within

our scope, though it is quite possible that some collectors
might regard them as objects of legitimate interest. Such,
for example, are the selections from Byron in Moxon's
"Miniature Poets," 1865; Rossetti's "Notes on the Royal
Academy Exhibition for 1868," part ii. of which is by
Swinburne; and Shelley's "Epipsychidion," published for
the Shelley Society in 1887, which contains a note by the
same author. Mr. Swinburne also wrote the introductory
matter to an edition of George Chapman's works, published
in 1874; to C. J. Wells's "Joseph and his Brethren," 1876;
to "Thomas Middleton" in Ellis's "Best Plays of the Old
Dramatists," 1887. He has also translated the "Parabasis"
of Aristophanes, 1883, and selected and arranged the poems
of Coleridge (1869), and various modern poets (1880).

In 1884, what was called a "Complete Edition of Swinburne's Works" appeared in New York, and in 1886 a
volume of "Miscellanies" (Chatto & Windus, London). The
former of these is not complete despite its title, and the
latter is merely a selection of notes on English poets, which
had for the most part already appeared in the pages of the
periodicals. In 1887 Mr. Swinburne himself published a
series of "Selections" from his poetical works, but so far
as I am aware no complete edition of the latter has as yet
been issued.

It may be mentioned at this point that the scarcest of
all Mr. Swinburne's separate writings is a demy 8vo, of
some 30 pages, printed by Moxon in 1866 under the title
"Laus Veneris." This was printed in "Poems and Ballads"
the same year, and why Moxon circulated it alone is now
a matter of conjecture. Some say that he had a few copies
printed off privately with the object of obtaining several
independent opinions on this representative specimen of
the author's poetry, with which apparently he was not
satisfied. However that may be, the poem "Laus Veneris"

was never *published* separately, and copies of Moxon's privately issued booklet are now hardly to be met with at all. Some £20 or £25 would probably be asked for any stray example that came on the market.

1. The Queen-Mother : Rosamond. Two Plays. By Algernon Charles Swinburne. London. Basil Montagu Pickering, Piccadilly. 1860.

This is a small book (fcap. 8vo) of 217 pages. A half-title should precede title as above, and a dedication to Dante Gabriel Rossetti follows on an unpaged leaf. Then follows "Persons Represented," and another half-title; there is also a half-title to face p. 160, and the collector must be specially careful to see that a leaf of "Errata" follows, p. 217. This leaf is not numbered, and is often wanting.

Value about £5 10s. (original cloth, auction).

Some copies of this book have Moxon's title. These are of much less value, some 25s. or 30s. being ample in most cases. A third title bears Hotten's imprint, and these are of less value still.

2. The Children of the Chapel. A Tale. By the author of "Mark Dennis." London. Joseph Masters. 1864.

The author of "Mark Dennis" here referred to was Miss Gordon, who published the work through Rivingtons in 1858 The volume is interesting, as the verse which appears here and there is all by Swinburne, Miss Gordon being sole author of the prose portion. It was published in 12mo at 2s.

This book is not easily procurable, and is worth probably some 10s. or 15s.

3. Dead Love.   By Algernon C. Swinburne.
   London.   John W. Parker & Son, West
   Strand.   1864.

A half-title precedes the title as above, and the text, which is
entirely in prose, occupies pp. 5–15.   Crown 8vo.   This is a very
scarce piece.

It is difficult, if not impossible, to say what a clean copy would
be worth, but probably not less than £5.   "Dead Love" appeared
originally in 1862 in the columns of *Once a Week*.   It is one of
the two prose stories written by Mr. Swinburne, the other being
entitled "A Year's Letters," which appeared in the *Tatler* at a
later period.

4. Atalanta in Calydon : a Tragedy.   By Algernon
   Charles Swinburne. . . . London.   Edward
   Moxon & Co., 44 Dover Street.   1865.

A 4to book in white cloth cover, ornamented with Rossetti's
designs, having half-title before title, and dedication to the memory
of Walter Savage Landor on a blank leaf following title.   Then
follows a Greek poem of twenty lines on unpaged leaf, and another
of fifty-six lines on the following leaf (also unpaged), list of " The
Persons " on an unpaged leaf, " The Argument " (pp. xi–xii), and
text, pp. 1–111.

Value about £5 (as issued, uncut).

5. Chastelard : a Tragedy.   By Algernon Charles
   Swinburne. . . . London.   Edward Moxon &
   Co., Dover Street.   1865.

This is a fcap. 8vo book, having half-title before title, dedica-
cation, " Persons," half-title, and text, pp. 3–219.   This tragedy is

written in five acts, and there is properly a half-title before each
of them.

Value about £1 (original cloth, auction).

6. Cleopatra.   By Algernon Charles Swinburne.
   London.   John Camden Hotten, Piccadilly.
   1866.

This book is technically described as a small crown 8vo, though
it exactly resembles a small 4to.   The original wrappers consist of
very thin paper (brown), in curious contrast to the quality of the
printed pages.   The wrappers contain no letterpress.   There is,
however, a half-title, and a quotation from T. Hayman on an unpaged leaf before and after the title respectively, and text, pp. 7–17.

This is one of the scarcest of Swinburne's publications.   The
copy in the British Museum Library cost £7 10s. (uncut, bound
by Tout, with the original wrappers inserted), but is likely to be
worth more now.

7. Poems and Ballads.   By Algernon Charles
   Swinburne.   London.   Edward Moxon & Co.,
   Dover Street.   1866.

In this case there is no half-title before title, but a dedication
to Edward Burne Jones follows it.   There is also a table of
contents on pp. v–vii, and the text of sixty-two different poems
occupies pp. 1–344.   The book is a fcap. 8vo, and forms the first
volume of the series of Mr. Swinburne's "Poems and Ballads"
(see *post*, Nos. 24 and 38).   It was suppressed by the author.

The series comprising 3 vols. 8vo, 1866–89, clean, in the original
binding, sells by auction for about £2, more or less.

8. Notes on Poems and Reviews.   By Algernon
   Charles   Swinburne. · .   .   . London.   John
   Camden Hotten, Piccadilly.   1866.

This is a rare pamphlet of 23 demy 8vo pages, in paper wrapper. A half-title ("Notes on Poems and Reviews") precedes title.

Value about 15s. (in wrapper as published).

9. A Song of Italy. By Algernon Charles Swinburne. London. John Camden Hotten, Piccadilly. 1867.

This small book (fcap. 8vo) was published in light-green cloth, lettered on the face in gilt. It is curiously made up, for there should first of all be eight numbered pages of opinions of the press, such as are usually found at the *end* of a work ; then follows a blank leaf, title as above, inscription to Joseph Mazzini, and text of poem, pp. 7–66. At the end of the volume are more press notices on pp. 1–8, all numbered. "A Song of Italy" was reprinted in the "Songs of Two Nations," 1875 (see *post*, No. 20).

Value about 5s. (original cloth). At one time this work was worth considerably more than at present, the reason of the depreciation being that two lots of "remainders," numbering some thousands of copies, have been discovered and thrown on the market. This of course materially affects the price.

10. An Appeal to England against the Execution of the Condemned Fenians. By Algernon Charles Swinburne. . . . Manchester. Reprinted from the *Morning Star*. 1867.

As the title discloses, this poem of twelve stanzas first appeared in the columns of the *Morning Star*. This reprint was given away or, in some instances, sold in the streets of Manchester prior to the execution of Allen, Larkin, and Gould, for the murder of Sergeant Brett near that city. It is in a slate-coloured wrapper, with half-title before title, and pp. 5–11. Some copies were bound up in a bright blue limp cloth cover, unlettered, and contain the whole pamphlet (cover and all) within. It is difficult to say what this pamphlet is worth, but probably about £1 5s.

11. William Blake : a Critical Essay. By Algernon Charles Swinburne. . . . With Illustrations from Blake's Designs in Facsimile. . . . London. John Camden Hotten, Piccadilly. 1868.

This book, which is of crown 8vo size, contains illustrations from Blake's designs in facsimile (some coloured), and pp. viii–304. Two editions were published the same year, but they cannot be mistaken.

The auction value of an uncut copy of the first edition is about £1 5s. (as issued).

12. Siena. By Algernon Charles Swinburne. London. John Camden Hotten, Piccadilly. 1868.

This is a scarce publication, very few copies having been issued, and none of those placed on the market. "Siena" is a crown 8vo pamphlet in a wrapper. After title as above, follows pp. 3–15 of text.

A good copy would sell by auction for about £10 or £12, and it is worthy of note that the market value of genuine copies of the work has at least doubled within the last three or four years.

A pirated reprint is occasionally to be met with, and, having been very carefully executed, it is almost impossible to detect it from the original. It is in every respect but one a masterly production, the only apparent defect being in the description of the paper, which it was probably found impossible to match exactly. There is no doubt that many of these forged copies are on the market.

13. Ode on the Proclamation of the French Republic, September 4, 1870. By Algernon Charles Swinburne. . . . London. F. S. Ellis, 33 King Street, Covent Garden. 1870.

This is a demy 8vo pamphlet of 23 pp. in an orange-coloured cover, on which the words of the title, as above, are repeated. Then follows half-title, title, a dedication to Victor Hugo, and text, pp. 7–23.

The published price was 1s., and the present value is some 8s. or 10s.

14. Songs before Sunrise. By Algernon Charles Swinburne. London. F. S. Ellis, 33 King Street, Covent Garden. 1871.

A crown 8vo book containing half-title, title, dedication to Joseph Mazzini in verse (v–vi), contents (vii–viii), and text of the various poems (thirty-seven in number), pp. 1–287.

Value from 21s. to 25s. (original cloth, auction).

Twenty-five copies of this book were printed on large paper for private circulation. Imperial 8vo. These are very scarce, selling by auction for as much as £10 each.

15. Under the Microscope. By Algernon Charles Swinburne. London. D. White, 22 Coventry Street, W. 1872.

In crown 8vo, half-title, title, and text, pp. 1–88. Published at 2s. 6d. This work, which is entirely in prose, made its appearance in a light-coloured paper wrapper, lettered with title as above.

Value from 25s. to 30s. (as issued, auction).

16. Le Tombeau de Théophile Gautier.　Paris.
Alphonse Lemerre. . . . Editeur.　1873.

This work is mentioned here because several of the poems—to
be precise, six poems—are by Mr. Swinburne.　The book is a 4to,
consisting of 179 pages.

Value about £1 10s. (in the original parchment wrapper,
auction), or £3 with the portrait.

17. Bothwell : a Tragedy.　By Algernon Charles
Swinburne.　London.　Chatto & Windus,
Piccadilly.　1874.

This is a crown 8vo book of 532 pages.　A half-title (with
Greek verses on the reverse) precedes title, which is followed by
a dedication to Victor Hugo in French verse.　Then follows
"Dramatis Personæ" on blank leaf, half-title, and finally the
Tragedy, in five acts, each of which has its appropriate half-title.

Value about 15s. (original cloth).

18. George Chapman : a Critical Essay.　By
Algernon Charles Swinburne. London. Chatto
& Windus, Piccadilly.　1875.

A crown 8vo book in smooth navy-blue cloth.　A half-title
precedes title, and there are 187 pages of text.

Value about 8s. (original cloth).

19. Essays and Studies.　By Algernon Charles
Swinburne.　London.　Chatto & Windus,
Piccadilly.　1875.

This work is made up as follows :—Half-title, title, dedication
on blank leaf, preface (pp. vii–xii), contents, and text, pp. 1–380.

Most of these essays were reprinted from the *Fortnightly Review*, and the rest from other periodicals. The preface, however, is quite new.

Value about 12s. (original cloth).

20. Songs of Two Nations. By Algernon Charles Swinburne. I. A Song of Italy. II. Ode on the Proclamation of the French Republic. III. Diræ. London. Chatto & Windus, Piccadilly. 1875.

Published in smooth navy-blue cloth, lettered in gilt on face. Crown 8vo. A half-title precedes, then follows title, two verses on unpaged leaf, contents (vii–viii), half-title ("A Song of Italy"), inscription to Mazzini, and text of the poems. pp. 5–78. Each of the three divisions, as mentioned on the title, is preceded by its appropriate half-title.

Value about 8s. (original cloth).

21. Erechtheus : a Tragedy. By Algernon Charles Swinburne. . . . London. Chatto & Windus. Piccadilly. 1876.

Published in the same binding as the last-named book. A leaf precedes, giving a list of Mr. Swinburne's works, then follows half-title, title as above, dedication, and list of "Persons," text pp. 1–105. There is a separate unpaged leaf of "Notes" following p. 105. None of the preliminary pages are numbered.

Value about 7s. 6d. (original cloth).

22. Note of an English Republican on the Muscovite Crusade. By Algernon Charles Swinburne. . . . London. Chatto & Windus, Piccadilly. 1876.

This pamphlet of 24 pages, crown 8vo, was published at 1s. in
slate-coloured wrappers.
Value about 7s. 6d. (as issued).

23. A Note on Charlotte Brontë. By Algernon
     Charles Swinburne. London. Chatto &
     Windus, Piccadilly. 1877.

Crown 8vo, containing half-title, title as above, dedication
to Theodore Watts, and text, pp. 1–97.
Value about 7s. (cloth, as issued).

24. Poems and Ballads. Second Series. By Alger-
     non Charles Swinburne. London. Chatto &
     Windus, Piccadilly. 1878.

Bound in smooth navy-blue cloth, crown 8vo. A half-title
precedes title, which is followed by an inscription to Captain R. F.
Burton, table of contents (pp. vii.–ix), and text of poems (58 in
number), pp. 1–240.
For value see *ante*, No. 7 in this article.

25. A Study of Shakespeare. By Algernon Charles
     Swinburne. London. Chatto & Windus.
     Piccadilly. 1880.

Bound as in the case of No. 24. A half-title precedes title, which
is followed by dedication to Mr. J. O. Halliwell-Phillipps, contents, and text, pp. 1–309.
Value about 12s. (cloth, as issued).

26. Songs of the Springtides. By Algernon Charles
     Swinburne. London. Chatto & Windus,
     Piccadilly. 1880.

Crown 8vo, bound in smooth navy-blue cloth, lettered on face in gilt. A half-title precedes title, which is followed by contents, another half-title, dedication to E. J. Trelawny, another half-title, and text, pp. 3–131. Half-titles precede pp. 37, 67, and 97, and an unpaged leaf containing a sonnet follows p. 91. At the end of the book there are 3 pp. of "Notes."

Value about 18s. (original cloth).

27. In the Album of Adah Menken.

This trifle consists simply of the title as above on one leaf, and two verses in French, headed "Dolorida," on a second. One of these verses is at one side of the page, and the other on the reverse side. The last page is numbered "iv." No date is mentioned, but the *brochure* was privately printed in 1880. The size is crown 8vo. No copies that I have seen have had any wrappers.

Value about £2 10s.

28. Studies in Song. By Algernon Charles Swinburne. London. Chatto & Windus. Piccadilly. 1880.

Crown 8vo, bound in smooth navy-blue cloth, lettered on face in gold. Half-title precedes title, which is followed by table of contents, another half-title ("Song for the Centenary," &c.), dedication in verse, and text, pp. 5–212. Every poem is preceded by its appropriate half-title.

Value about 6s. (cloth, as issued).

29. Mary Stuart : a Tragedy. By Algernon Charles Swinburne. London. Chatto & Windus, Piccadilly. 1881.

This volume is bound, like most of the others, in smooth navy-blue cloth. A half-title precedes title, and dedication to Victor

Hugo follows, then comes "Dramatis Personæ" on unpaged leaf,
and another half-title. Half-titles precede each of the remaining
four acts. Text, pp. 3–203. Crown 8vo.

Value 12s. to 15s. (as issued).

30. Tristram of Lyonesse, and other Poems. By
Algernon   Charles   Swinburne.   London.
Chatto & Windus, Piccadilly. 1882.

A crown 8vo volume, bound as usual in smooth navy-blue cloth.
Half-title precedes title, which is followed by dedication, a sonnet
on an unpaged leaf, contents (ix–xi), another half-title, and text of
poems (pp. 3–361). Another half-title should face p. 202, and
a fourth should follow p. 299.

Value from 15s. to £1 (cloth, as issued).

31. A Century of Roundels.   By Algernon Charles
Swinburne.   London.   Chatto & Windus,
Piccadilly.   1883.

This volume is a crown 4to, bound in the usual dark-blue cloth.
A half-title precedes title as above, which is followed by a dedication in verse to Christina Rossetti, contents (vii–xi), and text
(1–100). Three copies of this book appear to have been printed
on cartridge paper of a larger size than the ordinary issue. They
were prepared at the request of Miss Isabella Swinburne for
illustration purposes.

Value about 10s. (cloth, as issued). I have not seen a copy on
superior paper, nor heard of one being offered for sale.

32. A Midsummer Holiday, and other Poems.
By Algernon Charles Swinburne.   London.
Chatto & Windus, Piccadilly.   1884.

This is a crown 8vo book bound in the usual dark-blue cloth, and having the preliminary half-title.   There is a table of contents, followed by half-title, and text (pp. 3–189), embracing thirty-six separate poems.

Value 8s. or 10s. (cloth, as issued).

33. Marino Faliero: a Tragedy.   By Algernon Charles Swinburne.   London.   Chatto & Windus, Piccadilly.   1885.

Bound in the usual dark-blue cloth, and having the preliminary half-title; a dedication in verse occupies pp. v–viii, after which follows "Dramatis Personæ" on unpaged leaf, and text (pp. 3–151). There are, in this case, no half-titles before the different acts.

Value 8s. or 10s. (cloth, as issued).

34. A Study of Victor Hugo.   By Algernon Charles Swinburne.   London.   Chatto & Windus, Piccadilly.   1886.

A half-title precedes title, which is followed by preface (v–vi), and text (pp. 1–148).

Value about 5s. (cloth, as issued).

35. A Word for the Navy.   By Algernon Charles Swinburne.   London.   George Redway.   MDCCCLXXXVI.

This is a pamphlet of 16 pages, each page containing a separate stanza of 8 lines.   The cover is white, lettered on the side "A Word for the Navy."   Only 250 copies of this pamphlet were published, and there is reason to believe that some few bear date "MDCCCLXXXVII."

A copy of "A Word for the Navy" might be expected to sell by auction for about 7s. 6d., or £2 (earliest issue, green wrappers).

36. The Jubilee. MDCCCLXXXVII. By Algernon
Charles Swinburne. London. Charles Ottley,
Landon & Co. 1887.

A 4to pamphlet of 21 pages in green wrappers, lettered on side
"The Jubilee." A half-title precedes title, and there are two blank
leaves at the beginning and three at the end of the book. This
poem appeared originally in the *Nineteenth Century* for June 1887.

Copies in pamphlet form are very scarce, but I do not think
they would be "cheap at £7 7s. each," as stated a little while
ago by a well-known collector of early editions.

37. Locrine : a Tragedy. By Algernon Charles
Swinburne. London. Chatto & Windus,
Piccadilly. 1887.

A half-title precedes title, which is followed by a lengthy dedication in verse occupying pp. v–viii ; then follows table of
"Persons Represented" and text, pp. 3–138. Usual binding of
navy-blue cloth. Crown 8vo.

Value about 8s. (original cloth).

38. Poems and Ballads. Third Series. By Algernon Charles Swinburne. London. Chatto &
Windus, Piccadilly. 1889.

A half-title precedes title, which is followed by dedication on
unpaged leaf, table of contents (vii–viii), and poems, pp. 1–181.
Usual navy-blue cloth binding, with gilt letters on face.

For value see *ante*, No. 7 in this article.

39. The Ballad of Dead Men's Bay. By Algernon Charles Swinburne. London. Printed
Privately. 1889.

This is a fcap. 8vo pamphlet of 14 pages in a brown-paper cover.
A half-title precedes title.

Copies might be expected to sell for about £4.

40. A Study of Ben Jonson. By Algernon Charles Swinburne. London. Chatto & Windus, Piccadilly. 1889.

Bound in the usual navy-blue cloth. A half-title precedes title; contents and a half-title follow. The text occupies pp. 3–181, and half-titles follow pp. 89 and 125. Crown 8vo.

Value about 6s. (original cloth).

41. A Sequence of Sonnets on the Death of Robert Browning. By A. C. Swinburne. London. Printed for Private Circulation. MDCCCXC.

A 4to pamphlet of 13 pages, each page containing a separate sonnet. A half-title precedes title, which is followed by a "Note" as follows:—"What the author of 'Atalanta' felt impelled to utter on the death of the author of 'The Ring and the Book' appeared in the *Fortnightly Review* for January 1890. A few copies only have been printed in this separate form more befitting the occasion."

Probable value some £6 or £8 (as issued).

42. The Sisters: a Tragedy. By Algernon Charles Swinburne. London. Chatto & Windus, Piccadilly. 1892.

Crown 8vo, bound in smooth navy-blue cloth, gilt-lettered on the face. A half-title precedes title, and a dedication to Lady Mary Gordon follows. Then follows a long dedication in verse, occupying pp. vii–x, and list of "Persons Represented." Text of the Tragedy, pp. 3–107.

Value about 5s. (original cloth).

ALFRED, BARON TENNYSON.

Lord Tennyson's practice of re-writing his poems, and often of suppressing them entirely, very seriously affected, even in his lifetime, the well-known general rule, that of two editions of any given work, the first is to be preferred. In his case, the rule was broken in upon by so many exceptions that a subsidiary one had to be formulated, and on judging of the importance of any work bearing the name of the late Poet Laureate, we have to ask ourselves, not so much whether it belongs to a first or subsequent edition, as whether it contains anything that was afterwards altered or suppressed, or any variation from an edition previously published. "The Princess" of 1847, for example, differs greatly from the third edition of 1850, and still more from the fourth edition, while "The Lover's Tale" of 1833 is a totally distinct poem from "The Lover's Tale" of 1879.

Between the years 1833 and 1842 Lord Tennyson published nothing except a few stanzas which appeared in the *Tribute* for 1837, but during this period he was revising what he had already written, with the result that the "Poems" of 1842 are widely different from those of 1830 and 1833, even where a similarity of title would warrant us in assuming that they are substantially the same. It is these variations and distinctions which sometimes make a second edition or a second issue of equal importance with the first.

There is, however, one broad rule which is unfailing, and it is this. In judging of the importance of any of Tennyson's works —the importance here spoken of has reference to the wants of the collector only—it may be taken for granted that all first, and some later editions up to and including "In Memoriam," 1850, are of very considerable value, but that after 1850, first editions and *à fortiori* later ones, are of no value beyond a few shillings, with seven exceptions, three of which are hardly worth remembering at all by reason of the infrequency of their occurrence. These exceptions are, "Helen's Tower," N.D. (1861), "Poems MDCCCXXX.–MDCCCXXXIII.," 1862, "The Widow," 1867, "The Victim," 1867, "The Passing of Arthur," 1884, a few copies of which were issued for examination purposes, but never published, a trial issue of two Idylls called "Enid and Nimuë, the True and the False" (E. Moxon, 1857), of which only six copies were issued, and only one known to be extant; and the "Idylls of the Hearth" (E. Moxon, 1864), which is a first edition of "Enoch Arden," &c., with a different title-page. So far as I am aware, Lord Tennyson published nothing else after 1850 which is much sought for by collectors, the reason being the poet's popularity and the immense number of copies that were issued of each new work.

Thus, the "Ode on the Death of the Duke of Wellington," 1852, "Maud and other Poems," 1855, "Idylls of the King," 1859, "Enoch Arden," 1864, "The Holy Grail," 1870, and all the rest of Lord Tennyson's works down to "The Death of Œnone, Akbar's Dream and other Poems," 1892, are, with the seven notable exceptions mentioned, of no importance from a bibliographical point of view, and of very little value.

These remarks have reference solely to editions *quâ* early editions, and do not apply to instances where, for some extraneous reason, a special value is placed upon any particular copy or even issue. Thus, the "Idylls of the King," 1868, folio, worth now some 30s. or 35s. by auction, owes its importance solely to Doré's illustrations; so do the separate editions of "Elaine," "Enid," "Guinevere" and "Vivien," 1867–69, illustrated by the same artist, some copies of which contain signed engraver's proofs on India paper.

In like manner "The Lady of Shalott" was published in folio, 1852, illustrated by "A Lady;" "Dora" in 1856, folio, illustrated by Mrs. Mildmay; "The Miller's Daughter" in 1857, 4to, with plates by A. L. Bond; "The May Queen" in 1860, post 8vo, and 1861, crown 4to, illustrated respectively by "E. V. B." (the Hon. Mrs. Boyle) and Mrs. W. H. Hartley; and "Mariana" in 1863, with illustrations by Mary Montgomerie Lamb. Some of these are costly, the last especially, which sells by auction for close on £3 in the original wrappers.

But all these, and doubtless others as well, hardly interest us as being good editions of the poems themselves. Whatever interest they do possess is due to the excellence of the plates, and the books cannot be said to disprove the rule by reason of their existence.

1. Poems by Two Brothers . . . London. Printed for W. Simpkin & R. Marshall, Stationers' Hall Court, and J. & J. Jackson, Louth. MDCCCXXVII.

The "Two Brothers" were Alfred and Charles Tennyson, though a third brother was associated in the authorship of the poems. This scarce book was printed in two sizes, 12mo and 8vo, and contains title as above, advertisement, preliminary verses (v–vii), contents (ix–xii), and poems (pp. 1–228).

At the present time a good copy in 12mo, originally published at 5s., sells for about £14 or £15 by auction, and the large-paper copies (published at 7s.) for about £30, both original cloth as

issued. In May 1893 Messrs. Macmillan & Co. published a
reprint at 6s.

It is interesting to note that at a sale held at Messrs. Sotheby's
rooms in December 1892, the original MS. of "Poems by Two
Brothers" produced no less a sum than £480. It consisted of
eighty-eight leaves, the greater part being in the handwriting of
the late Lord Tennyson. The lot contained the receipt given by
the publishers for the copyright (£20), and three poems which
were not included in the printed book. The MS. has since been
resold at a high premium to an American collector.

2. Timbuctoo.   A Poem which obtained the Chan-
     cellor's Medal at the Cambridge Commence-
     ment, MDCCCXXIX.   By A. Tennyson of Trinity
     College.   N.D. (but 1829).

This is a demy 8vo pamphlet in blue wrappers, containing title
as above, and text of poem (pp. 5–13). It was printed by John
Smith under the common University title, " Prolusiones Academicæ
præmiis annuis dignatæ et in curiâ Cantabrigiensi recitatæ comitiis
magnis."

Reprints of this scarce pamphlet, of which there are several,
may be known by reference to the concluding lines of the poem,
where the words "ravished sense," as they should be, are made to
read "lavished sense."

It should be mentioned that " Timbuctoo " had previously
appeared in a local newspaper.

Value from £7 to £9 (original wrappers, auction). Though
copies are scarce in any condition, the value of such as have been
rebound without the blue wrapper, but with Smith's University
imprint, is much less than the sums quoted.

3. Poems, chiefly Lyrical.   By Alfred Tennyson.
     London.   Effingham Wilson, Royal Exchange,
     Cornhill.   1830.

Good copies of this book are very rare. It was published in boards, fcap. 8vo, at 5s., and contains title, leaf of "Errata" (unpaged), and pp. 1–154. There is no table of contents.

Value about £7 7s. (original boards, auction), though very good copies sometimes bring considerably more. Thus on one occasion £13 was realised at auction, and on another no less than £26 5s.

4. Poems by Alfred Tennyson. London. Edward Moxon, 64 New Bond Street. MDCCCXXXIII.

Though the title-page of this collection of "Poems" is dated 1833, the work was published at the latter end of 1832. It was published in fcap. 8vo, at 5s., and contains half-title, title, contents (leaf unpaged), and text, pp. 1–163.

Three sonnets and two other pieces published in this volume were afterwards suppressed.

Value from £5 to £6 (original cloth, auction). Here, again, prices vary greatly, for though the book is not so scarce as the last named, it has realised £15 15s. on one occasion and £26 on another (March 8, 1893, at Sotheby's).

5. The Lover's Tale. By Alfred Tennyson. London. Edward Moxon, 64 New Bond Street. MDCCCXXXIII.

This, the scarcest by far of all original copies of Tennyson's works, is a small book containing title and text pp. 3–60, which was practically suppressed before publication. A few copies were, however, saved and given away to friends, and of these probably the majority have altogether disappeared. Twenty years ago a copy bound up with "Poems, chiefly Lyrical," 1830, and "Poems," 1833, was sold at Sotheby's for £4 odd, a price which affords a curious contrast to that which would be obtained now under similar circumstances. Prior to 1870 it was seriously doubted whether such a book as "The Lover's Tale" really existed at all, but speculation was finally set at rest on the appearance of an undoubted copy of the work in the auction room on the date in question. Should another make its appearance about the present time, it would probably realise the best part of £100.

Mr. Locker-Lampson, in whose library is a copy of the original "Lover's Tale," says that it was written by the author in his nineteenth year, and that the edition was almost immediately recalled. In 1870 Mr. Tennyson again revised and printed some five or six copies without a title-page, with a view to publication, but this issue was also suppressed. Mr. Locker-Lampson has a second copy of the original issue with many corrections in Lord Tennyson's handwriting, which probably served as a draft for this second issue.

In 1879 Messrs. Kegan Paul & Co. published a poem by Tennyson under the same title, but it had been so entirely re-modelled as to bear only the slightest resemblance to the original work. The value of this reprint does not exceed a few shillings.

6. Poems. By Alfred Tennyson. London. Edward Moxon, Dover Street. MDCCCXLII.

In 2 vols. fcap. 8vo, published at 12s. The first volume consists of a number of selections from "Poems, chiefly Lyrical," 1830, and "Poems," 1833, the latter very much altered from their original form. Seven new pieces written in 1833 were added. The second volume consists, with one exception ("The Sleeping Beauty"), of poems now published for the first time.

Vol. i. contains half-title, title, contents (v–vii), a second half-title, and pp. 3–233.

Vol. ii. contains half-title, title, contents (v–vii) and pp. 1–231.

Value about £10 (original boards, auction).

Second Edition, 1843, 2 vols. fcap. 8vo, containing further alterations; from 20s. to 25s. (as issued).

Third Edition, 1845, 2 vols. fcap. 8vo, containing still further alterations; from 15s. to 20s. (as issued).

Fourth Edition, 1847, 2 vols. fcap. 8vo, the last edition published in 2 vols.; about 15s. (as issued).

Several of the poems appearing in these collections were published separately, with illustrations by various artists. Some of these are referred to *ante*, p. 306, which see.

7. The Princess; a Medley. By Alfred Tennyson. London. Edward Moxon, Dover Street. MDCCCXLVII.

Fcap. 8vo, in green cloth, lettered in gilt on face. It contains half-title, title, and text, pp. 1–164.

Value from £1 10s. to £2 10s. (original cloth, auction). Very choice copies sell for more.

The second edition of " The Princess " differs but little from the first, but the third edition contains several new poems, and for the fourth edition several additions and alterations were made in the text. A passage was added in the Prologue to the fifth edition.

Second Edition, 1848, fcap. 8vo, pp. vi–164, with dedication to Henry Lushington.

Value 10s. or 12s. (as issued).

Third Edition, 1850, fcap. 8vo, pp. 180.

Value about 5s. (as issued).

" The Princess " forms one of the volumes in the series known as " The Parchment Library." Large-paper copies (of which only 50 were issued) are scarce, realising at auction about 10s. or 12s. each.

The poem has also been published in folio, 1850, with ten plates (the borders in gold and colours), by Mrs. S. C. Lee. This edition was published at £2 2s. Another edition of 1866 in 4to (Moxon), was printed on thick toned paper, with 26 illustrations by Maclise.

Value about 10s. (morocco extra).

8. In Memoriam. London. Edward Moxon, Dover Street. 1850.

Fcap. 8vo, half-title, title, introductory stanzas (v–vii), and on the reverse of vii the words following, " In Memoriam A. H. H. obiit MDCCCXXXIII." The poem occupies pp. 1–210. Brown cloth, lettered in gilt on face. Published at 6s.

Value about £4 (original cloth, auction). None of the later editions are of any importance except the fourth, of 1851, fcap. 8vo, which contained a new stanza (lviii.). Copies of this edition have brought as much as £1 ·5s. by auction, but the average amount realised is less.

"In Memoriam" forms one of the volumes in the series known as "The Parchment Library." Large-paper copies (of which 50 were printed) realise 10s. or 12s. by auction.

"A. H. H.," to whom the poem is dedicated, is identified with Arthur Henry Hallam, son of the historian, who died at Vienna in 1833.

9. Helen's Tower. Clandeboye . . . Privately Printed. N.D. (1861).

This scarce book is a large 4to in glazed pink wrapper, with gilt edges. A perfect copy should collate as follows :—Glazed preliminary leaf printed to a pattern, the reverse white, blank white leaf. Title (with etching of Helen's Tower), leaf printed in black with red initial letters (unpaged) as follows :—" 11th day of November MDCCCL. Thursday at 3 of yᵉ clock did I Catherine Hamilton christen this Tower by yᵉ name style and title of Helen's Tower." Text pp. 3–8, the reverse of p. 5 blank. A blank white leaf follows p. 8, glazed end paper to pattern.

So far as I am aware, no copy of "Helen's Tower" has been sold at auction within the last five or six years. The value of a perfect copy would probably amount to £25 or £30.

10. Poems MDCCCXXX.–MDCCCXXXIII. Privately Printed. 1862.

This volume was probably printed in Canada. It consists of the poems in "Poems, chiefly Lyrical," 1830, and "Poems," 1833 (*ante*, Nos. 3 and 4), which were suppressed by Lord Tennyson, and gives the alterations made in those that were retained. This book is scarce, as its publication was prohibited by the Court of Chancery, though a few copies seem to have been distributed.

It is a fcap. 8vo in light green wrappers, lettered on the side in black as above, containing title, half-title (MDCCCXXX.), contents (v–viii), and poems, pp. 1–112. A half-title (MDCCCXXXIII.) follows, p. 44.

Value about £3 3s. (original paper covers, as issued, auction).

11. The Window, or The Loves of the Wrens. By Alfred Tennyson, D.C.L., Poet Laureate. . . . MDCCCLXVII.

Large 4to, bound in limp red cloth, lettered on side "The Window," in a lozenge. Two blank leaves precede the title, which has an etching of Canford Manor, then follows a leaf with monogram "J. G." in black, half-title, dedication, 12 stanzas on 15 unpaged leaves, printed on one side only. Two blank leaves follow. Only six copies of this book were privately printed by Sir J. and Miss Guest.

Value about £30 (as issued, auction).

Another Edition, 1871, 4to, with music to the words, by Sullivan ; published at 21s., and now worth about its original price.

12. The Victim. By Alfred Tennyson, D.C.L., Poet Laureate . . . MDCCCLXVII.

Large 4to, bound in limp red cloth, lettered on side "The Victim," in a lozenge. Two blank leaves precede title, which has an etching of Canford Manor. Then follows a leaf with monogram "J. G." in black, half-title, text consisting of vii. stanzas on six unpaged leaves printed on one side only. Two blank leaves follow. The work was privately printed by Sir J. and Miss Guest, and only a very small number of copies were distributed.

Value about £30 (as issued, auction).

13. Order of Service at the Funeral of Alfred, Lord Tennyson, on October 12, 1892.

This order of service is on a single sheet, folio (London, Harrison & Sons), and was presented to the mourners assembled at Westminster Abbey on Wednesday the 12th October 1892. It contains the text of two poems by Lord Tennyson, "Crossing the Bar," and "The Silent Voices."

WILLIAM MAKEPEACE THACKERAY.

A HOSTILE criticism on "The Kickleburys on the Rhine," which appeared in the *Times* newspaper, stated that Thackeray was intended by nature for an artist rather than an author, and, indeed, he appears at one period of his career to have been of a similar opinion himself.

When the "Pickwick Papers" originally appeared in the well-known monthly parts, Seymour commenced to illustrate it, but after he had made eight plates he committed suicide. Then Dickens gave the task to Buss, whose rough and slovenly work created such dissatisfaction, that he was compelled to sever his connection with him, and look around for another and a better artist. It is said, though with what degree of truth it is perhaps impossible to estimate, that Thackeray and Hablot Browne were both competitors for the vacant post, and that sketches were submitted by both of them, with the result, as all the world knows, that "Phiz" proved successful, to the great gain of letters; for, had the issue been otherwise, it is possible, and indeed probable, that Thackeray's wonderful literary skill might never have asserted itself.

Thackeray's first separately printed production, though by no means his first attempt at authorship, was the "Paris Sketch-Book," published by Macrone in 1840. Prior to this, he had contributed to the *Snob* and perhaps the *Gownsman*—two Cambridge periodicals subsequently noted—to Cruikshank's *Comic Almanack*, and other periodicals, though prior to the publication of the "Sketch-Book" his efforts had mainly been artistic. In 1838 he illustrated Addison's "Damascus and Palmyra," Douglas Jerrold's "Man of Character" in 1838, "Flore et Zephyr" in 1836, "Sketches by Spec" in 1840, and other works, which are valued mainly perhaps for this very reason. The last three are mentioned in the following list, in common with Thackeray's literary works.

In 1891, Mr. C. P. Johnson, who is the recognised authority on all matters relating to Thackeray's writings, discovered in the British Museum Library, the first volume of a periodical called *Britannia: a Weekly Journal of News, Politics, and Literature,* printed in the year 1840. He pointed out that one article in that volume was undoubtedly the work of Thackeray, and having subsequently acquired the remaining volumes, published in 1841 and 1842, he found that four original articles at least, all signed "M. A. Titmarsh," were from his pen. These have never been reprinted, and do not seem to have been recorded in any bibliography of Thackeray's writings. In May 1893, a set of the three volumes was sold by auction at Sotheby's, and realised £24 10s.

At this point it is perhaps better to mention that there are one or two light periodicals with which Thackeray's name is sometimes associated, though on what evidence I have been unable to discover. In March 1889, Messrs. Sotheby, Wilkinson & Hodge, in dispersing the library of Mr. John Mansfield Mackenzie of Edinburgh, catalogued the following periodicals under the name of Thackeray :—

The Snob, Nos. 3, 4, 5, 6, 9, 10 and 11, with title and preliminary leaves, Cambridge, 1829.

The Gownsman (formerly called) The Snob, Nos. 3 to 17, with title and preliminary leaves, *ibid.,* 1830.

Cambridge Odes, by Peter Persius, *ibid.,* N.D.

The Individual, Nos. 1 to 15, printed on different coloured papers, 1836–37.

The Progress to B.A. ; a Poem, by a Member of the University, *ibid.*, 1830.

The Fellow, No. 11, 1836.

The Tripos, No. 1, N.D.

Granta ; a Fragment, by a Freshman, edited by the Rev. J. Snodgrass, 1841.

A Few More Words to Freshmen, by the Rev. T. T., Cambridge, 1841, in 1 vol. 8vo.

The *Snob* and the *Gownsman* entries are intelligible, but I confess I do not understand the other references, nor do Mr. Shepherd and Mr. Johnson, Thackeray's bibliographers, refer to them in any way. The book sold for £9 exactly, with which remark we pass to firmer ground.

1. The Snob; a Literary and Scientific Journal. Not "Conducted by Members of the University." (Quotation from Virgil.) Cambridge. Published by W. H. Smith, Rose Crescent. 1829.

This 8vo periodical, to which Thackeray contributed *inter alia* "Timbuctoo," a skit on Tennyson's prize poem, is complete in 11 numbers, printed on variously tinted papers. When bound, there should be title as above, a dedication to Alderman Abbott, preface, index (vii–ix), and 64 pages of matter. All copies of these numbers hitherto discovered are headed with the words "Second Edition," "Third Edition," and so on, at the top of the first page. As to value, see next entry.

2. The Gownsman, formerly called The Snob; a Literary and Scientific Journal. Now Conducted by Members of the University. . . . Cambridge. Published by W. H. Smith, Rose Crescent, and sold by Simpkin & Marshall. London, and may be had of all Booksellers. 1830.

It is probable, though by no means certain, that Thackeray was the editor of the *Gownsman*.   Articles signed ⊙ are supposed to be from his pen, though this again appears to be a mere matter of speculation.   The periodical was not continued after the 17th number.

Complete copies of the *Snob* and the *Gownsman* are excessively scarce, as much as £91, and at another time even £125 having been paid for a set of both in the original printed covers.   The 17 numbers of the *Gownsman*, also in the original covers, once brought £37, the *Snob* being therefore the more valuable of the two.   Odd numbers of either periodical are more frequent, and do not seem to realise more than 8s. or 10s. each, sometimes not that.

3. Flore et Zephyr : Ballet Mythologique Dedie à (Sketch of a Ballet Girl).   Par Théophile Wagstaff.   London.   Published March 1, 1836, by J. Mitchell, Library, 33 Old Bond Street.   À Paris, chez Rittner & Goupil, Boulevard Montmartre.   Printed by Graf & Soret.

This is another excessively rare publication.   It consists of a series of nine lithographed plates in folio, indicative of scenes in the life of a ballet girl, the cut on the title being included in this computation.   The plates are sometimes found slightly tinted. There is no letterpress.

A short time ago two copies of this book appeared in the sale-room at Wellington Street, one realising £90, and the other £56.

In the latter case, a plate had sustained an injury.

4. Man of Character.   By Douglas Jerrold. . . . London.   Henry Colburn. . . . MDCCCXXXVIII.

The plates, 12 in number, are by Thackeray.

A good copy in the original cloth (3 vols. post 8vo) sells by auction for about £2 10s., but copies in later bindings usually bring considerably less. On one occasion a very fair example in cloth as issued only sold for £1 6s. Later editions cannot be mistaken, as they are so described.

5. Sketches by Spec. Published by Hugh Cunningham, 3 St. James's Square. N.D. (but 1840).

Mr. R. H. Shepherd, in his bibliography of Thackeray, says that it is doubtful whether this work was actually published, and that the only copy of the only number known to exist is in the possession of Mr. C. P. Johnson, who reproduced it in facsimile in 1885. This solitary number is stated by the same authority to bear the title "Britannia Protecting the Drama," and to consist of a print with letterpress description. I have never seen either original or reproduction.

6. The Paris Sketch-Book. By Mr. Titmarsh. . . . London. John Macrone, 1 St. Martin's Place, Trafalgar Square. 1840.

This work, which is noticeable as being Thackeray's first printed book, is in 2 vols. post 8vo, both dated 1840, and originally issued in cloth.

Vol. i. has contents, note, and a dedication to M. Aretz, all unnumbered, pp. 304, five full-page plates, and a frontispiece by the author.

Vol. ii. consists of contents, pp. 298, and five full-page plates and a frontispiece by the author.

A second edition, which appeared the same year, contains exactly the same matter and plates, but is described as such on the title.

Good copies in the original cloth as issued are seldom met with ; £8 or £9 being by no means an unusual price for the work to bring at auction under such circumstances. Rebound copies are worth much less, bringing no more than £1 10s. or £2, unless quite uncut and very clean.

7. An Essay on the Genius of George Cruikshank,
   with Numerous Illustrations of his Works.
   (From the "Westminster Review," No. LXVI.),
   with Additional Etchings.   Henry Hooper, 13
   Pall Mall East.   MDCCCXL.

This essay is reprinted from the 66th number of the *West-minster Review* (vol. xxxiv., 1840), for the first time.   It is a demy 8vo book, with two preliminary pages, containing a list of 17 full-page plates, 38 woodcuts, and 59 pages of text.   It must be remembered that some copies do not contain all the illustrations . above mentioned, and a plate entitled "Philoprogenitiveness," is in particular often wanting.   That plate is included in the 17 above quoted.

The value of this book varies according to its condition and the number of plates to be found in any particular copy.   If complete as above, an average auction price is from 35s. to £2, original cloth, uncut.

8. Heads of the People; or, Portraits of the
   English.   Drawn by Kenny Meadows. . . .
   London.   Robert Tyas.   MDCCCXL.

This work consists of 43 plates after drawings by Kenny Meadows, and a number of descriptive essays by Thackeray and others.   Thackeray contributed "Captain Rook and Mr. Pigeon," "The Fashionable Authoress," and "The Artists," re-printed in Mr. Thackeray's "Miscellaneous Writings," post 8vo, 1856, and published separately in yellow wrappers (see *post*, No. 29).

The value of "Heads of the People," complete in two volumes, 8vo, original cloth, is about £2 10s. by auction.   Rebound copies often sell for about £1, though in this case the quality of the binding must be considered.

9. The Second Funeral of Napoleon : in Three
   Letters to Miss Smith of London, and the
   Chronicle of the Drum.   By Mr. M. A.
   Titmarsh.   London.   Hugh Cunningham, St.
   Martin's Place, Trafalgar Square.   1841.

A small 4to book in a dark-coloured wrapper, bearing an etching
of Napoleon, covered by an eagle with a pall.   There are 122
pages, and four full-page woodcuts (inclusive of frontispiece).

"Have you read Thackeray's little book—'The Second Funeral
of Napoleon?'   If not, pray do; and buy it, and ask others to
buy it : as each copy sold puts 7½d. in T.'s pocket : which is very
empty just now, I take it.   I think this book is the best thing he
has done."—Edward Fitzgerald to W. H. Thompson, 18th February
1841.

This little book, which was published at 2s. 6d., is now very
rare, copies selling by auction for as much as £30 or £40.

The "Chronicle of the Drum" was reprinted for the first time
in 1886, in 4to, value about 10s. (original cloth).

10. Comic Tales and Sketches.   Edited and Illus-
    trated by Mr. Michael Angelo Titmarsh,
    Author of the Paris Sketch-Book, &c.   Lon-
    don.   Hugh Cunningham, St. Martin's Place,
    Trafalgar Square.   1841.

Vol. i. contains pp. vii, 299, and vol. ii. contents, and pp. 370.
There are six full-page tinted plates in each volume (inclusive of
frontispiece), post 8vo.

This work hardly sold at all when first published, and the very
extensive remainder lay stored in the publisher's premises until
the success of *Vanity Fair* in 1848 created a demand for all
Thackeray's earlier works.   What remained of "Comic Tales and
Sketches" was then put on the market again, so that there are
two issues of this same edition.

As genuine copies of the first issue are worth as much as £20, and sometimes more when clean and in the original dark brown cloth, the variations between the two issues are matters of great importance, and great care must be taken that any copy offered for sale is not a second issue with a reprinted title-page, for it is only from the title-page that any difference can be detected between the two books. The title-page of copies of the true first issue reads as above, that of the second and inferior issue refers to the author as the "author of *Vanity Fair*," and bears no date. Reprinted, and of course fraudulent title-pages, can only be detected by reference to the texture of the paper.

A made up set consisting of the first issue of vol. i. and the second issue of vol. ii., or *vice versâ*, would realise about £10 by auction (original cloth).

11. The Irish Sketch Book. By Mr. M. A. Titmarsh. With numerous Engravings on Wood drawn by the Author. London. Chapman & Hall, 186 Strand. MDCCCXLIII.

Vol. i. consists of pp. vi–311, with full-page front; vol. ii. of pp. vi–327, with full-page front. Both volumes are post 8vo.
Value about £6 6s. (auction, original cloth, as issued).
Another Edition, 2 vols. 8vo, 1845, sells for about £1 10s. (*ibid.*).

12. Notes of a Journey from Cornhill to Grand Cairo, by way of Lisbon. . . . By Mr. M. A. Titmarsh, Author of the " Irish Sketch Book," &c. . . . London. Chapman & Hall, 186 Strand. MDCCCXLVI.

Published in pictorial cloth, pp. xiv–301, 8vo, and contains a few cuts and a coloured front by the author. Most copies of this original edition were issued without the front, and it is a common practice to take that belonging to a second and smaller sized edition to complete the first.

Value about £1 10s. (auction, cloth as issued, with genuine front).

13. L'Abbaye de·Penmarch.   Mélodrame en Trois Actes.   Par MM. P. Tournemine et Thackeray. 1840.

This pamphlet of 21 pages, imperial 8vo, constitutes No. 53 of the "Répertoire Dramatique des auteurs contemporains," published at Paris in yellow covers.   It is a great question whether Thackeray really had anything to do with it.

The value of a clean copy in the original wrappers is about £5 or £6 by auction.

14. Mrs. Perkins' Ball.   By M. A. Titmarsh. Chapman & Hall, 186 Strand.   N.D. (but 1847).

Three editions of this book were published in pink boards, crown 4to, 1847, but the first can be told by reason of the fact that it is the only one which contains no letterpress under the plate facing the title.   The cover to the original edition reads "Mrs. Perkins' Ball. By Mr. M. A. Titmarsh.   Mrs. Perkins at Home.   Friday Evening, 19th December, Pocklington Square.   London.   Chapman & Hall, 186 Strand.   MDCCCXLVII.   Price 7s. 6d. plain, or 10s. 6d. coloured." There are or should be 22 full-page illustrations by the author (including title-page and front).   This is one of the well-known "Christmas Books."

Copies in the original boards, with plates coloured, sell by auction for about £4 4s. ; of plates not coloured, about £1 12s.

There is a later edition of 1864, in crown 8vo, worth some 12s. or 14s. coloured, or about 6s. if uncoloured.

15. Our Street. By Mr. M. A. Titmarsh. London. Chapman & Hall, 186 Strand. MDCCCXLVIII.

Published in pink boards, fcap. 4to, with 16 full-page illustrations (including title-page and front) by the author, pp. 54.
Value about £1 10s. (original boards, coloured plates, auction).
Second Edition, 1848, about 6s. (plates plain).
This is one of the " Christmas Books."

16. The Book of Snobs. By W. M. Thackeray, Author of " A Journey from Cornhill to Grand Cairo." . . . London. Punch Office, 85 Fleet Street. MDCCCXLVIII.

A post 8vo book, containing pp. vi-180, and woodcuts by the author. The stiff green pictorial wrappers in which the book was originally issued were also designed by the author. The "Book of Snobs" is a reprint of some (most, but not all) of the papers which appeared in *Punch* during the years 1846–7, under the title "The Snobs of England." It was re-issued in yellow wrappers in 1855 (see *post*, No. 29).
Value of the original edition of 1848, about £3 15s. or £4 (original wrappers, auction), though prices vary greatly.

17. Vanity Fair: a Novel without a Hero. By William Makepeace Thackeray. With Illustrations on Steel and Wood by the Author. London. Bradbury. & Evans, 11 Bouverie Street. 1848.

This work was issued originally in 20 monthly parts (January 1847 to July 1848), in yellow wrappers (bearing a title somewhat different from the above), and afterwards in cloth, pp. xvi-624, demy 8vo. The illustrations comprise 40 full-page plates and numerous woodcuts, and a complete and perfect copy of the work should contain two title-pages, each dated 1848, and an illustrated advertisement of "The Great Hoggarty Diamond," which, however, did not appear until 1849.

As is well known, there are two distinct issues of the first edition of this work. The first and best has the short title "Vanity Fair" on p. 1, in small rustic open lettered type, and there is a woodcut of the "Marquess of Steyne" on p. 336. These features appear in no other issue or edition.

The following are some recent auction values : £21 10s. (original parts, complete), £5 10s. (first issue, original cloth), £1 1s. (second issue, half calf), £2 5s. (first issue, half calf).

18. The Three Sailors, with Reminiscences of Michael Angelo Titmarsh at Rome [printed in Samuel Bevan's Sand and Canvas; a Narrative of Adventures in Egypt, with a Sojourn among the Artists at Rome. London. Charles Gilpin, 5 Bishopsgate Street Without. 1849.]

This work was published in cloth, 8vo, with coloured plates and woodcuts.

A copy as issued is worth about £1 10s. (auction).

19. The History of Pendennis : His Fortunes and Misfortunes : His Friends and his Greatest Enemy. By William Makepeace Thackeray. With Illustrations on Steel and Wood by the Author. Bradbury & Evans, 11 Bouverie Street. 1849.

Originally issued in 24 monthly parts in yellow wrappers, with 48 full-page etchings and many woodcuts by the author. Afterwards in 2 vols. demy 8vo, cloth.

Vol. i. is dated 1849, and contains pp. viii–384.

Vol. ii. is dated 1850, and contains pp. xii–372.

Value about £2 10s. (original parts) ; £1 10s. (cloth, as issued).

20. The History of Samuel Titmarsh and the Great Hoggarty Diamond. By W. M. Thackeray, Author of " Pendennis," " Vanity Fair," &c. &c. London. Bradbury & Evans, 11 Bouverie Street. MDCCCXLIX.

Published in pictorial boards, post 8vo, and contains 9 full-page etchings and illustrated title by the author. The complete work contains two title-pages, the first illustrated and the second plain ; a half-title precedes both, with full-page plate, " The Rosolio," to face. Unless a copy exactly answers this description it is not complete.

Value about £3 10s. (original boards, auction) ; considerably less, as usual, if rebound.

Another Edition of this work appeared without date (but 1860), in post 8vo. It contains the same plates. A reprint appeared among the " Miscellanies " in 1857 (see *post*, No. 29).

The story of " Samuel Titmarsh and the Great Hoggarty Diamond " originally appeared in *Fraser's Magazine.*

21. Doctor Birch and his Young Friends. By Mr. M. A. Titmarsh. London. Chapman & Hall, 186 Strand. 1849.

This is one of Thackeray's " Christmas Books." There should be one unnumbered page containing a list of the illustrations (16 in number, inclusive of first title and front) by the author. There are two title-pages, the first coloured and the second plain (even in copies described as coloured throughout), and a coloured front. The book is in crown 4to.

Value about £3 10s. (original pink boards, auction).

An edition of 1864, in yellow boards, crown 8vo, is worth
about 5s.

22. Rebecca and Rowena : a Romance upon
    Romance. By Mr. M. A. Titmarsh. With
    Illustrations by Richard Doyle. London.
    Chapman & Hall, 186 Strand. 1850.

Contains pp. viii–102, crown 4to. The 8 illustrations include
the frontispiece. The cuts on the title are generally left plain,
even in coloured copies.

Value about £2 (plates coloured, original pictorial boards,
auction).

This work is one of Thackeray's "Christmas Books," and was
reprinted in 1856 among the "Miscellanies" (see *post*, No. 29).

23. The Kickleburys on the Rhine. By Mr. M.
    A. Titmarsh. London. Smith, Elder & Co.,
    65 Cornhill. MDCCCL.

This work contains 15 full-page etchings (sometimes tinted),
including front ("The Interior of Hades"), and sketch on title.
There are, or should be, one preliminary leaf containing list of
illustrations, and 87 pages of text, square 8vo.

Value about £2 (original pink boards, coloured, auction).

A second edition of this book, much valued by collectors on
account of the preface entitled "Essay on Thunder and Small
Beer," now appearing for the first time, was published in 1851,
and is worth about £1 (pink boards, as issued).

24. The History of Henry Esmond, Esq., a
    Colonel in the Service of Her Majesty Q.
    Anne. Written by Himself. . . . London.
    Printed for Smith, Elder & Company, over
    against St. Peter's Church in Cornhill. 1852.

The three volumes which complete this work were published in post 8vo, cloth, with white labels, and when in that condition and clean, sell by auction for about £2 10s. A second edition of 1853, also in 3 vols. post 8vo, has a different title-page, but is in other respects very similar to the first.

25. The English Humourists of the Eighteenth Century: a series of Lectures delivered in England. . . . By W. M. Thackeray, Author of "Esmond." . . . London. Smith, Elder & Co., 65 Cornhill. Bombay. Smith, Taylor & Co. 1853.

Published in cloth, and made up of contents and errata, 2 pp. (not numbered), and pp. 322, post 8vo.

Value from 17s. 6d. to £1 (auction, cloth, as issued).

There is a second edition of the same date, but it is described as such on the title.

26. The Newcomes: Memoirs of a Most Respectable Family. Edited by Arthur Pendennis, Esq. With Illustrations on Steel and Wood by Richard Doyle. London. Bradbury & Evans, 11 Bouverie Street. 1854.

This work was issued originally in 24 monthly parts (October 1853 to August 1855), in pictorial yellow wrappers, and contains 48 full-page etchings and many woodcuts. Afterwards published in 2 vols. demy 8vo, 1854-5, slate-coloured cloth.

The value of a set of the numbers ranges from about £1 5s. to £4, according to their condition. A copy in cloth sells as a rule for about 15s.

27. Sketches after English Landscape Painters. By L. Marvy. . . . London. David Bogue. N.D. (but 1854 ?).

The text is by Thackeray. The plates number 20, preceded by title, preface, and table of contents. Bright blue cloth, lettered in gilt on side within gilt scroll.

Value of a copy in the original cloth, as issued, about £7 (auction).

Another and much inferior edition was issued without date (but 1854) by Griffin & Co.

28. The Rose and the Ring; or the History of Prince Giglio and Prince Bulbo: a Fireside Pantomime for Great and Small Children. By Mr. M. A. Titmarsh. . . . London. Smith, Elder & Co., 65 Cornhill. 1855.

This Christmas Book was published in pink boards, square 8vo, at 5s. It contains 8 full-page plates (including title), and numerous woodcuts, all by Thackeray. The plates are never found coloured.

Value about £3 3s. (boards, as issued).

A third edition also appeared in 1855, and what is known as the first New York edition appeared in that city during the same year.

29. Mr. Thackeray's Miscellaneous Writings: Miscellanies in Prose and Verse. London. Bradbury & Evans, 11 Bouverie Street. 1855–57.

This, the first collective edition of the "Miscellanies," is in 4 vols., post 8vo. Selections from the miscellaneous writings of Thackeray were also published at intervals during the years 1855,

1856, and 1857. Some of these selections had been previously published in book form, but others had not. Under any circumstances, however, the following list is worthy of note.

All the books referred to were published in yellow wrappers, and inasmuch as later editions, also in the same yellow wrappers, afterwards appeared, care must be taken to observe that the date of any copy offered for sale is correct, according to the following table :—

I. The Snob Papers. 1855. Appeared originally in *Punch* (1846–47), and had already been separately published under the title of "The Book of Snobs" (see *ante*, No. 16). Value about 5s.

II. The Fatal Boots and Cox's Diary. 1855. First appeared in Cruikshank's *Comic Almanack*. "The Fatal Boots" is to be found in the "Comic Tales and Sketches" (see *ante*, No. 10). Value about 8s.

III. Ballads. 1855. These had appeared in various periodicals, and were now published in a collective form for the first time. Value about 10s.

IV. Novels by Eminent Hands and Character Sketches. 1856. The "Character Sketches" appeared in Kenny Meadows' "Heads of the People" (see *ante*, No. 8). The "Novels by Eminent Hands" appeared originally in *Punch*, and were now published in separate form for the first time. Value about 10s.

V. Burlesques: a Legend of the Rhine; Rebecca and Rowena. 1856. The "Legend of the Rhine" was now published separately for the first time. "Rebecca and Rowena" first appeared in 1850 (see *ante*, No. 22). Value about 6s.

VI. A Little Dinner at Timmins's; The Bedford Row Conspiracy. 1856. The former sketch originally appeared in *Punch*. "The Bedford Row Conspiracy" is one of the "Comic Tales and Sketches" (see *ante*, No. 10). Value about 10s.

VII. Major Gahagan's Tremendous Adventures. 1856. One of the "Comic Tales and Sketches" now reprinted for the first time. Value about 8s.

VIII. Memoirs of Mr. Charles James Yellowplush; the Diary of C. Jeames De La Pluche, Esq. 1856. The "Diary" now appears in separate form for the first time. It appeared originally in *Punch*. The memoirs are reprinted from "Comic Tales and Sketches." Value about 12s.

IX. Sketches and Travels in London. 1856. This first appeared in *Punch* under another title, and is published separately for the first time. Value about 10s.

X. Memoirs of Barry Lyndon, Esq. 1856. Now published in a separate form for the first time. The Memoirs originally appeared in *Fraser's Magazine* (vols. xxix. and xxx.) under the title " The Luck of Barry Lyndon," &c. Value about 12s.

XI. A Shabby Genteel Story. 1857. Appeared previously in *Fraser's Magazine* (vols. xxi. and xxii.). Value about 10s.

XII. The History of Samuel Titmarsh and the Great Hoggarty Diamond. 1857. Already separately published (see *ante*, No. 20). Value about 5s.

XIII. The Fitz-Boodle Papers ; Men's Wives. 1857. Both of these were contributed to *Fraser's Magazine* (vols. xxv., xxvi., and xxvii.), and now appear for the first time in a separate form. Value about 10s.

30. The Virginians : a Tale of the Last Century. By W. M. Thackeray, Author of " Esmond." . . . With Illustrations on Steel and Wood by the Author. London. Bradbury & Evans, 11 Bouverie Street. 1858.

This novel appeared originally in 24 monthly parts in the usual yellow wrappers (November 1857 to September 1859), and was afterwards published in 2 vols. demy 8vo, cloth, dated respectively 1858 and 1859. Each volume has two title-pages, one engraved and the other plain, and in each case the engraved title is faced by a full-page plate. There should be 48 full-page etchings and many woodcuts by the author.

Value about £2 (original parts, auction), or about £1 1s. (original cloth, auction).

31. Mr. Thackeray, Mr. Yates, and the Garrick
    Club. The Correspondence and Facts stated
    by Edmund Yates. Printed for Private Circu-
    lation. 1859.

A scarce post 8vo pamphlet of 15 pages, worth about £10 by
auction. The pagination runs 3–15.

32. Lovel the Widower.   By W. M. Thackeray.
    With Illustrations. London. Smith, Elder &
    Co., 65 Cornhill. MDCCCLXI.

Published in embossed violet cloth, post 8vo, with 6 full-page
plates by the author. This work originally appeared in the pages
of the *Cornhill Magazine*. The title-pages of later editions are
dated accordingly, but in other respects the arrangement and
nature of the contents are the same.
    Value from 17s. 6d. to £1 (original cloth).

33. The Four Georges: Sketches of Manners,
    Morals, Court and Town Life.   By W. M.
    Thackeray, Author of "Lectures on the Eng-
    lish Humourists," &c. &c. With Illustrations.
    London. Smith, Elder & Co., 65 Cornhill.
    MDCCCLXI.

This work consists of 226 pp., and has 2 full-page illustrations, one as a frontispiece, and the other to face p. 59. It was
published in post 8vo, green cloth. There are two issues of the
first edition, of which the first is by far the best. Only the
genuine first issues have the words " Sketches of Manners, Morals,
Court and Town Life " on the title-pages themselves. All the
other issues have a half-title, on which the words appear.
    Value about £1 12s. (first issue, original cloth, auction).

34. Adventures of Philip on his way through the World, showing who robbed him, who helped him, and who passed him by. By W. M. Thackeray, Author of "Esmond." . . . London. Smith, Elder & Co., 65 Cornhill. MDCCCXLII.

Published in 3 vols. post 8vo, dark red cloth. When this tale originally appeared in the *Cornhill Magazine* it was illustrated, but the three volumes contain no plates.

Value about 17s. 6d. (original cloth).

35. Roundabout Papers. Reprinted from the "Cornhill Magazine." With Illustrations. By W. M. Thackeray, Author of "Esmond." . . . London. Smith, Elder & Co., 65 Cornhill. MDCCCLXIII.

This book was issued in post 8vo, cloth, and comprises contents and list of plates, one page with illustration entitled "On a Lazy Idle Boy," and 352 pages of text. Its peculiarity is that, although the list of illustrations only mentions two plates, there are in reality four, the extra ones being "The Lazy Idle Boy" to face p. 1, and "Latin Grammar" to face p. 120. The work, though dated 1863, was published the previous year.

Value about 15s. (original cloth).

36. The Students' Quarter; or Paris Five and Thirty Years since. By William Makepeace Thackeray. London. John Camden Hotten. N.D.

Published in cloth, post 8vo, in 1864, with coloured illustrations, but whether by Thackeray or not is uncertain.

Value about 10s. (original cloth).

37. Denis Duval.   By W. M. Thackeray, Author
    of " Vanity Fair." . . . London.   Smith,
    Elder & Co., 65 Cornhill.   1867.

This is Thackeray's last work.   It appeared in the *Cornhill
Magazine* for 1864, and though left incomplete, was now reprinted
for the first time.   The last page is numbered 253, and the " Notes "
occupy pp. 255-275, post 8vo.   This work is not illustrated.
Value about 17s. 6d. (original cloth).

———

38. Thackerayana : Notes and Anecdotes.   Illus-
    trated by nearly Six Hundred Sketches by
    William Makepeace Thackeray, depicting
    Humourous Incidents in his School Life.
    . . . London.   Chatto & Windus, Piccadilly.
    1875.

Pp. xx-492.   Pictorial red cloth.   This work (published in
1874) was suppressed as infringing copyright in certain particulars, and though reissued with alterations, no variation is observ-
able in the title-page.   The original issue contains 492 pages, the
reissue has five coloured plates.
Value about £1 1s. (original issue, auction).

39. The Orphan of Pimlico : a Moral Tale of Bel-
    gravian Life.   By Miss M. T. Wigglesworth.
    . . . and other Sketches, Fragments, and
    Drawings.   By William Makepeace Thackeray.
    . . . London.   Smith, Elder & Co., 15
    Waterloo Place.   1876.

This work (a large 4to) contains 195 pages, including plates,

which are, however, alone numbered. The earliest issue is in
slate-coloured boards, lettered in dark red ; the later issues appeared
in blue cloth. A very few coloured copies were published.

Value about £1 12s. (first issue, not coloured).

40. Etchings by the late William Makepeace
      Thackeray, while at Cambridge. Illustrative
      of University Life, &c. Now first published
      from the Original Plates. London. H.
      Sotheran & Co., Piccadilly. 1878.

Consists of engraved title, one page of "List of Subjects," and
11 plates on 8 pages. A few copies were coloured.

Value about 5s. plain, and 10s. or 12s. coloured (original boards).

The *Edition de Luxe* of Thackeray's works issued by Smith,
Elder & Co., in 26 vols., 1878–86, devotes the last two volumes to
"Miscellaneous Essays, Sketches, and Reviews, and Contributions
to *Punch* not previously reprinted."

It may be noted that the complete edition of 26 vols. sells by
auction for about £14 (cloth).

One of the rarest of Thackeray's separate pieces is entitled "An
Interesting Event." Only one copy with the wrappers is known,
but examples without have been sold on several occasions. On
one occasion £21 was paid for a copy in this condition.

INDEX

OF

BOOKS, &c., INCIDENTALLY MENTIONED IN THE TEXT.

THE END.